INANNA'S TEARS

VOLLMAR · mpMANN

ARCHAIA ENTERTAINMENT LLC
WWW.ARCHAIA.COM

INANNA'S TEARS

WRITTEN BY ROB VOLLMAR
ILLUSTRATED BY MPMANN

Book Design and Layout by
Brian Newman

Published by Archaia

Archaia Entertainment LLC
1680 Vine Street, Suite 912
Los Angeles, California, 90028, USA
www.archaia.com

ARCHAIA ™

INANNA'S TEARS

March 2011

FIRST PRINTING

10 9 8 7 6 5 4 3 2 1

ISBN: 1-932386-79-3
ISBN 13: 978-1-932386-79-0

TABLE of CONTENTS

FOREWORD *A. David Lewis*..........................5

INTRODUCTION *Rob Vollmar*....................6

CHAPTER ONE.......................................11

CHAPTER TWO.....................................37

CHAPTER THREE...............................63

CHAPTER FOUR.................................89

CHAPTER FIVE..................................115

AFTERWORD *mpMann*..........................143

ABOUT THE AUTHORS..................144

FOREWORD

"And within the darkness, Inanna lamented her fate. Sensing the form that she possessed, but could not know it in a world of unending darkness. Far did her spirit wander, see king an end to the void that she might discover her form…"

Y ou are a traitor to Inanna.
So is Rob Vollmar, though, and mpMann. And certainly myself. You hold the proof in your hands, because you hold a book in your hands. As much as Inanna's story bears telling – and as well as it is told here by Vollmar and Mann – you cannot overlook your culpability. You bought the book, you read the book, and, in doing do, you approve the Book, the medium.

I can't blame you, really. Certainly, I am a major enthusiast for the graphic novel medium, and, more largely, the written word. They deliver treasures. And I can't lay blame on Gutenberg's press nor even at Moses' tablets. It is a relatively alien offense to the post-Renaissance Westerner, but here we are nonetheless. You have put your faith in print.

Along with the social, spiritual, and sexual– as in chromosomes, not pheremones–issues compellingly treated by *Inanna's Tears*, I'm particularly drawn (no pun intended) to the textual conflict. That is, mark-making is already part of the culture in *Innana's Tears*, clerks asking needy citizens to imprint their symbol on a tablet in order to receive hand-outs. But this is more a mathematical system, a primitive form of accounting, than any sort of grammar. That, though, is exactly the direction which Entika– the current embodiment of sacred En for Inanna–fears when her loyal Dubsal Anarin presents his work to her. He has transcribed their prayers into phonetic symbols, and,

shocked, Entika accidentally smashes his tablet on the ground. "This is a sign of the Lady's displeasure," she says, and Anarin's experiment is terminated.

Not for long, though. It is soon made clear that Entika's opponents wish to have their tales written. It subverts the whole system, you see, of oral tradition, of practiced memorization, and even of social hegemony. Anyone can read what is printed; it presents its content to him wantonly. And, as scholars like Walter Benjamin have pointed out, it is disconnected from anyone's personal authority. Perhaps we question the speaker of a story, but we generally believe what we read.

Therefore, be a good reader, as best a reader as a traitor might be. Enjoy Mann's sensational art, and savor Vollmar's gripping story. But probe the work, going deeper than the surface of the page and passively accepting all you read. It's too good a story to ingest so crudely.

Maintain some loyalty to Inanna and to storytelling in general. Ask, as Entika will, why you believe what you believe: Because it is simply written, or because you hear the story's truth ringing in your eyes as well as filling your eyes.

"It's something completely new. Let me show you."

—A. DAVID LEWIS

INTRODUCTION

Inanna's Tears is not historical fiction.

History is often equated with the *past*; the things which occurred that led to this place in time where we are now. History, one might reasonably suggest, is an examination of this past that results in a narrative that explains essentially how we got here from there.

As long as the "we" in question is confined to very specific groups of human beings in the last 4500 years or so, history does a pretty able job of accomplishing this task and the closer you get to *this present moment*, the more able it becomes. As a species, we are mass-communicating on an unprecedented scale and, as a result, we are producing more *instant history* than ever before. To the people with the right technology and a clear vision of what they are looking for, the human life is utterly transparent in the Information Age and, for historians, has finally presented itself as the ideal subject for archiving, collating, and classifying.

But as we wander away from the 21st century and back across the millenia towards the dawn of human civilization, the journey has scarcely begun (a mere five thousand years!) before history simply runs out of fuel. Handing off the baton to a variety of other disciplines like archaeology and anthropology, history falls silent for the remaining 245,000 years of homo sapiens' existence on Planet Earth, to say nothing of the 3,699,975,500 years that life is widely thought to have existed without us, or the 1.5 billion years preceding that our planet somehow got by without any life on it at all.

It would, of course, be patently false to claim that nothing can be known about the world with any certainty further back than 5,000 years or so. Thanks to some of those fields mentioned above and a holy host of others, we know more about life on Earth before the dawn of human civilization than ever before. But don't thank history, because if you ask history, it will tell you something like this:

Humans wandered around lost in the wilderness for 250,000 years. Then, about 5,000 years ago, one group of them called the Sumerians got their act together and invented everything that makes modern culture work; specifically, agriculture, economics, math, writing, government, and law. Everyone, everywhere eventually followed suit, resulting in the perfect world, filled with history that we enjoy today.

Maybe I'm being unnecessarily harsh but, my own recollection of my *World Thought and Culture* textbook back at the old alma mater matches that description to a T. At best, it had a chapter covering "What Came Before" (a span of nearly a quarter of a million years), followed by 1500 pages of "What Came After" (the 5,000 that followed).

Before what? After what?

Writing, of course.

History starts with Sumer because, like all historical societies that followed in their example, they had the decency to write it all down in a way that could not be easily eradicated by the passage of time. Unlike the Egyptians, who entrusted the bulk of their cultural context to fragile papyrii, the Sumerians captured their own narrative in wedge shaped marks etched on to a clay tablet that was dried and sometimes fired in a kiln to ensure its near eternal influence. The body of extant Sumerian writing is very large and, at present, mostly untranslated but that which has been made comprehensible to the modern is remarkably rich in comparison to other cultures from the period, like the Egyptians, that despite the obvious influence of writing on their culture, didn't transmit that communication to the future effectively. Whether by virtue of dumb luck or extreme foresight, Sumer's importance in the historical community has gone in roughly 150 years from non-existence to primal importance, eclipsing even Egypt who, with her showy monuments and compelling funereal art, so dominated the birth of human interest in antiquity, and all thanks to the power of the written word.

Inanna's Tears, though, isn't about any of that. It's about what came before.

More specifically, it's about what came right before; a culture one is tempted to think of as transitional, sandwiched between the nomadic hunter-gatherers that populated the space between the Tigris and Euphrates rivers for 30,000 years and the everything else that follows. It hardly does them justice. It was a thousand years of unparalleled human ingenuity in action. They were the first true masters of agriculture, understanding perfectly its lessons of producing more than is needed and creating magic from the surplus. They developed fundamental concepts of mathematics that shape the way that every person alive today thinks about counting and time. And, from their rigorous accounting, they eventually developed the oldest known form of writing.

As a result, history is able to look just beyond its own borders to rightly suggest to us that the achievements of these pre-literate Sumerians changed the very essence of humanity and how we exist in relation to the natural environment of which once we were but an inseparable component.

Inanna's Tears is a thought-picture of that seam joining "What Came Before" with "What Came After." As history was,

uniquely in this case, both written and invented by the victor, it serves here as only a counterbalance to the ambitious goal of re-animating the spirit of this otherwise unknowable age. Though not our primary focus, we have endeavored not to trample the meager flowers of history that have sprouted in this ancient and dusty soil. Given the right tools and a willingness to search, one will undoubtedly discover such footprints anyway. With another ten years to prepare, we might have been able to create something more complete, more accurate, more whatever you like.

Having been among these people and their world, however distorted from the one in which the actual Sumerians may have lived, we've come to believe that their story is an important one for us to tell. For us all to start telling; right here and right now and however we're able. While its beginning may stretch just beyond what is permissable to be known, its conclusion has yet to be reached, though like *Inanna's Tears*, it has all the landmarks of a tragedy in progress. We only hope that you are able to hear the urgency in their voices as clearly as they emerge from 5,000 years of silence.

—ROB VOLLMAR

"Beyond this there is nothing but prodigies and fictions, the only inhabitants are the poets and inventors of fables; there is no credit, or certainty further."

—PLUTARCH "THESEUS"

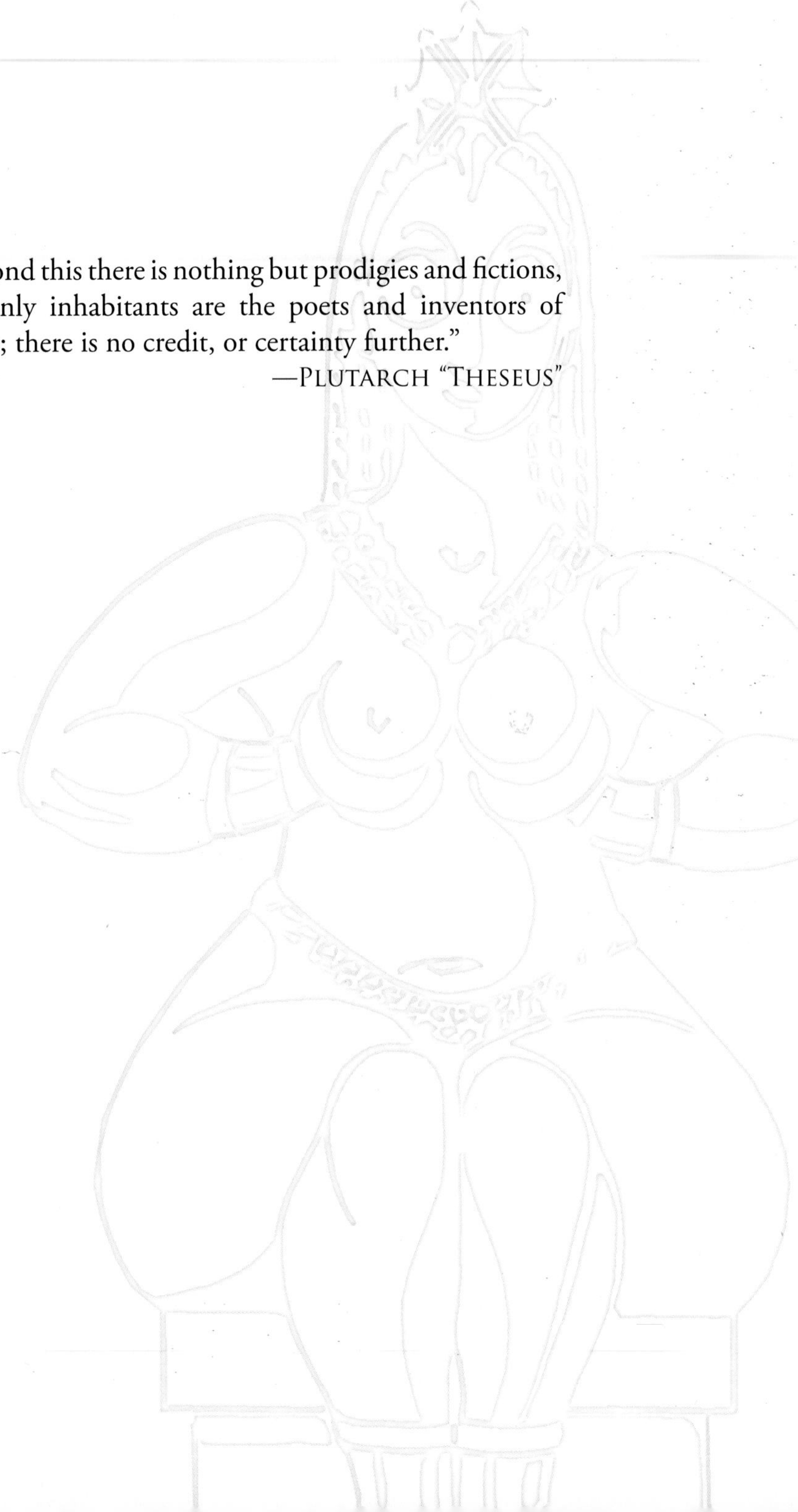

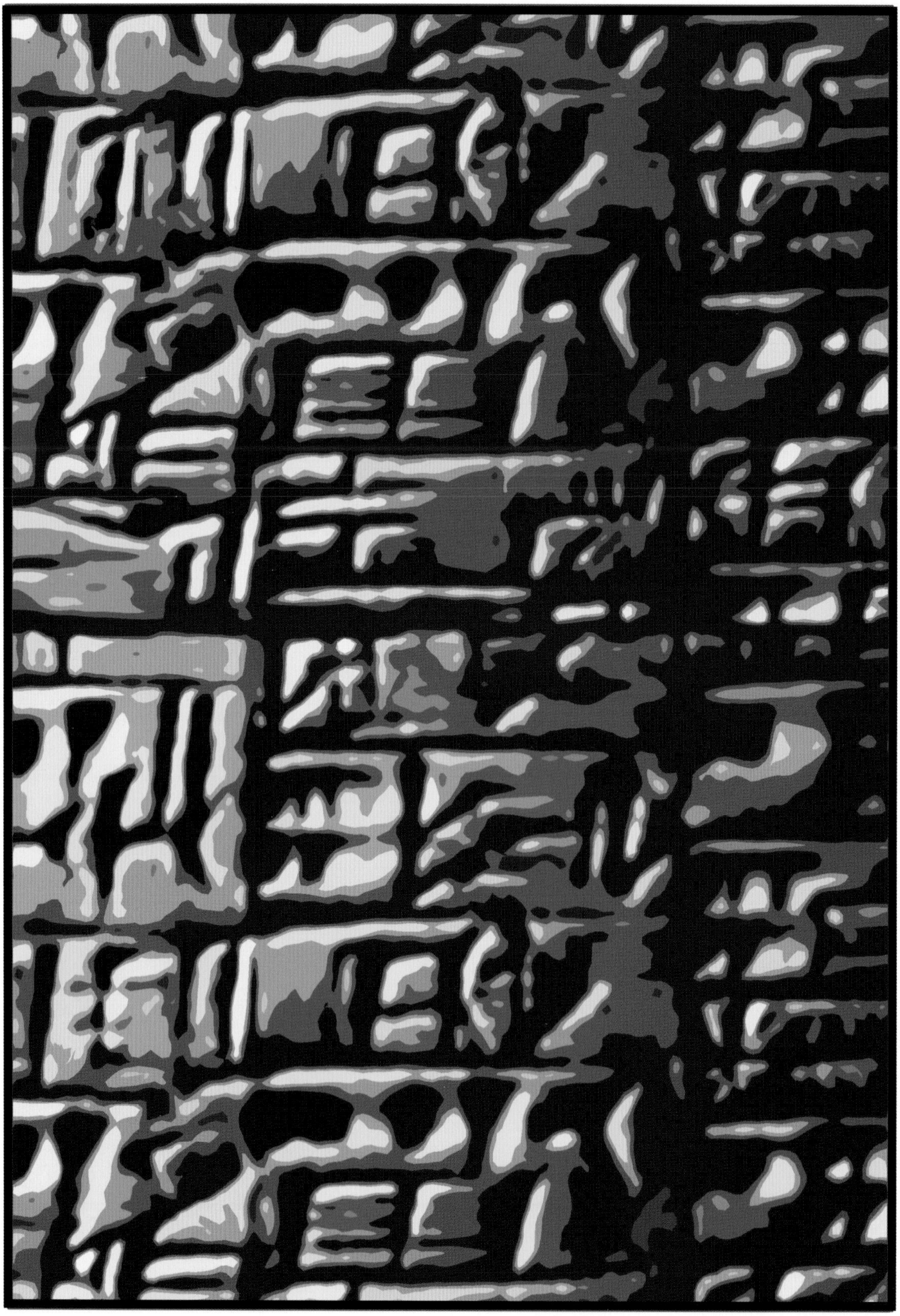

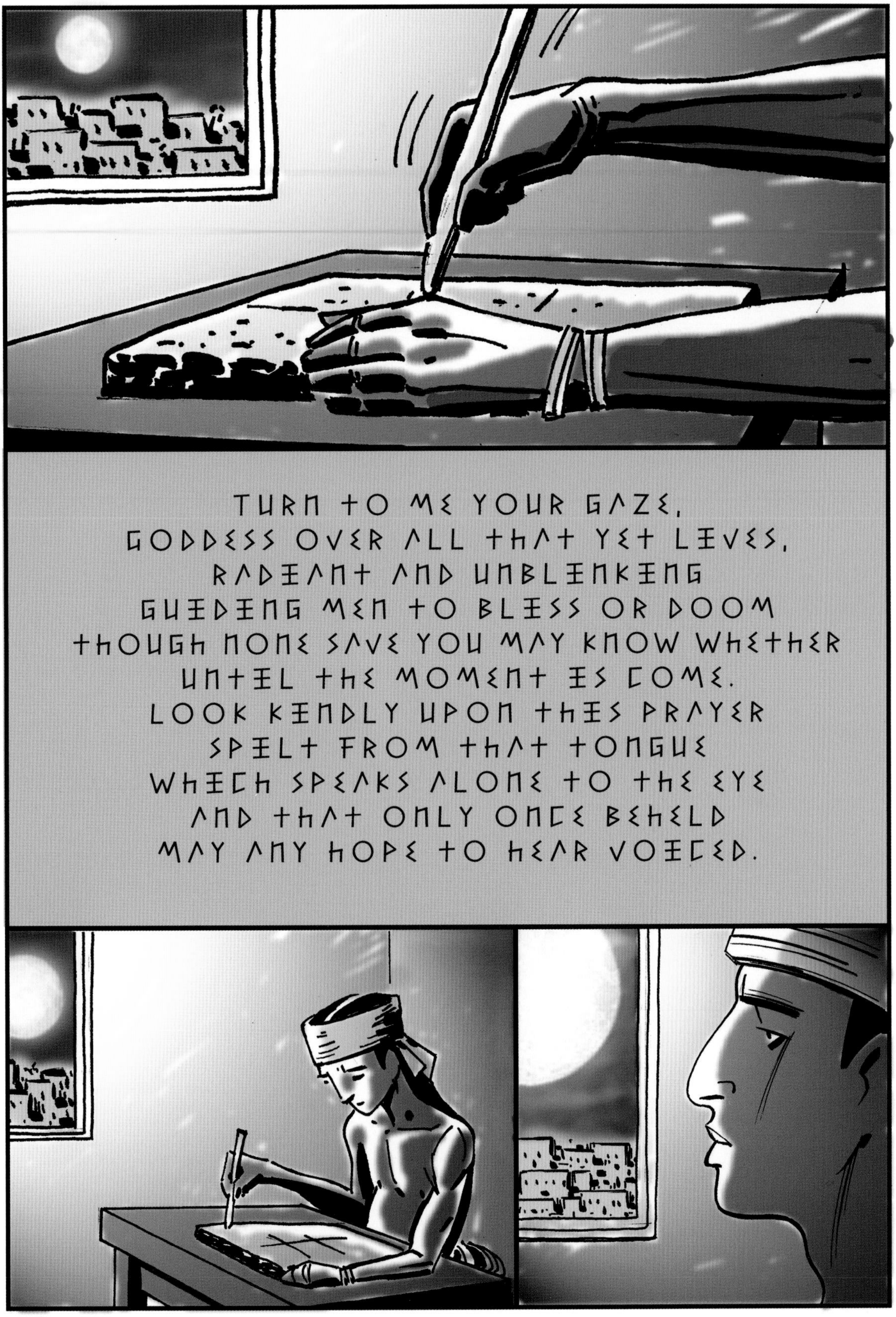
TURN TO ME YOUR GAZE,
GODDESS OVER ALL THAT YET LIVES,
RADIANT AND UNBLINKING
GUIDING MEN TO BLESS OR DOOM
THOUGH NONE SAVE YOU MAY KNOW WHETHER
UNTIL THE MOMENT IS COME.
LOOK KINDLY UPON THIS PRAYER
SPELT FROM THAT TONGUE
WHICH SPEAKS ALONE TO THE EYE
AND THAT ONLY ONCE BEHELD
MAY ANY HOPE TO HEAR VOICED.

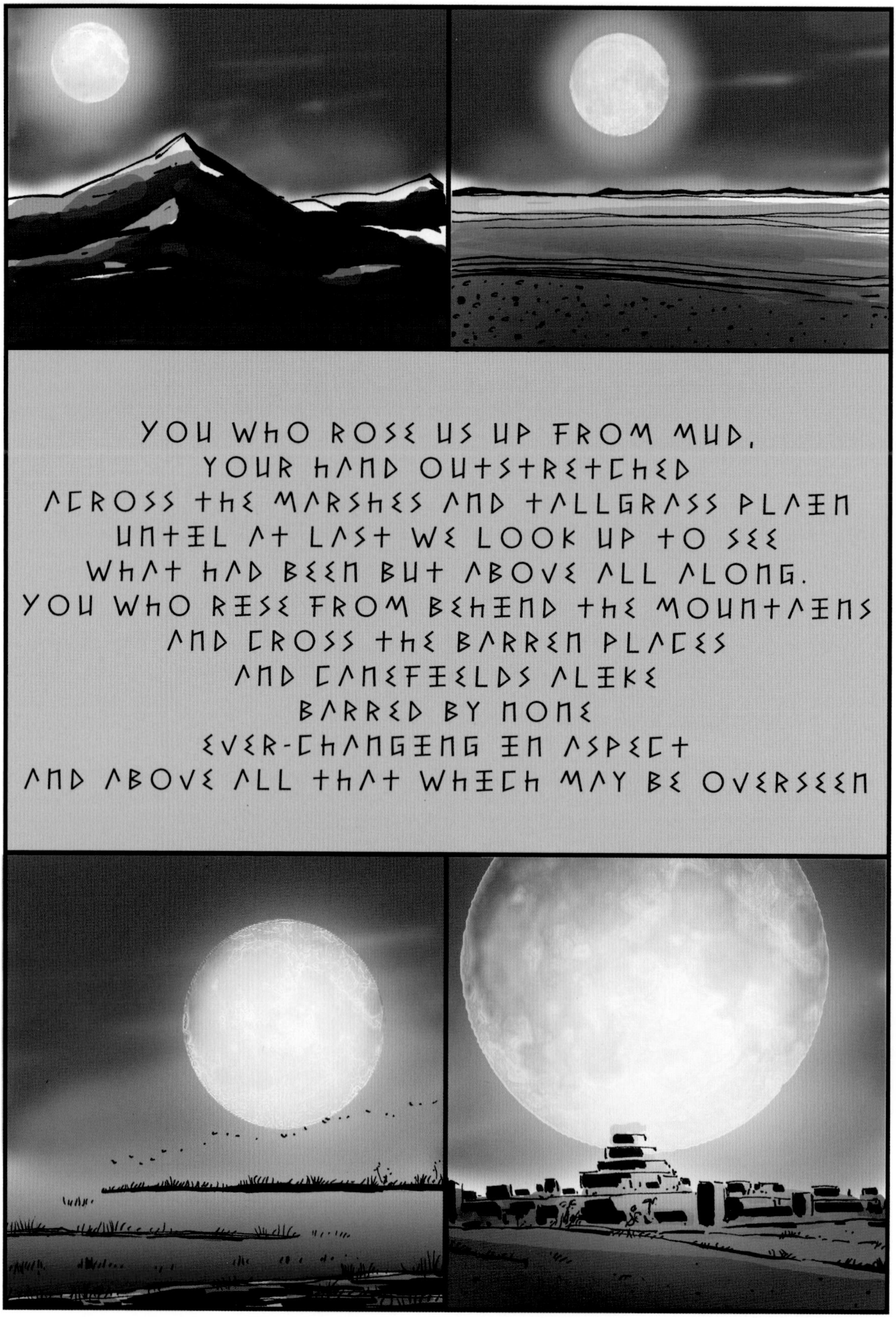
YOU WHO ROSE US UP FROM MUD,
YOUR HAND OUTSTRETCHED
ACROSS THE MARSHES AND TALLGRASS PLAIN
UNTIL AT LAST WE LOOK UP TO SEE
WHAT HAD BEEN BUT ABOVE ALL ALONG.
YOU WHO RISE FROM BEHIND THE MOUNTAINS
AND CROSS THE BARREN PLACES
AND CANEFIELDS ALIKE
BARRED BY NONE
EVER-CHANGING IN ASPECT
AND ABOVE ALL THAT WHICH MAY BE OVERSEEN

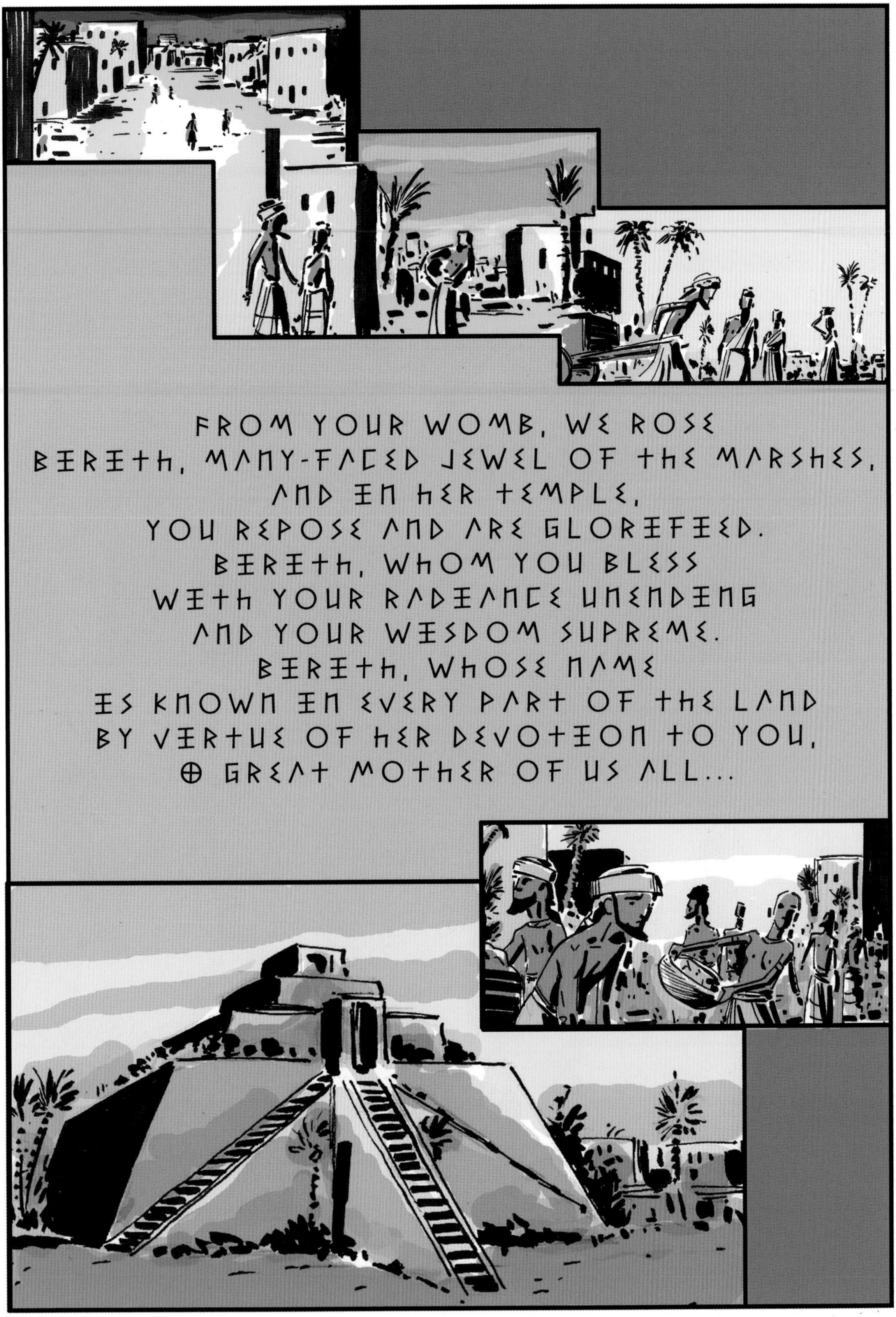
FROM YOUR WOMB, WE ROSE
BIRITH, MANY-FACED JEWEL OF THE MARSHES,
AND IN HER TEMPLE,
YOU REPOSE AND ARE GLORIFIED.
BIRITH, WHOM YOU BLESS
WITH YOUR RADIANCE UNENDING
AND YOUR WISDOM SUPREME.
BIRITH, WHOSE NAME
IS KNOWN IN EVERY PART OF THE LAND
BY VIRTUE OF HER DEVOTION TO YOU,
O GREAT MOTHER OF US ALL...

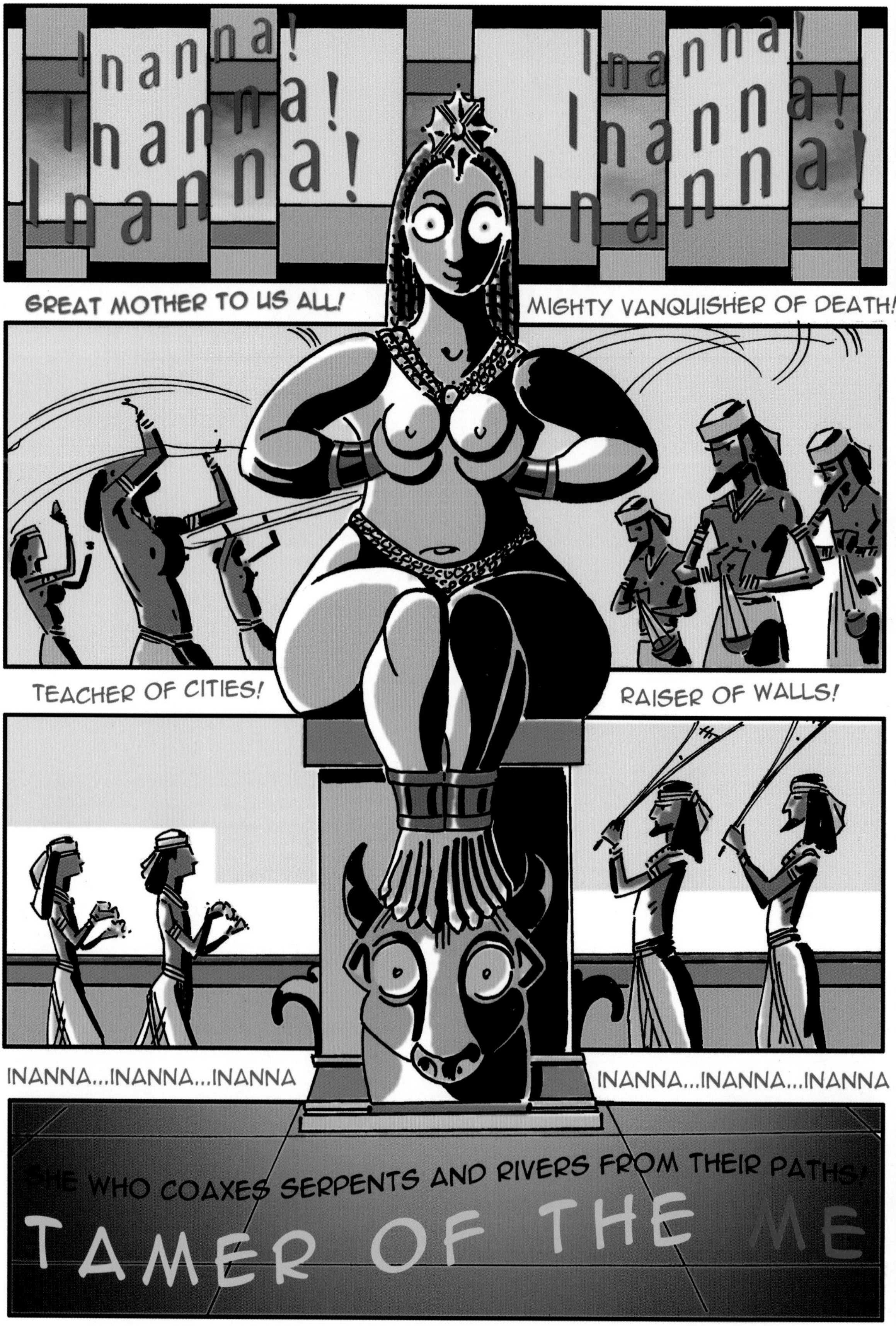
Inanna! Inanna! Inanna!
Inanna! Inanna! Inanna!
GREAT MOTHER TO US ALL!
MIGHTY VANQUISHER OF DEATH!
TEACHER OF CITIES!
RAISER OF WALLS!
INANNA...INANNA...INANNA
INANNA...INANNA...INANNA
SHE WHO COAXES SERPENTS AND RIVERS FROM THEIR PATHS!
TAMER OF THE ME

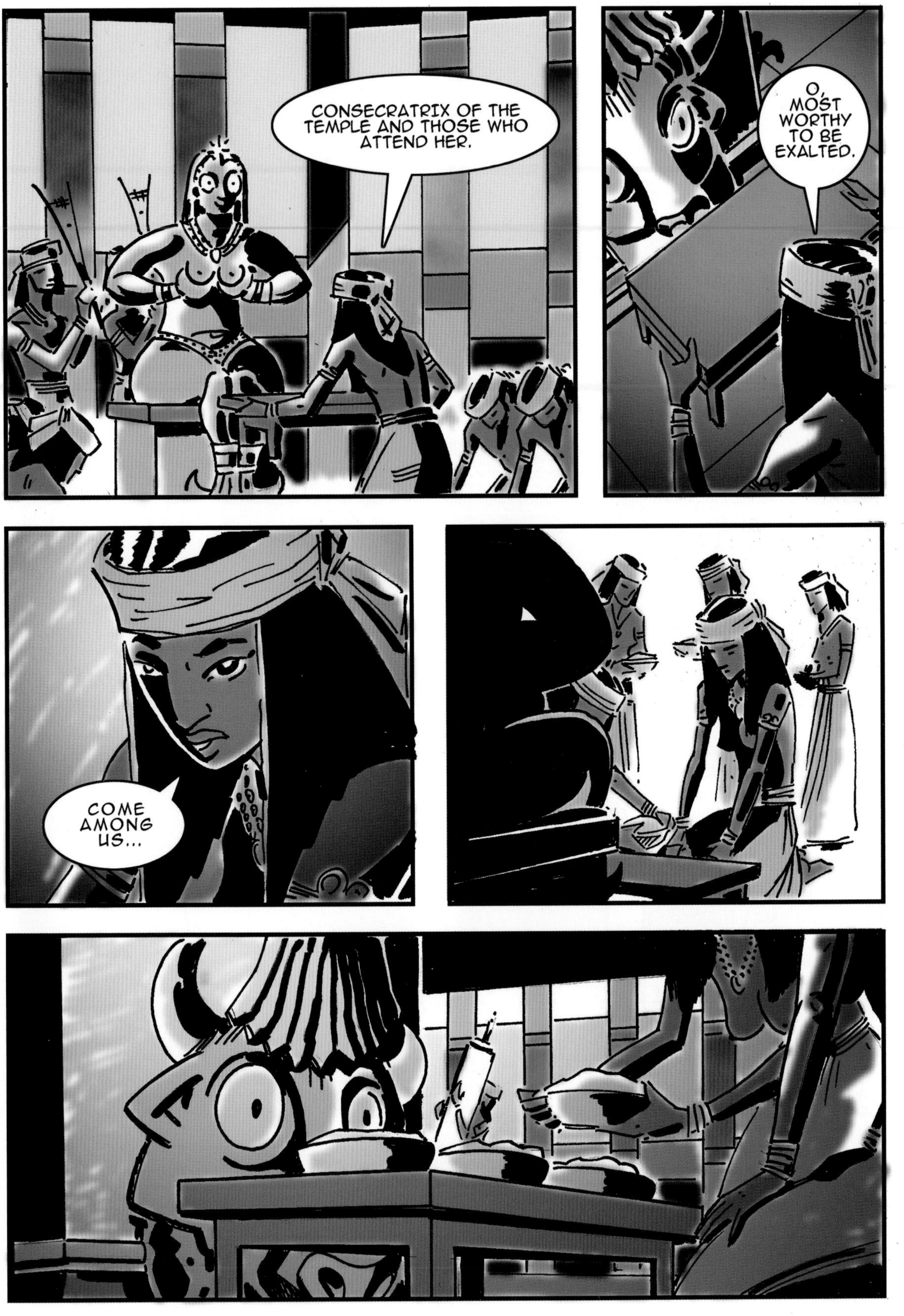
CONSECRATRIX OF THE TEMPLE AND THOSE WHO ATTEND HER.
O, MOST WORTHY TO BE EXALTED.
COME AMONG US...

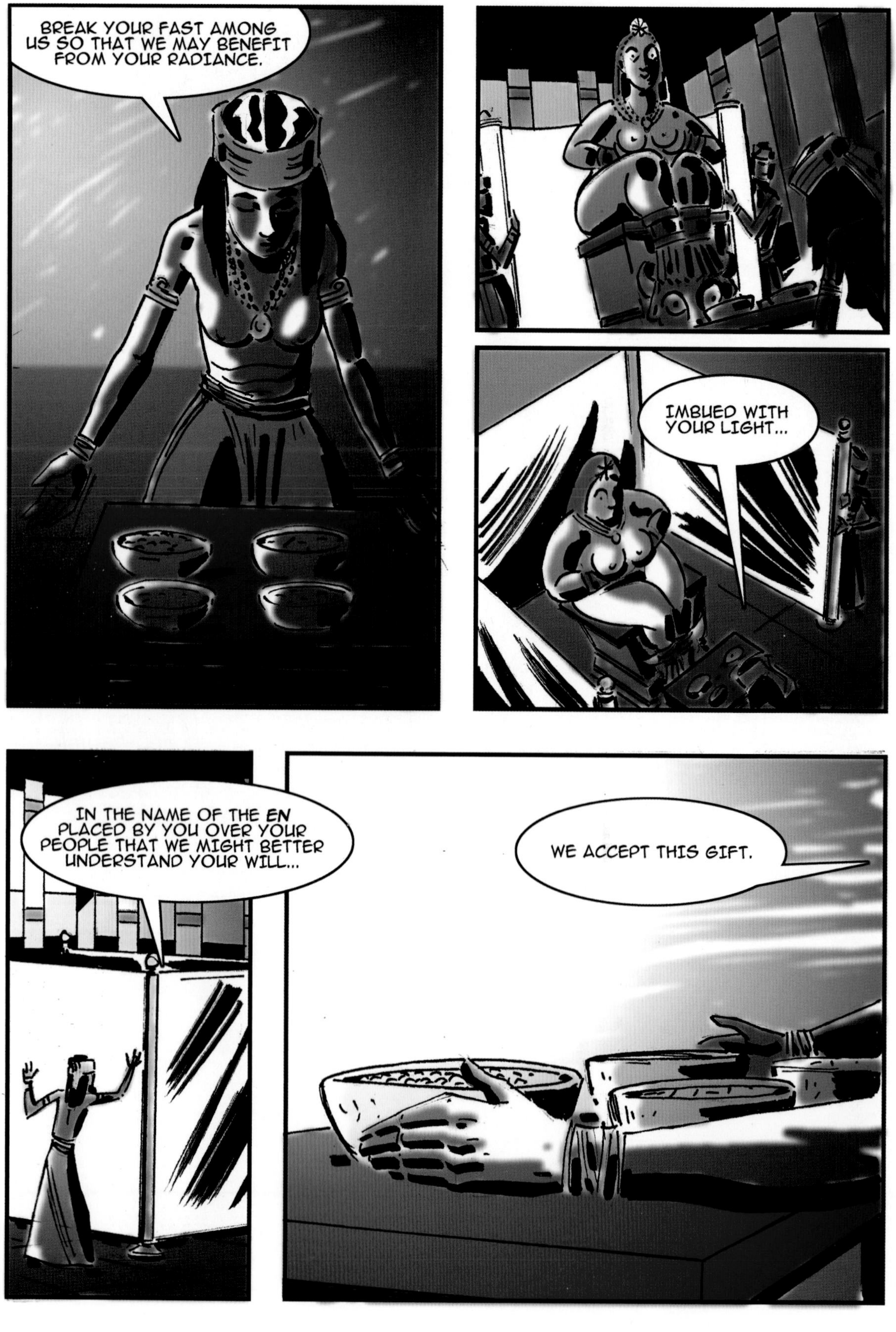
BREAK YOUR FAST AMONG US SO THAT WE MAY BENEFIT FROM YOUR RADIANCE.
IMBUED WITH YOUR LIGHT...
IN THE NAME OF THE *EN* PLACED BY YOU OVER YOUR PEOPLE THAT WE MIGHT BETTER UNDERSTAND YOUR WILL...
WE ACCEPT THIS GIFT.

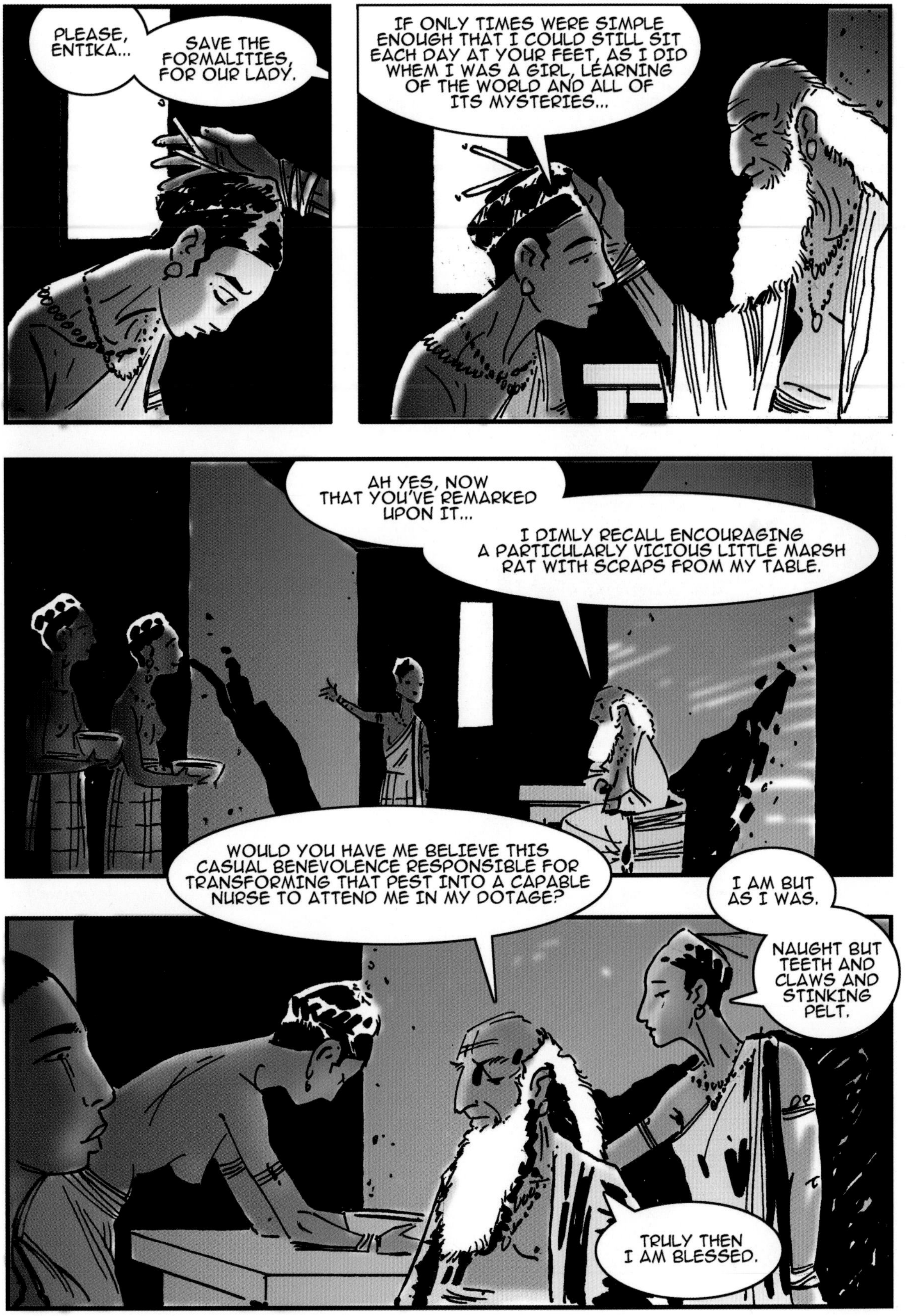
PLEASE, ENTIKA...
SAVE THE FORMALITIES, FOR OUR LADY.
IF ONLY TIMES WERE SIMPLE ENOUGH THAT I COULD STILL SIT EACH DAY AT YOUR FEET, AS I DID WHEM I WAS A GIRL, LEARNING OF THE WORLD AND ALL OF ITS MYSTERIES...
AH YES, NOW THAT YOU'VE REMARKED UPON IT...
I DIMLY RECALL ENCOURAGING A PARTICULARLY VICIOUS LITTLE MARSH RAT WITH SCRAPS FROM MY TABLE.
WOULD YOU HAVE ME BELIEVE THIS CASUAL BENEVOLENCE RESPONSIBLE FOR TRANSFORMING THAT PEST INTO A CAPABLE NURSE TO ATTEND ME IN MY DOTAGE?
I AM BUT AS I WAS.
NAUGHT BUT TEETH AND CLAWS AND STINKING PELT.
TRULY THEN I AM BLESSED.

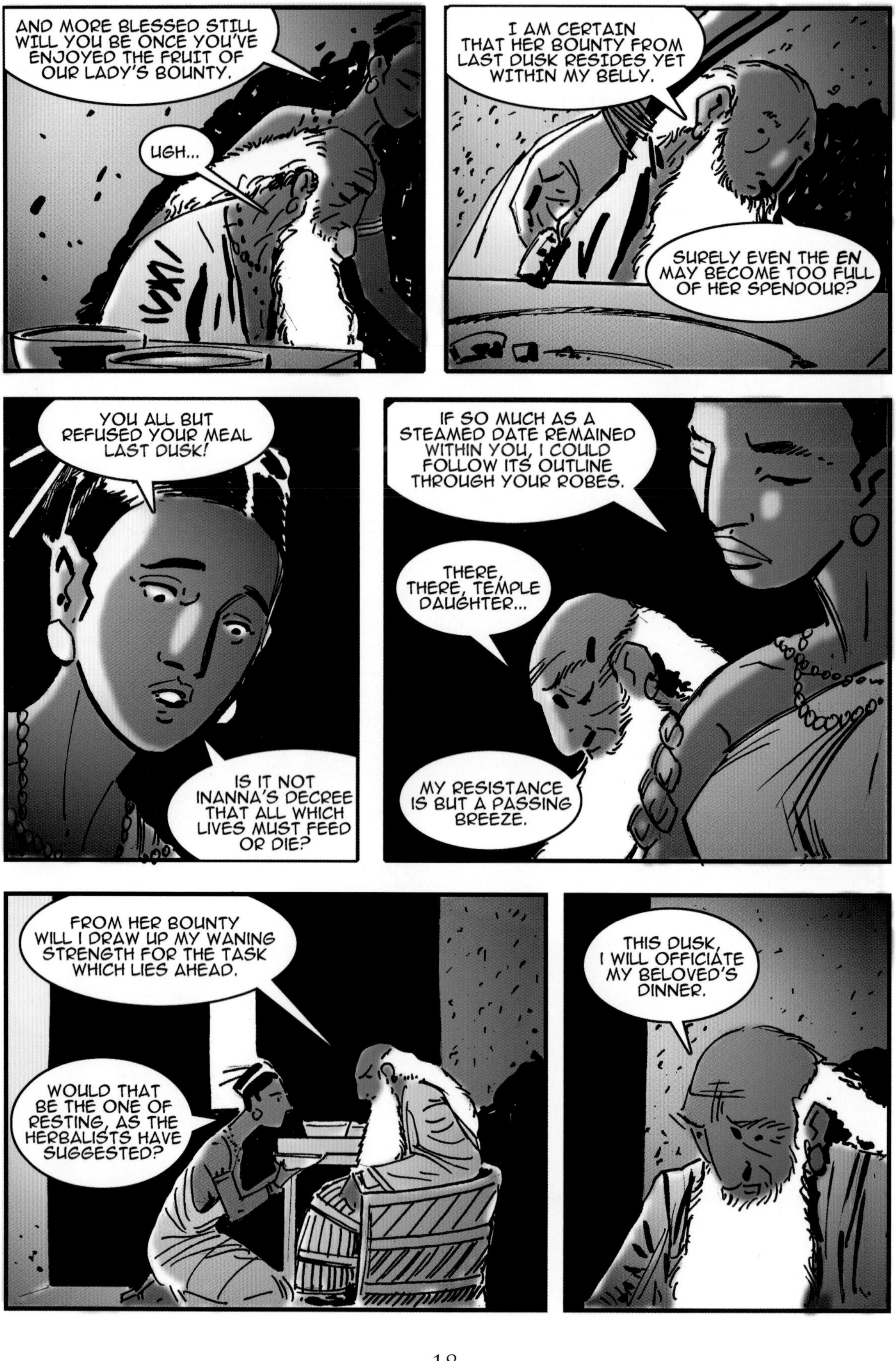
AND MORE BLESSED STILL WILL YOU BE ONCE YOU'VE ENJOYED THE FRUIT OF OUR LADY'S BOUNTY.
UGH...
I AM CERTAIN THAT HER BOUNTY FROM LAST DUSK RESIDES YET WITHIN MY BELLY.
SURELY EVEN THE EN MAY BECOME TOO FULL OF HER SPENDOUR?
YOU ALL BUT REFUSED YOUR MEAL LAST DUSK!
IS IT NOT INANNA'S DECREE THAT ALL WHICH LIVES MUST FEED OR DIE?
IF SO MUCH AS A STEAMED DATE REMAINED WITHIN YOU, I COULD FOLLOW ITS OUTLINE THROUGH YOUR ROBES.
THERE, THERE, TEMPLE DAUGHTER...
MY RESISTANCE IS BUT A PASSING BREEZE.
FROM HER BOUNTY WILL I DRAW UP MY WANING STRENGTH FOR THE TASK WHICH LIES AHEAD.
WOULD THAT BE THE ONE OF RESTING, AS THE HERBALISTS HAVE SUGGESTED?
THIS DUSK, I WILL OFFICIATE MY BELOVED'S DINNER.

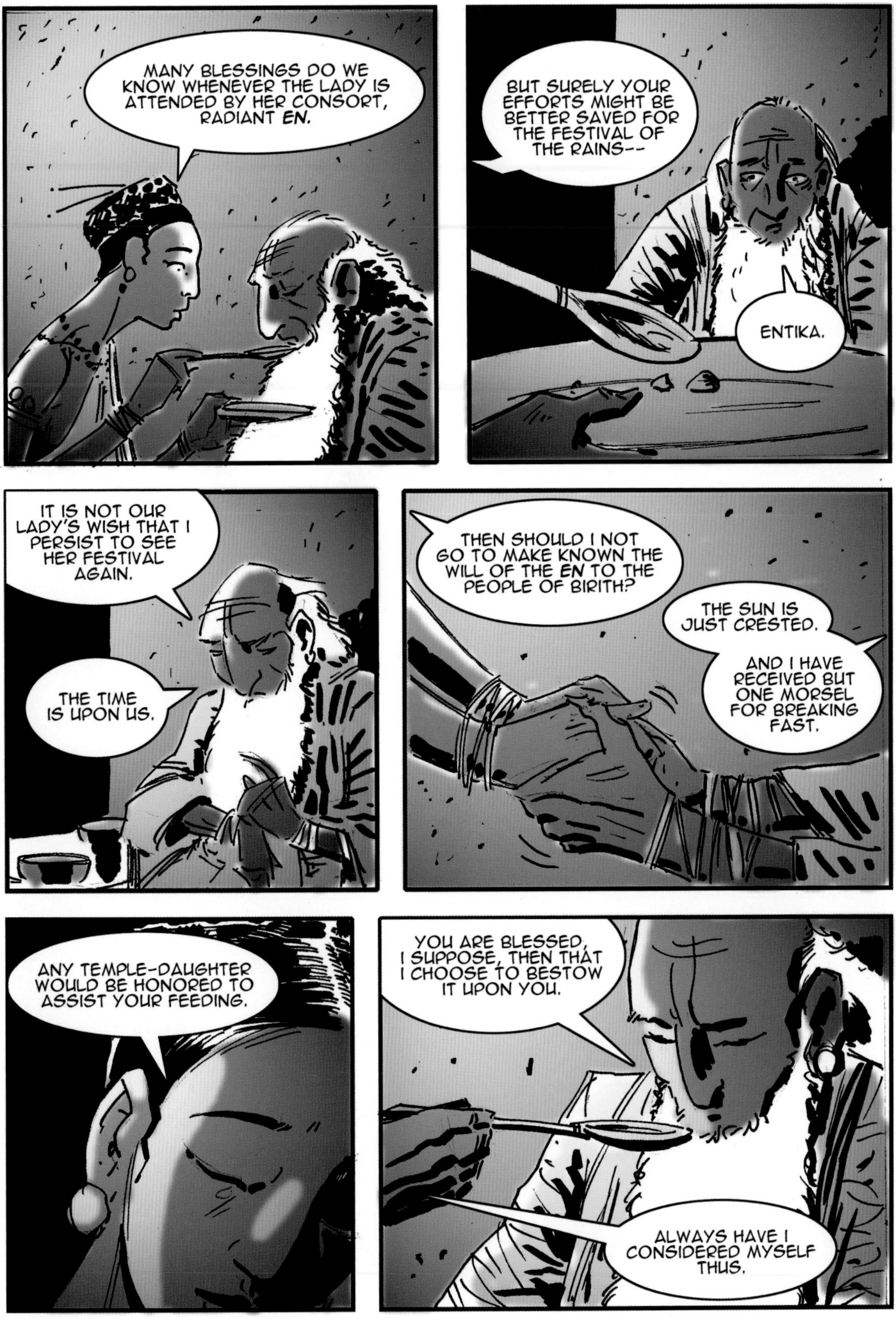
MANY BLESSINGS DO WE KNOW WHENEVER THE LADY IS ATTENDED BY HER CONSORT, RADIANT **EN.**
BUT SURELY YOUR EFFORTS MIGHT BE BETTER SAVED FOR THE FESTIVAL OF THE RAINS--
ENTIKA.
IT IS NOT OUR LADY'S WISH THAT I PERSIST TO SEE HER FESTIVAL AGAIN.
THE TIME IS UPON US.
THEN SHOULD I NOT GO TO MAKE KNOWN THE WILL OF THE **EN** TO THE PEOPLE OF BIRITH?
THE SUN IS JUST CRESTED.
AND I HAVE RECEIVED BUT ONE MORSEL FOR BREAKING FAST.
ANY TEMPLE-DAUGHTER WOULD BE HONORED TO ASSIST YOUR FEEDING.
YOU ARE BLESSED, I SUPPOSE, THEN THAT I CHOOSE TO BESTOW IT UPON YOU.
ALWAYS HAVE I CONSIDERED MYSELF THUS.

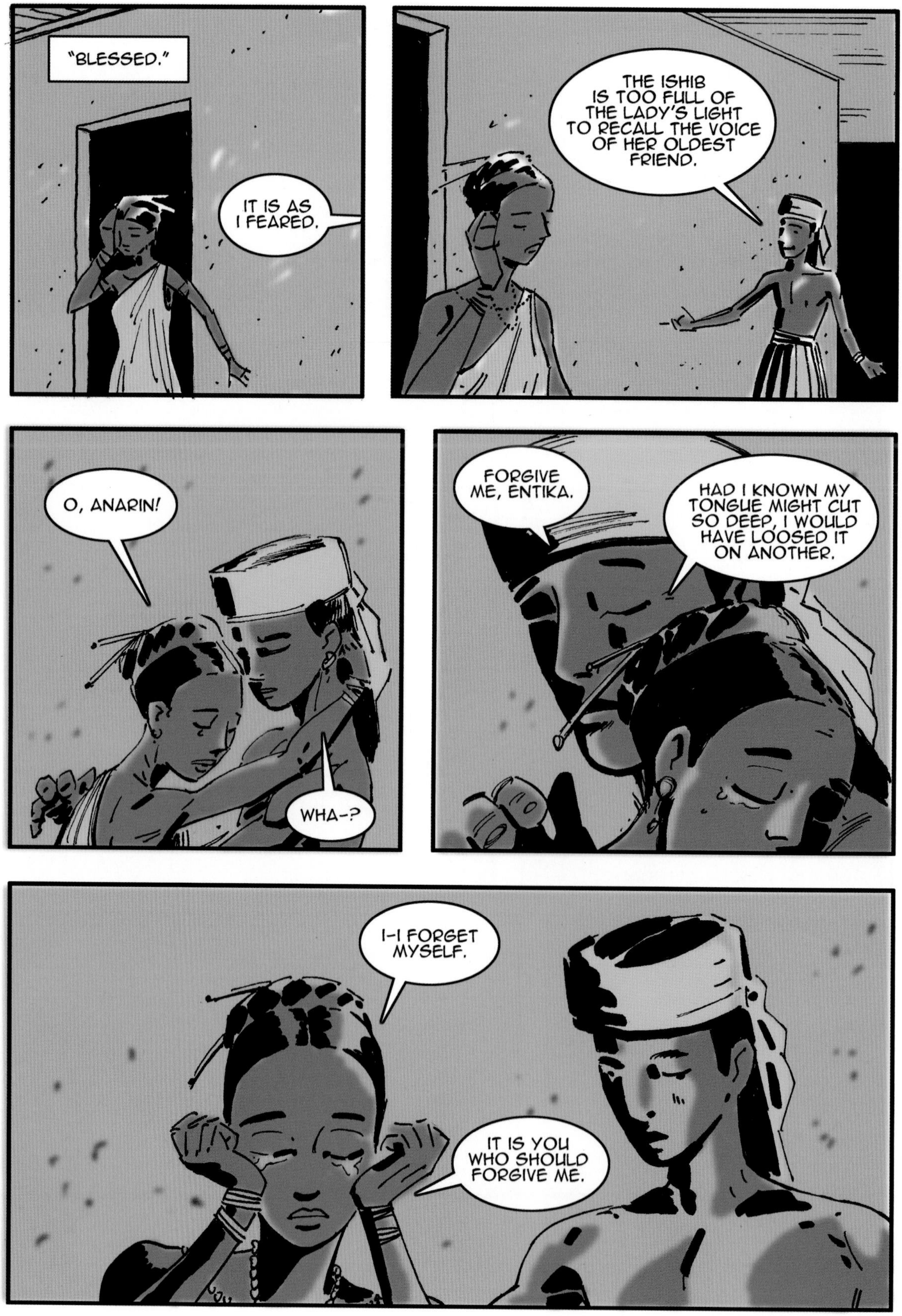
"BLESSED."
IT IS AS I FEARED.
THE ISHIB IS TOO FULL OF THE LADY'S LIGHT TO RECALL THE VOICE OF HER OLDEST FRIEND.
O, ANARIN!
WHA-?
FORGIVE ME, ENTIKA.
HAD I KNOWN MY TONGUE MIGHT CUT SO DEEP, I WOULD HAVE LOOSED IT ON ANOTHER.
I-I FORGET MYSELF.
IT IS YOU WHO SHOULD FORGIVE ME.

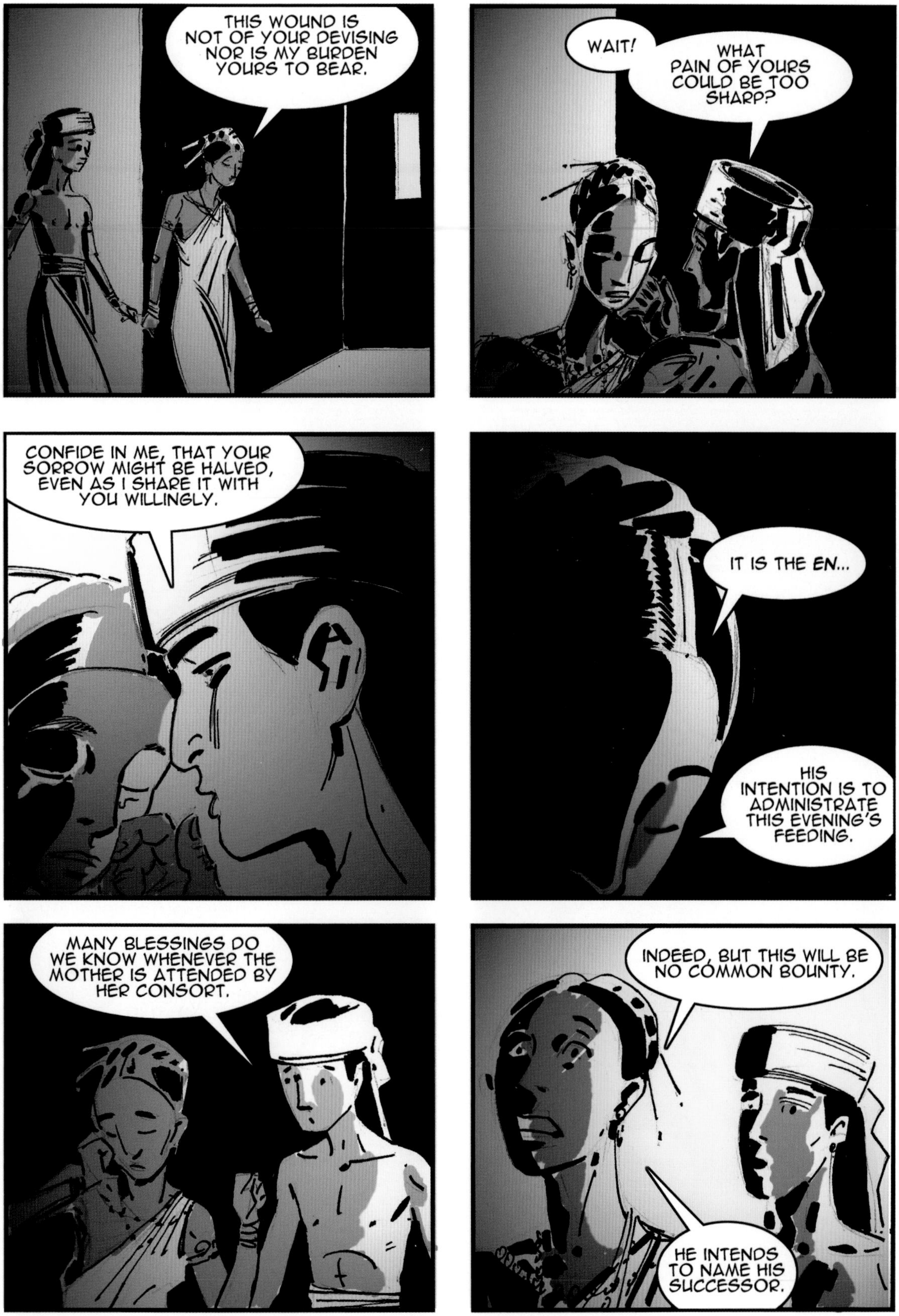
THIS WOUND IS NOT OF YOUR DEVISING NOR IS MY BURDEN YOURS TO BEAR.
WAIT!
WHAT PAIN OF YOURS COULD BE TOO SHARP?
CONFIDE IN ME, THAT YOUR SORROW MIGHT BE HALVED, EVEN AS I SHARE IT WITH YOU WILLINGLY.
IT IS THE EN...
HIS INTENTION IS TO ADMINISTRATE THIS EVENING'S FEEDING.
MANY BLESSINGS DO WE KNOW WHENEVER THE MOTHER IS ATTENDED BY HER CONSORT.
INDEED, BUT THIS WILL BE NO COMMON BOUNTY.
HE INTENDS TO NAME HIS SUCCESSOR.

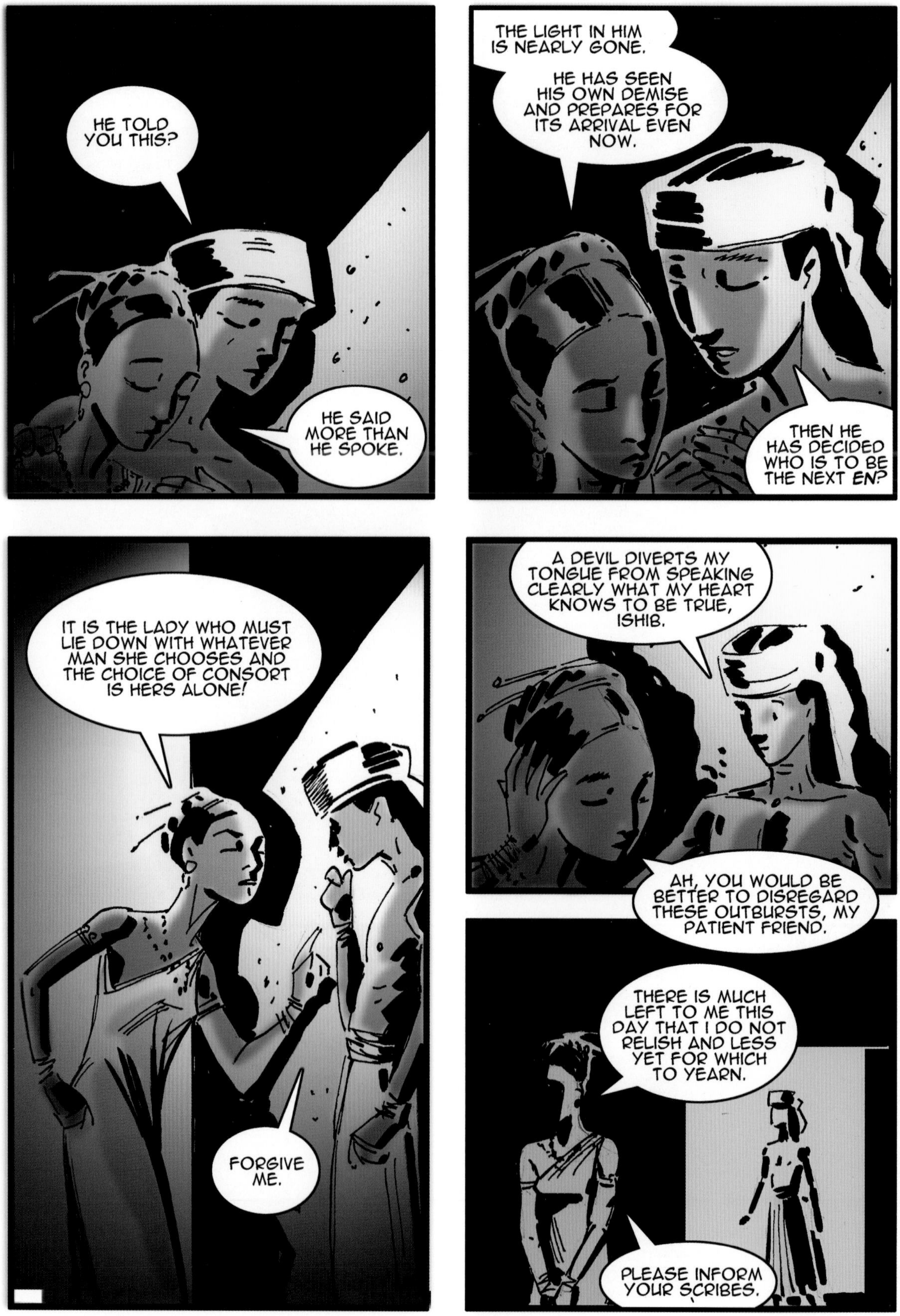
HE TOLD YOU THIS?
HE SAID MORE THAN HE SPOKE.
THE LIGHT IN HIM IS NEARLY GONE.
HE HAS SEEN HIS OWN DEMISE AND PREPARES FOR ITS ARRIVAL EVEN NOW.
THEN HE HAS DECIDED WHO IS TO BE THE NEXT *EN*?
IT IS THE LADY WHO MUST LIE DOWN WITH WHATEVER MAN SHE CHOOSES AND THE CHOICE OF CONSORT IS HERS ALONE!
FORGIVE ME.
A DEVIL DIVERTS MY TONGUE FROM SPEAKING CLEARLY WHAT MY HEART KNOWS TO BE TRUE, ISHIB.
AH, YOU WOULD BE BETTER TO DISREGARD THESE OUTBURSTS, MY PATIENT FRIEND.
THERE IS MUCH LEFT TO ME THIS DAY THAT I DO NOT RELISH AND LESS YET FOR WHICH TO YEARN.
PLEASE INFORM YOUR SCRIBES.

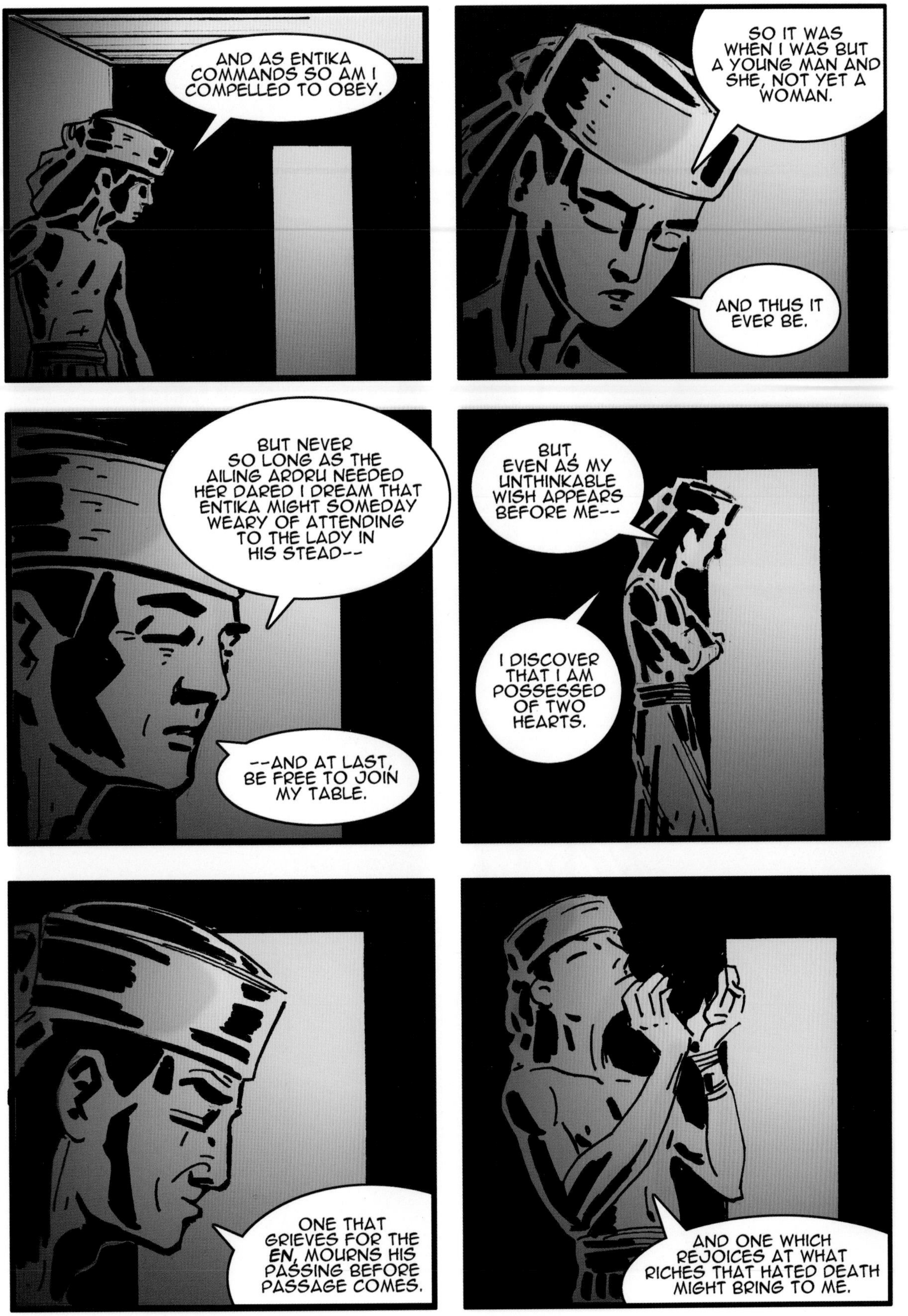
AND AS ENTIKA COMMANDS SO AM I COMPELLED TO OBEY.
SO IT WAS WHEN I WAS BUT A YOUNG MAN AND SHE, NOT YET A WOMAN.
AND THUS IT EVER BE.
BUT NEVER SO LONG AS THE AILING ARDRU NEEDED HER DARED I DREAM THAT ENTIKA MIGHT SOMEDAY WEARY OF ATTENDING TO THE LADY IN HIS STEAD--
--AND AT LAST, BE FREE TO JOIN MY TABLE.
BUT, EVEN AS MY UNTHINKABLE WISH APPEARS BEFORE ME--
I DISCOVER THAT I AM POSSESSED OF TWO HEARTS.
ONE THAT GRIEVES FOR THE EN, MOURNS HIS PASSING BEFORE PASSAGE COMES.
AND ONE WHICH REJOICES AT WHAT RICHES THAT HATED DEATH MIGHT BRING TO ME.

IS IT THE LADY'S WISH THAT I BE CURSED OR BLESSED?
OR IS IT LIKELIER STILL THAT I AM OF NO CONCERN TO HER AT ALL?

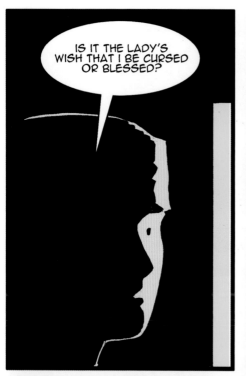

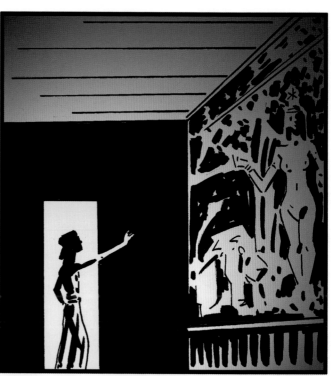

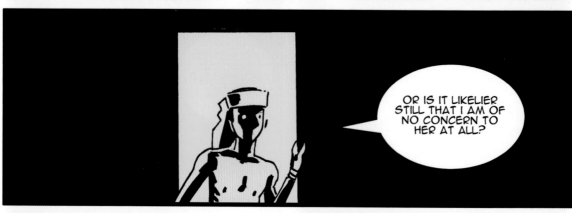

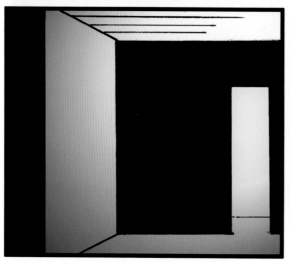

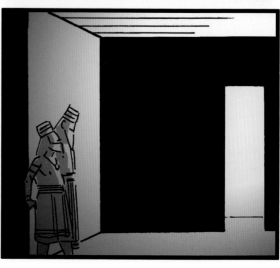

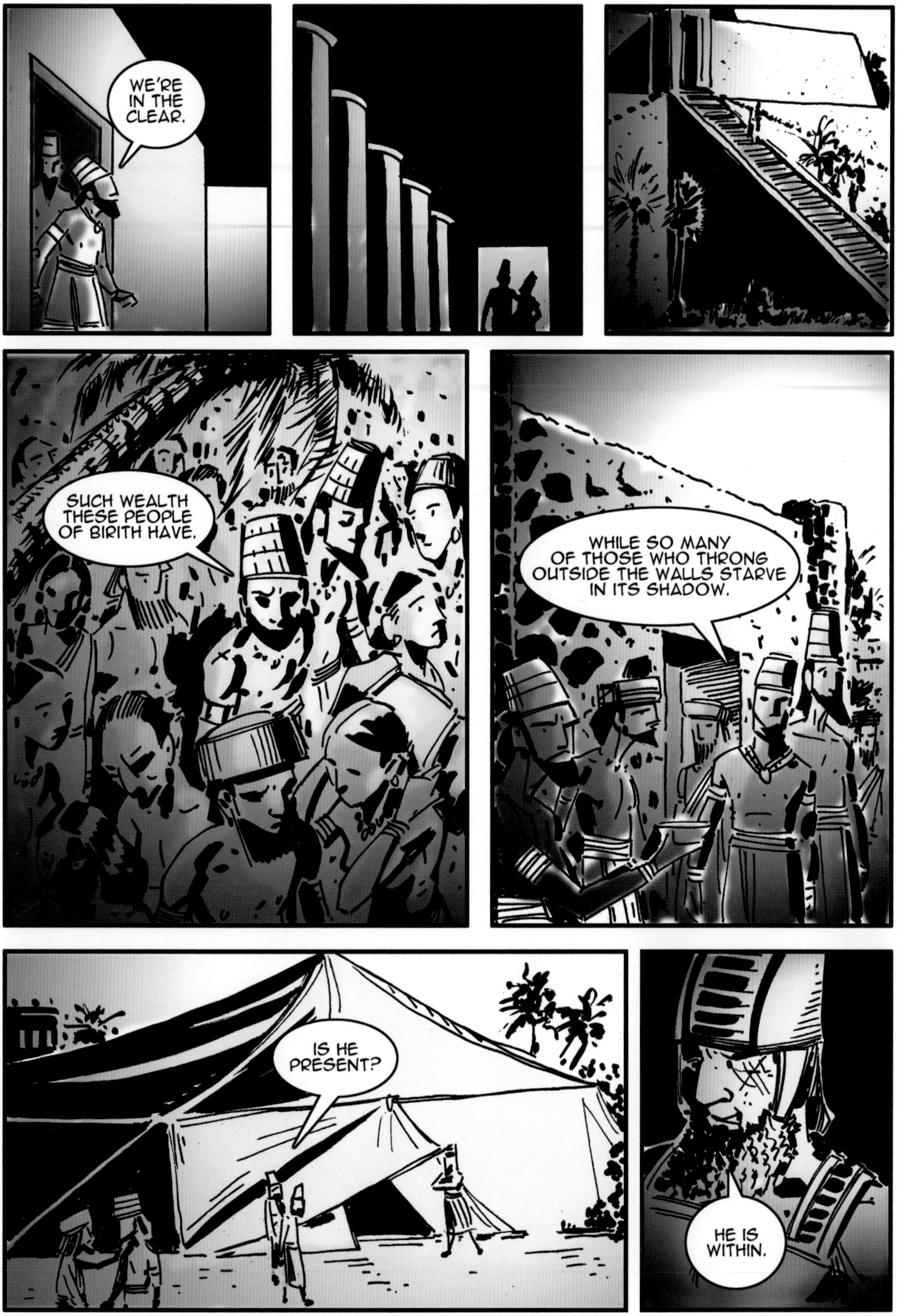
WE'RE IN THE CLEAR.
SUCH WEALTH THESE PEOPLE OF BIRITH HAVE.
WHILE SO MANY OF THOSE WHO THRONG OUTSIDE THE WALLS STARVE IN ITS SHADOW.
IS HE PRESENT?
HE IS WITHIN.

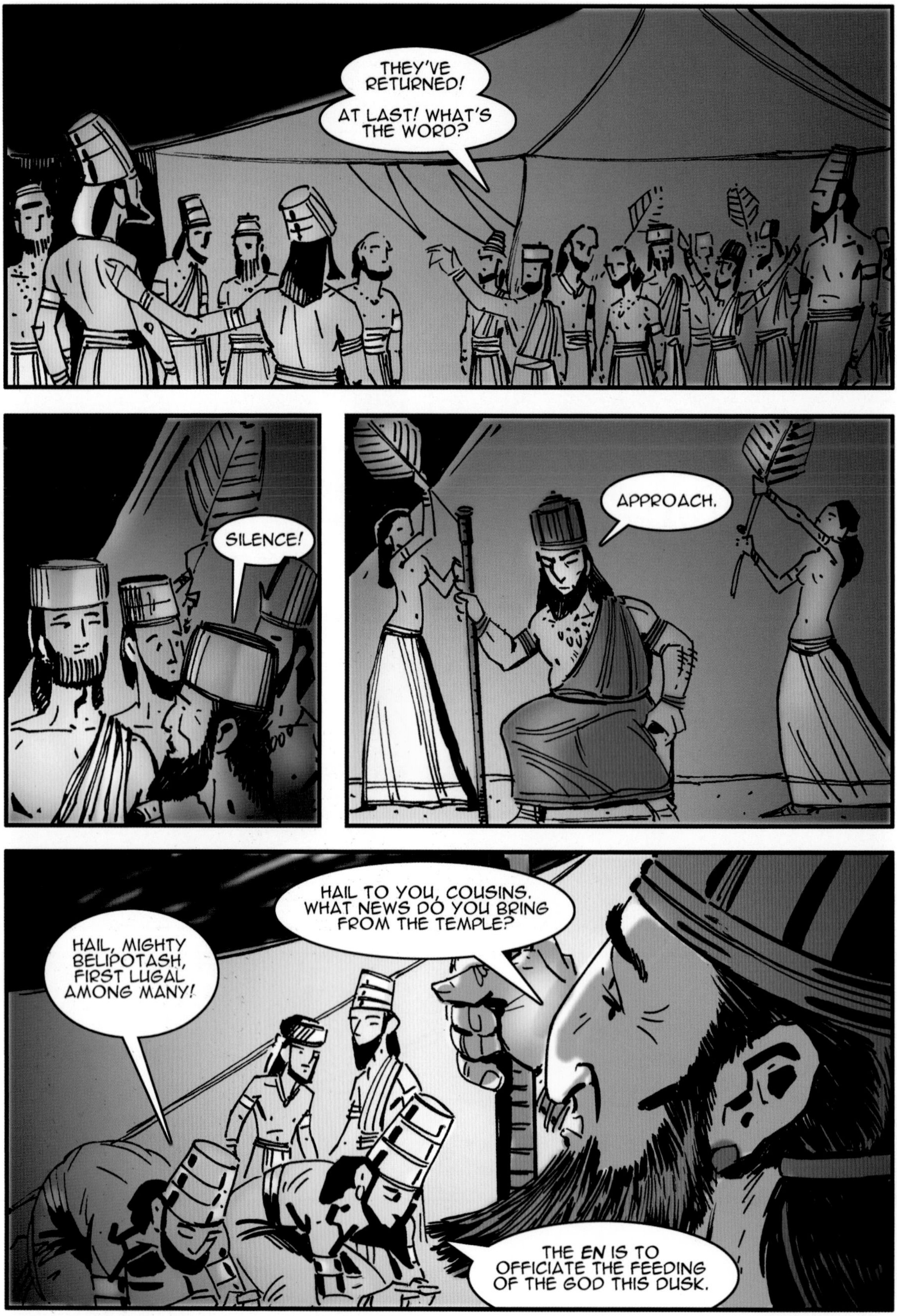
THEY'VE RETURNED!
AT LAST! WHAT'S THE WORD?
SILENCE!
APPROACH.
HAIL TO YOU, COUSINS. WHAT NEWS DO YOU BRING FROM THE TEMPLE?
HAIL, MIGHTY BELIPOTASH, FIRST LUGAL AMONG MANY!
THE *EN* IS TO OFFICIATE THE FEEDING OF THE GOD THIS DUSK.

THEN IT IS AS THEY SAY.

ARDRU IS NOT LONG FOR THIS LIFE.

BUT HOW CAN WE BE CERTAIN HE MEANS TO NAME A SUCCESSOR?

PERHAPS THE LADY HAS RETURNED HIS STRENGTH TO HIM?

HIS BODY IS A SHATTERED URN.

EVEN THE GODS CANNOT FILL THAT WHICH HOLDS NO FORM.

FROM WHOSE LIPS DID YOU HEAR THIS?

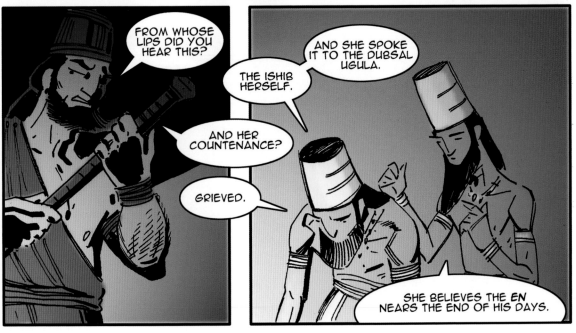

AND SHE SPOKE IT TO THE DUBSAL UGULA.

THE ISHIB HERSELF.

AND HER COUNTENANCE?

GRIEVED.

SHE BELIEVES THE *EN* NEARS THE END OF HIS DAYS.

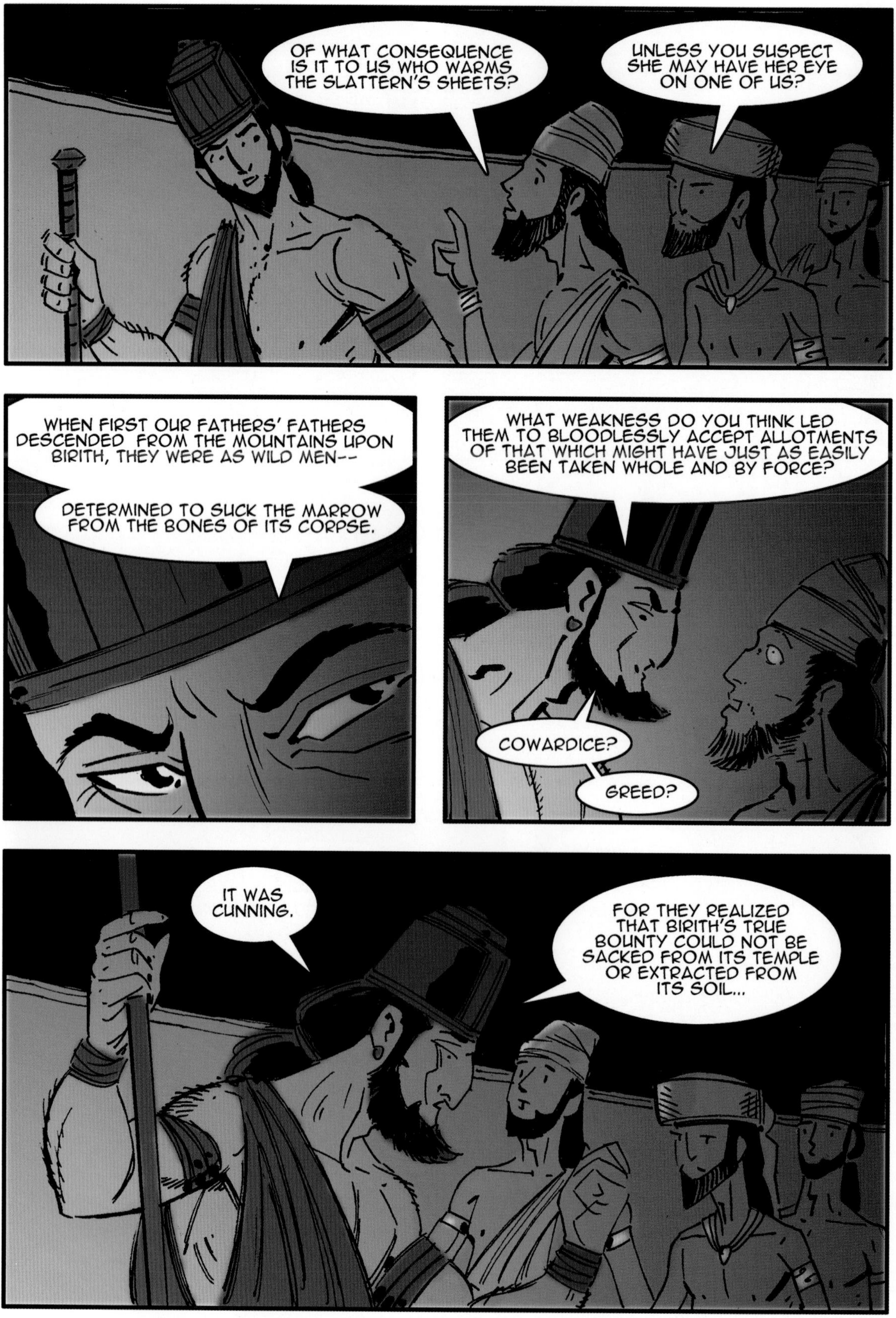
OF WHAT CONSEQUENCE IS IT TO US WHO WARMS THE SLATTERN'S SHEETS?
UNLESS YOU SUSPECT SHE MAY HAVE HER EYE ON ONE OF US?
WHEN FIRST OUR FATHERS' FATHERS DESCENDED FROM THE MOUNTAINS UPON BIRITH, THEY WERE AS WILD MEN--
DETERMINED TO SUCK THE MARROW FROM THE BONES OF ITS CORPSE.
WHAT WEAKNESS DO YOU THINK LED THEM TO BLOODLESSLY ACCEPT ALLOTMENTS OF THAT WHICH MIGHT HAVE JUST AS EASILY BEEN TAKEN WHOLE AND BY FORCE?
COWARDICE?
GREED?
IT WAS CUNNING.
FOR THEY REALIZED THAT BIRITH'S TRUE BOUNTY COULD NOT BE SACKED FROM ITS TEMPLE OR EXTRACTED FROM ITS SOIL...

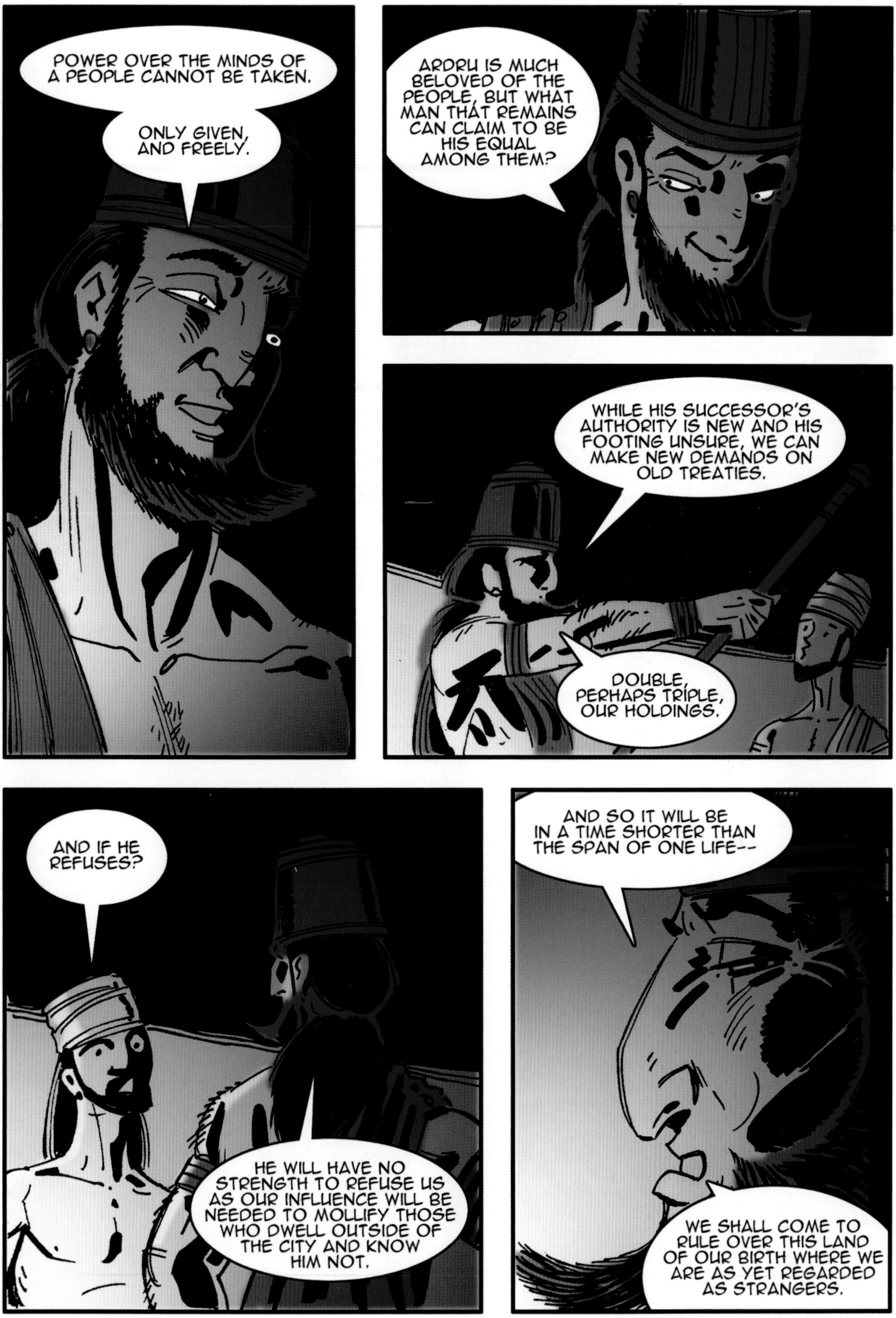
POWER OVER THE MINDS OF A PEOPLE CANNOT BE TAKEN.
ONLY GIVEN, AND FREELY.
ARDRU IS MUCH BELOVED OF THE PEOPLE, BUT WHAT MAN THAT REMAINS CAN CLAIM TO BE HIS EQUAL AMONG THEM?
WHILE HIS SUCCESSOR'S AUTHORITY IS NEW AND HIS FOOTING UNSURE, WE CAN MAKE NEW DEMANDS ON OLD TREATIES.
DOUBLE, PERHAPS TRIPLE, OUR HOLDINGS.
AND IF HE REFUSES?
HE WILL HAVE NO STRENGTH TO REFUSE US AS OUR INFLUENCE WILL BE NEEDED TO MOLLIFY THOSE WHO DWELL OUTSIDE OF THE CITY AND KNOW HIM NOT.
AND SO IT WILL BE IN A TIME SHORTER THAN THE SPAN OF ONE LIFE--
WE SHALL COME TO RULE OVER THIS LAND OF OUR BIRTH WHERE WE ARE AS YET REGARDED AS STRANGERS.

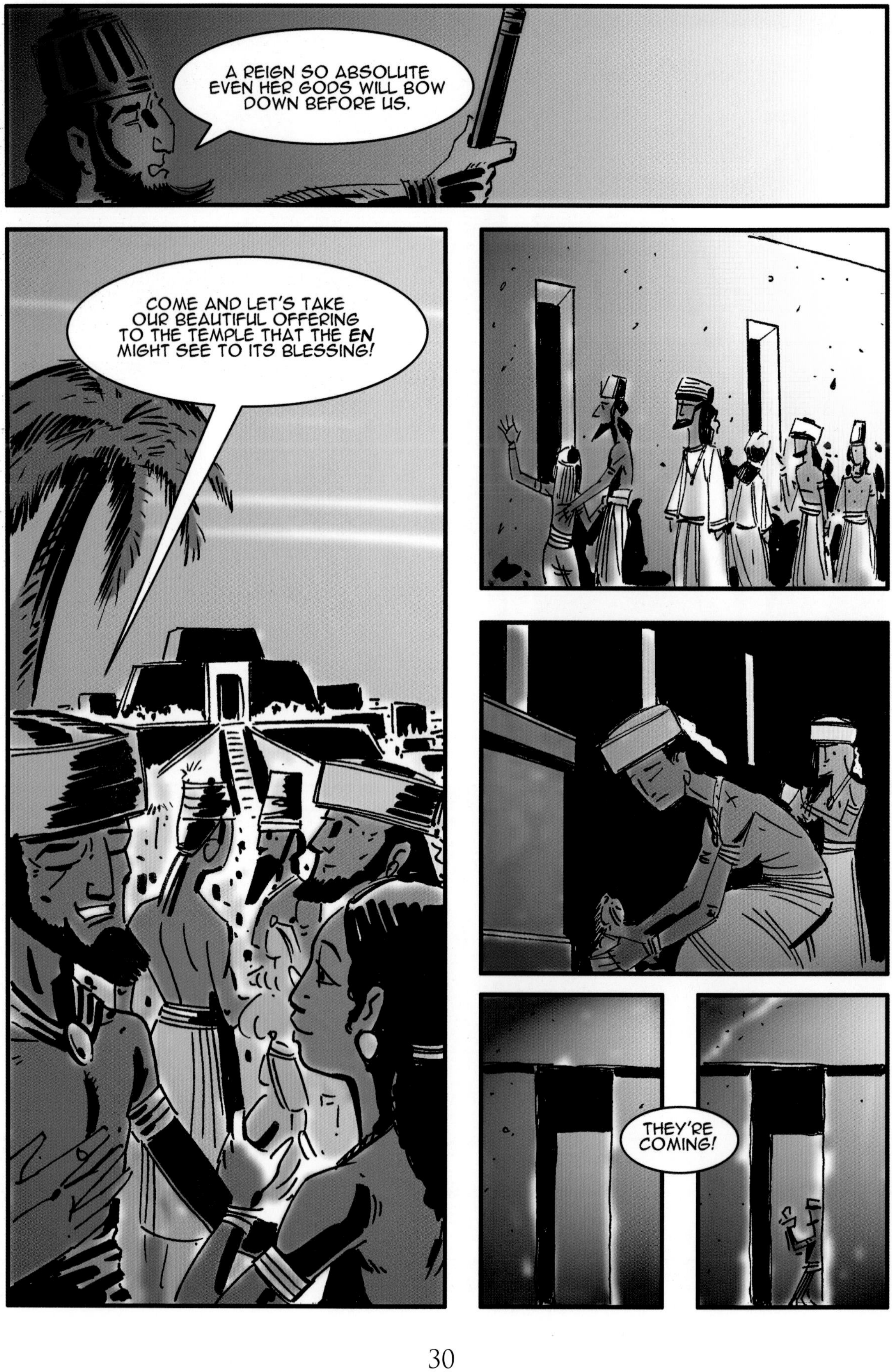
A REIGN SO ABSOLUTE EVEN HER GODS WILL BOW DOWN BEFORE US.
COME AND LET'S TAKE OUR BEAUTIFUL OFFERING TO THE TEMPLE THAT THE EN MIGHT SEE TO ITS BLESSING!
THEY'RE COMING!

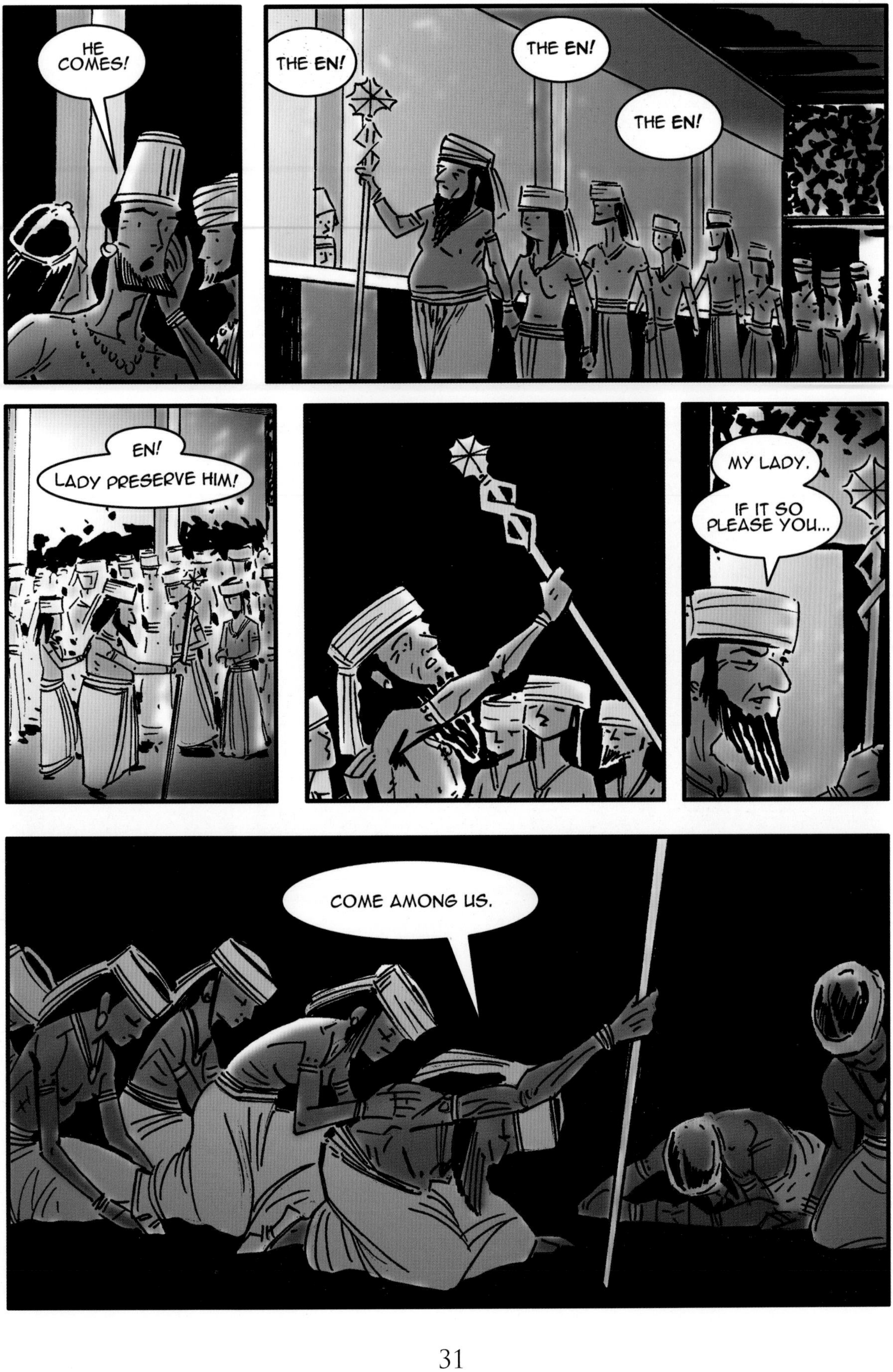
HE COMES!
THE EN!
THE EN!
THE EN!
EN!
LADY PRESERVE HIM!
MY LADY.
IF IT SO PLEASE YOU...
COME AMONG US.

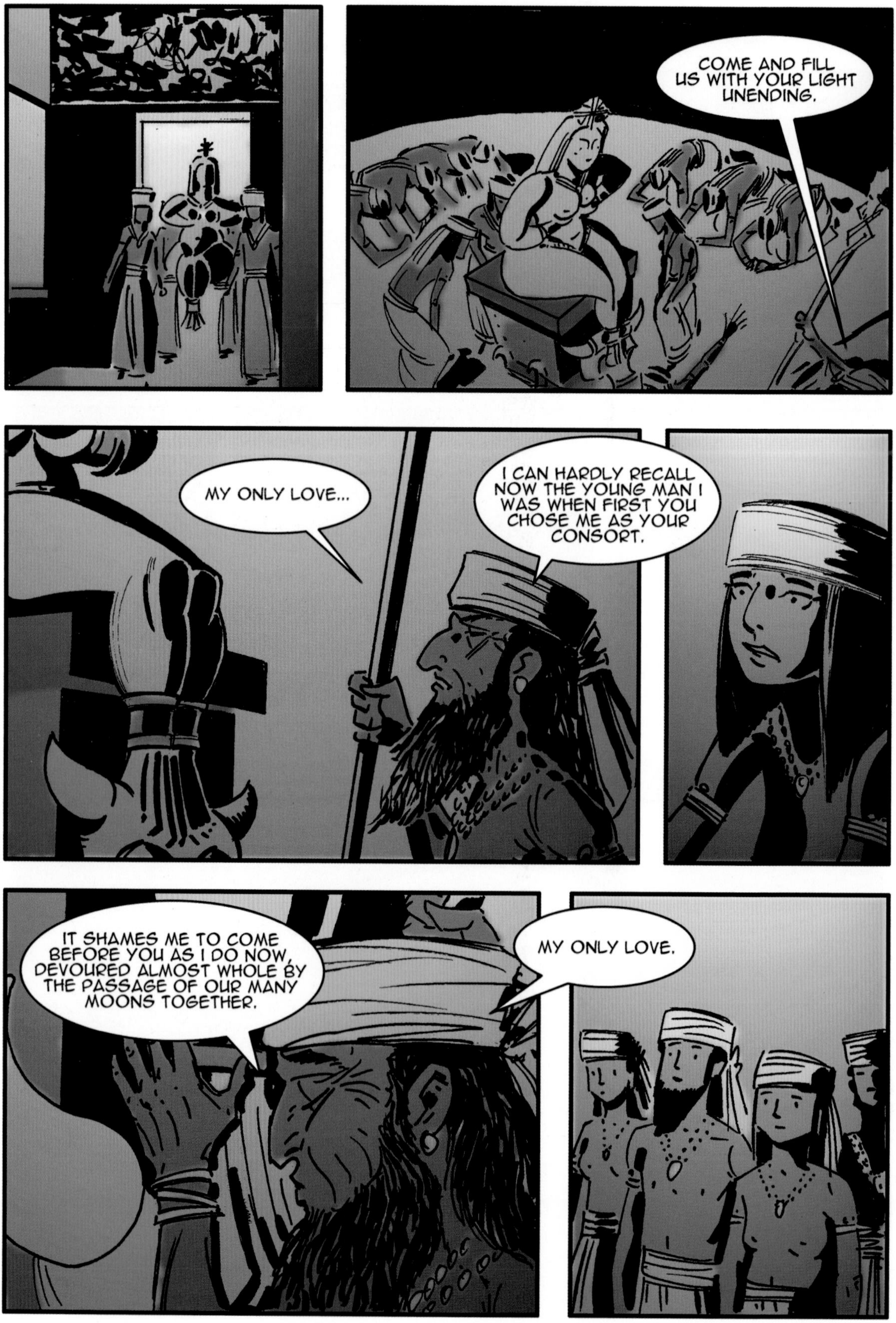
COME AND FILL US WITH YOUR LIGHT UNENDING.
MY ONLY LOVE...
I CAN HARDLY RECALL NOW THE YOUNG MAN I WAS WHEN FIRST YOU CHOSE ME AS YOUR CONSORT.
IT SHAMES ME TO COME BEFORE YOU AS I DO NOW, DEVOURED ALMOST WHOLE BY THE PASSAGE OF OUR MANY MOONS TOGETHER.
MY ONLY LOVE.

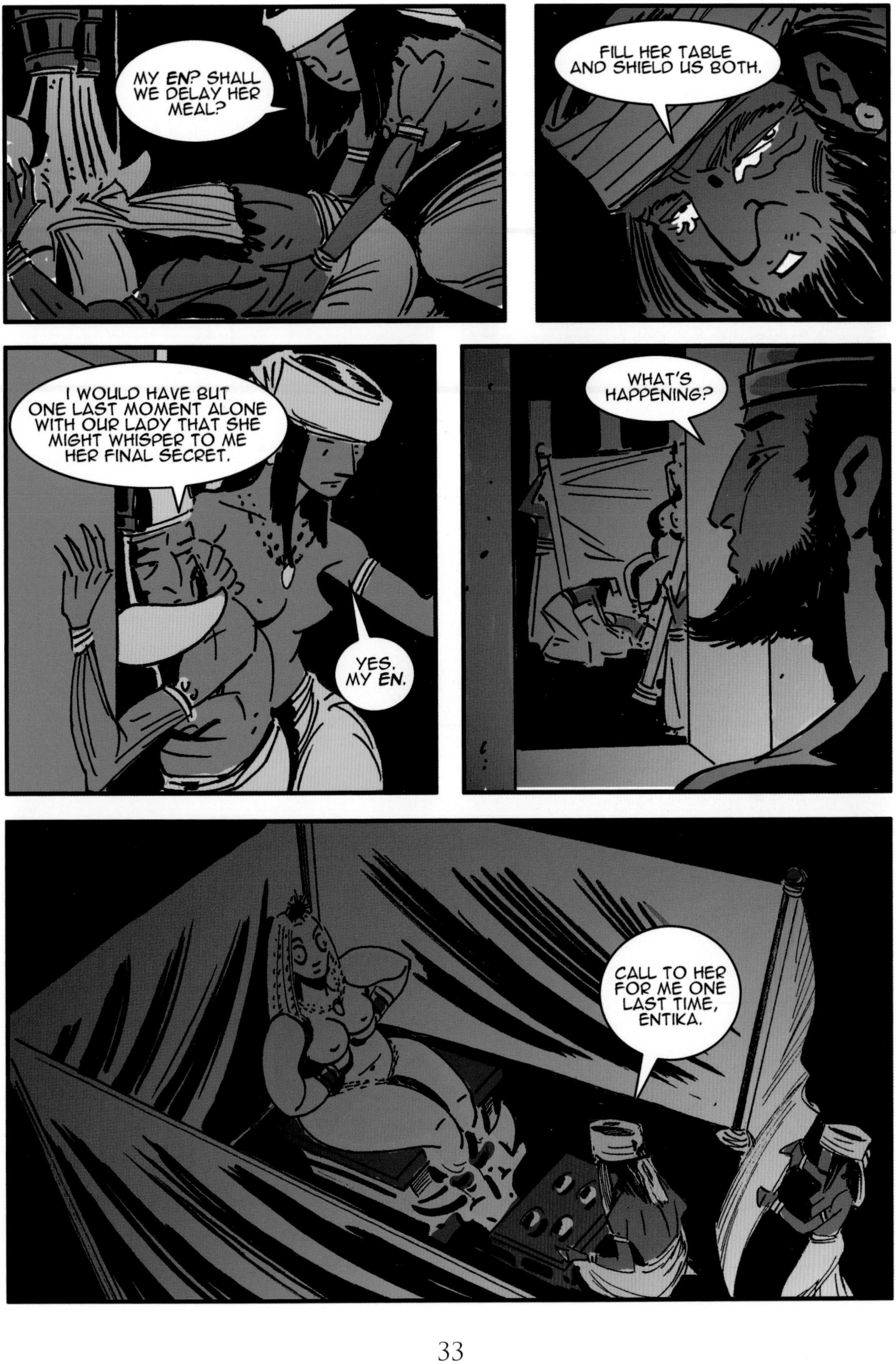
MY EN? SHALL WE DELAY HER MEAL?
FILL HER TABLE AND SHIELD US BOTH.
I WOULD HAVE BUT ONE LAST MOMENT ALONE WITH OUR LADY THAT SHE MIGHT WHISPER TO ME HER FINAL SECRET.
YES, MY EN.
WHAT'S HAPPENING?
CALL TO HER FOR ME ONE LAST TIME, ENTIKA.

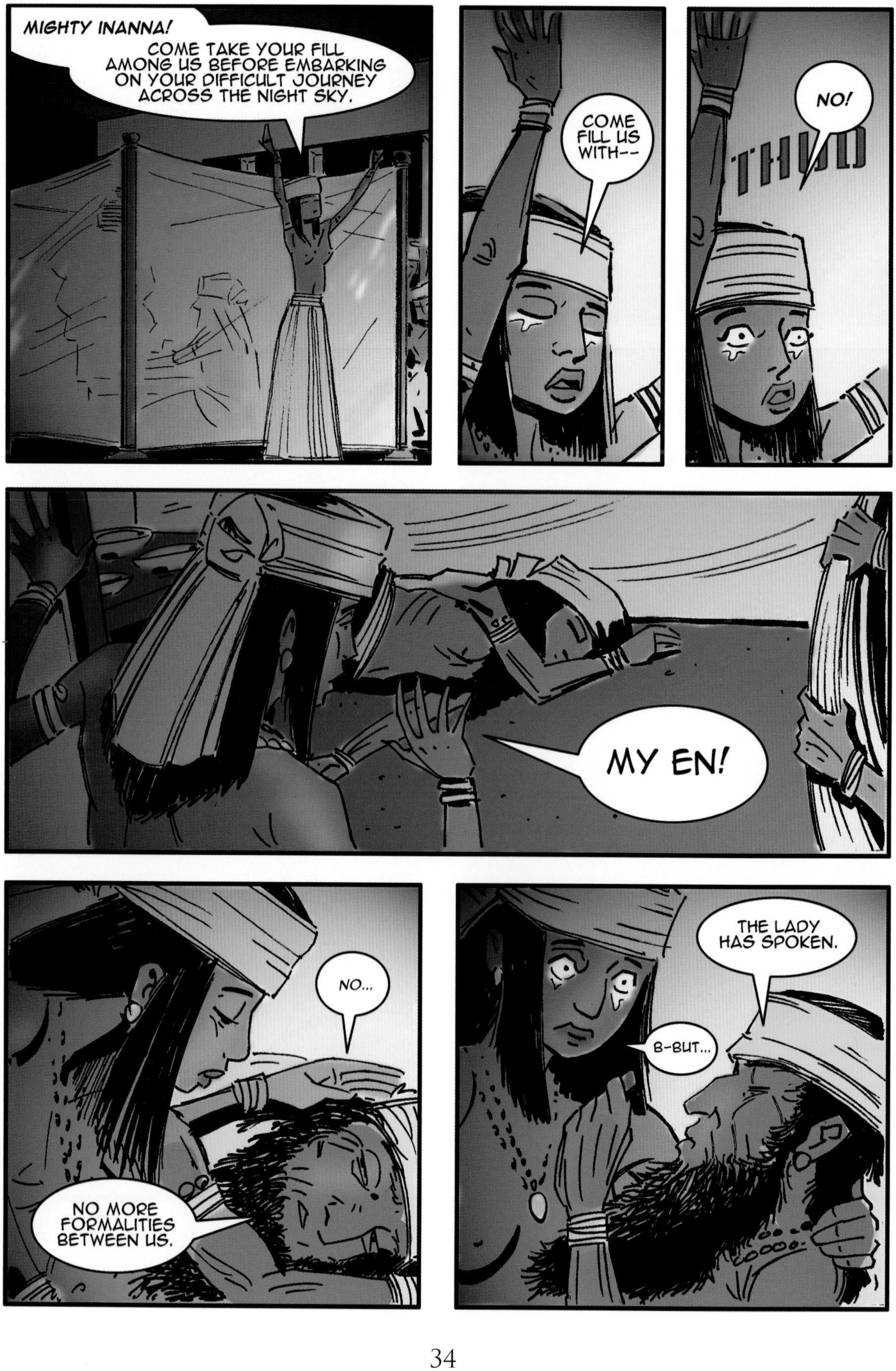
MIGHTY INANNA!
COME TAKE YOUR FILL AMONG US BEFORE EMBARKING ON YOUR DIFFICULT JOURNEY ACROSS THE NIGHT SKY.
COME FILL US WITH--
THUD
NO!
MY EN!
NO...
NO MORE FORMALITIES BETWEEN US.
THE LADY HAS SPOKEN.
B-BUT...

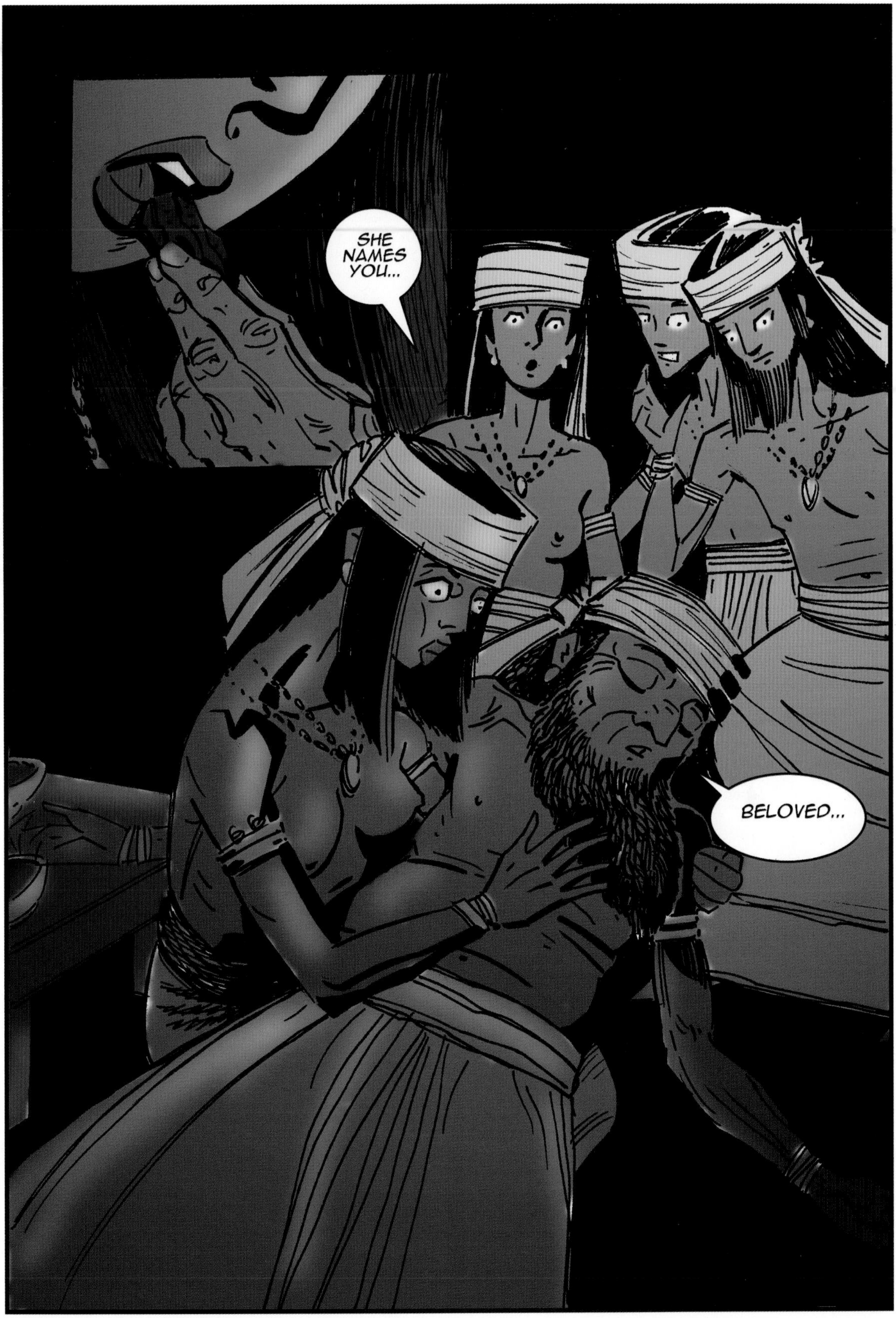
SHE NAMES YOU...
BELOVED...

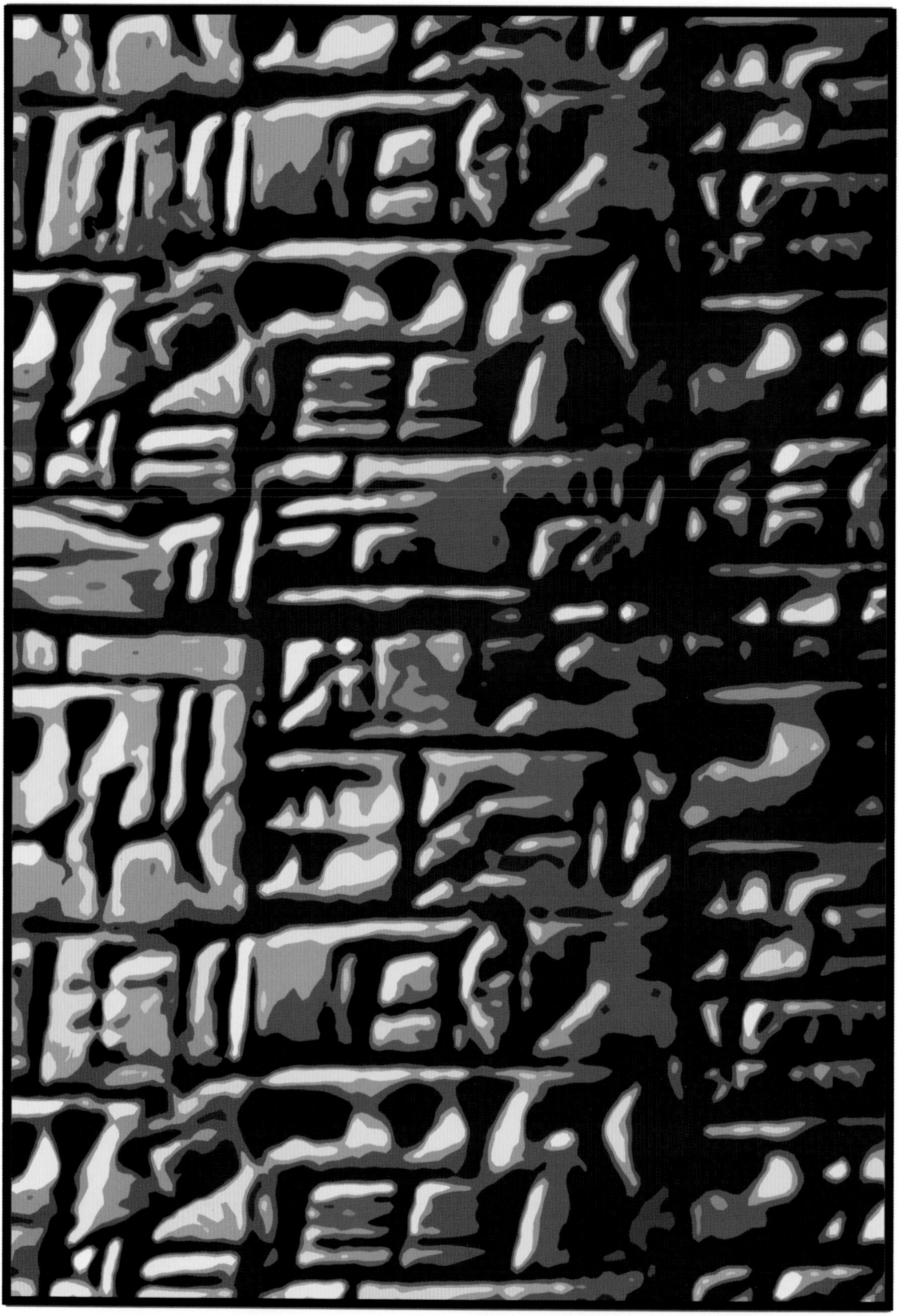

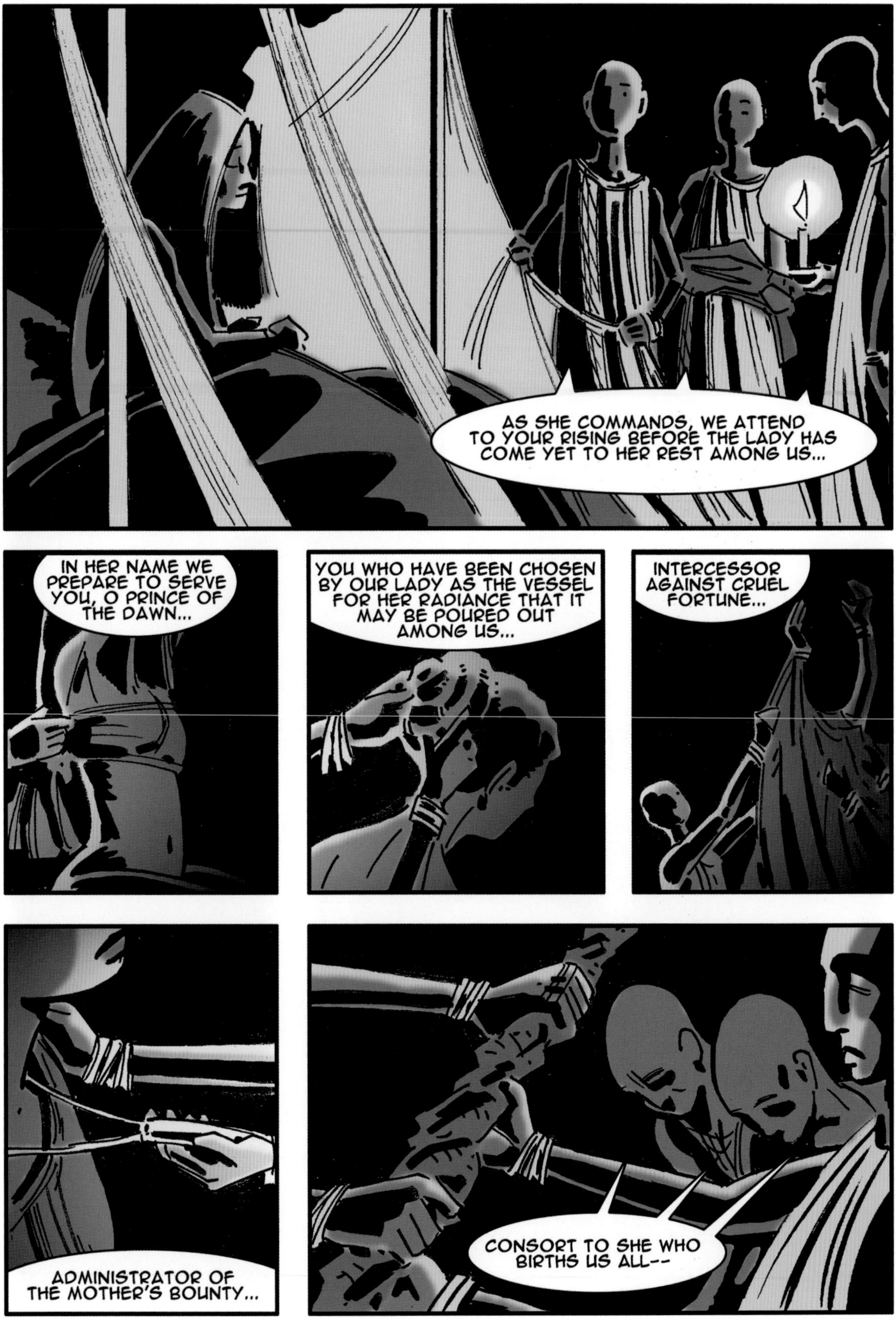
AS SHE COMMANDS, WE ATTEND TO YOUR RISING BEFORE THE LADY HAS COME YET TO HER REST AMONG US...
IN HER NAME WE PREPARE TO SERVE YOU, O PRINCE OF THE DAWN...
YOU WHO HAVE BEEN CHOSEN BY OUR LADY AS THE VESSEL FOR HER RADIANCE THAT IT MAY BE POURED OUT AMONG US...
INTERCESSOR AGAINST CRUEL FORTUNE...
ADMINISTRATOR OF THE MOTHER'S BOUNTY...
CONSORT TO SHE WHO BIRTHS US ALL--

RISE, SANGA...

O GLORIOUS *EN!*

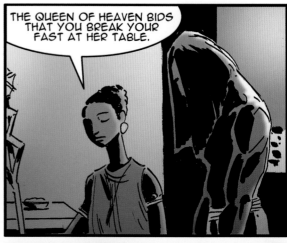

THE QUEEN OF HEAVEN BIDS THAT YOU BREAK YOUR FAST AT HER TABLE.

HER GRACES ARE WITHOUT MEASURE.

YOU HAVE BLESSED THE TEMPLE FOR MANY YEARS WITH THE EFFICACY OF YOUR ADMINISTRATIVE ABILITIES.

IT IS ONLY FITTING THAT YOU BE REWARDED FOR THAT ABLE SERVICE.

LEAVE US.

ARDRU SPOKE TO ME OFTEN OF YOU IN HIS FINAL CYCLES.

HE TOLD ME YOU WERE A MAN OF GREAT INTEGRITY WITH WHOM HE ENTRUSTED THE WELFARE OF THIS CITY AND ITS PEOPLE.

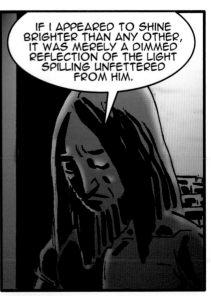

IF I APPEARED TO SHINE BRIGHTER THAN ANY OTHER, IT WAS MERELY A DIMMED REFLECTION OF THE LIGHT SPILLING UNFETTERED FROM HIM.

HOW TRUE OF US ALL...

MY LORD?

AM I, SANGÁ?

OR MERELY, PERHAPS, HIS SHADOW?

WHICH DO YOU SERVE, THE IDEA OR THE MAN?

I SERVE NONE BUT THE QUEEN OF HEAVEN.

BUT IN THIS SERVICE, I AM LOYAL UNTO MY DEATH TO THE EN'S INTERPRETATION OF HER DESIRES.

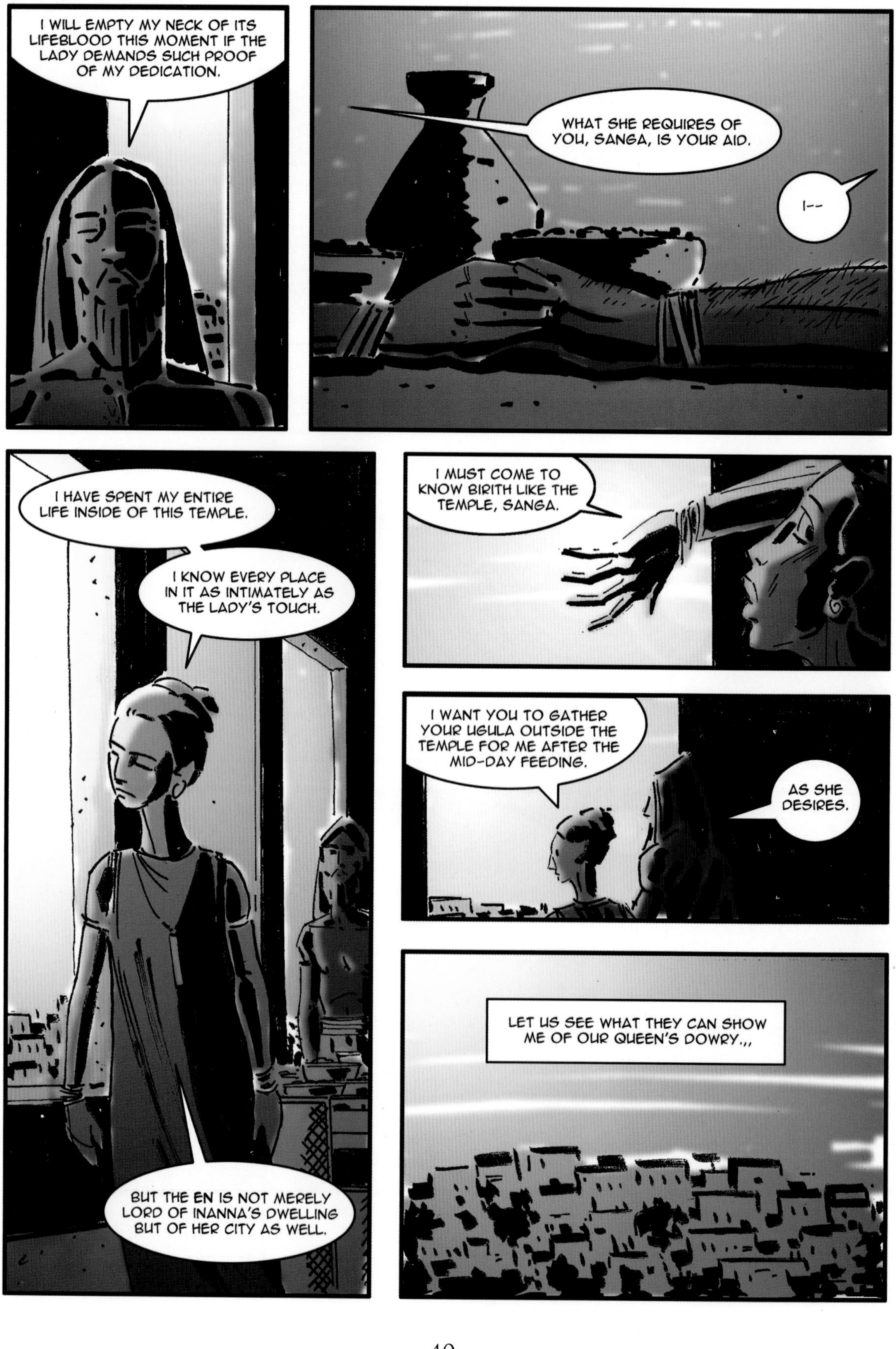
I WILL EMPTY MY NECK OF ITS LIFEBLOOD THIS MOMENT IF THE LADY DEMANDS SUCH PROOF OF MY DEDICATION.
WHAT SHE REQUIRES OF YOU, SANGA, IS YOUR AID.
I--
I HAVE SPENT MY ENTIRE LIFE INSIDE OF THIS TEMPLE.
I KNOW EVERY PLACE IN IT AS INTIMATELY AS THE LADY'S TOUCH.
BUT THE EN IS NOT MERELY LORD OF INANNA'S DWELLING BUT OF HER CITY AS WELL.
I MUST COME TO KNOW BIRITH LIKE THE TEMPLE, SANGA.
I WANT YOU TO GATHER YOUR UGULA OUTSIDE THE TEMPLE FOR ME AFTER THE MID-DAY FEEDING.
AS SHE DESIRES.
LET US SEE WHAT THEY CAN SHOW ME OF OUR QUEEN'S DOWRY.,,

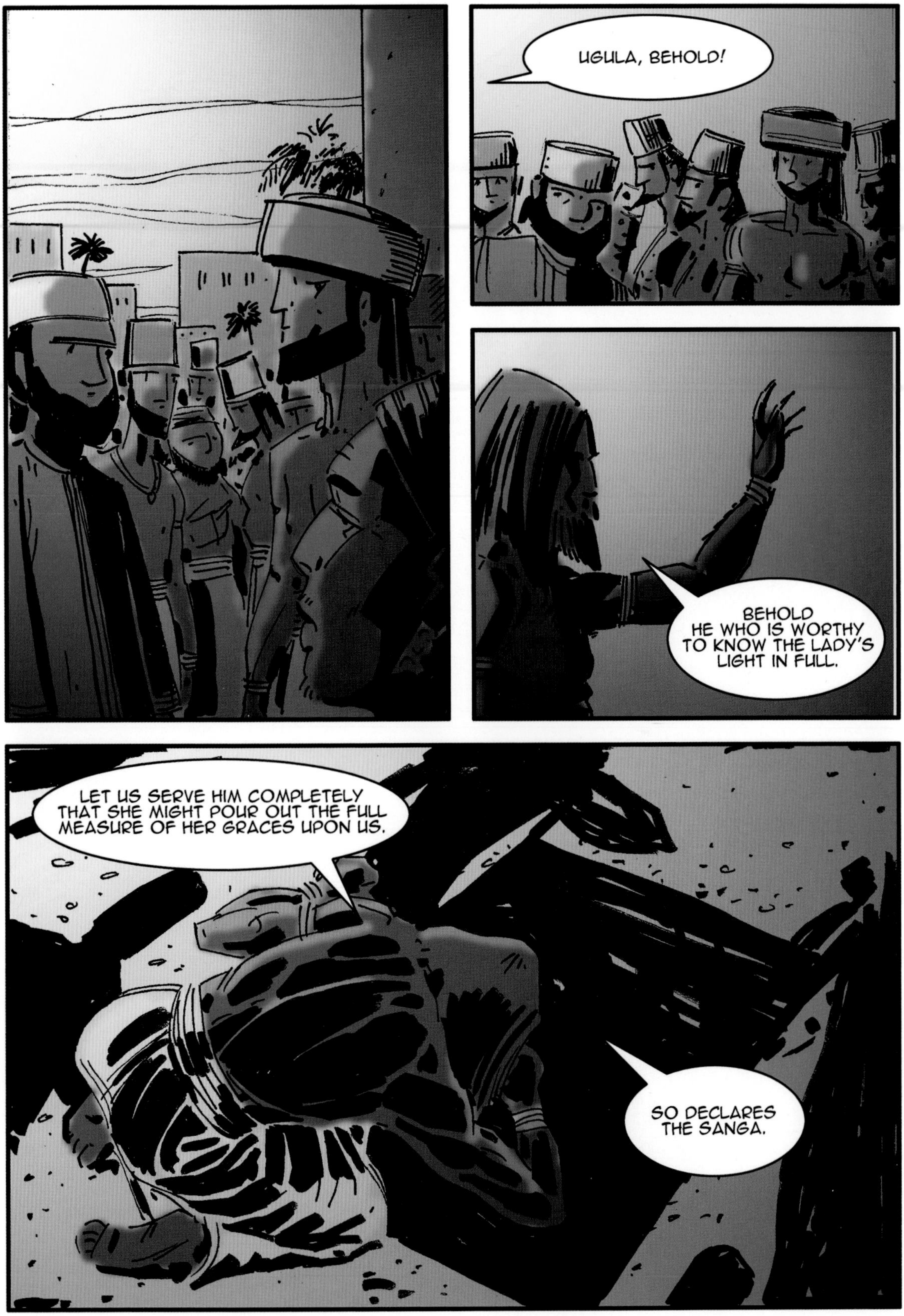
UGULA, BEHOLD!
BEHOLD HE WHO IS WORTHY TO KNOW THE LADY'S LIGHT IN FULL.
LET US SERVE HIM COMPLETELY THAT SHE MIGHT POUR OUT THE FULL MEASURE OF HER GRACES UPON US.
SO DECLARES THE SANGA.

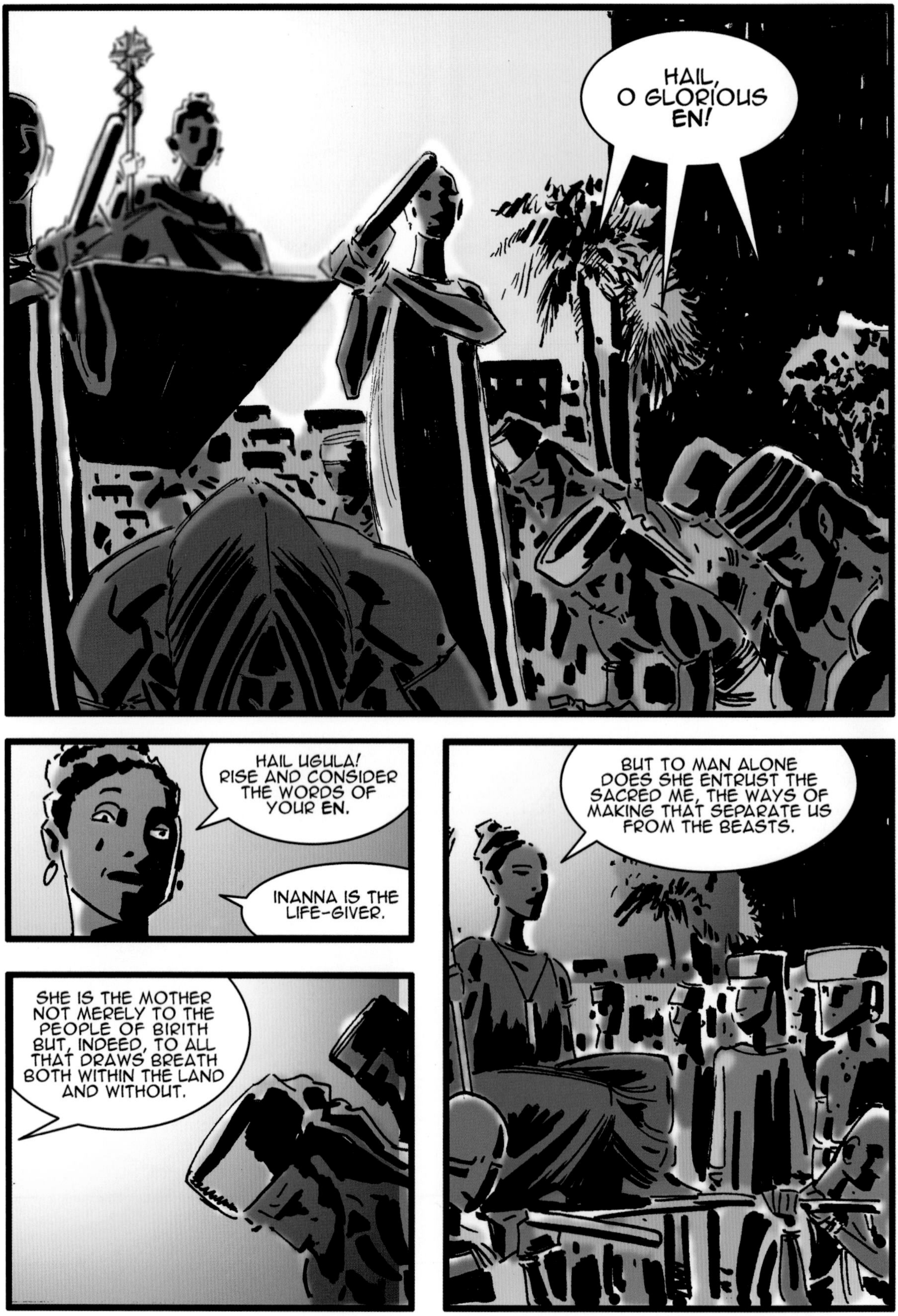
HAIL, O GLORIOUS EN!
HAIL UGULA! RISE AND CONSIDER THE WORDS OF YOUR EN.
INANNA IS THE LIFE-GIVER.
SHE IS THE MOTHER NOT MERELY TO THE PEOPLE OF BIRITH BUT, INDEED, TO ALL THAT DRAWS BREATH BOTH WITHIN THE LAND AND WITHOUT.
BUT TO MAN ALONE DOES SHE ENTRUST THE SACRED ME, THE WAYS OF MAKING THAT SEPARATE US FROM THE BEASTS.

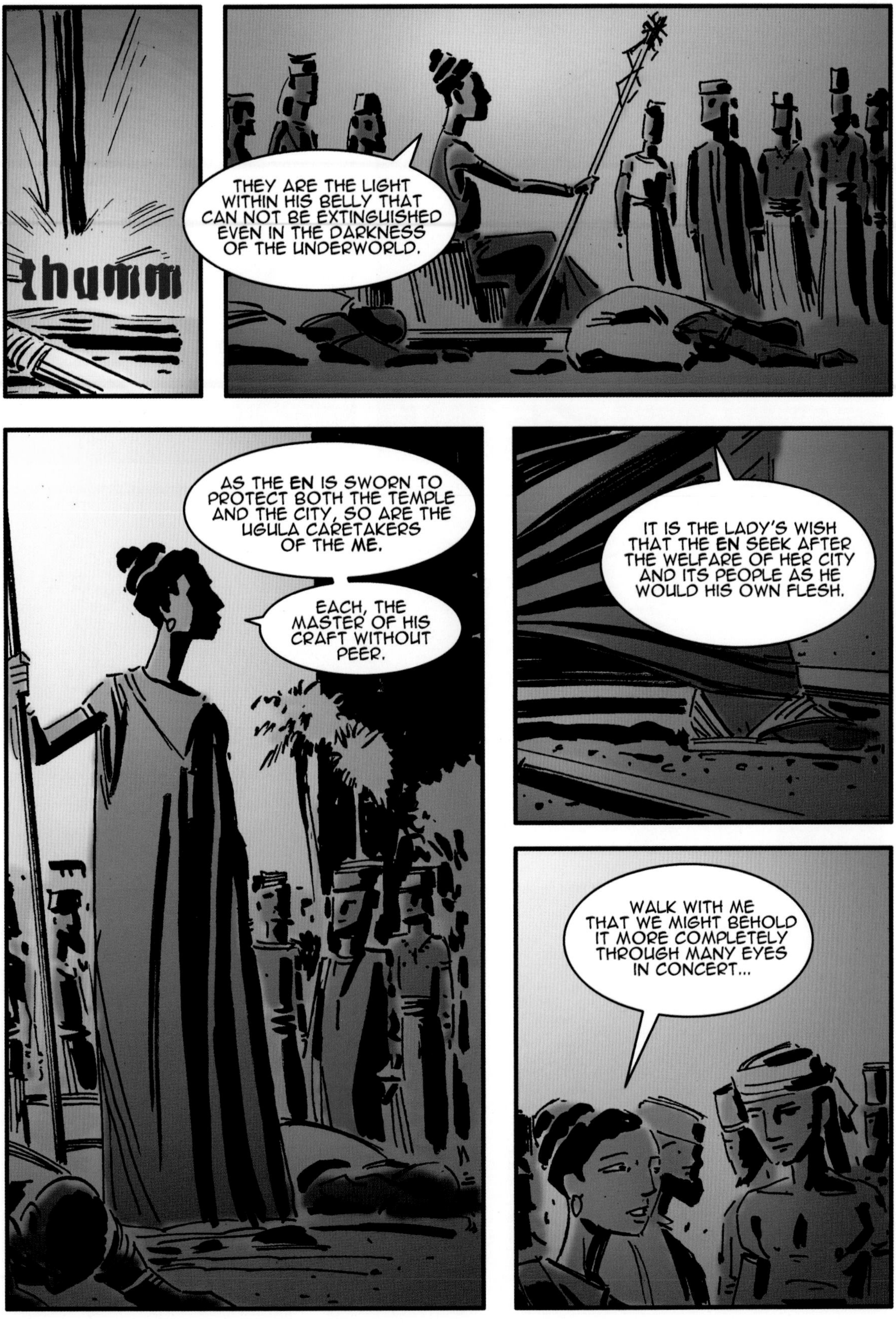
thumm
THEY ARE THE LIGHT WITHIN HIS BELLY THAT CAN NOT BE EXTINGUISHED EVEN IN THE DARKNESS OF THE UNDERWORLD.
AS THE EN IS SWORN TO PROTECT BOTH THE TEMPLE AND THE CITY, SO ARE THE UGULA CARETAKERS OF THE ME.
EACH, THE MASTER OF HIS CRAFT WITHOUT PEER.
IT IS THE LADY'S WISH THAT THE EN SEEK AFTER THE WELFARE OF HER CITY AND ITS PEOPLE AS HE WOULD HIS OWN FLESH.
WALK WITH ME THAT WE MIGHT BEHOLD IT MORE COMPLETELY THROUGH MANY EYES IN CONCERT...

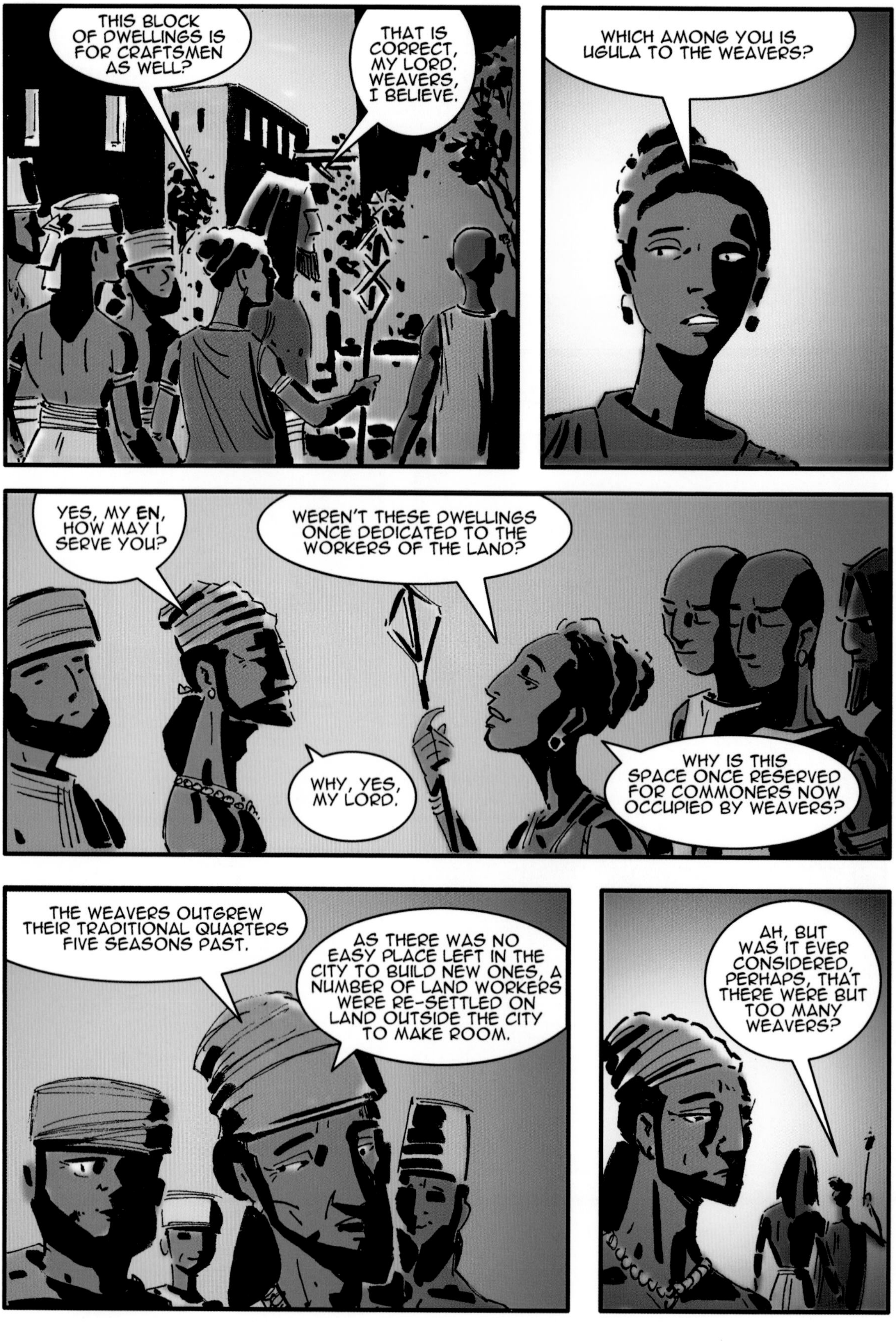
THIS BLOCK OF DWELLINGS IS FOR CRAFTSMEN AS WELL?
THAT IS CORRECT, MY LORD. WEAVERS, I BELIEVE.
WHICH AMONG YOU IS UGULA TO THE WEAVERS?
YES, MY EN, HOW MAY I SERVE YOU?
WEREN'T THESE DWELLINGS ONCE DEDICATED TO THE WORKERS OF THE LAND?
WHY, YES, MY LORD.
WHY IS THIS SPACE ONCE RESERVED FOR COMMONERS NOW OCCUPIED BY WEAVERS?
THE WEAVERS OUTGREW THEIR TRADITIONAL QUARTERS FIVE SEASONS PAST.
AS THERE WAS NO EASY PLACE LEFT IN THE CITY TO BUILD NEW ONES, A NUMBER OF LAND WORKERS WERE RE-SETTLED ON LAND OUTSIDE THE CITY TO MAKE ROOM.
AH, BUT WAS IT EVER CONSIDERED, PERHAPS, THAT THERE WERE BUT TOO MANY WEAVERS?

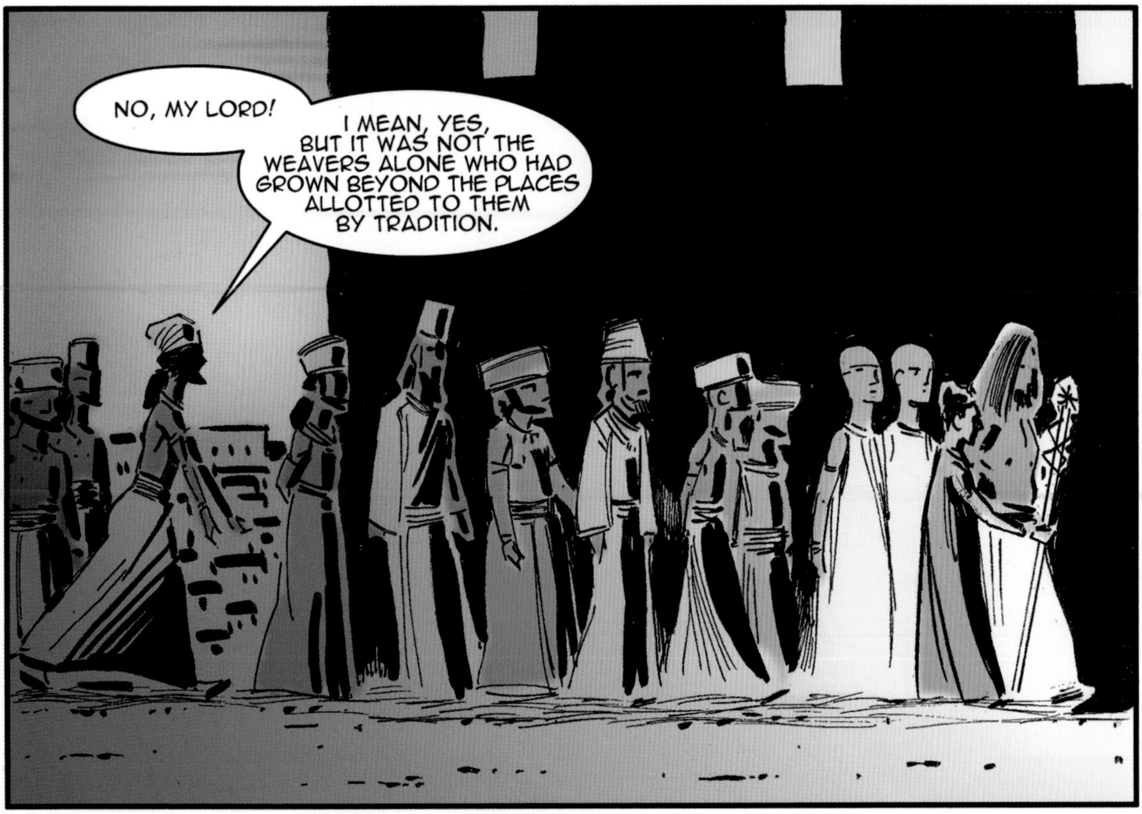
NO, MY LORD!
I MEAN, YES, BUT IT WAS NOT THE WEAVERS ALONE WHO HAD GROWN BEYOND THE PLACES ALLOTTED TO THEM BY TRADITION.

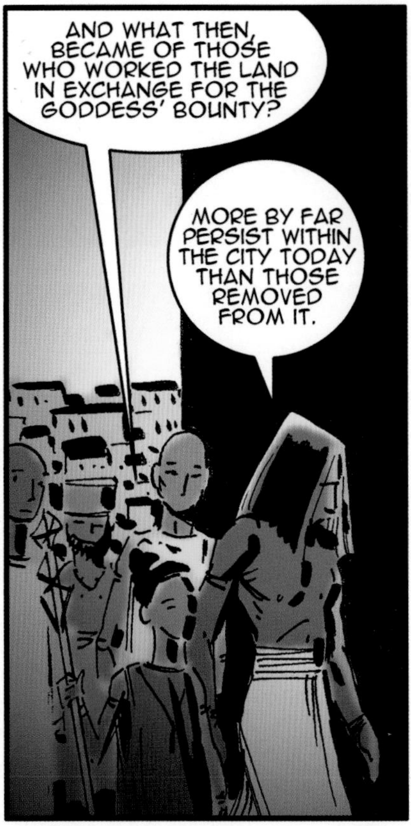
AND WHAT THEN, BECAME OF THOSE WHO WORKED THE LAND IN EXCHANGE FOR THE GODDESS' BOUNTY?
MORE BY FAR PERSIST WITHIN THE CITY TODAY THAN THOSE REMOVED FROM IT.

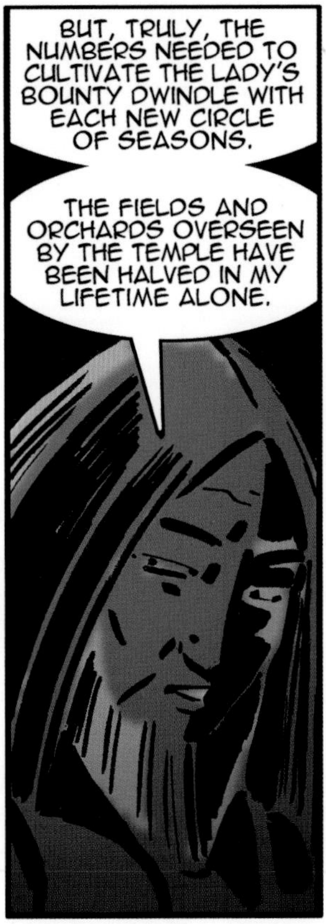
BUT, TRULY, THE NUMBERS NEEDED TO CULTIVATE THE LADY'S BOUNTY DWINDLE WITH EACH NEW CIRCLE OF SEASONS.
THE FIELDS AND ORCHARDS OVERSEEN BY THE TEMPLE HAVE BEEN HALVED IN MY LIFETIME ALONE.

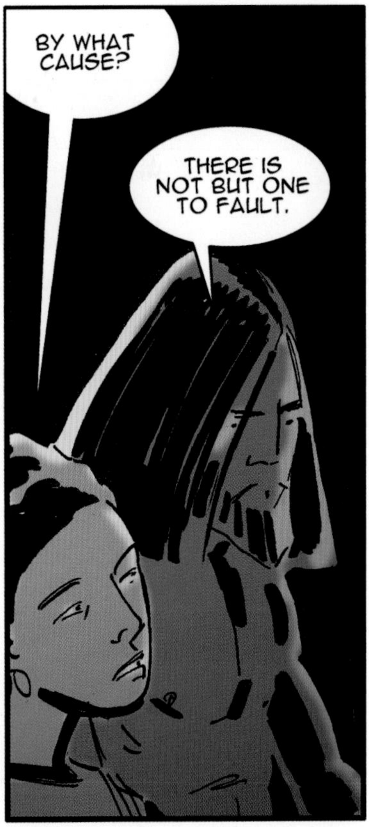
BY WHAT CAUSE?
THERE IS NOT BUT ONE TO FAULT.

"MANY FIELDS ONCE CONSIDERED THE TEMPLE'S RICHEST--

CAME TO REJECT THE SEEDS SOWN IN THEIR SOIL AND, IN TIME--

WERE SWALLOWED UP THE DRY GRASS AND CREEPING SANDS."

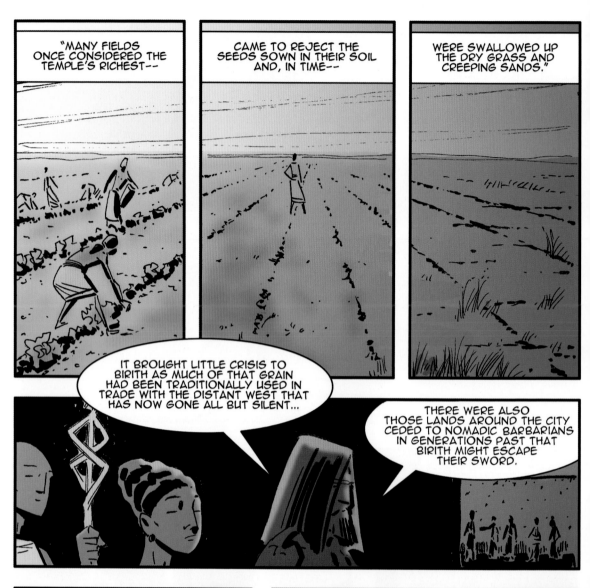

IT BROUGHT LITTLE CRISIS TO BIRITH AS MUCH OF THAT GRAIN HAD BEEN TRADITIONALLY USED IN TRADE WITH THE DISTANT WEST THAT HAS NOW GONE ALL BUT SILENT...

THERE WERE ALSO THOSE LANDS AROUND THE CITY CEDED TO NOMADIC BARBARIANS IN GENERATIONS PAST THAT BIRITH MIGHT ESCAPE THEIR SWORD.

SOME OF THOSE EXPELLED NOW TOIL IN THE FIELDS OF THESE NEW MASTERS.

AH YES, THE LUGALS.

PERHAPS THE ANSWERS WE SEEK AS TO BIRITH'S TRUE WELFARE LIE WHERE WE MIGHT BE LAST INCLINED TO SEARCH?

OUTSIDE THE SAFETY OF HER WALLS.

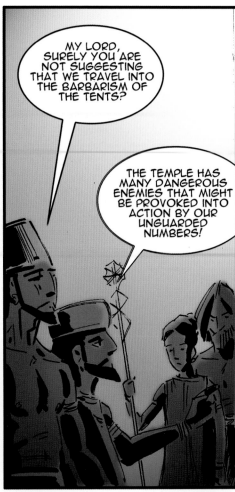

MY LORD, SURELY YOU ARE NOT SUGGESTING THAT WE TRAVEL INTO THE BARBARISM OF THE TENTS?

THE TEMPLE HAS MANY DANGEROUS ENEMIES THAT MIGHT BE PROVOKED INTO ACTION BY OUR UNGUARDED NUMBERS!

HOLD YOUR INSOLENT TONGUES!

NONE MAY PRESUME TO KNOW THE LADY'S MIND SAVE THE EN!

WE HAVE TASK ENOUGH YET BEFORE US TO CATALOG THE TROUBLES OF THE CITY'S INTERIOR.

WE CAN ONLY PRAY THAT THE PRESSURES ON HER OUTER SHELL WILL WAIT FOR ANOTHER SUN.

NEXT!
HOW MANY AT YOUR TABLE?
SIX INCLUDING MY WIFE'S MOTHER WHO IS FEEBLE.
IF SHE CAN'T WORK THEN SOMEONE ELSE WILL HAVE TO ASSUME HER OBLIGATION.
IMPRINT YOUR MARK ON THE TABLET.
YOUR TIME IN THE FIELDS WILL BEGIN IN THREE DAYS.

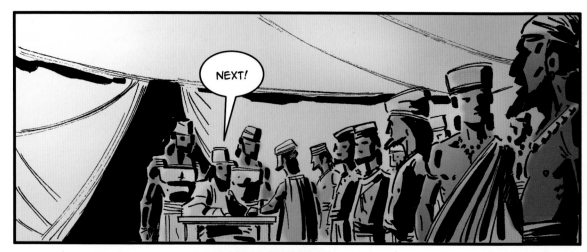

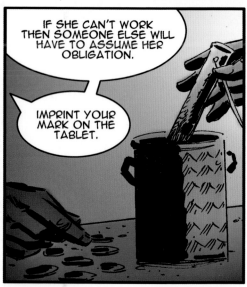

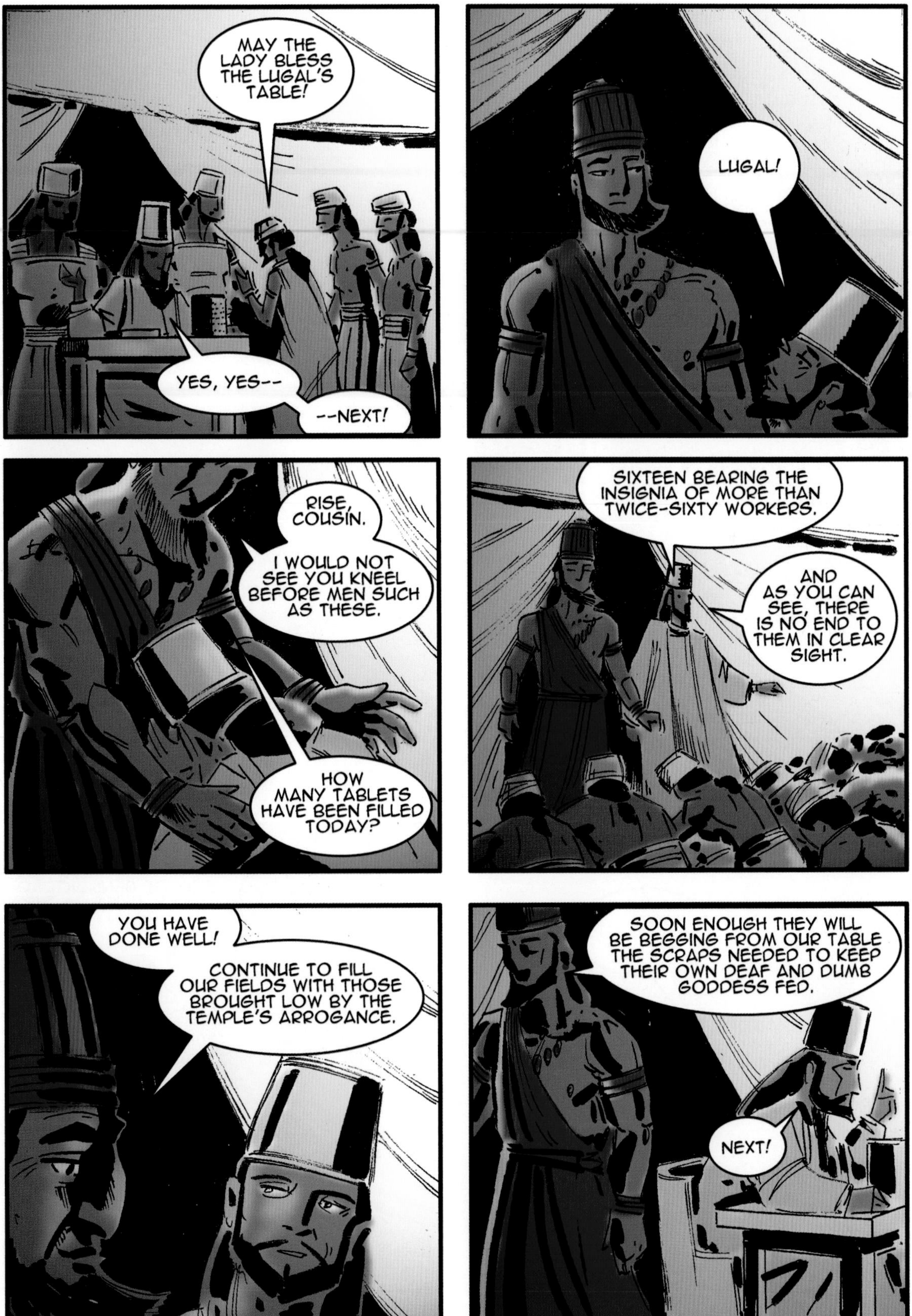
MAY THE LADY BLESS THE LUGAL'S TABLE!
YES, YES--
--NEXT!
LUGAL!
RISE, COUSIN.
I WOULD NOT SEE YOU KNEEL BEFORE MEN SUCH AS THESE.
HOW MANY TABLETS HAVE BEEN FILLED TODAY?
SIXTEEN BEARING THE INSIGNIA OF MORE THAN TWICE-SIXTY WORKERS.
AND AS YOU CAN SEE, THERE IS NO END TO THEM IN CLEAR SIGHT.
YOU HAVE DONE WELL!
CONTINUE TO FILL OUR FIELDS WITH THOSE BROUGHT LOW BY THE TEMPLE'S ARROGANCE.
SOON ENOUGH THEY WILL BE BEGGING FROM OUR TABLE THE SCRAPS NEEDED TO KEEP THEIR OWN DEAF AND DUMB GODDESS FED.
NEXT!

YOU ARE GUNNABARON, ELDEST SON OF GUNNABARASH THE DIVINER?
WHO SPEAKS THESE NAMES LONG FORGOTTEN TO THE PEOPLE OF THE MOUNTAIN?
MERELY A VOICE AMONG MANY UNTIL I AM CERTAIN THAT YOU ARE HE WHOM WE SEEK.
WHO BUT GUNNABARASH'S ELDEST SON WOULD BEAR THE WEIGHT OF THE DIVINER'S POUCH EVEN AS HIS PEOPLE CONTINUE TO FORSAKE THE OLD WAYS?
WHO ELSE COULD HAVE THE MISFORTUNE OF BEING FORCED TO BEG FOR SCRAPS WHEN HE SHOULD BE PREPARING THE SACRIFICES?
WAI--
I AM BELIPOTASH, ELDEST SON OF BENNIKOTTUL SON OF BENNIDODAR, ONCE-CHIEF OF THE MOUNTAIN PEOPLE.
WE COME SEEKING YOUR COUNSEL.

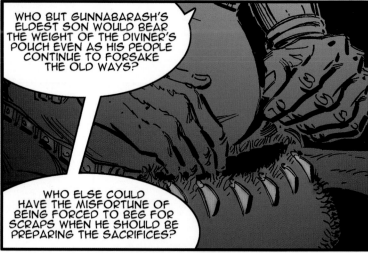

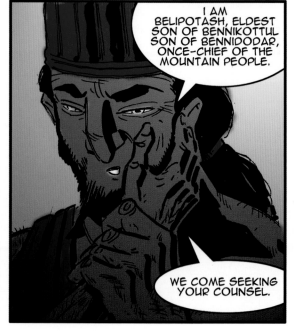

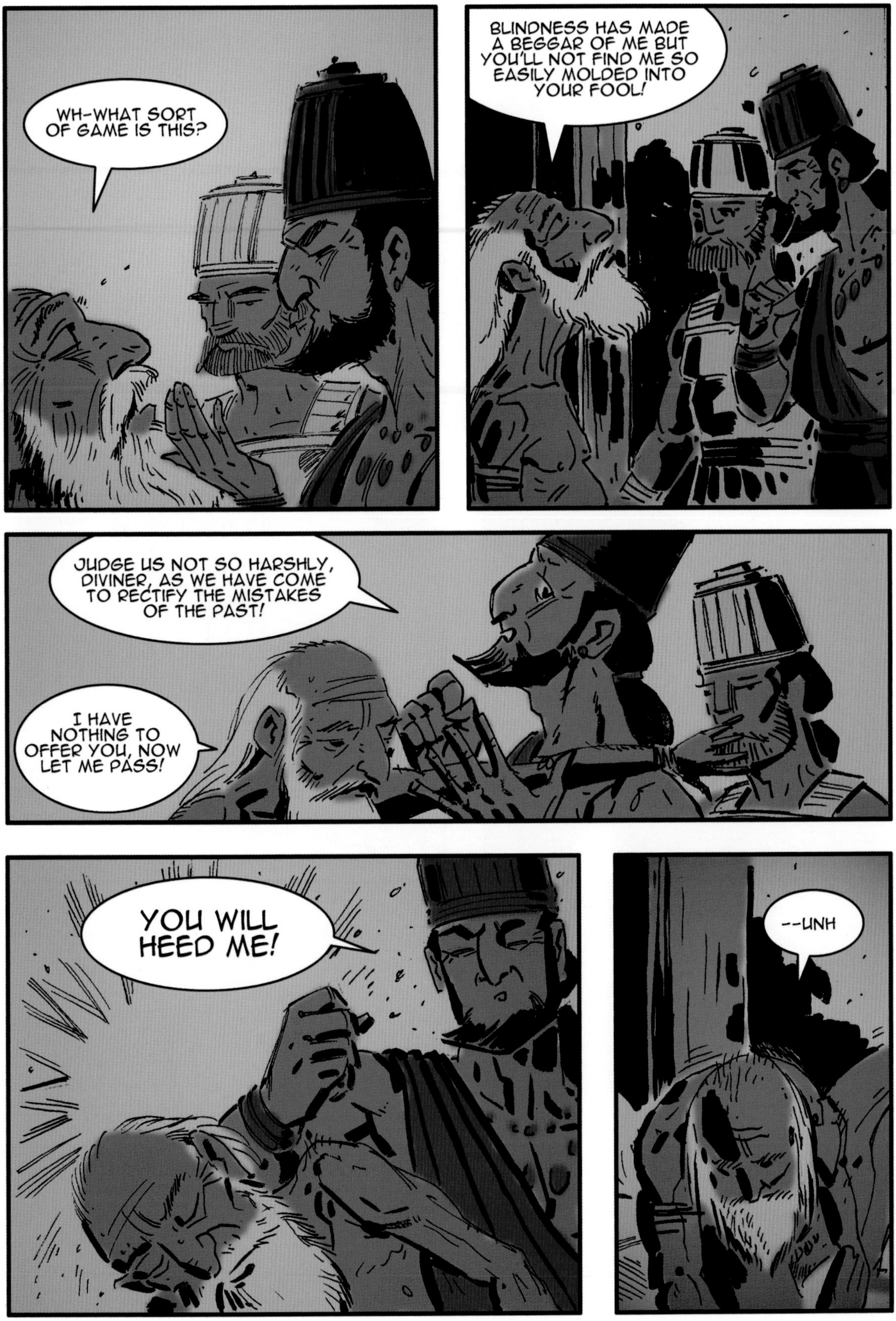
WH-WHAT SORT OF GAME IS THIS?
BLINDNESS HAS MADE A BEGGAR OF ME BUT YOU'LL NOT FIND ME SO EASILY MOLDED INTO YOUR FOOL!
JUDGE US NOT SO HARSHLY, DIVINER, AS WE HAVE COME TO RECTIFY THE MISTAKES OF THE PAST!
I HAVE NOTHING TO OFFER YOU, NOW LET ME PASS!
YOU WILL HEED ME!
--UNH

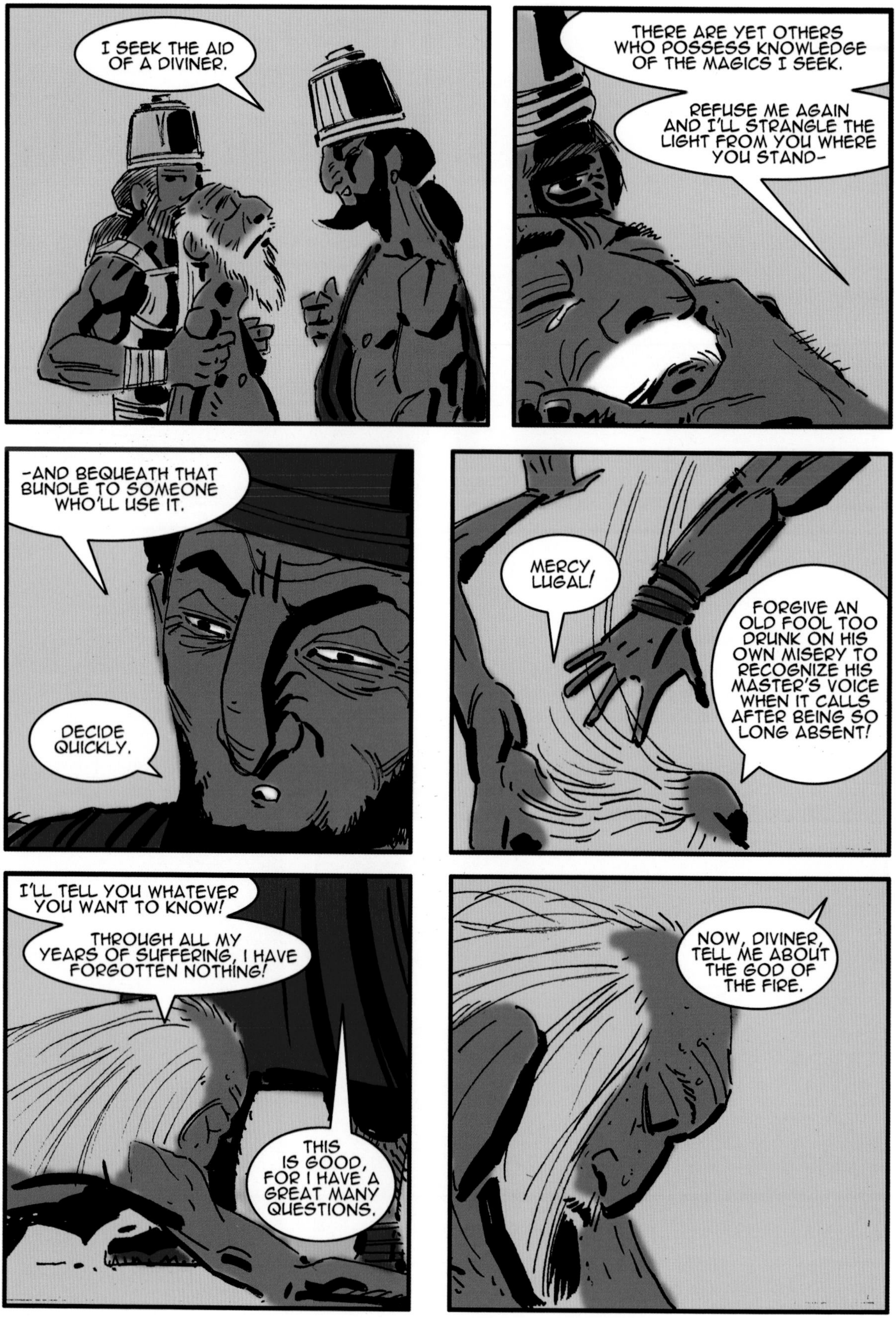
I SEEK THE AID OF A DIVINER.
THERE ARE YET OTHERS WHO POSSESS KNOWLEDGE OF THE MAGICS I SEEK.
REFUSE ME AGAIN AND I'LL STRANGLE THE LIGHT FROM YOU WHERE YOU STAND-
-AND BEQUEATH THAT BUNDLE TO SOMEONE WHO'LL USE IT.
DECIDE QUICKLY.
MERCY, LUGAL!
FORGIVE AN OLD FOOL TOO DRUNK ON HIS OWN MISERY TO RECOGNIZE HIS MASTER'S VOICE WHEN IT CALLS AFTER BEING SO LONG ABSENT!
I'LL TELL YOU WHATEVER YOU WANT TO KNOW!
THROUGH ALL MY YEARS OF SUFFERING, I HAVE FORGOTTEN NOTHING!
THIS IS GOOD, FOR I HAVE A GREAT MANY QUESTIONS.
NOW, DIVINER, TELL ME ABOUT THE GOD OF THE FIRE.

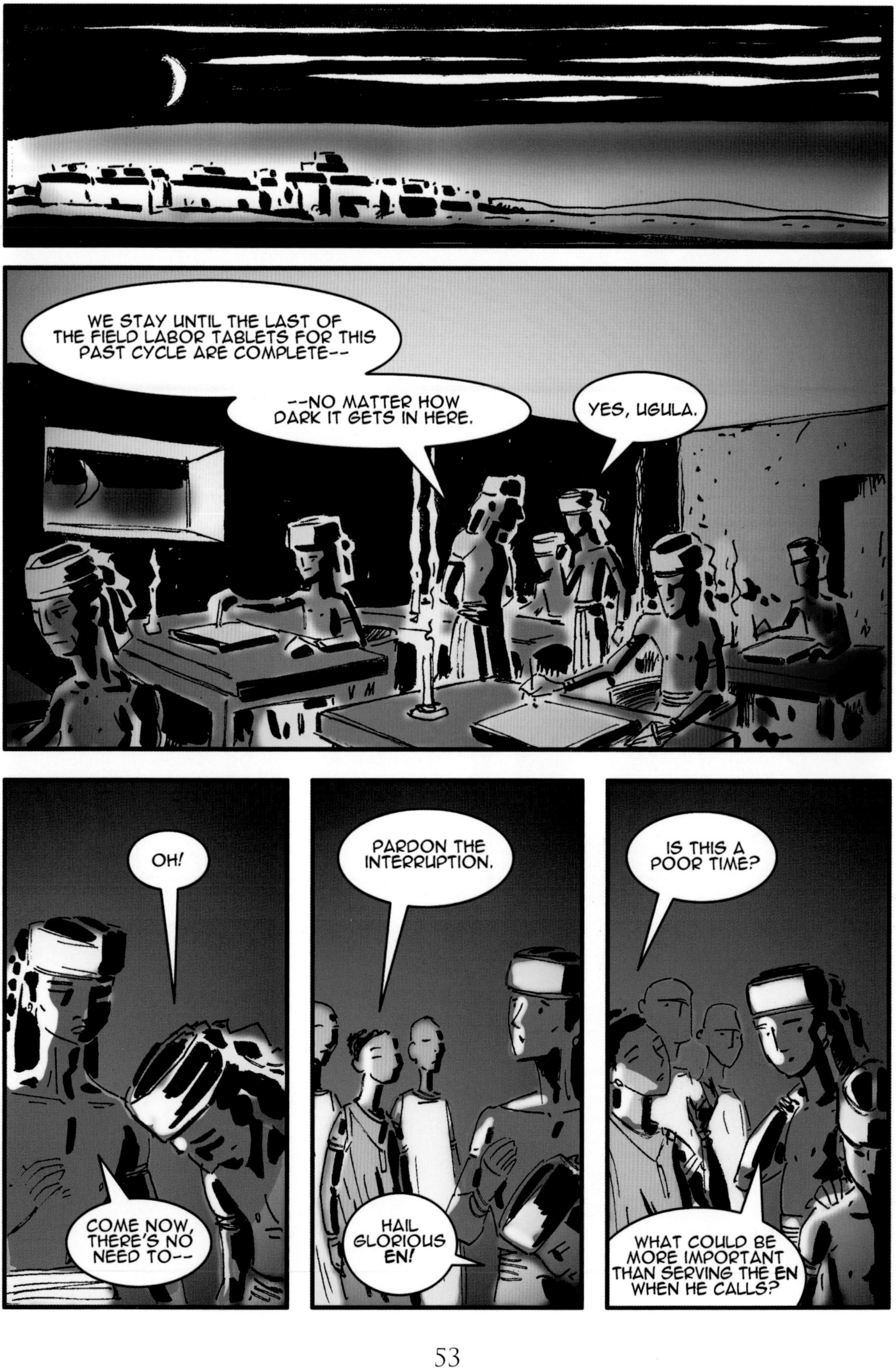
WE STAY UNTIL THE LAST OF THE FIELD LABOR TABLETS FOR THIS PAST CYCLE ARE COMPLETE--
--NO MATTER HOW DARK IT GETS IN HERE.
YES, UGULA.
OH!
COME NOW, THERE'S NO NEED TO--
PARDON THE INTERRUPTION.
HAIL GLORIOUS EN!
IS THIS A POOR TIME?
WHAT COULD BE MORE IMPORTANT THAN SERVING THE EN WHEN HE CALLS?

HA! YOU MAKE IT SEEM SO DIRE...

SOMETHING MORE AKIN TO SURPRISE.

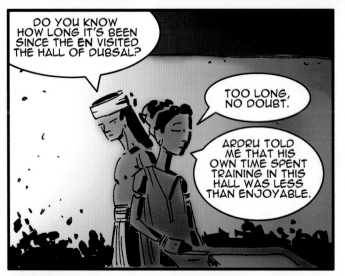

DO YOU KNOW HOW LONG IT'S BEEN SINCE THE EN VISITED THE HALL OF DUBSAL?

TOO LONG, NO DOUBT.

ARDRU TOLD ME THAT HIS OWN TIME SPENT TRAINING IN THIS HALL WAS LESS THAN ENJOYABLE.

THE DUBSAL UGULA OF HIS CHILDHOOD WAS BY ALL ACCOUNTS A DIFFICULT MAN.

I CAN ASSURE YOU THAT OUR METHODS ARE MORE IN LINE WITH THE SPIRIT OF THIS AGE.

BUT NO LESS VITAL, IT SEEMS, AS EVERY GUILDMASTER I QUESTIONED TODAY GAVE ME THE SAME ANSWER.

"CONSULT THE DUBSAL UGULA, OH GLORIOUS EN, AS HE HOLDS THE NUMBERS YOU SEEK..."

I BESEECH THE LADY DAWN TO DUSK TO SHIELD ME FROM THE PRAISE OF THOSE SEEKING TO REDIRECT UNWANTED ATTENTION AWAY FROM THEIR OWN AFFAIRS.

HA! HOW COULD A PRAYER SO EARNEST BE REFUSED?

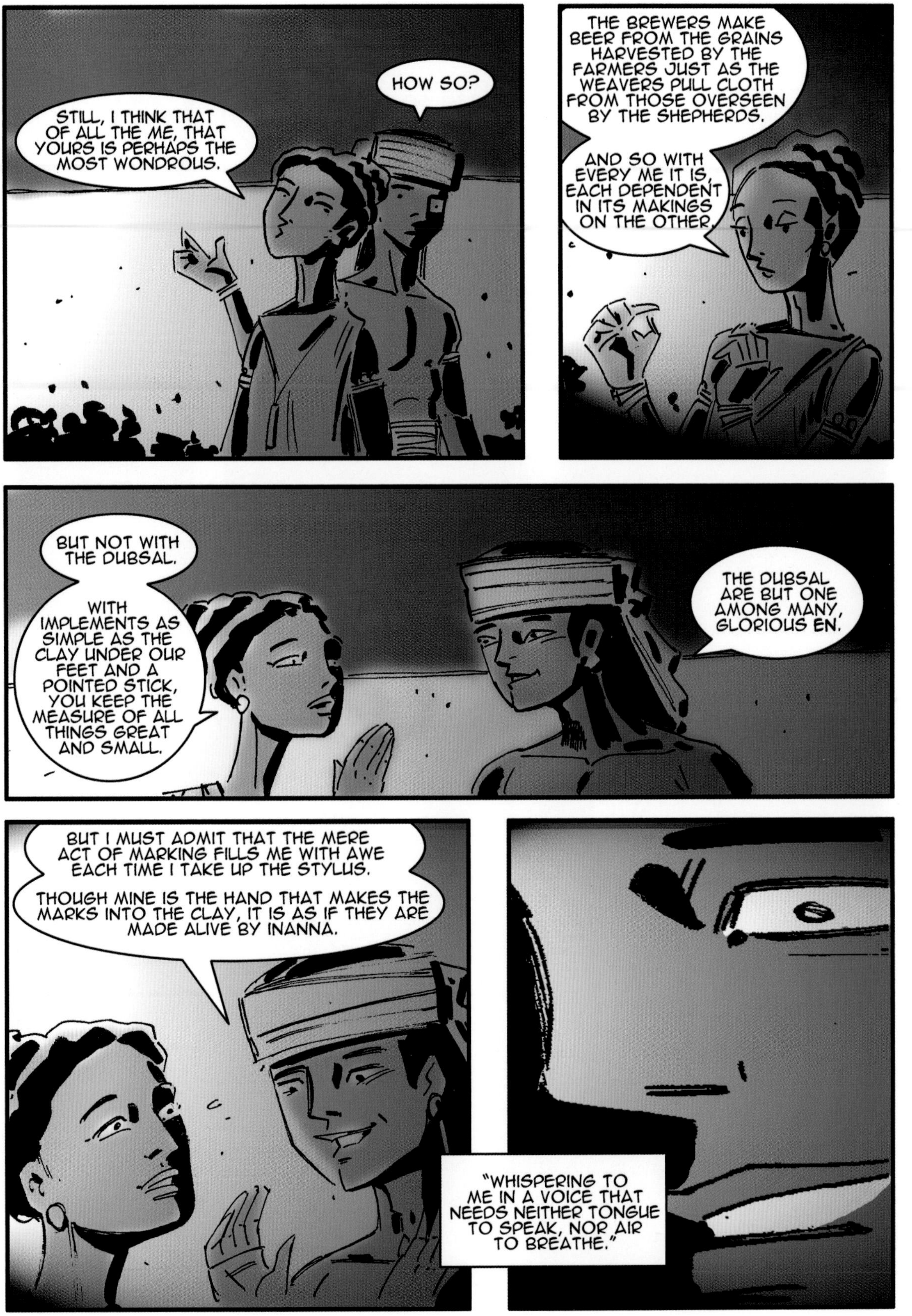
STILL, I THINK THAT OF ALL THE ME, THAT YOURS IS PERHAPS THE MOST WONDROUS.
HOW SO?
THE BREWERS MAKE BEER FROM THE GRAINS HARVESTED BY THE FARMERS JUST AS THE WEAVERS PULL CLOTH FROM THOSE OVERSEEN BY THE SHEPHERDS.
AND SO WITH EVERY ME IT IS, EACH DEPENDENT IN ITS MAKINGS ON THE OTHER.
BUT NOT WITH THE DUBSAL.
WITH IMPLEMENTS AS SIMPLE AS THE CLAY UNDER OUR FEET AND A POINTED STICK, YOU KEEP THE MEASURE OF ALL THINGS GREAT AND SMALL.
THE DUBSAL ARE BUT ONE AMONG MANY, GLORIOUS **EN**.
BUT I MUST ADMIT THAT THE MERE ACT OF MARKING FILLS ME WITH AWE EACH TIME I TAKE UP THE STYLUS.
THOUGH MINE IS THE HAND THAT MAKES THE MARKS INTO THE CLAY, IT IS AS IF THEY ARE MADE ALIVE BY INANNA.
"WHISPERING TO ME IN A VOICE THAT NEEDS NEITHER TONGUE TO SPEAK, NOR AIR TO BREATHE."

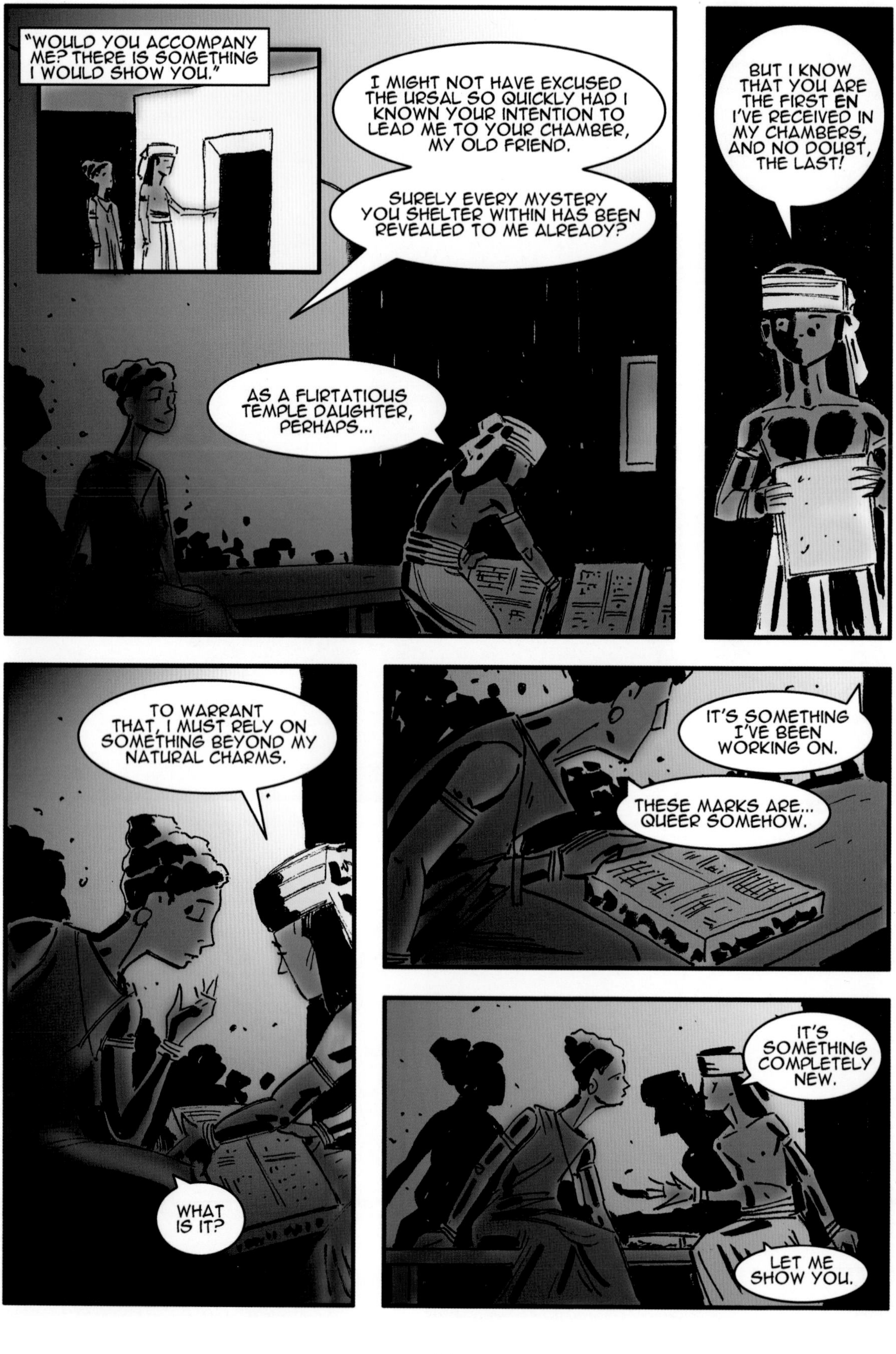
"WOULD YOU ACCOMPANY ME? THERE IS SOMETHING I WOULD SHOW YOU."
I MIGHT NOT HAVE EXCUSED THE URSAL SO QUICKLY HAD I KNOWN YOUR INTENTION TO LEAD ME TO YOUR CHAMBER, MY OLD FRIEND.
SURELY EVERY MYSTERY YOU SHELTER WITHIN HAS BEEN REVEALED TO ME ALREADY?
AS A FLIRTATIOUS TEMPLE DAUGHTER, PERHAPS...
BUT I KNOW THAT YOU ARE THE FIRST EN I'VE RECEIVED IN MY CHAMBERS, AND NO DOUBT, THE LAST!
TO WARRANT THAT, I MUST RELY ON SOMETHING BEYOND MY NATURAL CHARMS.
WHAT IS IT?
IT'S SOMETHING I'VE BEEN WORKING ON.
THESE MARKS ARE... QUEER SOMEHOW.
IT'S SOMETHING COMPLETELY NEW.
LET ME SHOW YOU.

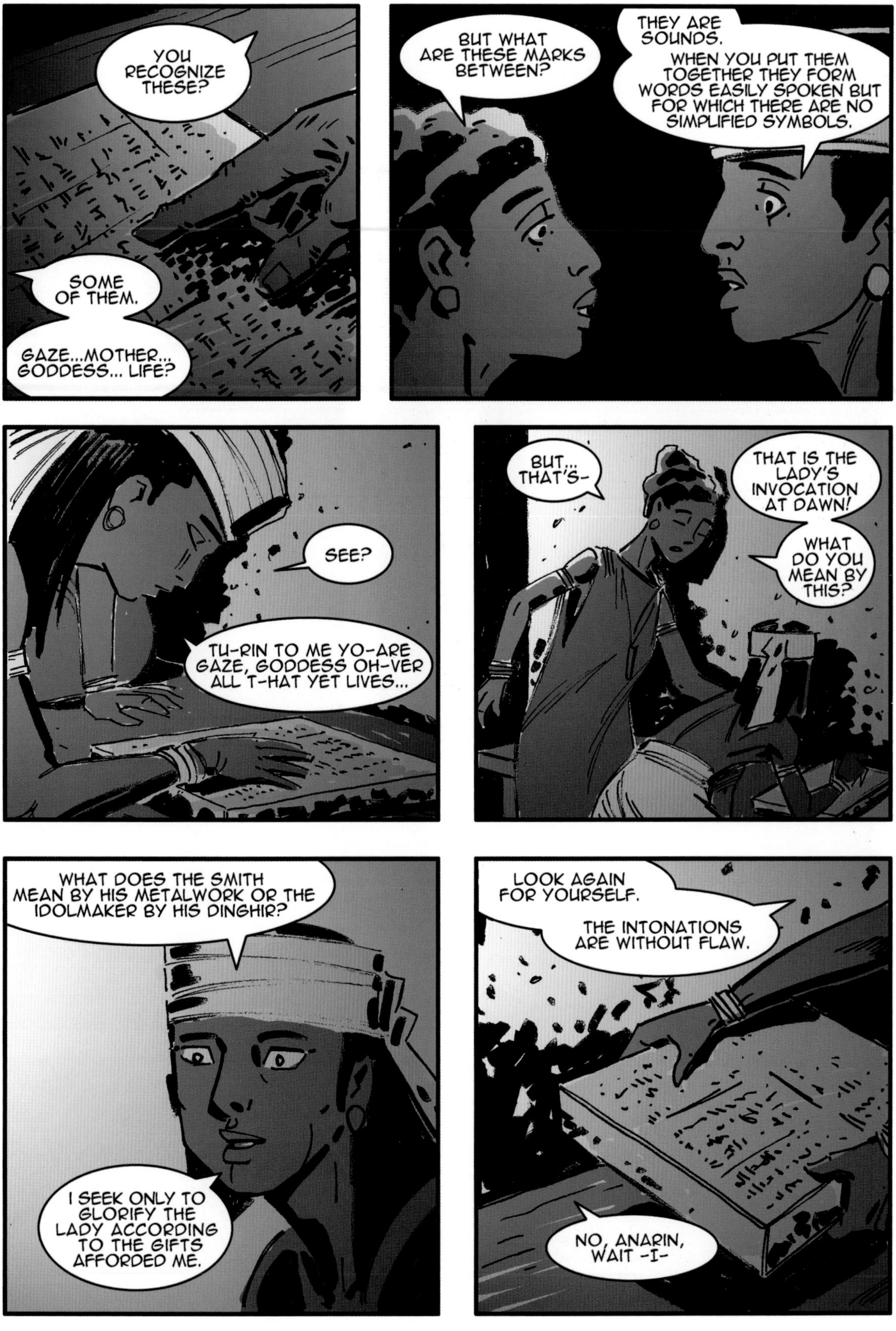
YOU RECOGNIZE THESE?
SOME OF THEM.
GAZE...MOTHER... GODDESS... LIFE?
BUT WHAT ARE THESE MARKS BETWEEN?
THEY ARE SOUNDS.
WHEN YOU PUT THEM TOGETHER THEY FORM WORDS EASILY SPOKEN BUT FOR WHICH THERE ARE NO SIMPLIFIED SYMBOLS.
SEE?
TU-RIN TO ME YO-ARE GAZE, GODDESS OH-VER ALL T-HAT YET LIVES...
BUT... THAT'S-
THAT IS THE LADY'S INVOCATION AT DAWN!
WHAT DO YOU MEAN BY THIS?
WHAT DOES THE SMITH MEAN BY HIS METALWORK OR THE IDOLMAKER BY HIS DINGHIR?
I SEEK ONLY TO GLORIFY THE LADY ACCORDING TO THE GIFTS AFFORDED ME.
LOOK AGAIN FOR YOURSELF.
THE INTONATIONS ARE WITHOUT FLAW.
NO, ANARIN, WAIT -I-

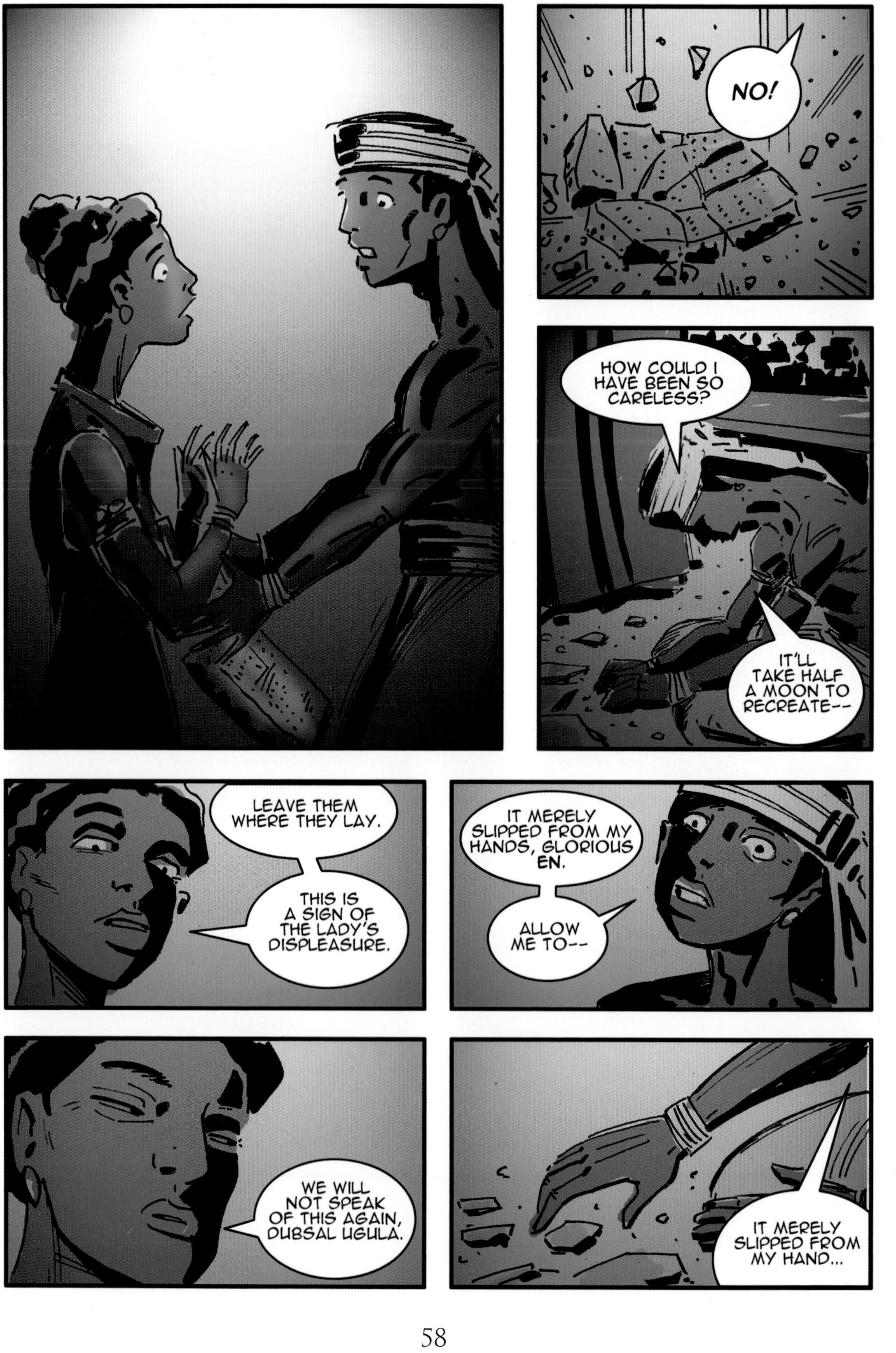
NO!
HOW COULD I HAVE BEEN SO CARELESS?
IT'LL TAKE HALF A MOON TO RECREATE--
LEAVE THEM WHERE THEY LAY.
THIS IS A SIGN OF THE LADY'S DISPLEASURE.
IT MERELY SLIPPED FROM MY HANDS, GLORIOUS EN.
ALLOW ME TO--
WE WILL NOT SPEAK OF THIS AGAIN, DUBSAL UGULA.
IT MERELY SLIPPED FROM MY HAND...

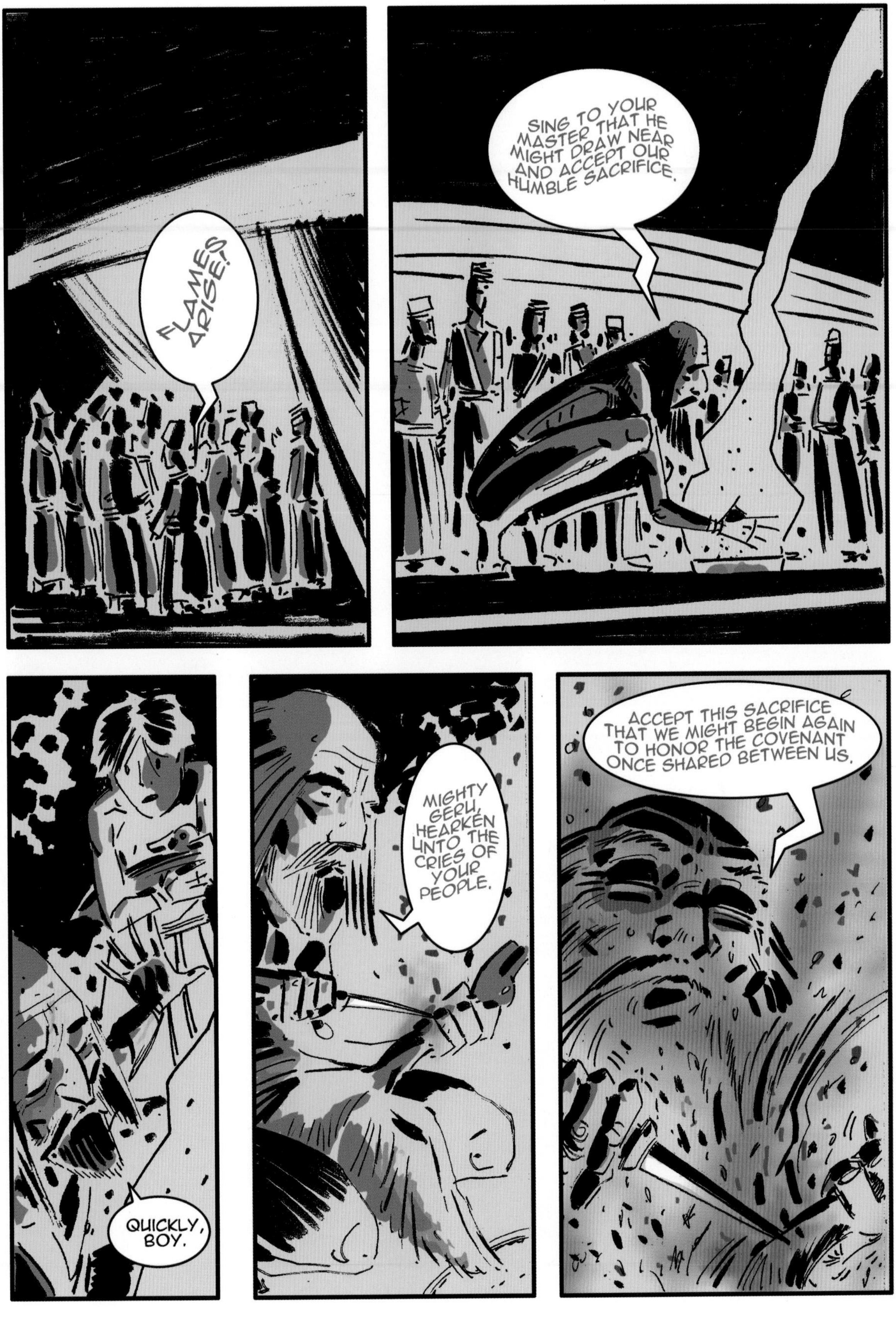
FLAMES ARISE!
SING TO YOUR MASTER THAT HE MIGHT DRAW NEAR AND ACCEPT OUR HUMBLE SACRIFICE.
QUICKLY, BOY.
MIGHTY GERU, HEARKEN UNTO THE CRIES OF YOUR PEOPLE.
ACCEPT THIS SACRIFICE THAT WE MIGHT BEGIN AGAIN TO HONOR THE COVENANT ONCE SHARED BETWEEN US.

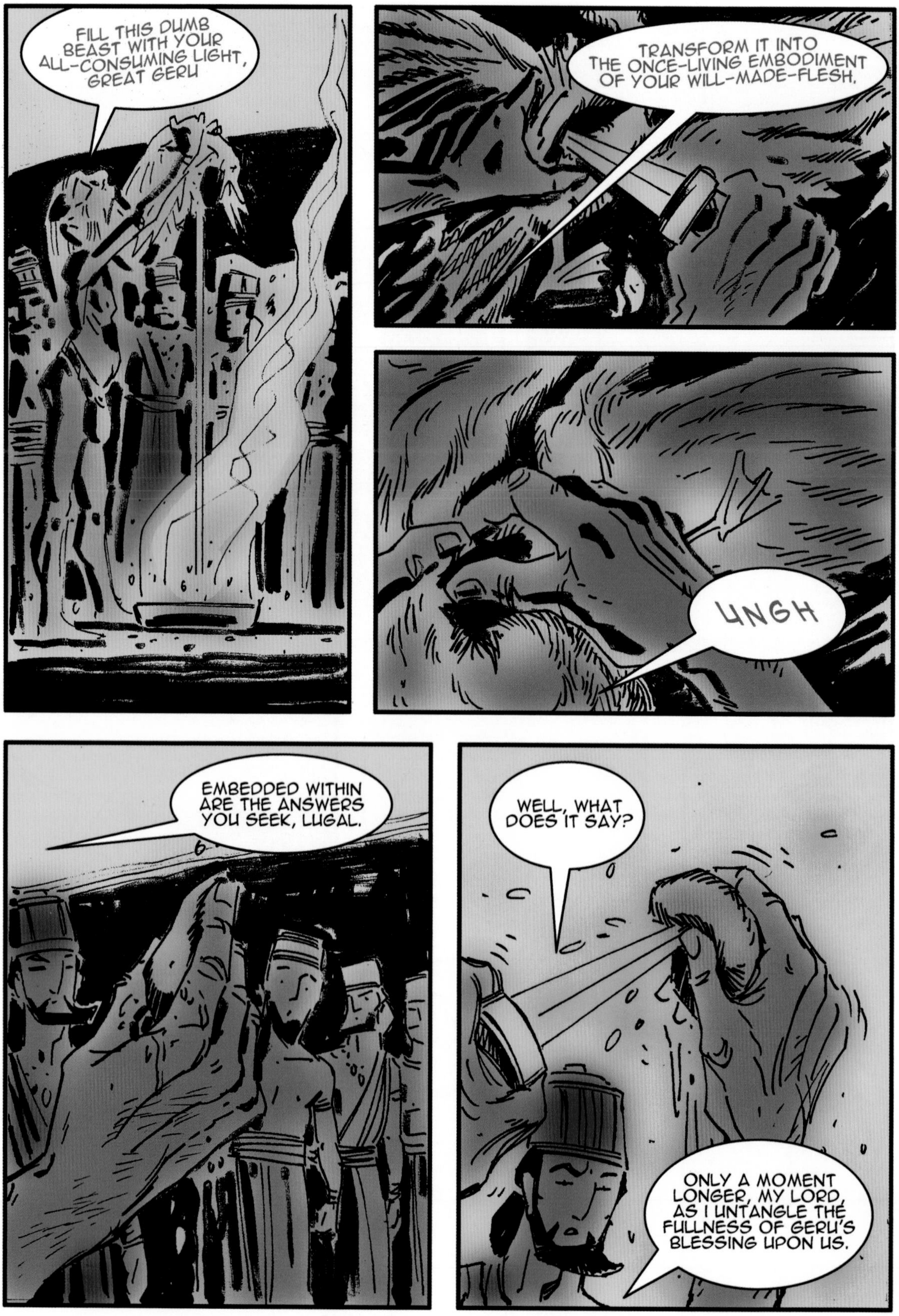
FILL THIS DUMB BEAST WITH YOUR ALL-CONSUMING LIGHT, GREAT GERU
TRANSFORM IT INTO THE ONCE-LIVING EMBODIMENT OF YOUR WILL-MADE-FLESH.
UNGH
EMBEDDED WITHIN ARE THE ANSWERS YOU SEEK, LUGAL.
WELL, WHAT DOES IT SAY?
ONLY A MOMENT LONGER, MY LORD, AS I UNTANGLE THE FULLNESS OF GERU'S BLESSING UPON US.

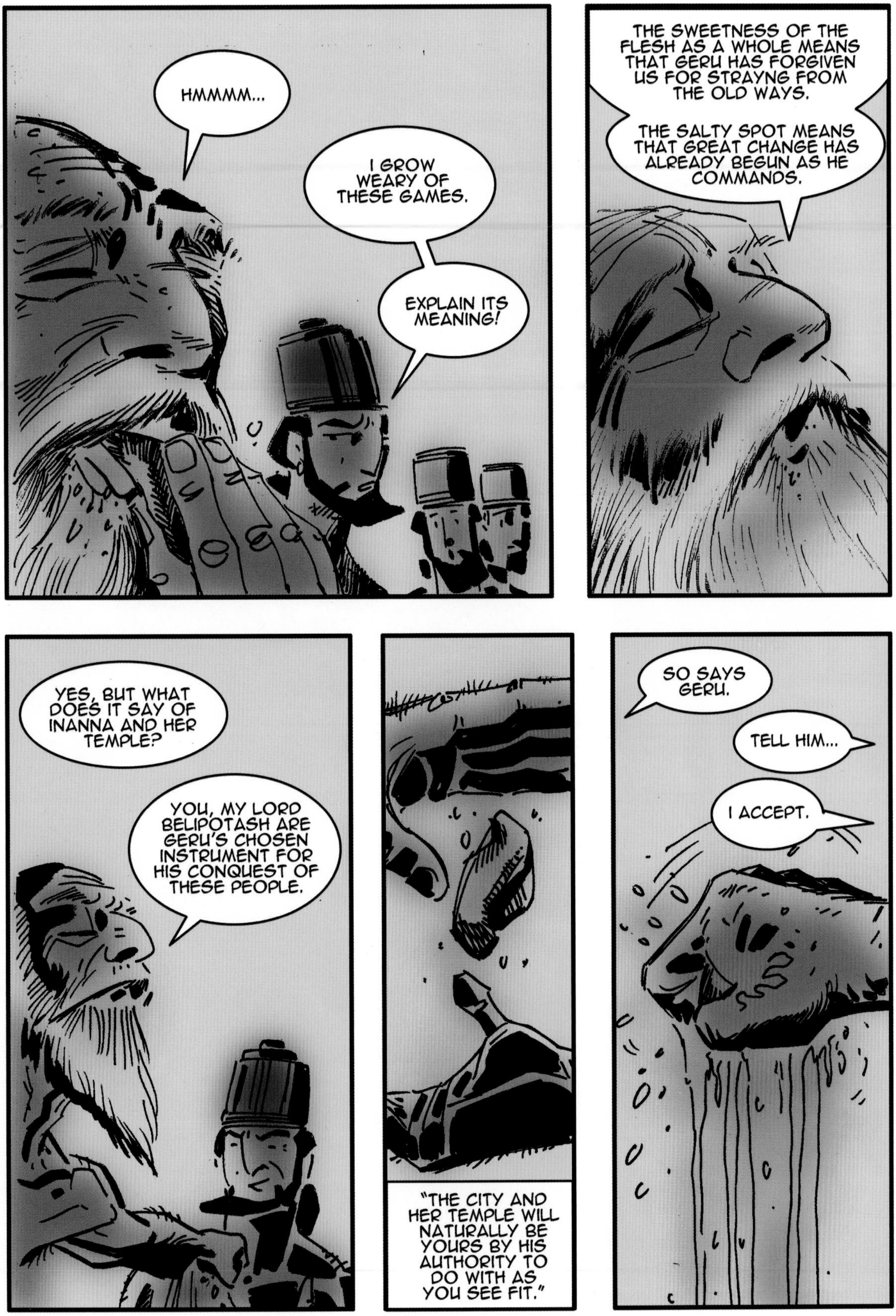
HMMMM...
I GROW WEARY OF THESE GAMES.
EXPLAIN ITS MEANING!
THE SWEETNESS OF THE FLESH AS A WHOLE MEANS THAT GERU HAS FORGIVEN US FOR STRAYNG FROM THE OLD WAYS.
THE SALTY SPOT MEANS THAT GREAT CHANGE HAS ALREADY BEGUN AS HE COMMANDS.
YES, BUT WHAT DOES IT SAY OF INANNA AND HER TEMPLE?
YOU, MY LORD BELIPOTASH ARE GERU'S CHOSEN INSTRUMENT FOR HIS CONQUEST OF THESE PEOPLE.
"THE CITY AND HER TEMPLE WILL NATURALLY BE YOURS BY HIS AUTHORITY TO DO WITH AS YOU SEE FIT."
SO SAYS GERU.
TELL HIM...
I ACCEPT.

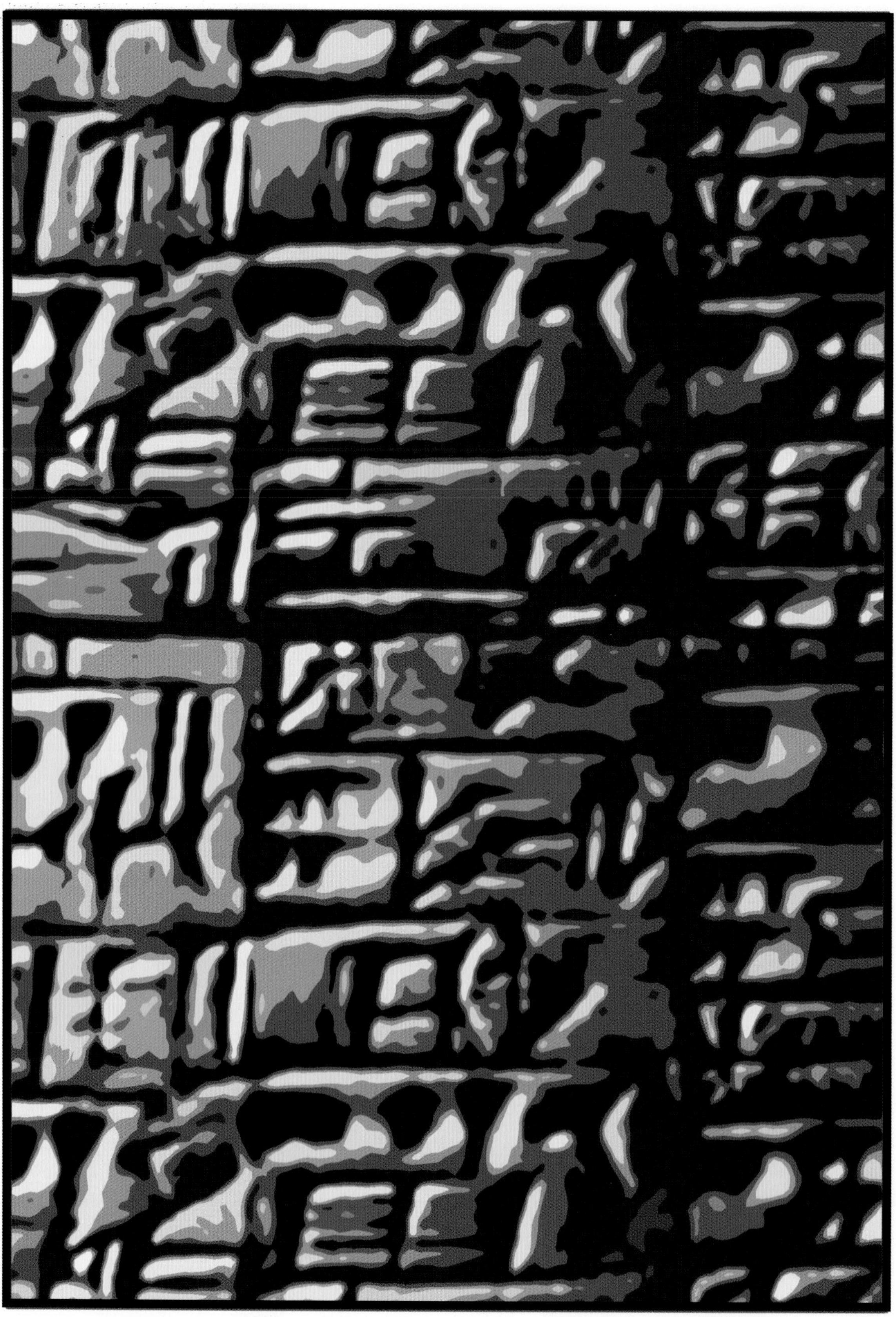

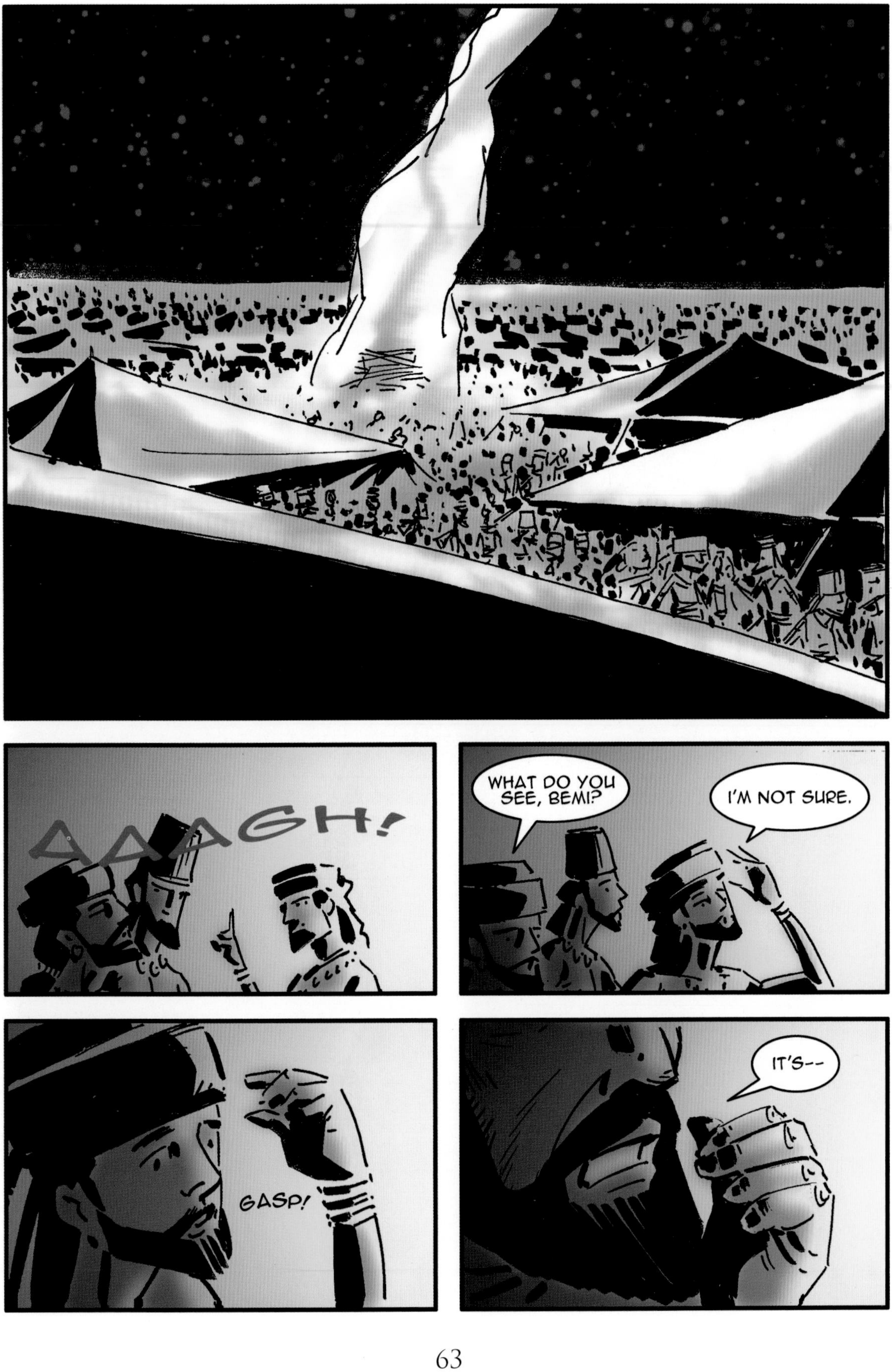
AAAGH!
WHAT DO YOU SEE, BEMI?
I'M NOT SURE.
GASP!
IT'S--

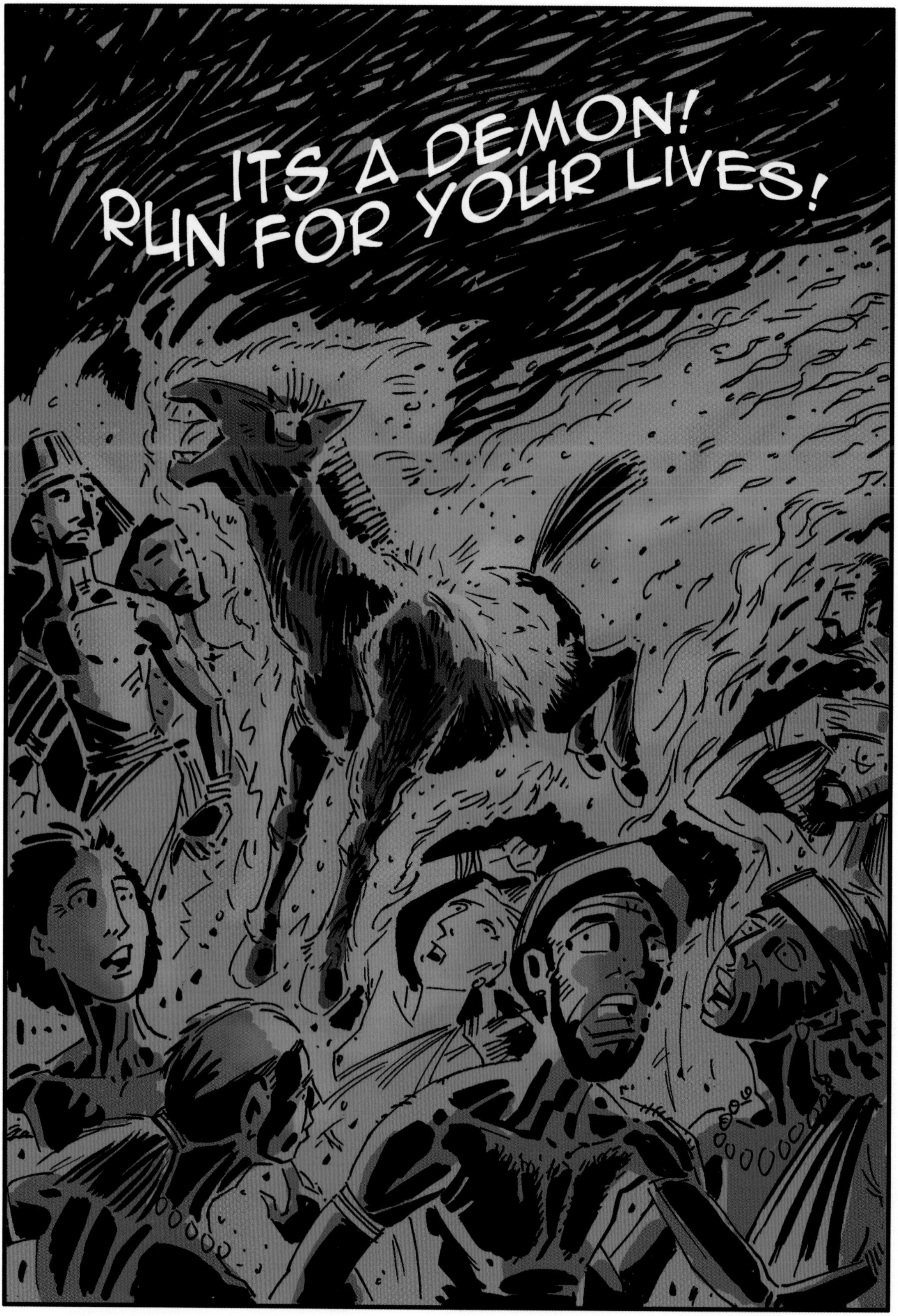
ITS A DEMON!
RUN FOR YOUR LIVES!

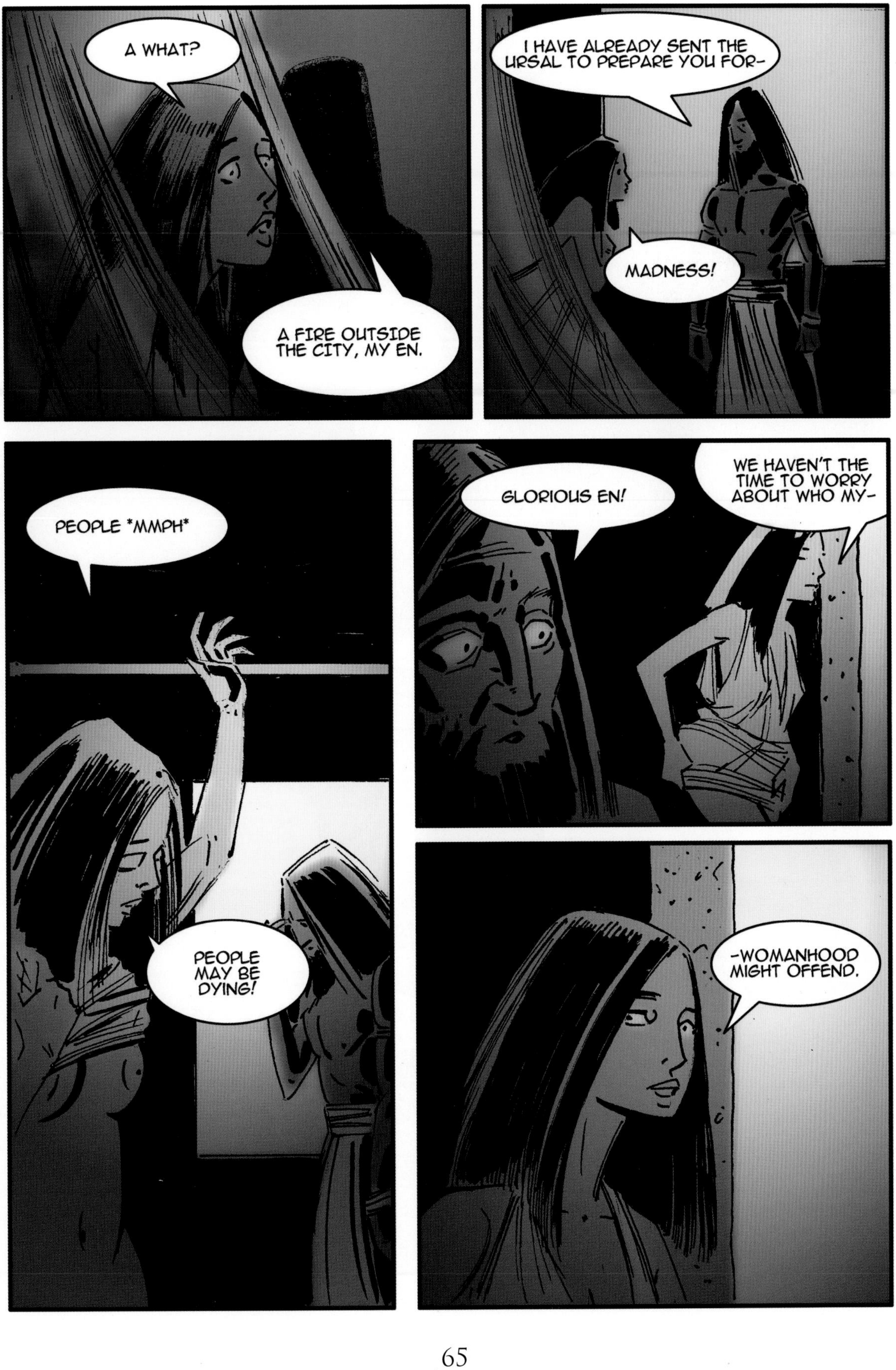
A WHAT?
A FIRE OUTSIDE THE CITY, MY EN.
I HAVE ALREADY SENT THE URSAL TO PREPARE YOU FOR-
MADNESS!
PEOPLE *MMPH*
PEOPLE MAY BE DYING!
GLORIOUS EN!
WE HAVEN'T THE TIME TO WORRY ABOUT WHO MY-
-WOMANHOOD MIGHT OFFEND.

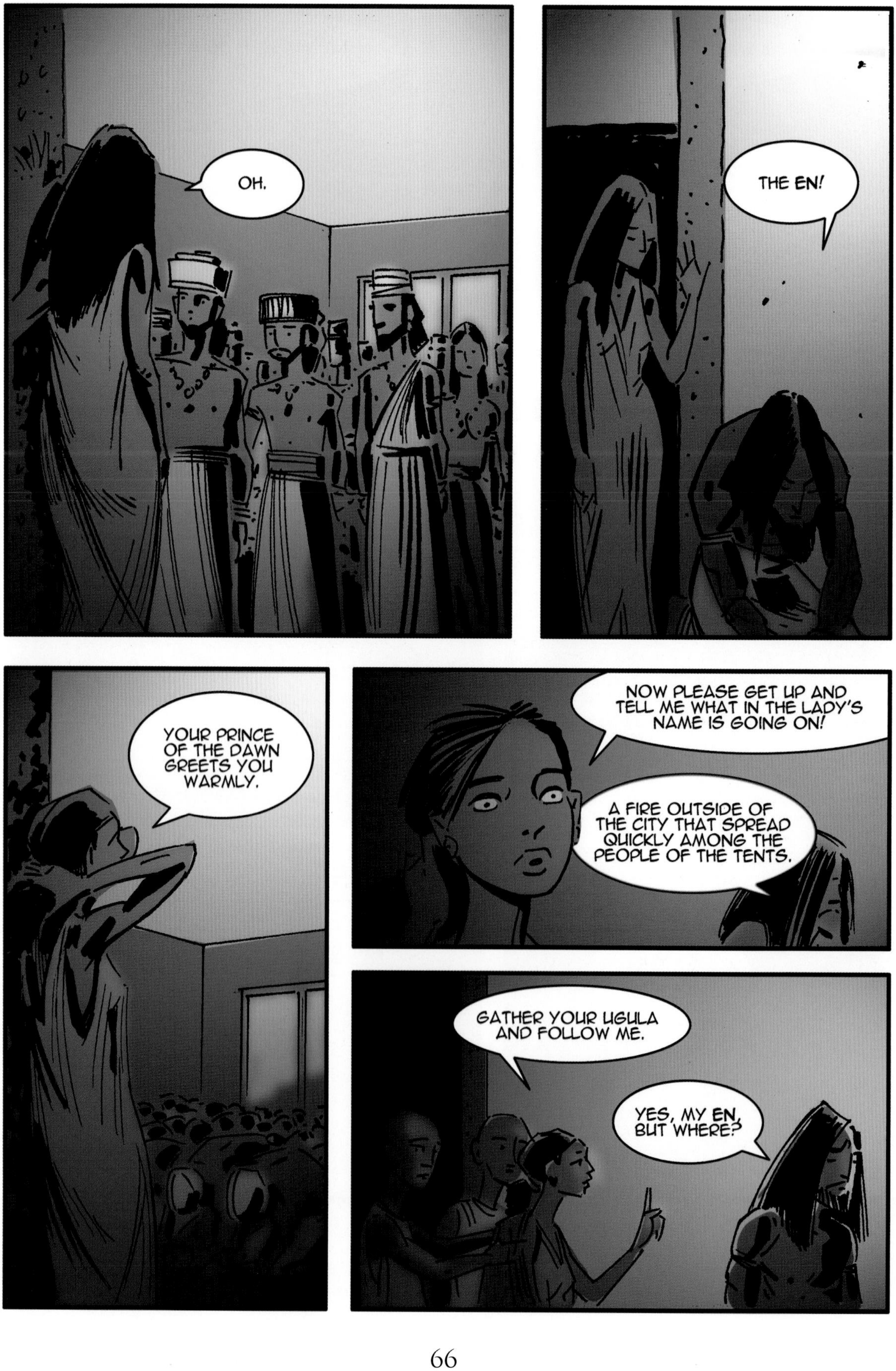
OH.
THE EN!
YOUR PRINCE OF THE DAWN GREETS YOU WARMLY.
NOW PLEASE GET UP AND TELL ME WHAT IN THE LADY'S NAME IS GOING ON!
A FIRE OUTSIDE OF THE CITY THAT SPREAD QUICKLY AMONG THE PEOPLE OF THE TENTS.
GATHER YOUR UGULA AND FOLLOW ME.
YES, MY EN, BUT WHERE?

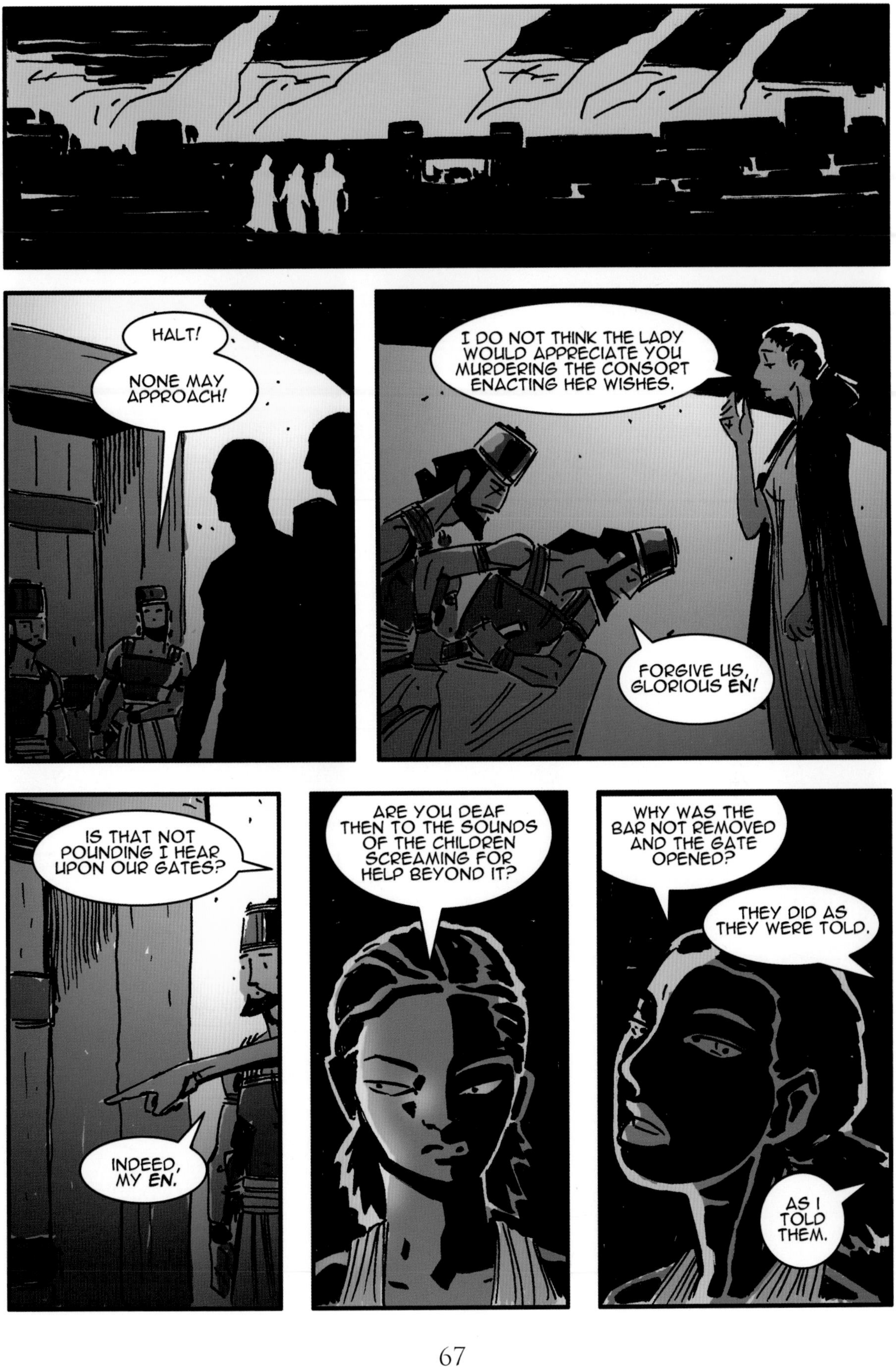
HALT!
NONE MAY APPROACH!
I DO NOT THINK THE LADY WOULD APPRECIATE YOU MURDERING THE CONSORT ENACTING HER WISHES.
FORGIVE US, GLORIOUS EN!
IS THAT NOT POUNDING I HEAR UPON OUR GATES?
INDEED, MY EN.
ARE YOU DEAF THEN TO THE SOUNDS OF THE CHILDREN SCREAMING FOR HELP BEYOND IT?
WHY WAS THE BAR NOT REMOVED AND THE GATE OPENED?
THEY DID AS THEY WERE TOLD.
AS I TOLD THEM.

AND WHY DID YOU TELL THEM THIS?

IT WAS BUT THREE CYCLES OF MAN AGO THAT THE OUTER CITY WAS SET AFIRE AS A PRELUDE TO A LARGER ATTACK UPON THE WALLS AND WITHIN.

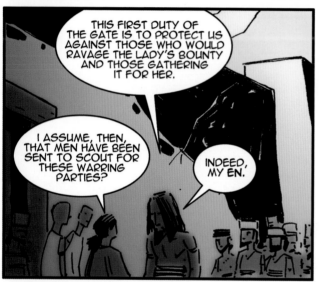

THIS FIRST DUTY OF THE GATE IS TO PROTECT US AGAINST THOSE WHO WOULD RAVAGE THE LADY'S BOUNTY AND THOSE GATHERING IT FOR HER.

I ASSUME, THEN, THAT MEN HAVE BEEN SENT TO SCOUT FOR THESE WARRING PARTIES?

INDEED, MY EN.

THERE IS NO SIGN OF ONE CLOSE ENOUGH TO STRIKE US TONIGHT.

INDEED.

MASTER CANALSMAN?

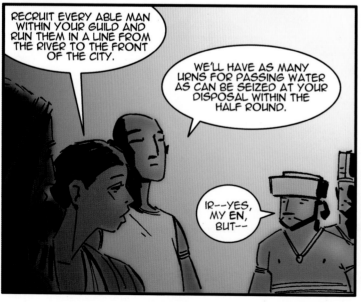

RECRUIT EVERY ABLE MAN WITHIN YOUR GUILD AND RUN THEM IN A LINE FROM THE RIVER TO THE FRONT OF THE CITY.

WE'LL HAVE AS MANY URNS FOR PASSING WATER AS CAN BE SEIZED AT YOUR DISPOSAL WITHIN THE HALF ROUND.

IR--YES, MY EN, BUT--

FOR THAT AMOUNT OF TIME AND MEN I COULD RUN YOU A DITCH THAT'D BRING ALL THE WATER YOU COULD USE.

THE LADY WOULD BE MOST GRATEFUL...

NOW, OPEN THE GATE!

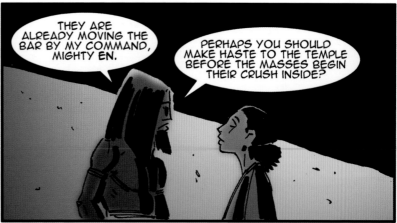

THEY ARE ALREADY MOVING THE BAR BY MY COMMAND, MIGHTY EN.

PERHAPS YOU SHOULD MAKE HASTE TO THE TEMPLE BEFORE THE MASSES BEGIN THEIR CRUSH INSIDE?

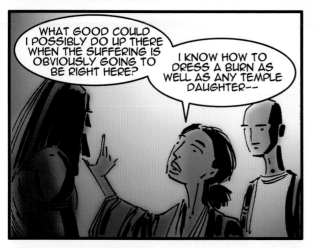

WHAT GOOD COULD I POSSIBLY DO UP THERE WHEN THE SUFFERING IS OBVIOUSLY GOING TO BE RIGHT HERE?

I KNOW HOW TO DRESS A BURN AS WELL AS ANY TEMPLE DAUGHTER--

I EXPECT YOU TO BRING ME NEWS AS IT IS KNOWN, GOOD SANGA.

OF COURSE, MY EN.

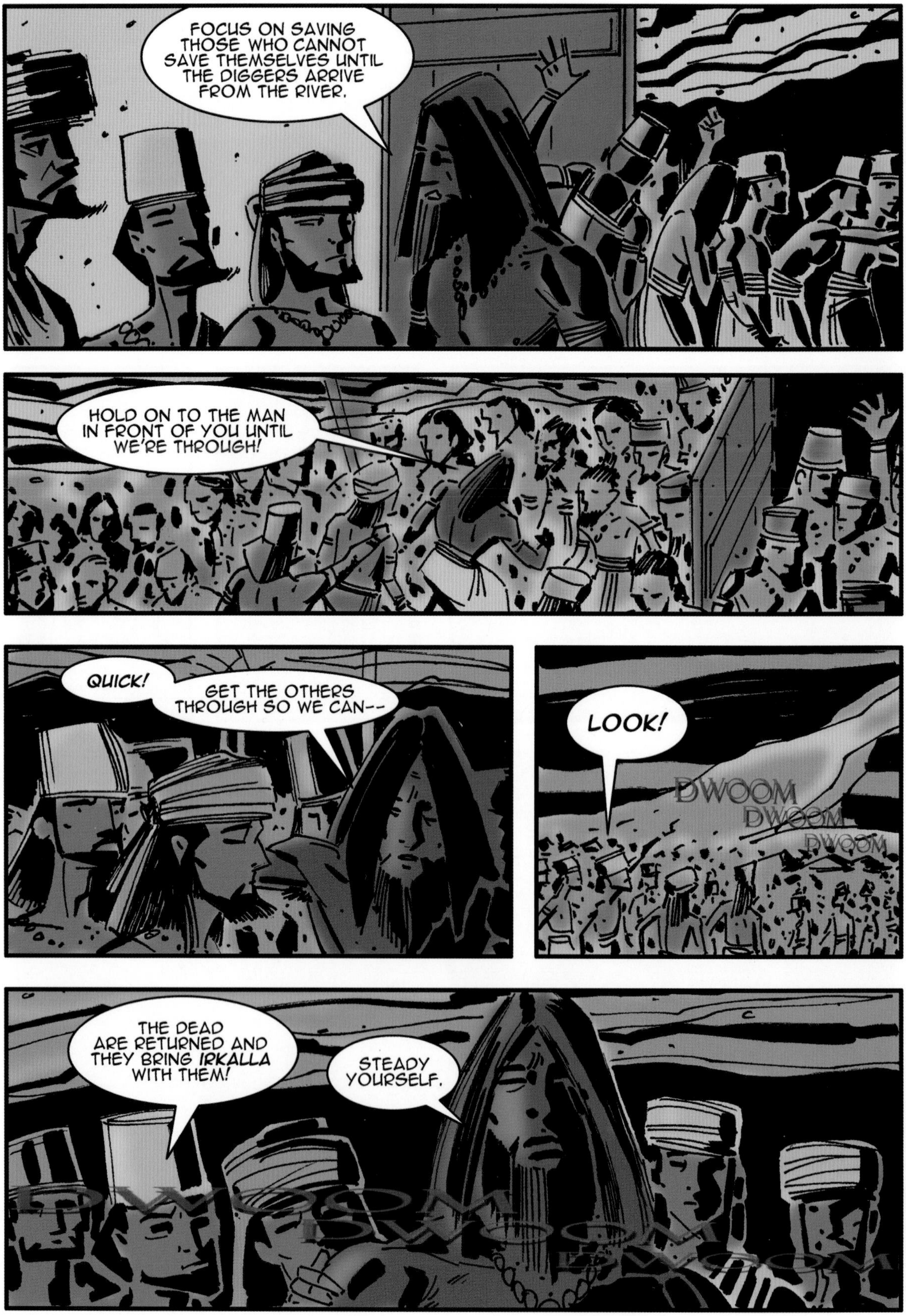
FOCUS ON SAVING THOSE WHO CANNOT SAVE THEMSELVES UNTIL THE DIGGERS ARRIVE FROM THE RIVER.
HOLD ON TO THE MAN IN FRONT OF YOU UNTIL WE'RE THROUGH!
QUICK!
GET THE OTHERS THROUGH SO WE CAN--
LOOK!
DWOOM
DWOOM
DWOOM
THE DEAD ARE RETURNED AND THEY BRING IRKALLA WITH THEM!
STEADY YOURSELF.

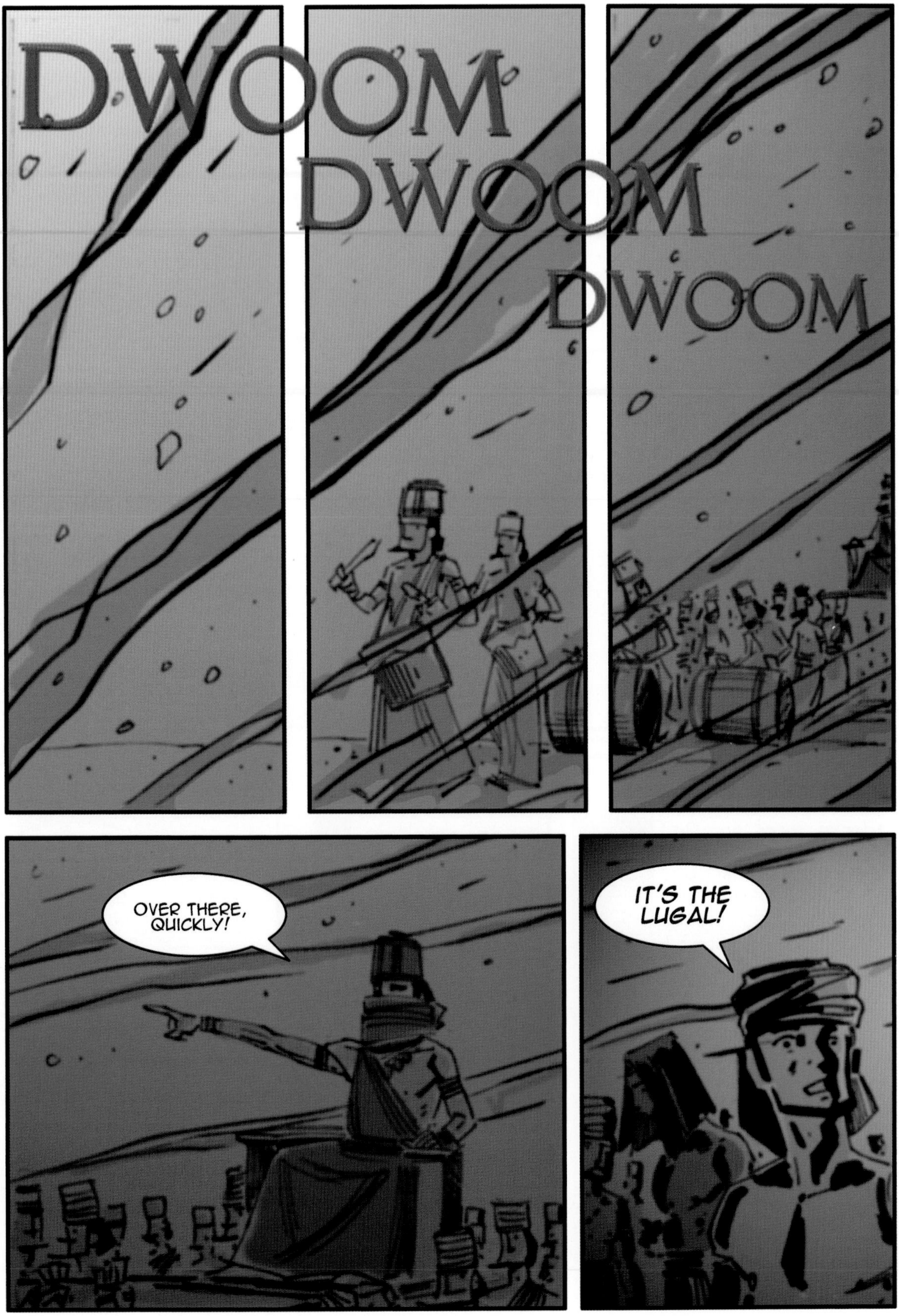
DWOOM
DWOOM
DWOOM
OVER THERE, QUICKLY!
IT'S THE LUGAL!

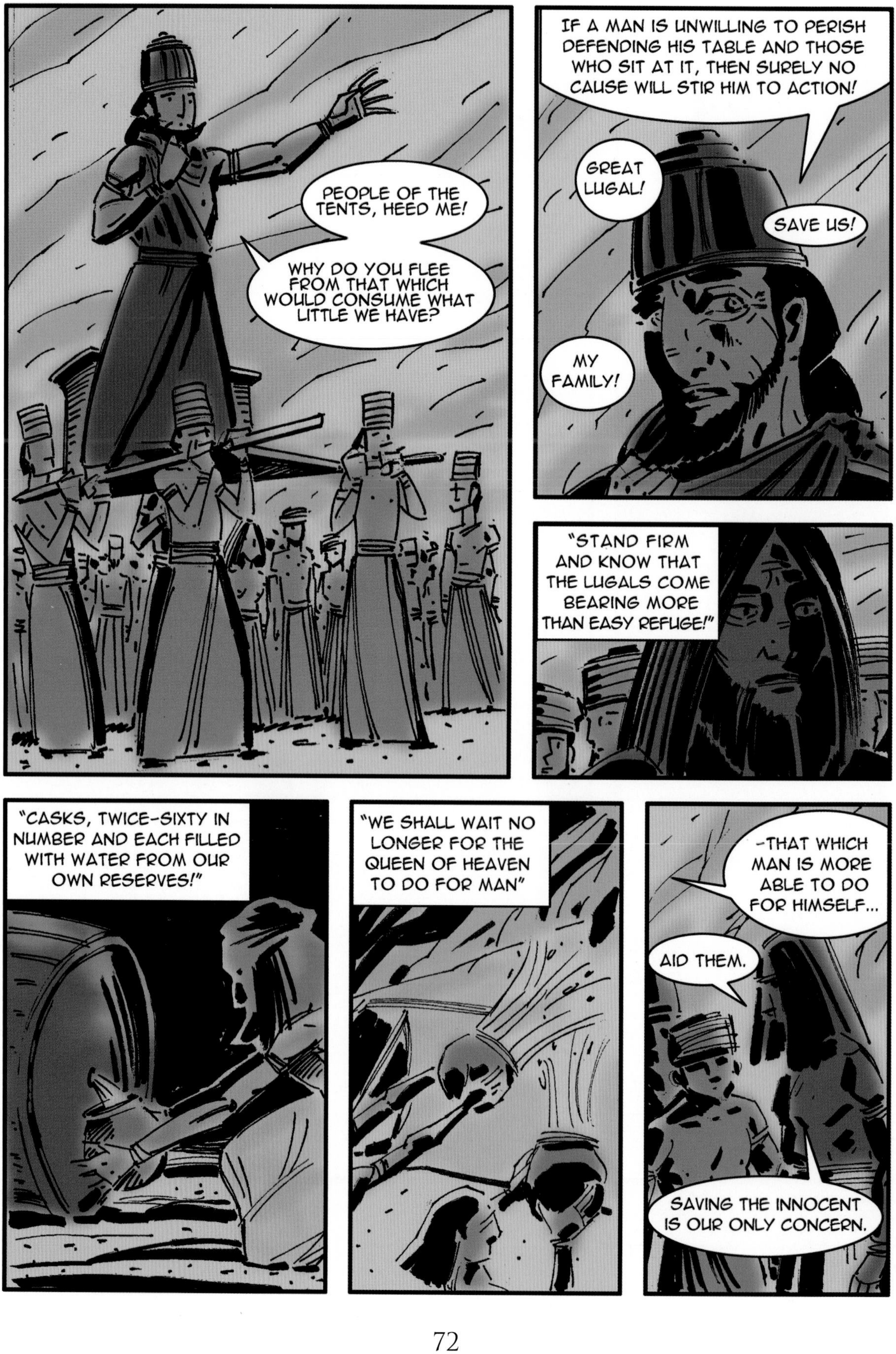
PEOPLE OF THE TENTS, HEED ME!
WHY DO YOU FLEE FROM THAT WHICH WOULD CONSUME WHAT LITTLE WE HAVE?
IF A MAN IS UNWILLING TO PERISH DEFENDING HIS TABLE AND THOSE WHO SIT AT IT, THEN SURELY NO CAUSE WILL STIR HIM TO ACTION!
GREAT LUGAL!
SAVE US!
MY FAMILY!
"STAND FIRM AND KNOW THAT THE LUGALS COME BEARING MORE THAN EASY REFUGE!"
"CASKS, TWICE-SIXTY IN NUMBER AND EACH FILLED WITH WATER FROM OUR OWN RESERVES!"
"WE SHALL WAIT NO LONGER FOR THE QUEEN OF HEAVEN TO DO FOR MAN"
-THAT WHICH MAN IS MORE ABLE TO DO FOR HIMSELF...
AID THEM.
SAVING THE INNOCENT IS OUR ONLY CONCERN.

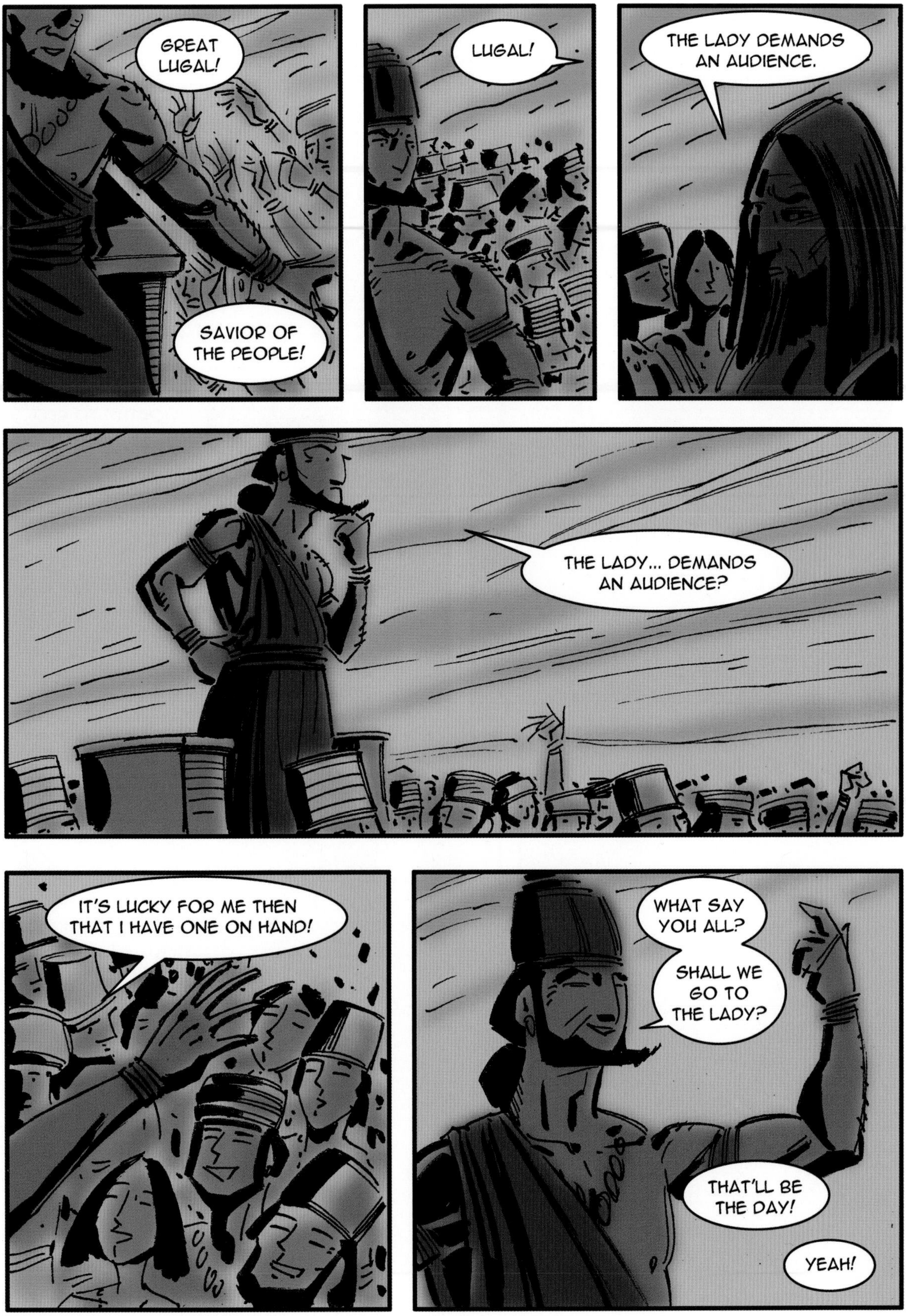
GREAT LUGAL!
SAVIOR OF THE PEOPLE!
LUGAL!
THE LADY DEMANDS AN AUDIENCE.
THE LADY... DEMANDS AN AUDIENCE?
IT'S LUCKY FOR ME THEN THAT I HAVE ONE ON HAND!
WHAT SAY YOU ALL?
SHALL WE GO TO THE LADY?
THAT'LL BE THE DAY!
YEAH!

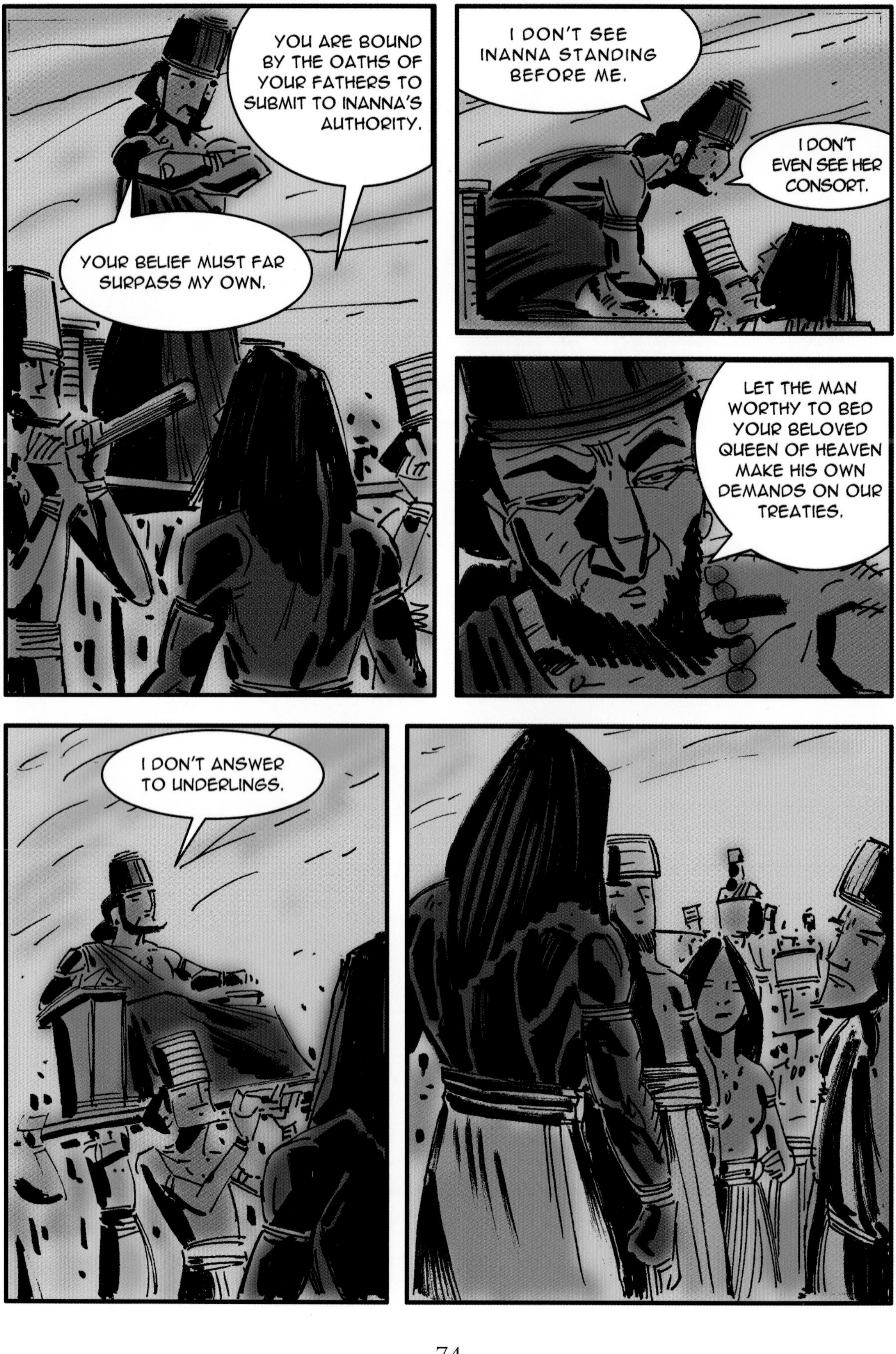
YOU ARE BOUND BY THE OATHS OF YOUR FATHERS TO SUBMIT TO INANNA'S AUTHORITY.
YOUR BELIEF MUST FAR SURPASS MY OWN.
I DON'T SEE INANNA STANDING BEFORE ME.
I DON'T EVEN SEE HER CONSORT.
LET THE MAN WORTHY TO BED YOUR BELOVED QUEEN OF HEAVEN MAKE HIS OWN DEMANDS ON OUR TREATIES.
I DON'T ANSWER TO UNDERLINGS.

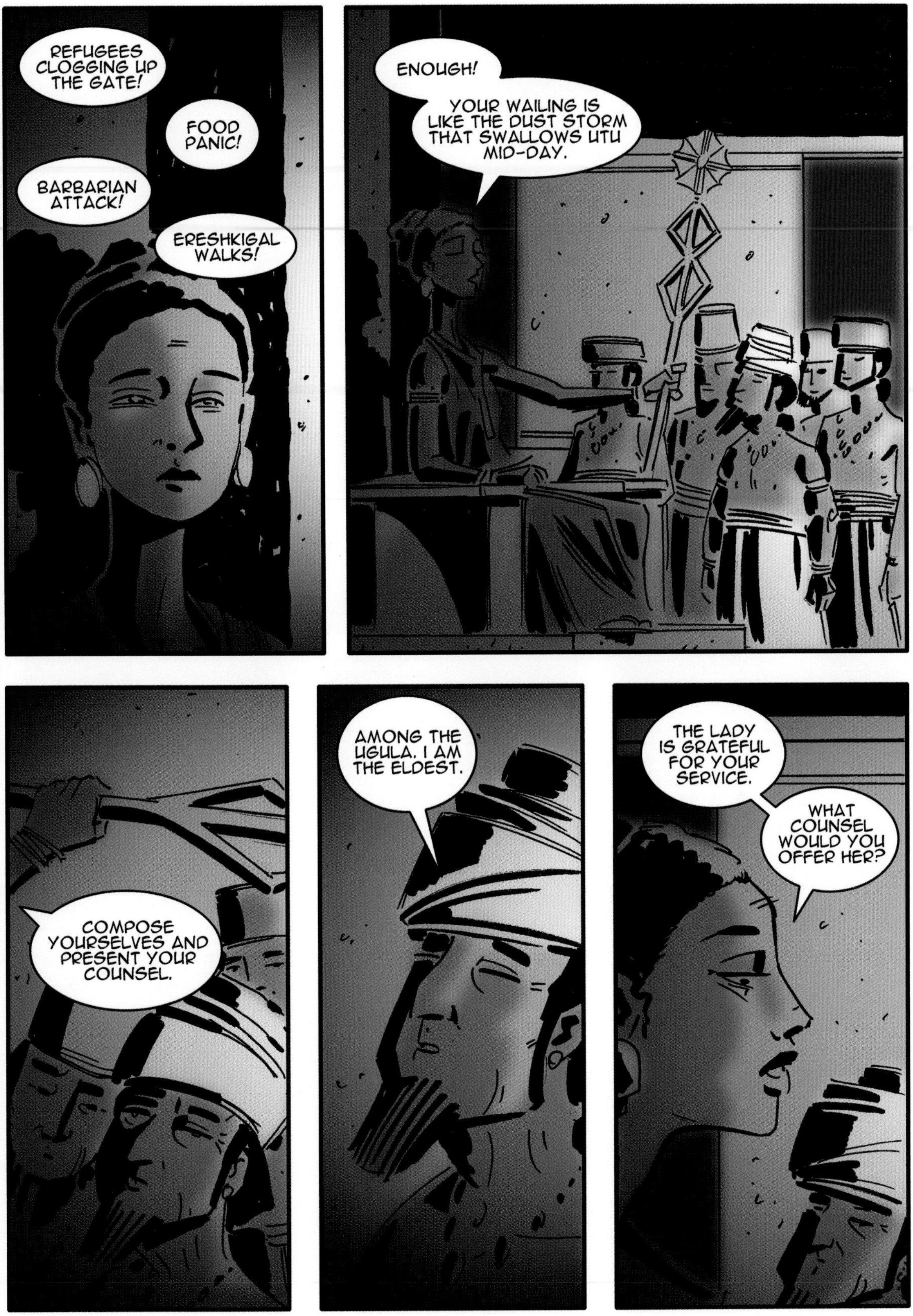
REFUGEES CLOGGING UP THE GATE!
FOOD PANIC!
BARBARIAN ATTACK!
ERESHKIGAL WALKS!
ENOUGH!
YOUR WAILING IS LIKE THE DUST STORM THAT SWALLOWS UTU MID-DAY.
COMPOSE YOURSELVES AND PRESENT YOUR COUNSEL.
AMONG THE UGULA, I AM THE ELDEST.
THE LADY IS GRATEFUL FOR YOUR SERVICE.
WHAT COUNSEL WOULD YOU OFFER HER?

THAT OF WITNESS, GLORIOUS *ÉN*, AS I HAVE SEEN MANY CHANGES TAKE THE LAND.

AS A BOY, MY FATHER WOULD TAKE ME ALONG TO THE OUTER CITY WHERE HE TRADED WITH MEN FROM ALL PARTS OF THE LAND AND BEYOND.

IT WAS VERY DIFFERENT FROM WHAT WE KNOW TODAY, A PLACE PEOPLED BY VISITORS.

NO ONE LIVED THERE.

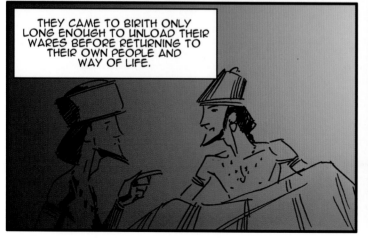

THEY CAME TO BIRITH ONLY LONG ENOUGH TO UNLOAD THEIR WARES BEFORE RETURNING TO THEIR OWN PEOPLE AND WAY OF LIFE.

AND THEN CAME THE INVADERS...

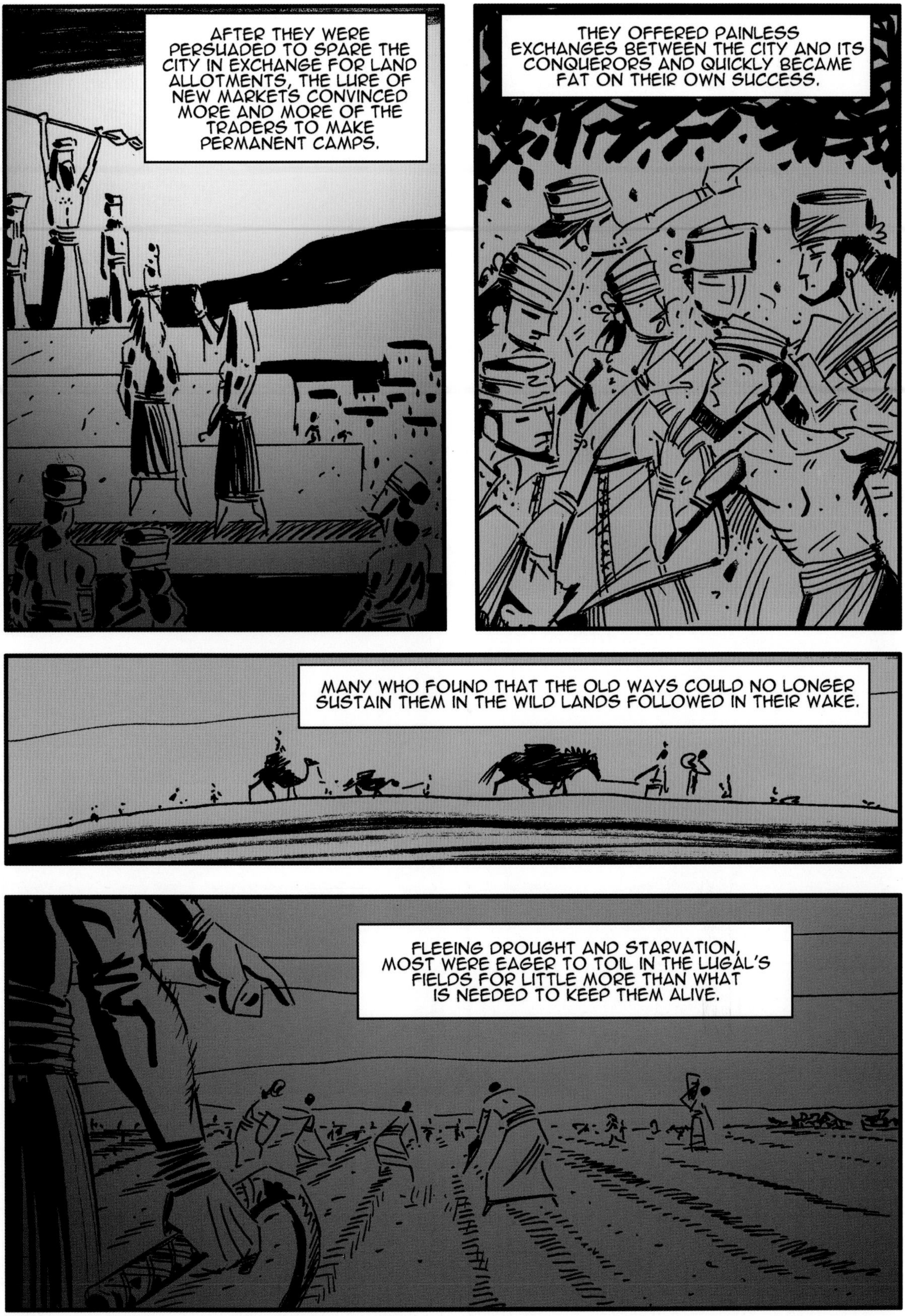
AFTER THEY WERE PERSUADED TO SPARE THE CITY IN EXCHANGE FOR LAND ALLOTMENTS, THE LURE OF NEW MARKETS CONVINCED MORE AND MORE OF THE TRADERS TO MAKE PERMANENT CAMPS.
THEY OFFERED PAINLESS EXCHANGES BETWEEN THE CITY AND ITS CONQUERORS AND QUICKLY BECAME FAT ON THEIR OWN SUCCESS.
MANY WHO FOUND THAT THE OLD WAYS COULD NO LONGER SUSTAIN THEM IN THE WILD LANDS FOLLOWED IN THEIR WAKE.
FLEEING DROUGHT AND STARVATION, MOST WERE EAGER TO TOIL IN THE LUGAL'S FIELDS FOR LITTLE MORE THAN WHAT IS NEEDED TO KEEP THEM ALIVE.

WITH FAR MORE HUDDLED AMONG THE TENTS THAN FIELDS TO PLOW OR CARAVANS TO GUARD, I SUSPECT THIS UNREST WILL ONLY ESCALATE.
YOUR COUNSEL IS WELL TAKEN, BREWER, BUT WHAT DO THE LAND WORKERS GAIN IN RAZING THEIR OWN DWELLINGS?
THIS FIRE WAS NOT SPREAD BY THE HAND OF A LAND WORKER.
PLEASE FORGIVE THE ABRUPTNESS OF MY INTRUSION.
YOU INTRUDE ONLY UPON MY WAITING FOR YOUR WORD, SANGA.
WHAT HAVE YOU LEARNED?
THE TENT CITY NO LONGER BURNS, MY **EN**.
THE FIRE HAS BEEN SMOTHERED.
PRAISE HER MERCY!
I WOULD SPEAK WITH THE ***EN*** ALONE.

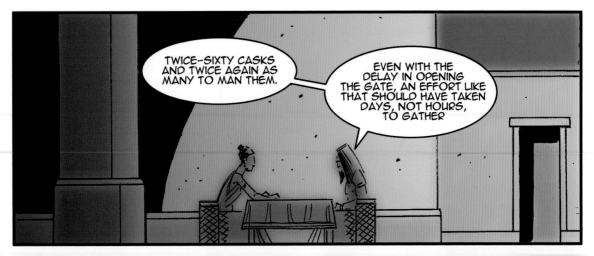

TWICE-SIXTY CASKS AND TWICE AGAIN AS MANY TO MAN THEM.

EVEN WITH THE DELAY IN OPENING THE GATE, AN EFFORT LIKE THAT SHOULD HAVE TAKEN DAYS, NOT HOURS, TO GATHER

UNLESS THEY KNEW IT WAS GOING TO HAPPEN AND HAD TIME TO PREPARE.

THAT IS MY BELIEF.

WHAT DO THEY HOPE TO GAIN BY BURNING OUT THEIR OWN?

THEY HAVE ALREADY GAINED MUCH.

THOUGH MANY ESCAPED INTO THE CITY, MORE YET PERISHED WHILE THE GATES REMAINED SHUT.

THOSE WHO SURVIVED WILL REMEMBER THAT IT WAS THE LUGALS WHO CAME TO THEIR RESCUE

PERHAPS IF WE COULD PROVIDE THEM WITH FOOD AND MATERIALS TO REBUILD THEIR HOMES?

I WILL SEE TO IT. THOUGH I FEAR THAT MANY WILL REFUSE OUR AID.

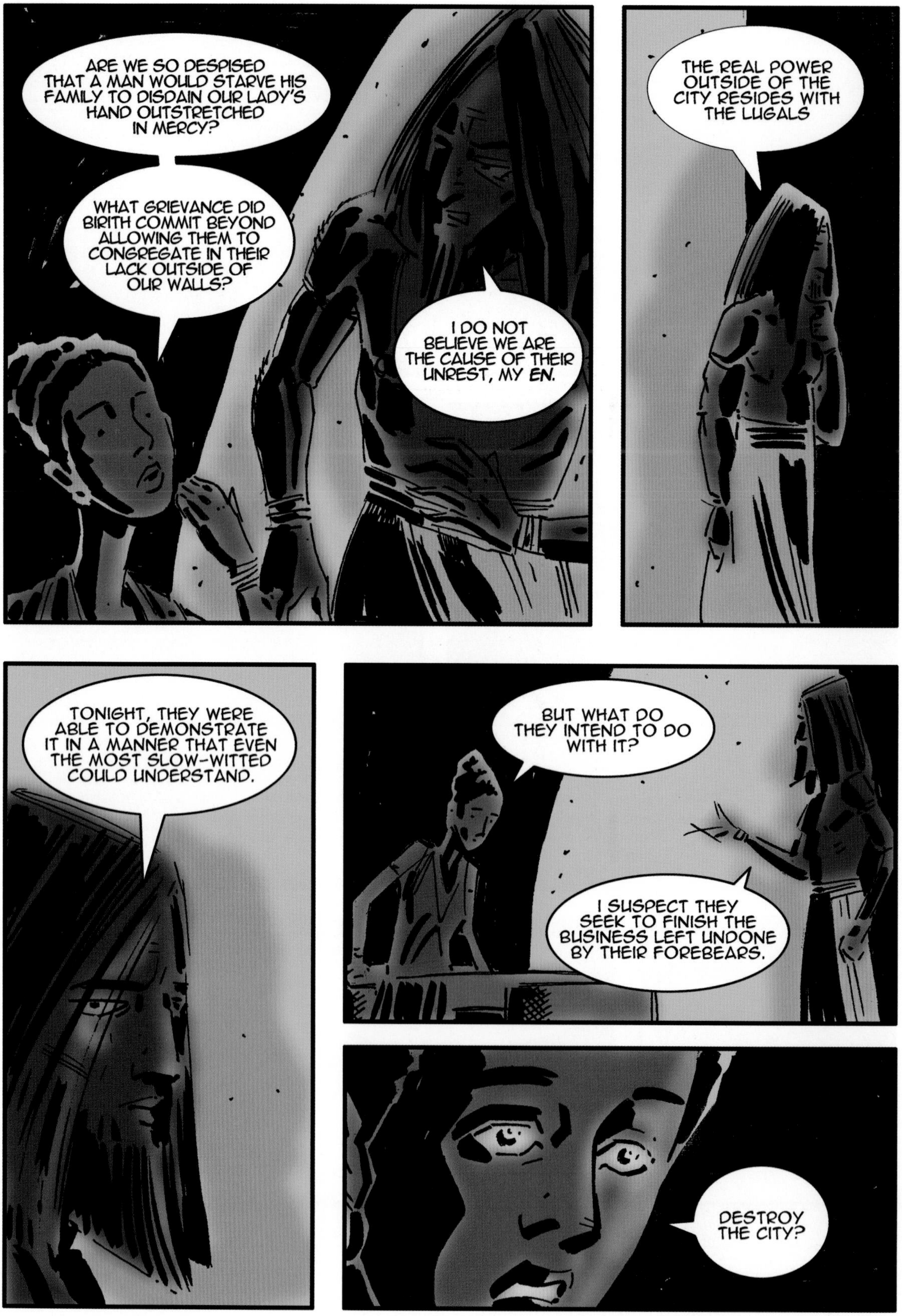
ARE WE SO DESPISED THAT A MAN WOULD STARVE HIS FAMILY TO DISDAIN OUR LADY'S HAND OUTSTRETCHED IN MERCY?
WHAT GRIEVANCE DID BIRITH COMMIT BEYOND ALLOWING THEM TO CONGREGATE IN THEIR LACK OUTSIDE OF OUR WALLS?
I DO NOT BELIEVE WE ARE THE CAUSE OF THEIR UNREST, MY EN.
THE REAL POWER OUTSIDE OF THE CITY RESIDES WITH THE LUGALS
TONIGHT, THEY WERE ABLE TO DEMONSTRATE IT IN A MANNER THAT EVEN THE MOST SLOW-WITTED COULD UNDERSTAND.
BUT WHAT DO THEY INTEND TO DO WITH IT?
I SUSPECT THEY SEEK TO FINISH THE BUSINESS LEFT UNDONE BY THEIR FOREBEARS.
DESTROY THE CITY?

DOUBTFUL...

THEY WILL NEED ITS RESOURCES TO LIVE IN THE MANNER TO WHICH THEY HAVE GROWN ACCUSTOMED.

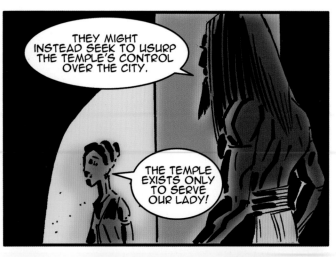

THEY MIGHT INSTEAD SEEK TO USURP THE TEMPLE'S CONTROL OVER THE CITY.

THE TEMPLE EXISTS ONLY TO SERVE OUR LADY!

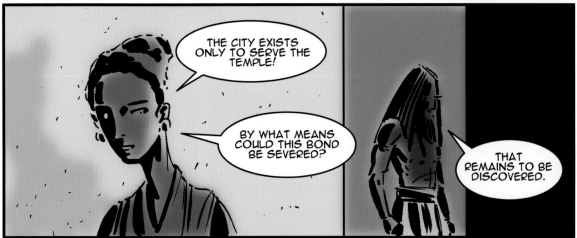

THE CITY EXISTS ONLY TO SERVE THE TEMPLE!

BY WHAT MEANS COULD THIS BOND BE SEVERED?

THAT REMAINS TO BE DISCOVERED.

IT SEEMS UNWISE TO GAMBLE BIRITH'S WELFARE ON THE CERTAINTY THAT WE WILL IN TIME.

COULD THEY INSTEAD BE PACIFIED BY GREATER LAND GRANTS?

NO ONE CAN SAY.

HAS ANYONE TRIED ASKING THEM?

THEY SAY THEY WILL CONSIDER THE OLD TREATIES ONLY WITH THE CONSORT PRESENT.

NONE WAIT IN THE HALL SEEKING AN AUDIENCE.

WHY HAVE THE URSAL NOT BEEN SUMMONED IF I AM TO JOURNEY OUTSIDE OF THE TEMPLE?

THERE IS TO BE NO JOURNEY.

FROM THEIR OWN TONGUE, THEY WILL SPEAK ONLY WITH THE MAN WORTHY TO BED THE QUEEN OF HEAVEN.

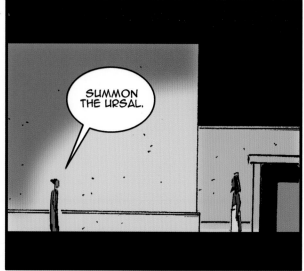

SUMMON THE URSAL.

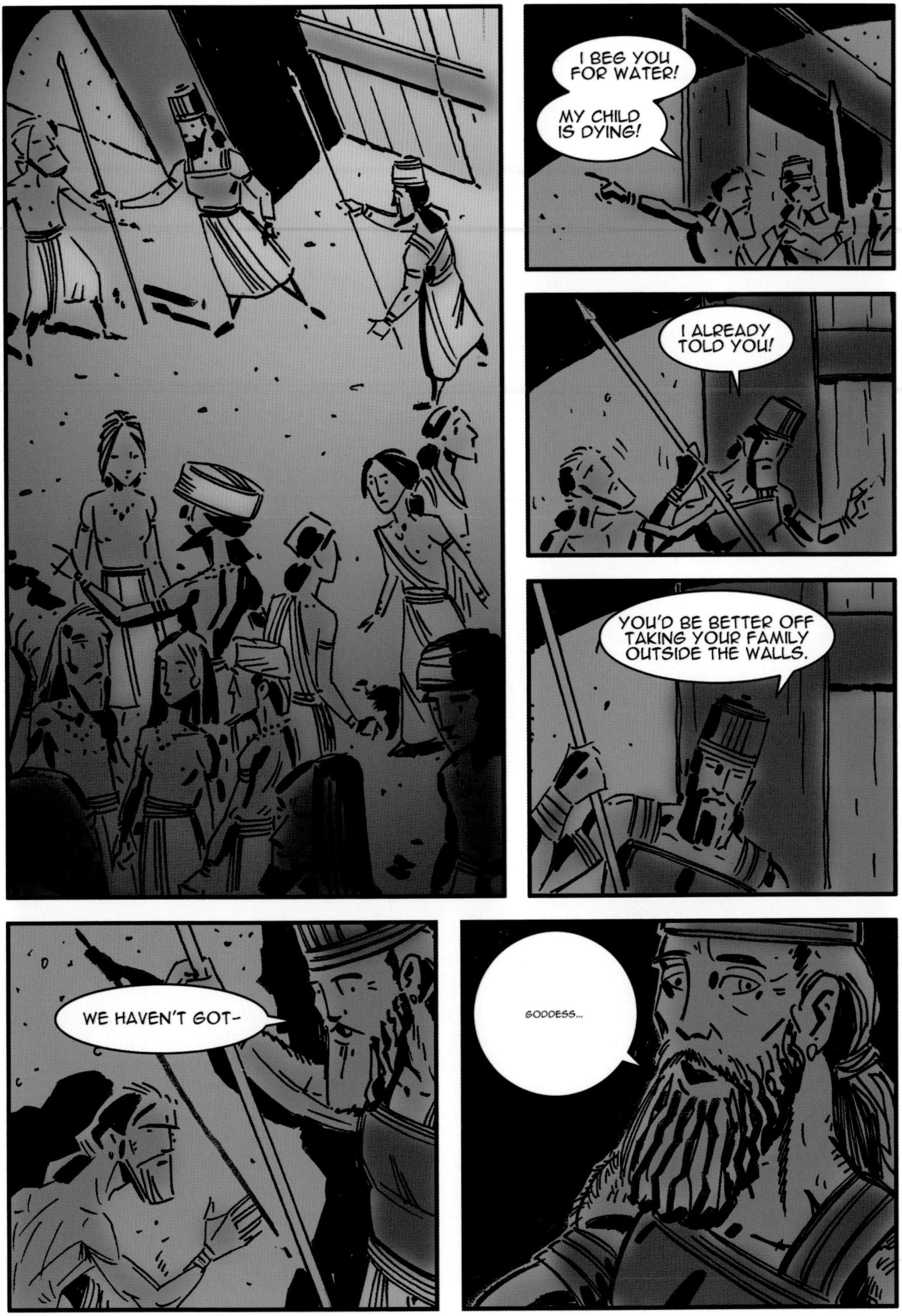
I BEG YOU FOR WATER!
MY CHILD IS DYING!
I ALREADY TOLD YOU!
YOU'D BE BETTER OFF TAKING YOUR FAMILY OUTSIDE THE WALLS.
WE HAVEN'T GOT-
GODDESS...

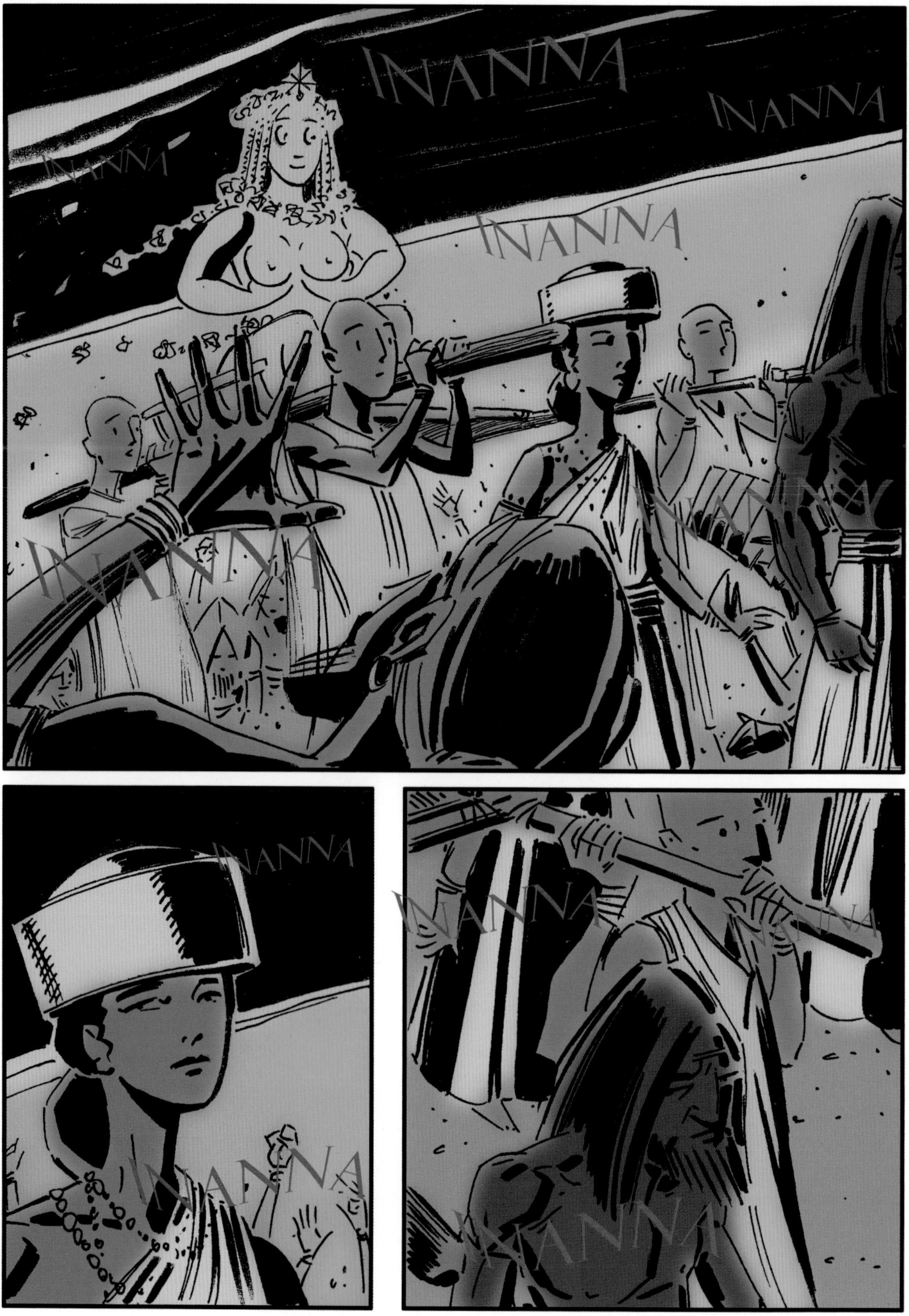
INANNA
INANNA
INANNA
INANNA
INANNA
INANNA
INANNA
INANNA
INANNA
INANNA
INANNA

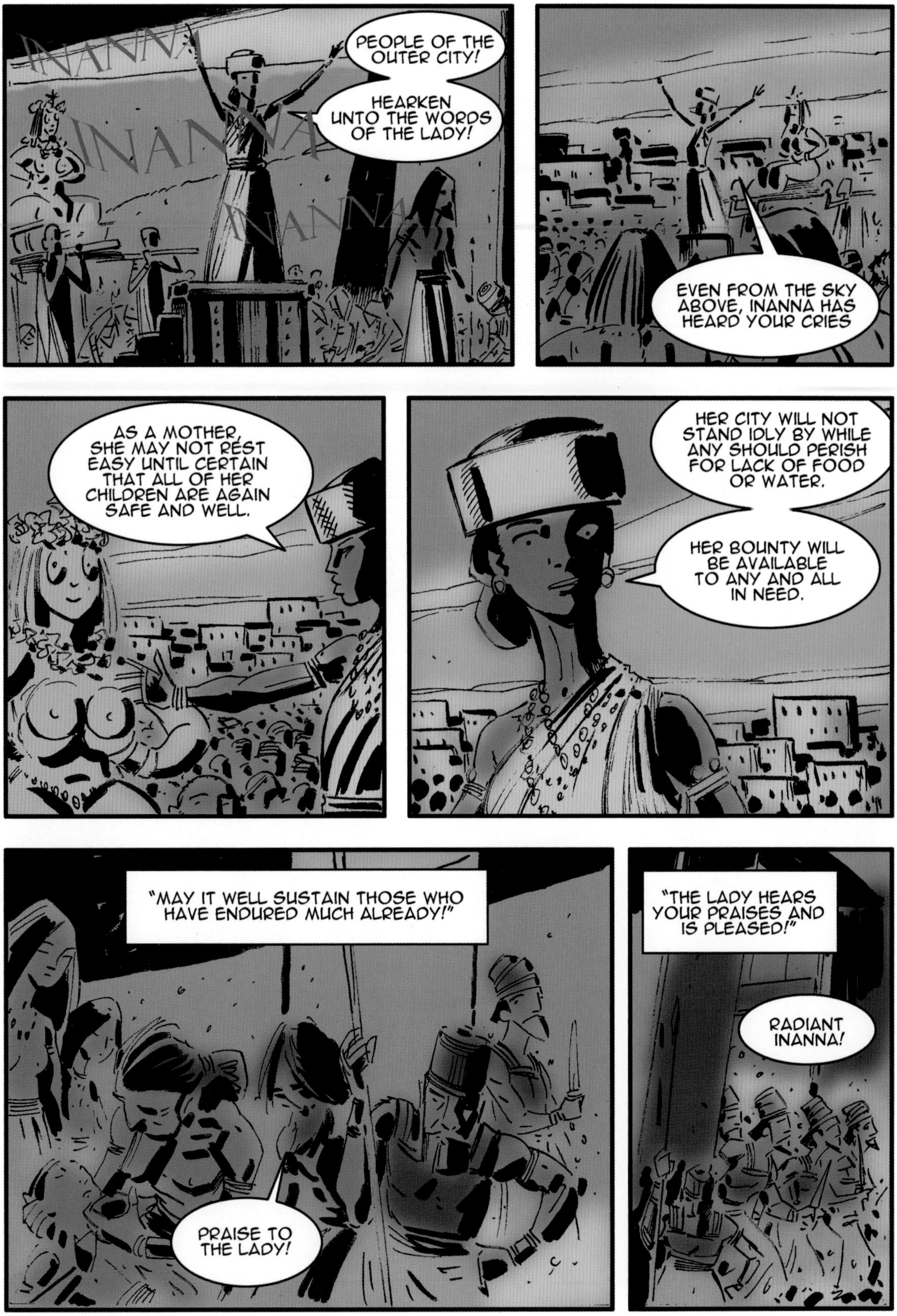
INANNA
INANNA
INANNA
PEOPLE OF THE OUTER CITY!
HEARKEN UNTO THE WORDS OF THE LADY!
EVEN FROM THE SKY ABOVE, INANNA HAS HEARD YOUR CRIES
AS A MOTHER, SHE MAY NOT REST EASY UNTIL CERTAIN THAT ALL OF HER CHILDREN ARE AGAIN SAFE AND WELL.
HER CITY WILL NOT STAND IDLY BY WHILE ANY SHOULD PERISH FOR LACK OF FOOD OR WATER.
HER BOUNTY WILL BE AVAILABLE TO ANY AND ALL IN NEED.
"MAY IT WELL SUSTAIN THOSE WHO HAVE ENDURED MUCH ALREADY!"
PRAISE TO THE LADY!
"THE LADY HEARS YOUR PRAISES AND IS PLEASED!"
RADIANT INANNA!

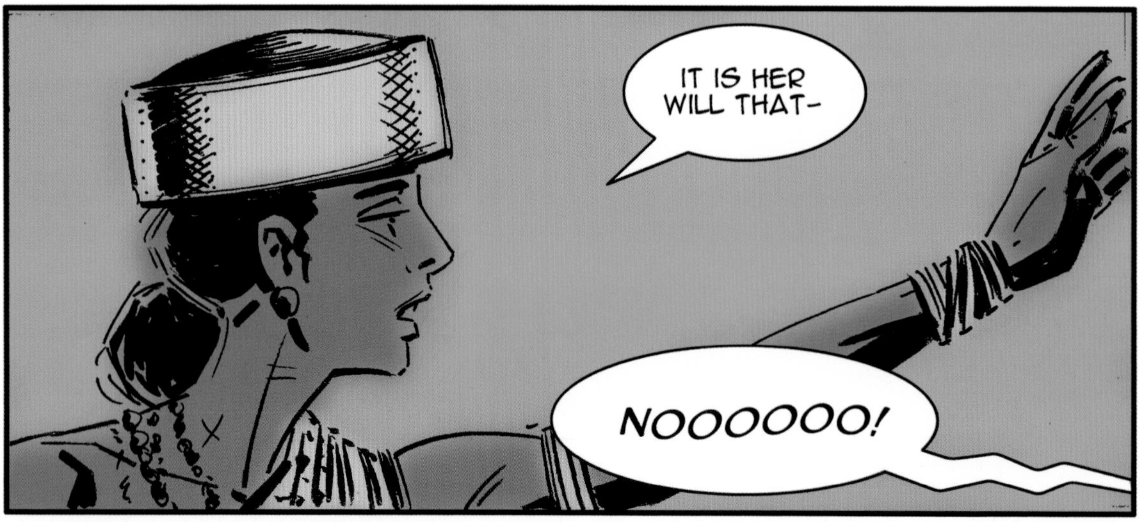
IT IS HER WILL THAT-
NOOOOOO!

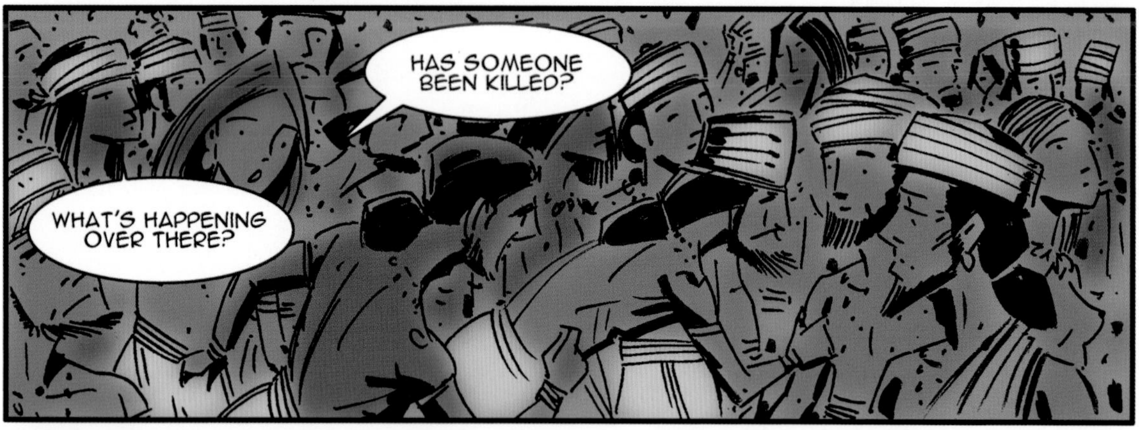
HAS SOMEONE BEEN KILLED?
WHAT'S HAPPENING OVER THERE?

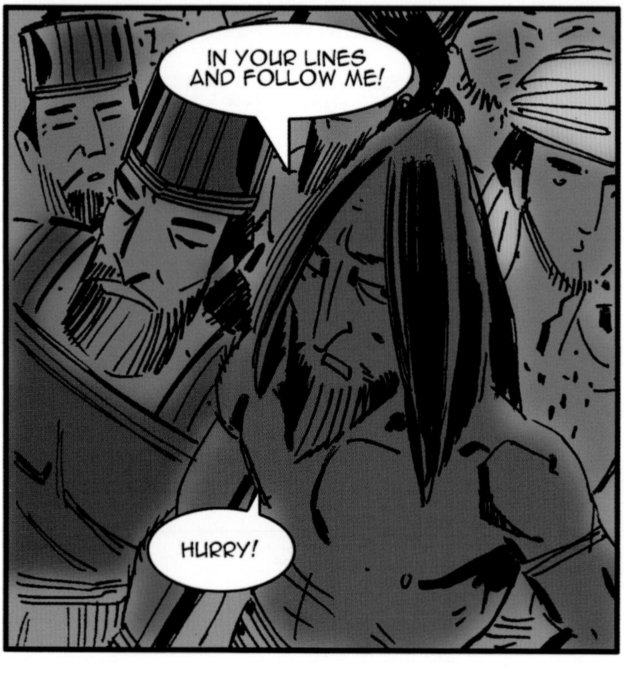
IN YOUR LINES AND FOLLOW ME!
HURRY!

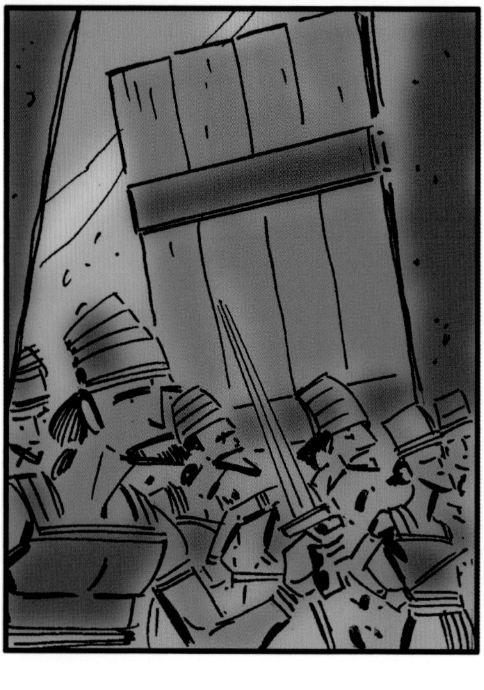

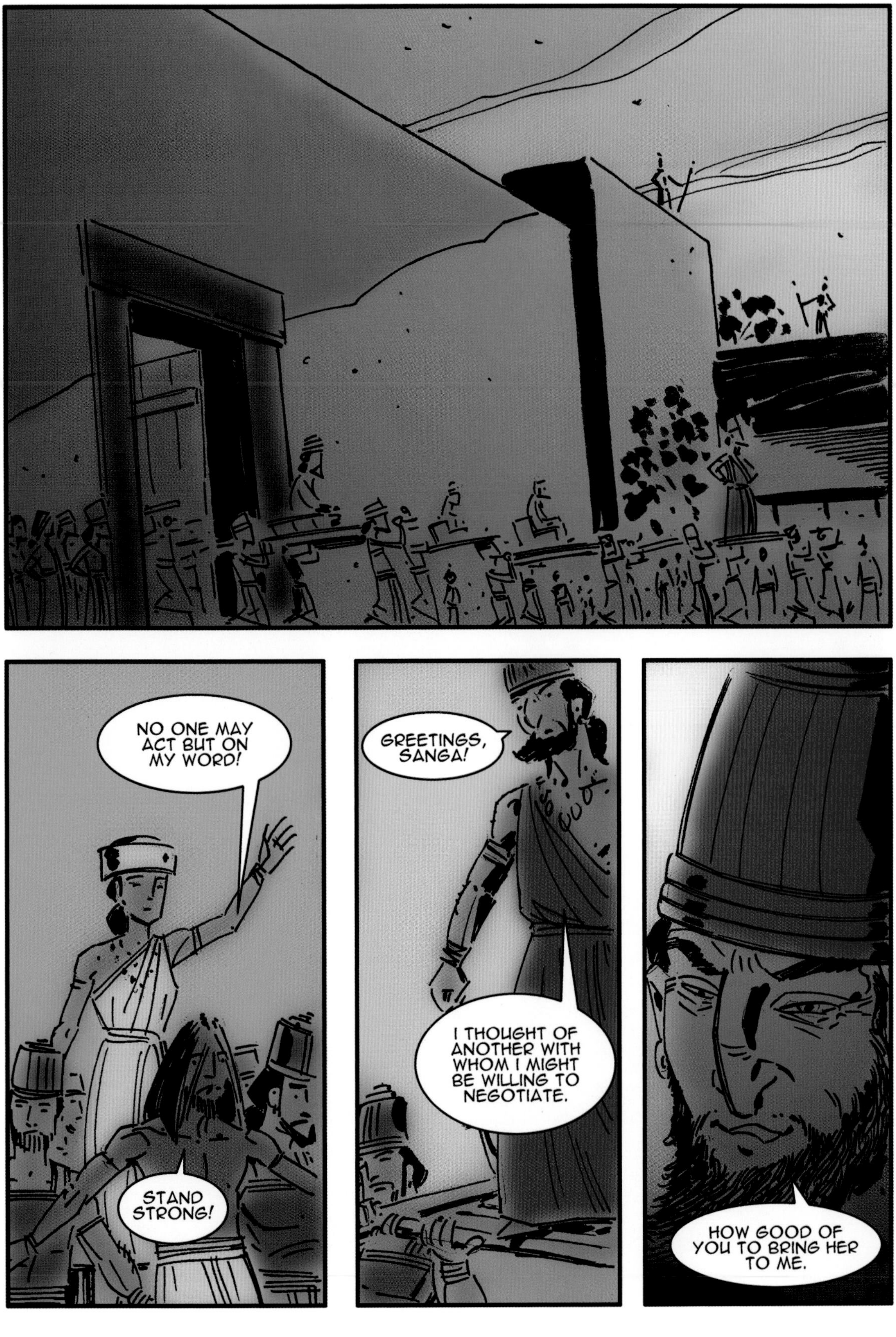
NO ONE MAY ACT BUT ON MY WORD!
STAND STRONG!
GREETINGS, SANGA!
I THOUGHT OF ANOTHER WITH WHOM I MIGHT BE WILLING TO NEGOTIATE.
HOW GOOD OF YOU TO BRING HER TO ME.

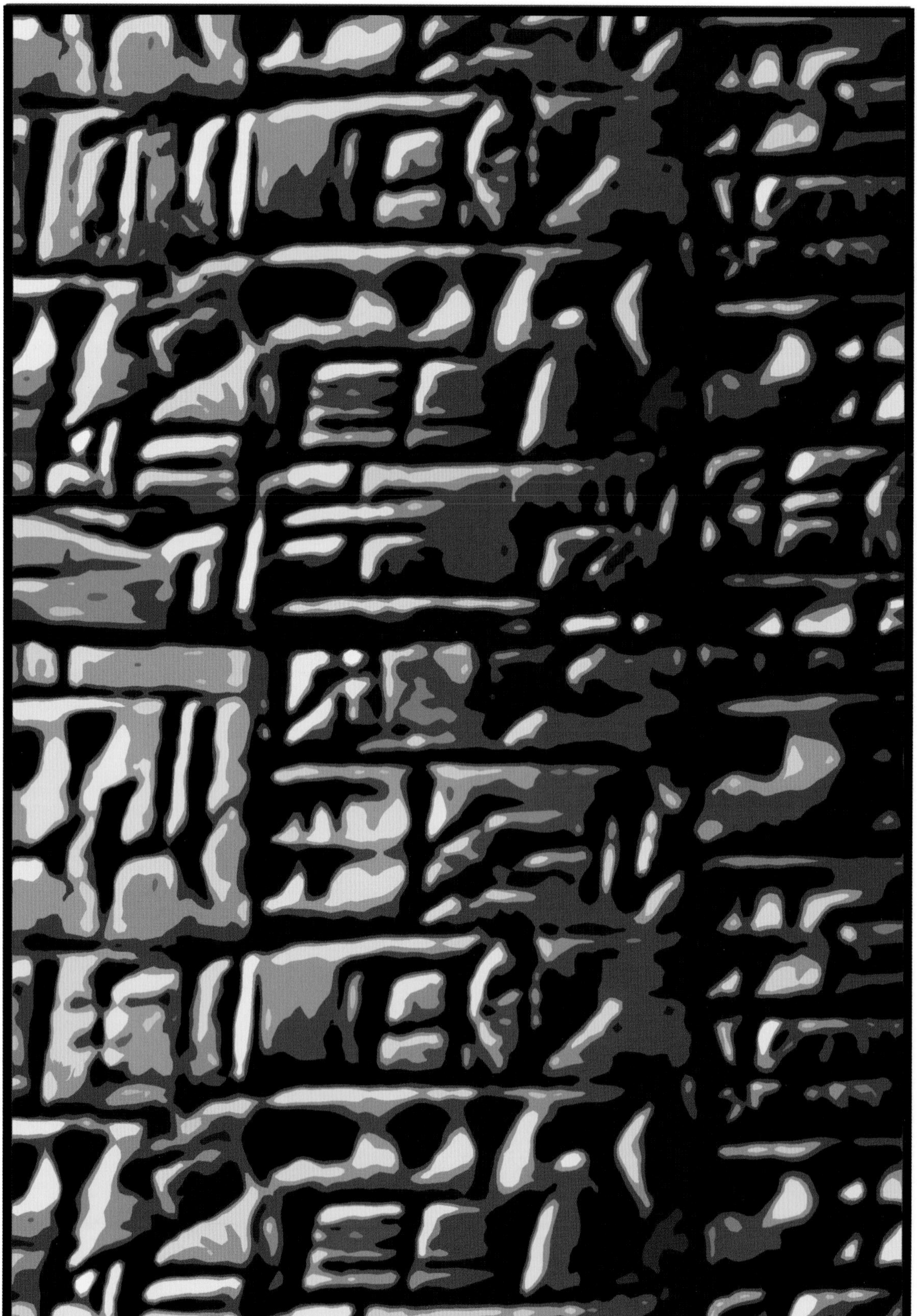

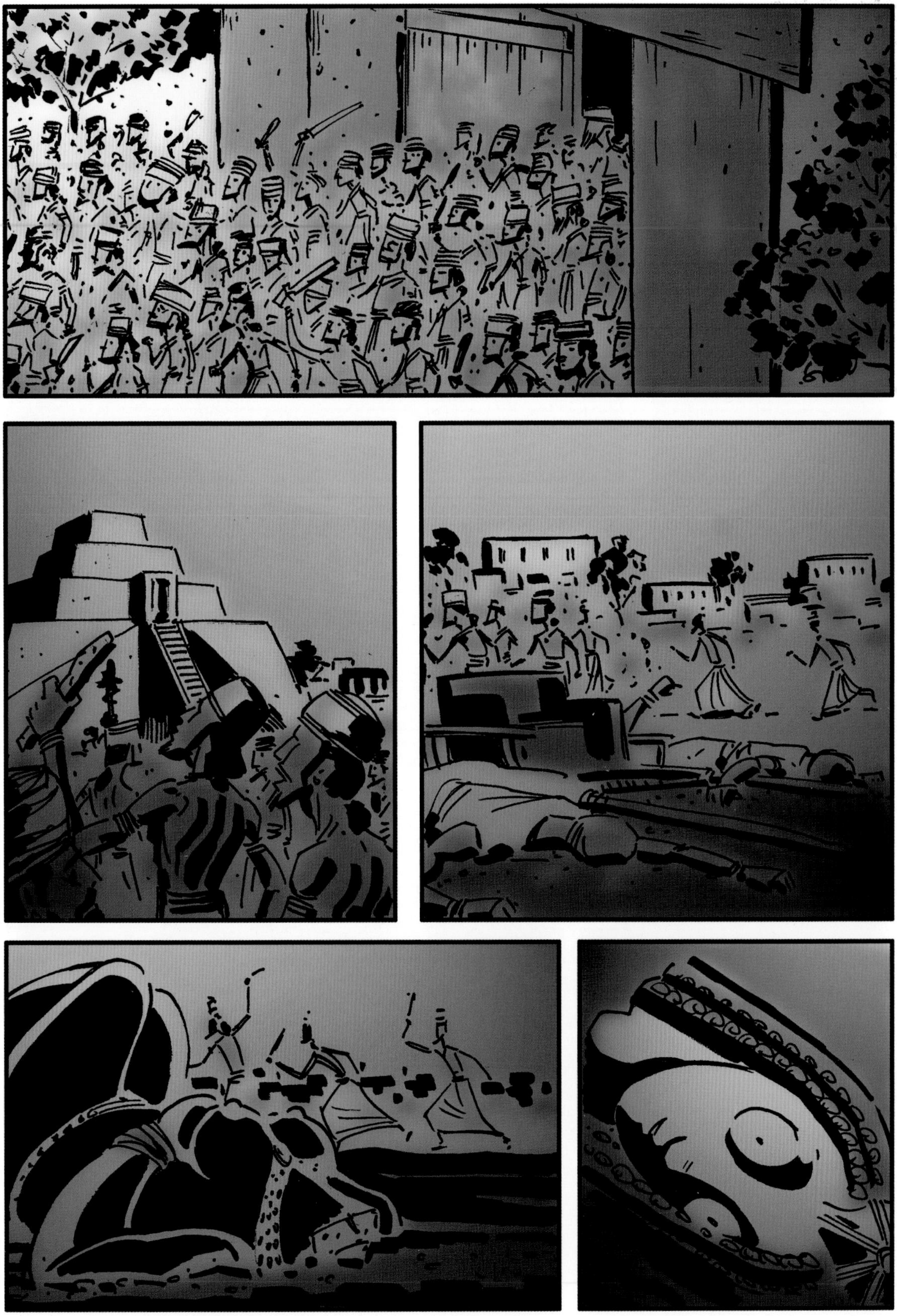

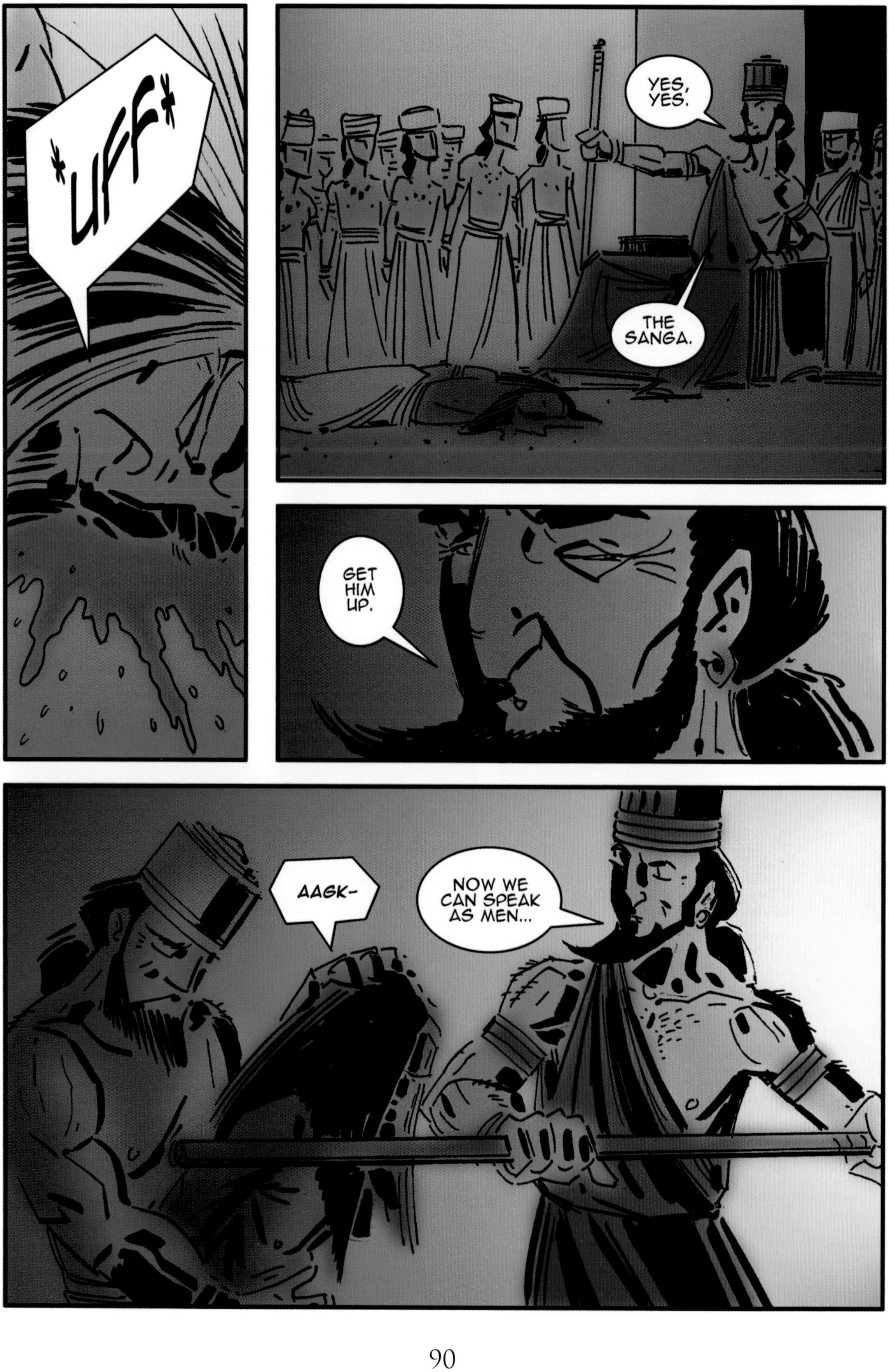
UFF
YES, YES.
THE SANGA.
GET HIM UP.
AAGK-
NOW WE CAN SPEAK AS MEN...

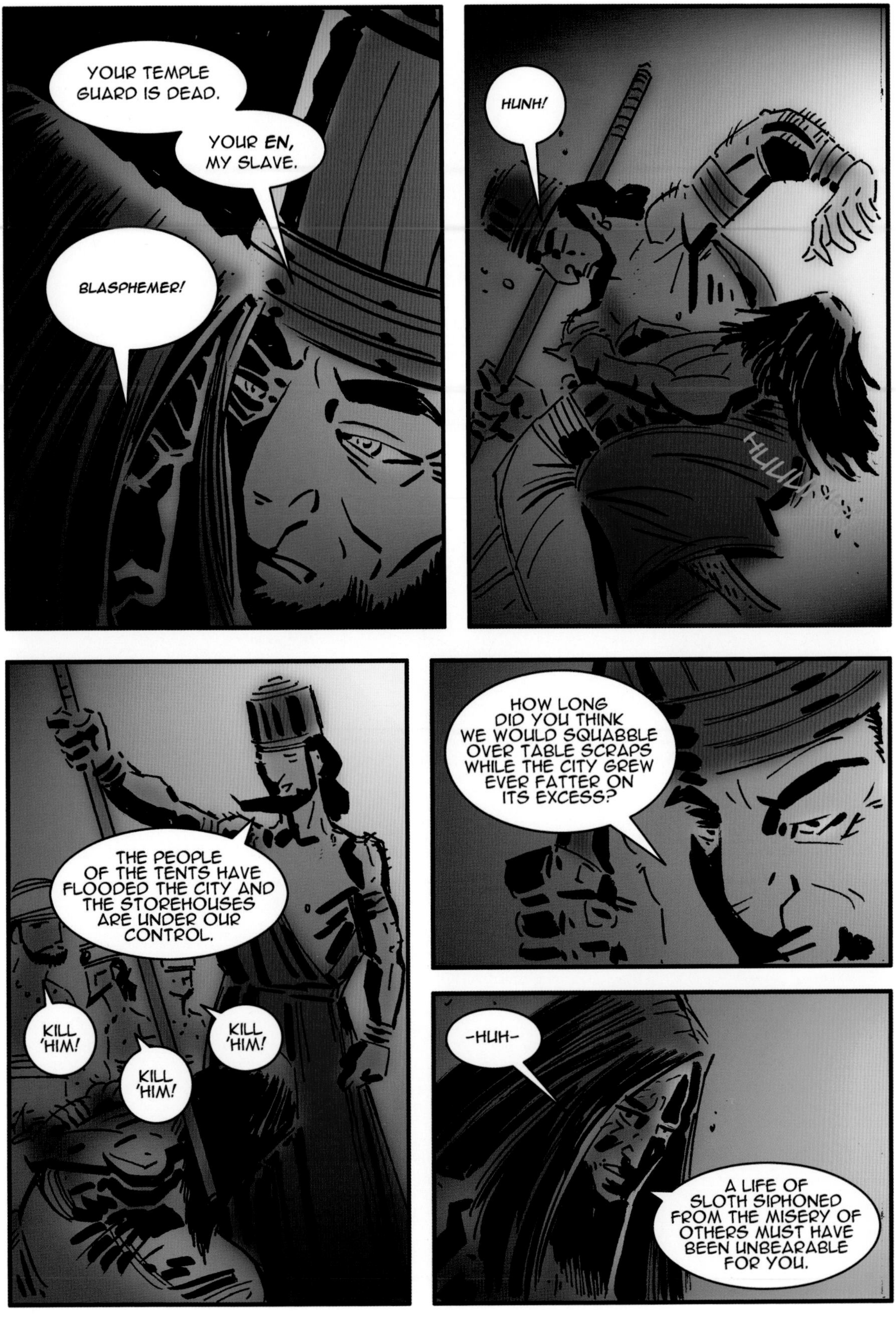
YOUR TEMPLE GUARD IS DEAD.
YOUR EN, MY SLAVE.
BLASPHEMER!
HUNH!
THE PEOPLE OF THE TENTS HAVE FLOODED THE CITY AND THE STOREHOUSES ARE UNDER OUR CONTROL.
KILL 'HIM!
KILL 'HIM!
KILL 'HIM!
HOW LONG DID YOU THINK WE WOULD SQUABBLE OVER TABLE SCRAPS WHILE THE CITY GREW EVER FATTER ON ITS EXCESS?
-HUH-
A LIFE OF SLOTH SIPHONED FROM THE MISERY OF OTHERS MUST HAVE BEEN UNBEARABLE FOR YOU.

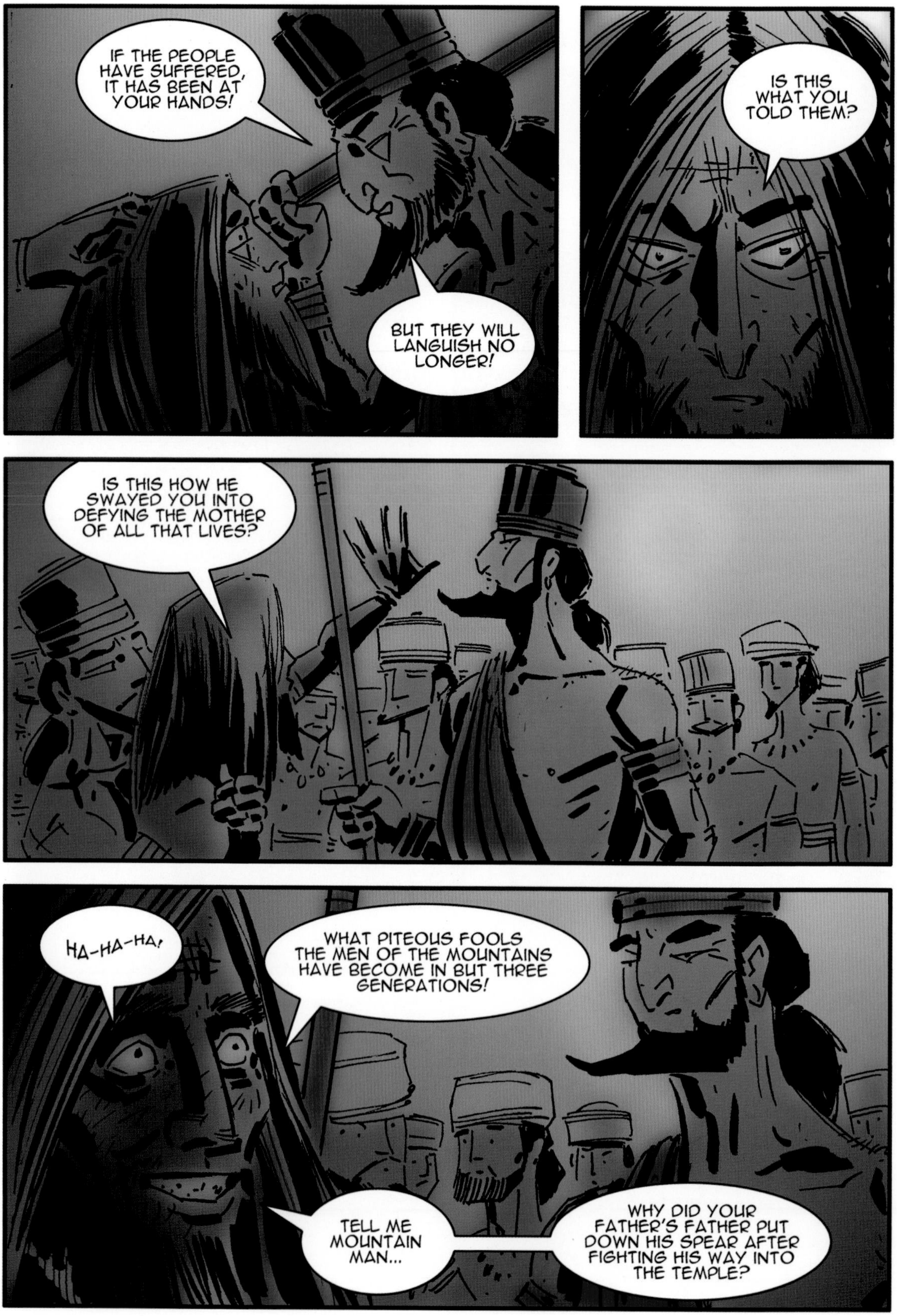
IF THE PEOPLE HAVE SUFFERED, IT HAS BEEN AT YOUR HANDS!
BUT THEY WILL LANGUISH NO LONGER!
IS THIS WHAT YOU TOLD THEM?
IS THIS HOW HE SWAYED YOU INTO DEFYING THE MOTHER OF ALL THAT LIVES?
HA-HA-HA!
WHAT PITEOUS FOOLS THE MEN OF THE MOUNTAINS HAVE BECOME IN BUT THREE GENERATIONS!
TELL ME MOUNTAIN MAN...
WHY DID YOUR FATHER'S FATHER PUT DOWN HIS SPEAR AFTER FIGHTING HIS WAY INTO THE TEMPLE?

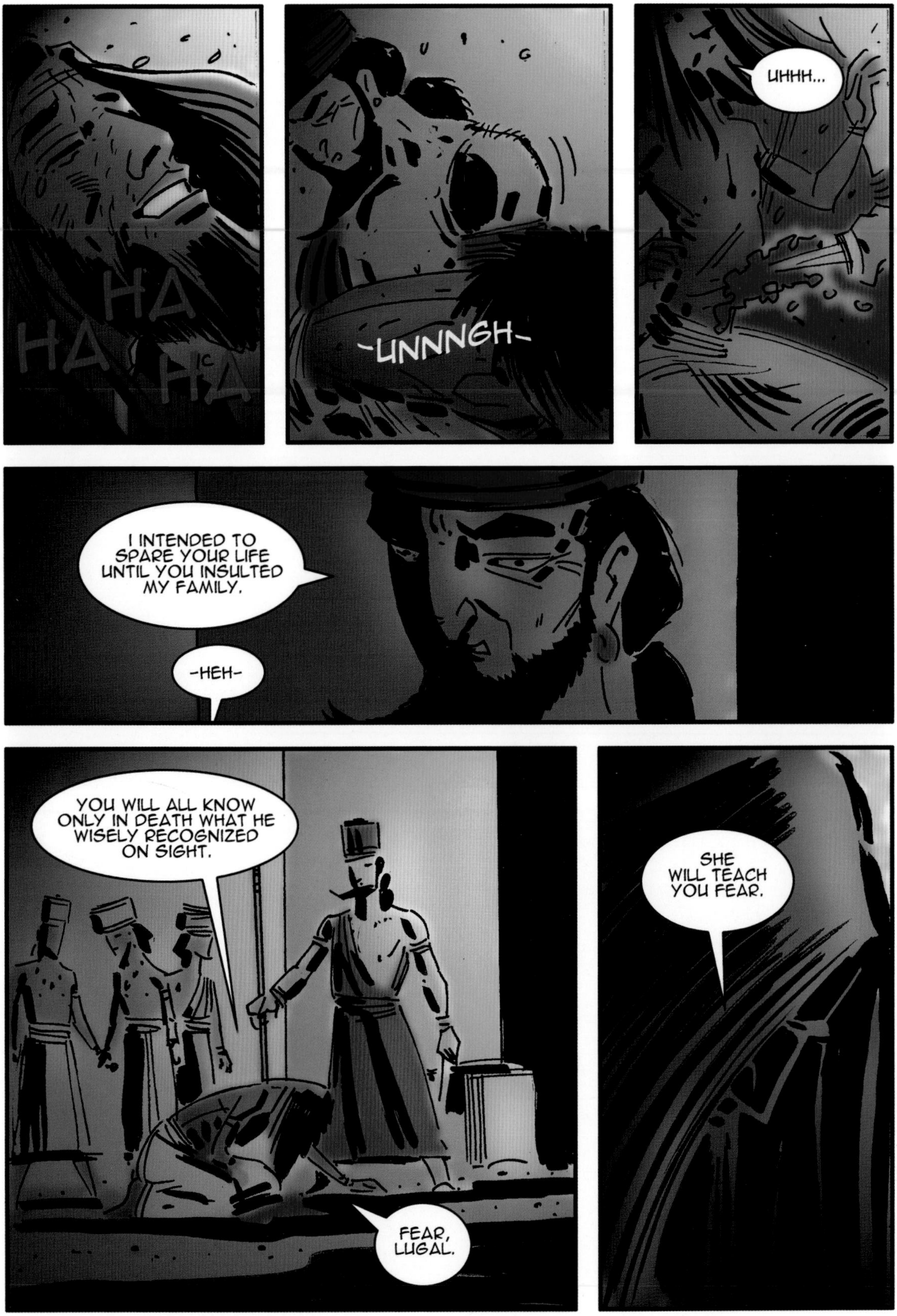
HA
HA
HA
HA
-UNNNGH-
UHHH...
I INTENDED TO SPARE YOUR LIFE UNTIL YOU INSULTED MY FAMILY.
-HEH-
YOU WILL ALL KNOW ONLY IN DEATH WHAT HE WISELY RECOGNIZED ON SIGHT.
FEAR, LUGAL.
SHE WILL TEACH YOU FEAR.

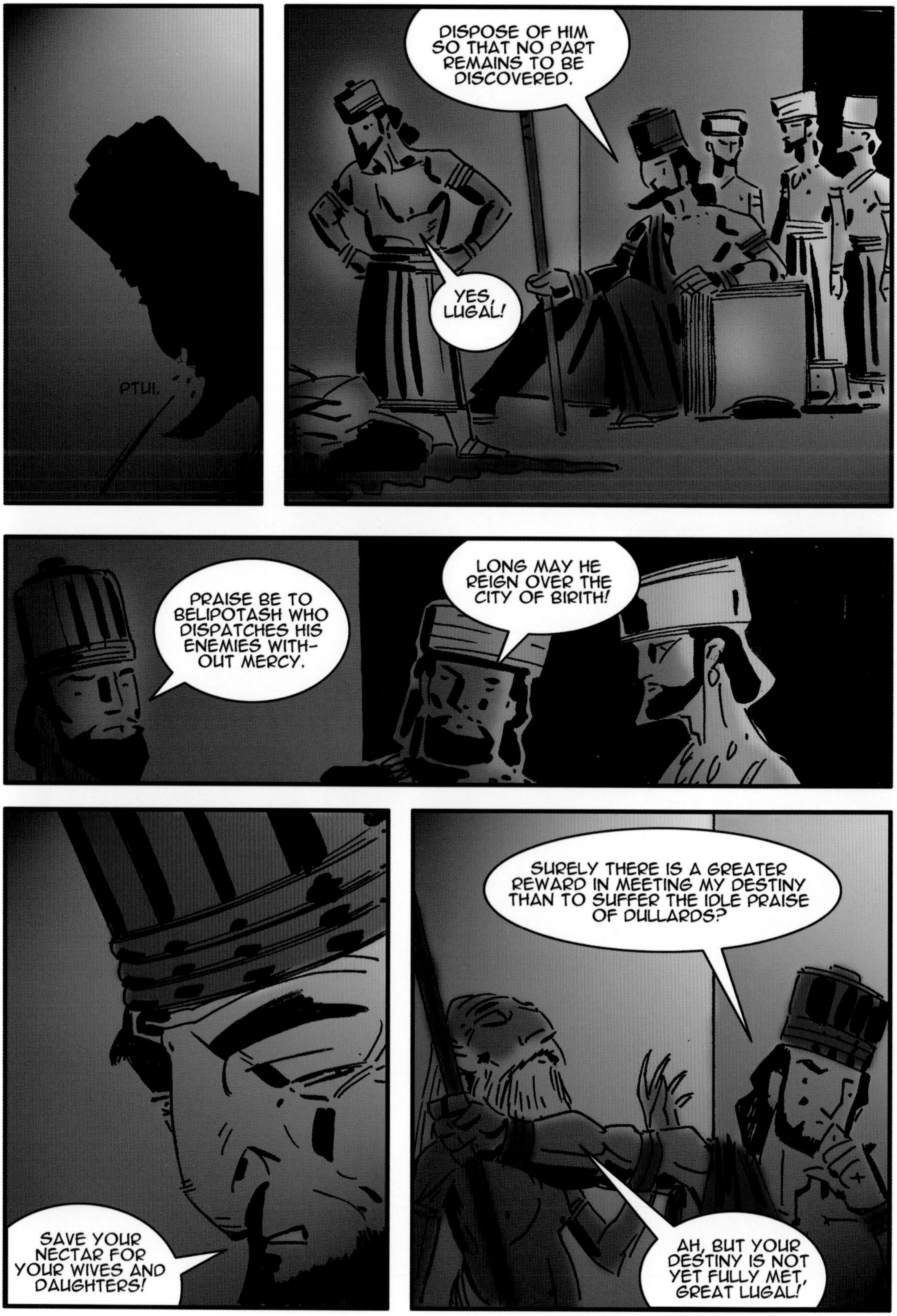
PTUI.
DISPOSE OF HIM SO THAT NO PART REMAINS TO BE DISCOVERED.
YES, LUGAL!
PRAISE BE TO BELIPOTASH WHO DISPATCHES HIS ENEMIES WITH-OUT MERCY.
LONG MAY HE REIGN OVER THE CITY OF BIRITH!
SAVE YOUR NECTAR FOR YOUR WIVES AND DAUGHTERS!
SURELY THERE IS A GREATER REWARD IN MEETING MY DESTINY THAN TO SUFFER THE IDLE PRAISE OF DULLARDS?
AH, BUT YOUR DESTINY IS NOT YET FULLY MET, GREAT LUGAL!

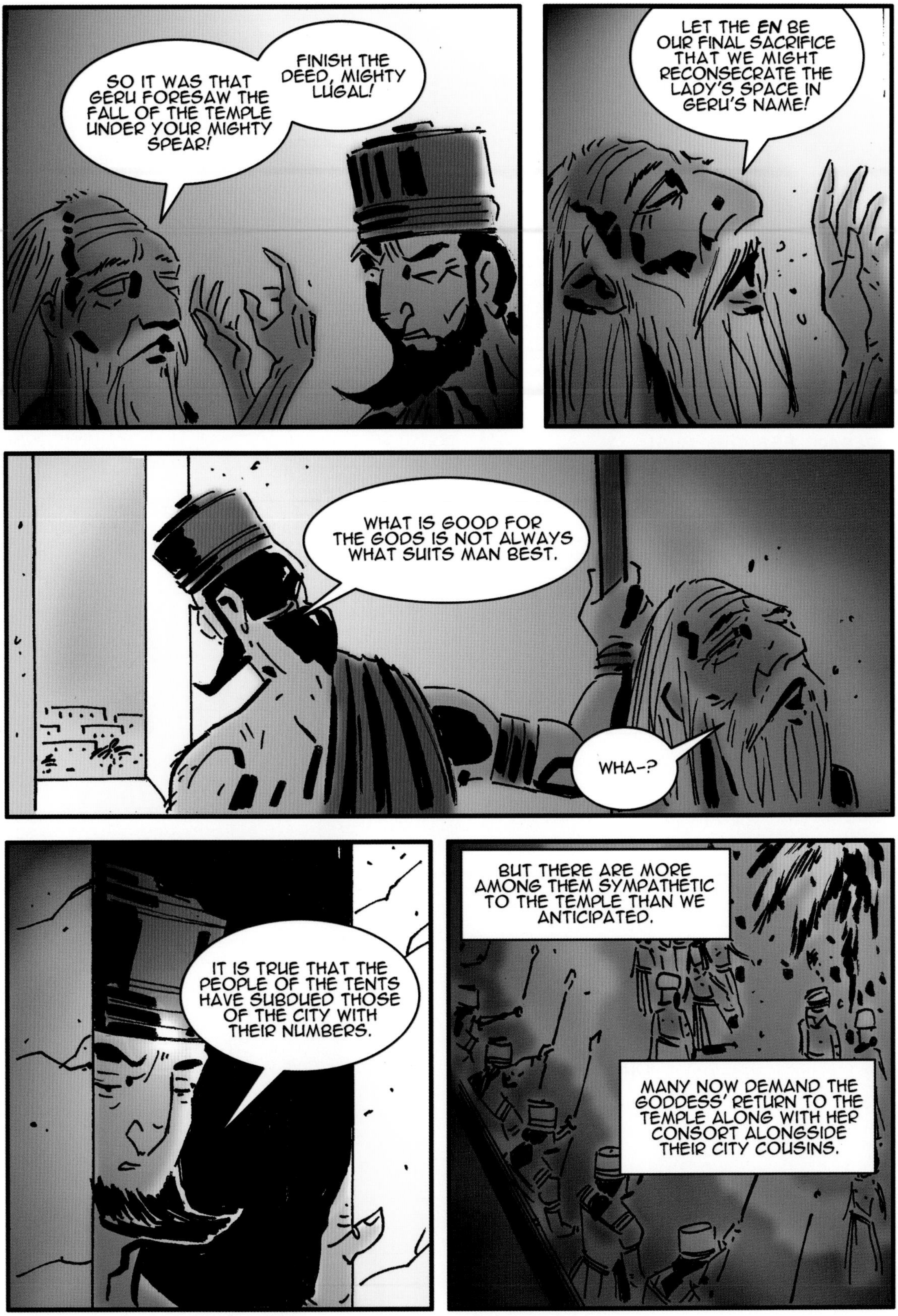
SO IT WAS THAT GERU FORESAW THE FALL OF THE TEMPLE UNDER YOUR MIGHTY SPEAR!
FINISH THE DEED, MIGHTY LUGAL!
LET THE EN BE OUR FINAL SACRIFICE THAT WE MIGHT RECONSECRATE THE LADY'S SPACE IN GERU'S NAME!
WHAT IS GOOD FOR THE GODS IS NOT ALWAYS WHAT SUITS MAN BEST.
WHA-?
IT IS TRUE THAT THE PEOPLE OF THE TENTS HAVE SUBDUED THOSE OF THE CITY WITH THEIR NUMBERS.
BUT THERE ARE MORE AMONG THEM SYMPATHETIC TO THE TEMPLE THAN WE ANTICIPATED.
MANY NOW DEMAND THE GODDESS' RETURN TO THE TEMPLE ALONG WITH HER CONSORT ALONGSIDE THEIR CITY COUSINS.

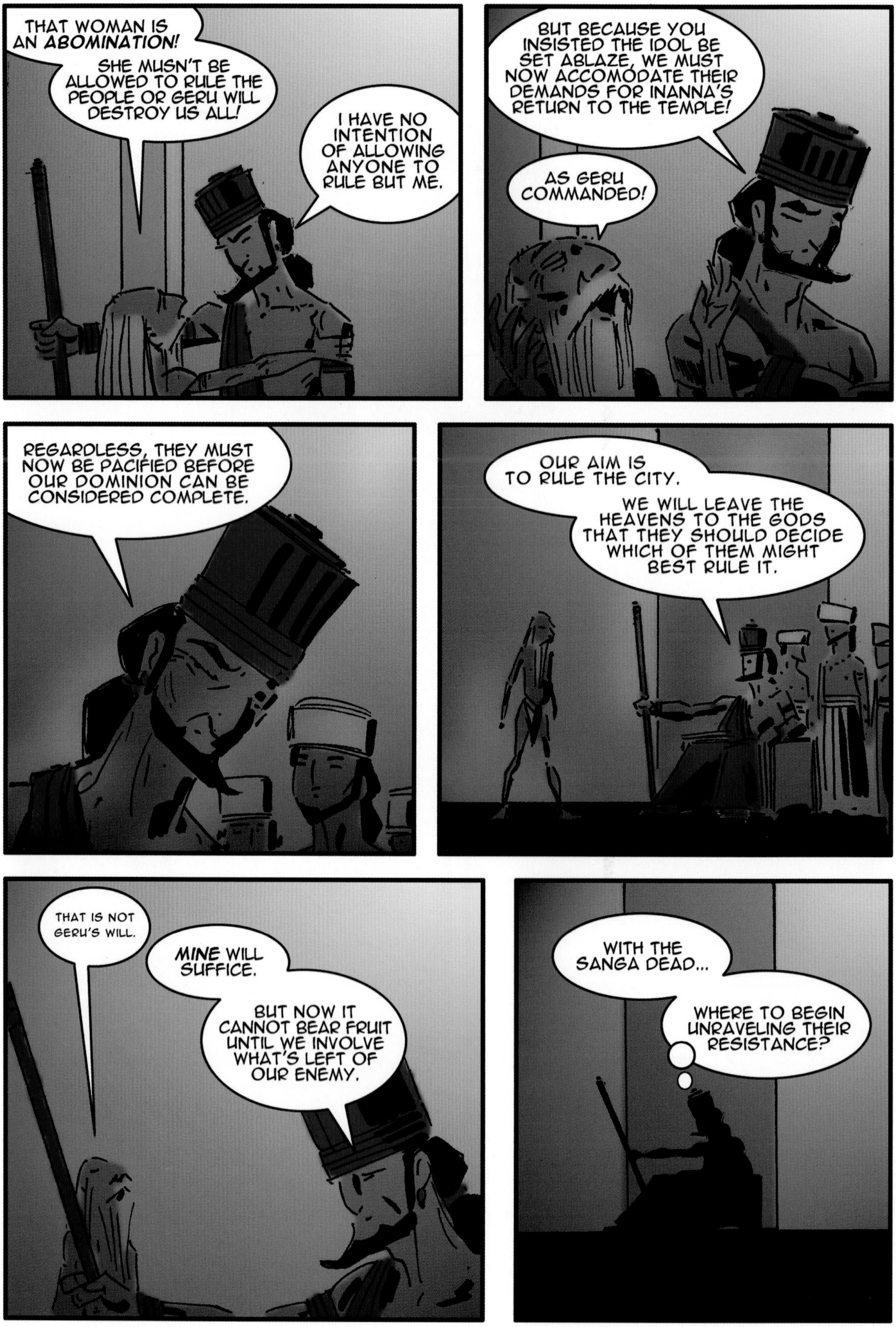
THAT WOMAN IS AN ABOMINATION!
SHE MUSN'T BE ALLOWED TO RULE THE PEOPLE OR GERU WILL DESTROY US ALL!
I HAVE NO INTENTION OF ALLOWING ANYONE TO RULE BUT ME.
BUT BECAUSE YOU INSISTED THE IDOL BE SET ABLAZE, WE MUST NOW ACCOMODATE THEIR DEMANDS FOR INANNA'S RETURN TO THE TEMPLE!
AS GERU COMMANDED!
REGARDLESS, THEY MUST NOW BE PACIFIED BEFORE OUR DOMINION CAN BE CONSIDERED COMPLETE.
OUR AIM IS TO RULE THE CITY.
WE WILL LEAVE THE HEAVENS TO THE GODS THAT THEY SHOULD DECIDE WHICH OF THEM MIGHT BEST RULE IT.
THAT IS NOT GERU'S WILL.
MINE WILL SUFFICE.
BUT NOW IT CANNOT BEAR FRUIT UNTIL WE INVOLVE WHAT'S LEFT OF OUR ENEMY.
WITH THE SANGA DEAD...
WHERE TO BEGIN UNRAVELING THEIR RESISTANCE?

ARE WE GUARDED?

I THINK THAT WE ARE LEFT ALONE FOR NOW.

AH, DUBSAL ANARIN...

WHO ELSE AMONG US REMAINS?

I KNOW THE WEAVER BY HIS COUGH AND THE BREWER BY HIS SMELL.

OF THE OTHERS, I AM UNSURE.

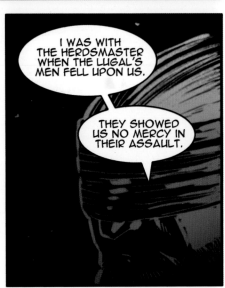

I WAS WITH THE HERDSMASTER WHEN THE LUGAL'S MEN FELL UPON US.

THEY SHOWED US NO MERCY IN THEIR ASSAULT.

HOW DO YOU FARE NOW?

WELL ENOUGH.

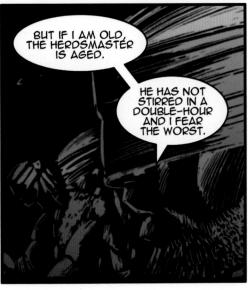

BUT IF I AM OLD, THE HERDSMASTER IS AGED.

HE HAS NOT STIRRED IN A DOUBLE-HOUR AND I FEAR THE WORST.

I DON'T UNDERSTAND ANY OF THIS.

WHAT OF THE *EN?* WHAT OF THE SANGA?

IF EITHER WERE ABLE TO SAVE US, WE WOULD NOT PERSIST IN BONDAGE.

AT BEST, THEY SHARE OUR PREDICAMENT.

I WILL NOT CONTEMPLATE THE WORST.

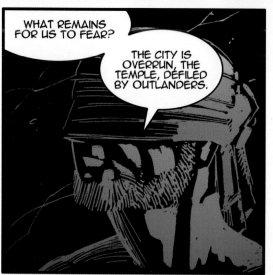

WHAT REMAINS FOR US TO FEAR?

THE CITY IS OVERRUN, THE TEMPLE, DEFILED BY OUTLANDERS.

INANNA HAS ABANDONED US UTTERLY.

ONLY THE EN MAY KNOW HER DISPOSITION!

AS LONG AS THERE IS THE POSSIBILITY THAT HE MIGHT YET ABIDE, HOPE MUST NOT BE FORSAKEN.

AS YOU SAY, DUBSAL.

WHAT OTHER OFFERING HAVE WE LEFT WITH WHICH TO ENTREAT HER MERCY?

SOMEONE'S COMING.

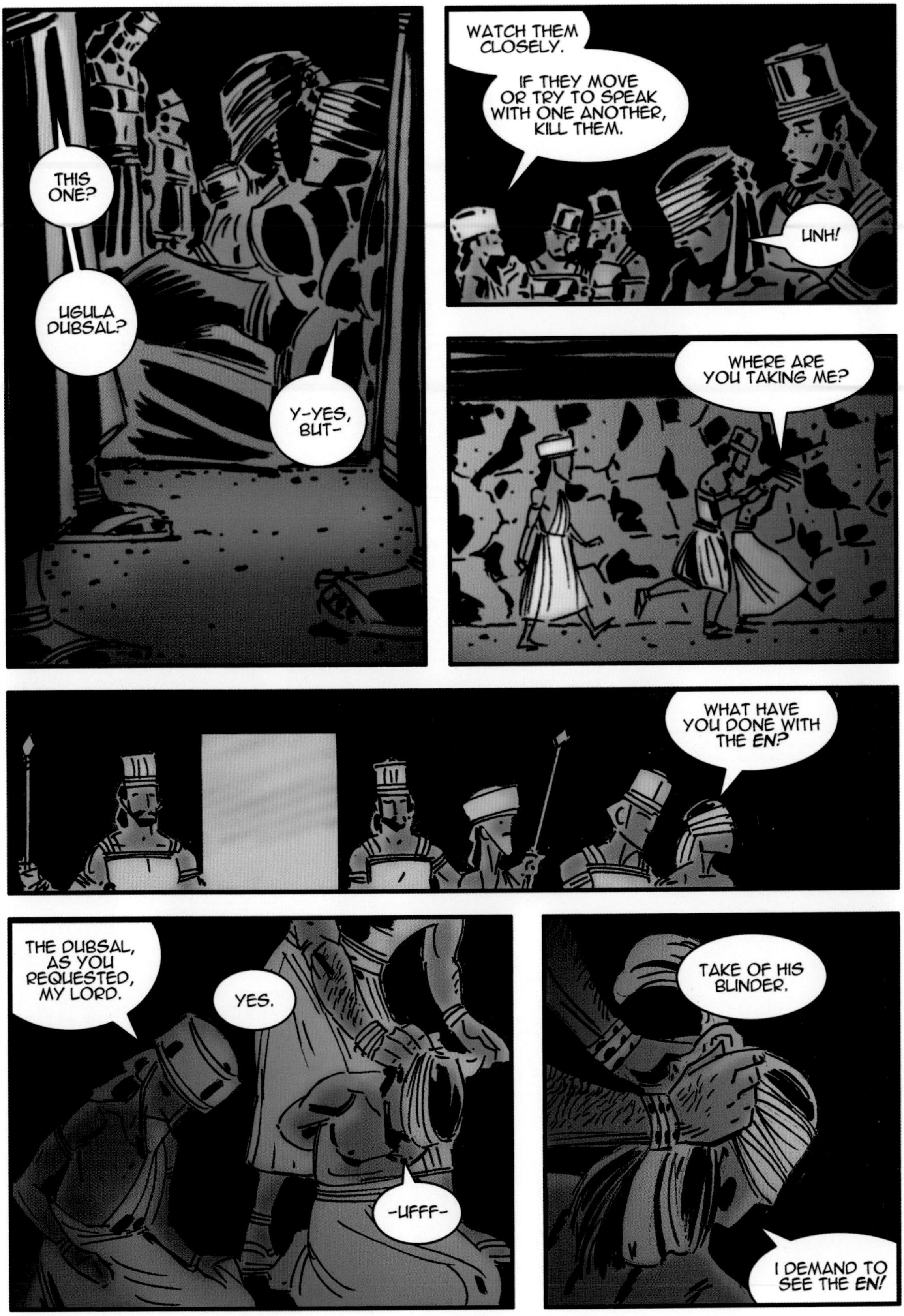
THIS ONE?
UGULA DUBSAL?
Y-YES, BUT-
WATCH THEM CLOSELY.
IF THEY MOVE OR TRY TO SPEAK WITH ONE ANOTHER, KILL THEM.
UNH!
WHERE ARE YOU TAKING ME?
WHAT HAVE YOU DONE WITH THE EN?
THE DUBSAL, AS YOU REQUESTED, MY LORD.
YES.
-UFFF-
TAKE OF HIS BLINDER.
I DEMAND TO SEE THE EN!

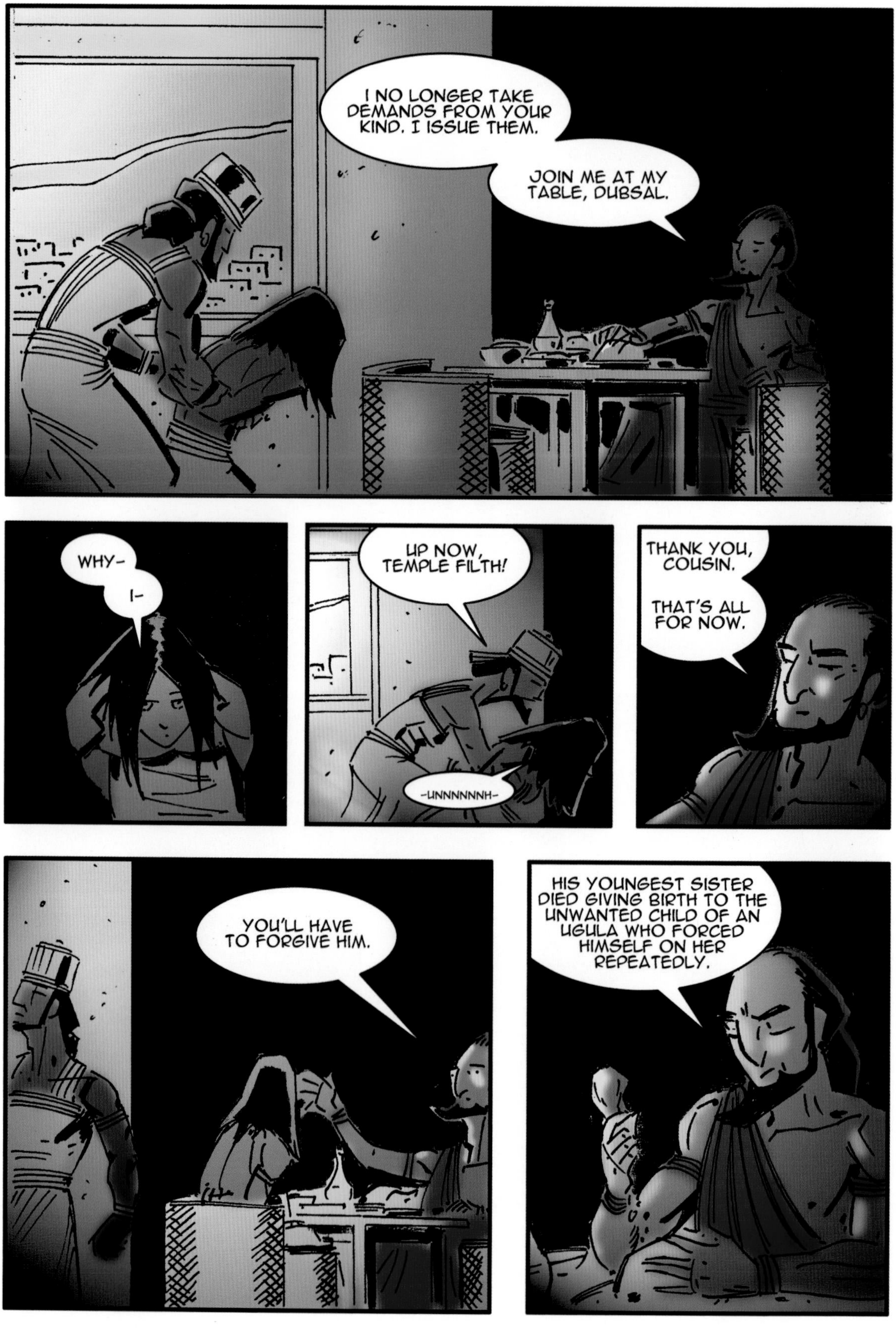
I NO LONGER TAKE DEMANDS FROM YOUR KIND. I ISSUE THEM.
JOIN ME AT MY TABLE, DUBSAL.
WHY-
I-
UP NOW, TEMPLE FILTH!
-UNNNNNNH-
THANK YOU, COUSIN.
THAT'S ALL FOR NOW.
YOU'LL HAVE TO FORGIVE HIM.
HIS YOUNGEST SISTER DIED GIVING BIRTH TO THE UNWANTED CHILD OF AN UGULA WHO FORCED HIMSELF ON HER REPEATEDLY.

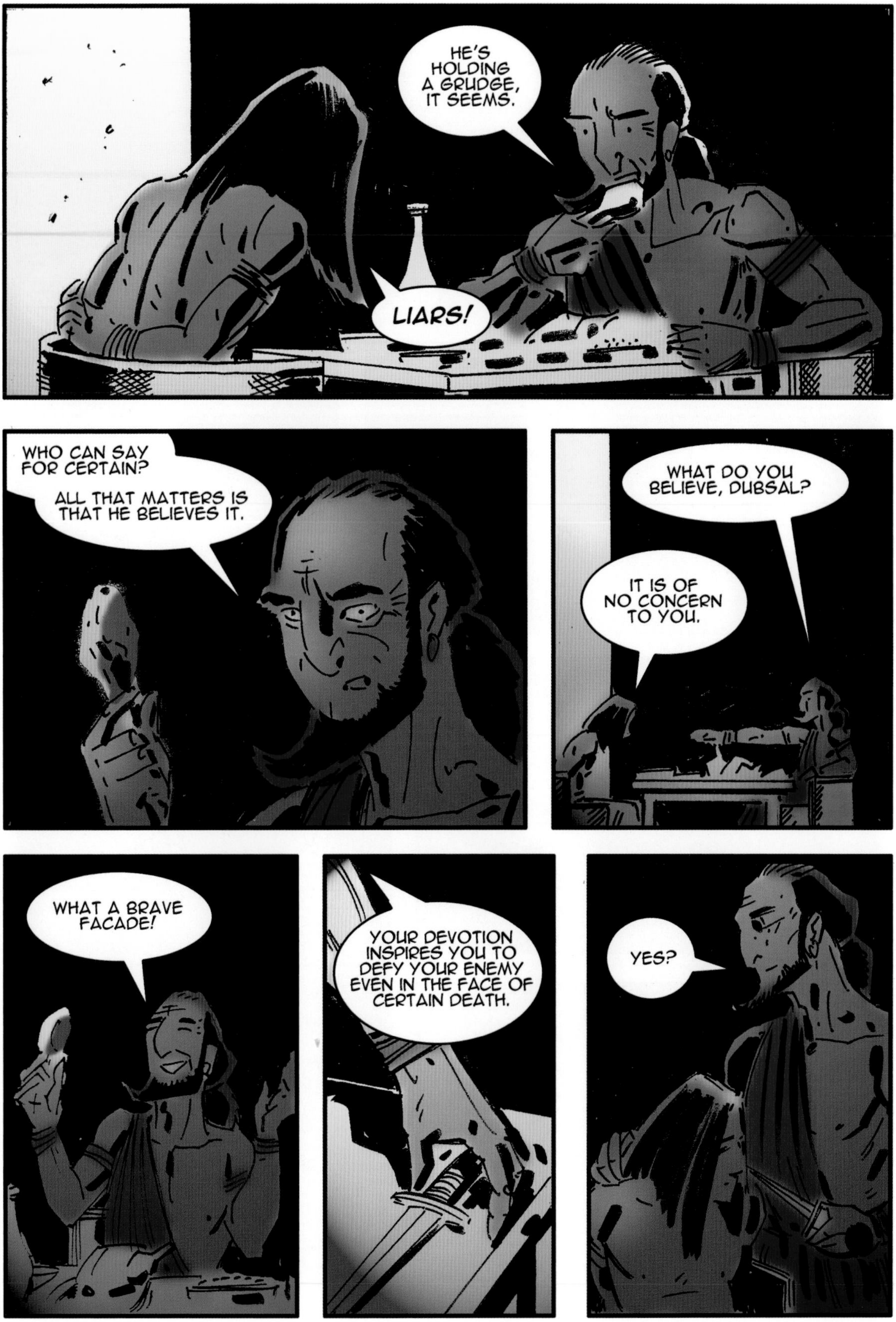
HE'S HOLDING A GRUDGE, IT SEEMS.
LIARS!
WHO CAN SAY FOR CERTAIN?
ALL THAT MATTERS IS THAT HE BELIEVES IT.
WHAT DO YOU BELIEVE, DUBSAL?
IT IS OF NO CONCERN TO YOU.
WHAT A BRAVE FACADE!
YOUR DEVOTION INSPIRES YOU TO DEFY YOUR ENEMY EVEN IN THE FACE OF CERTAIN DEATH.
YES?

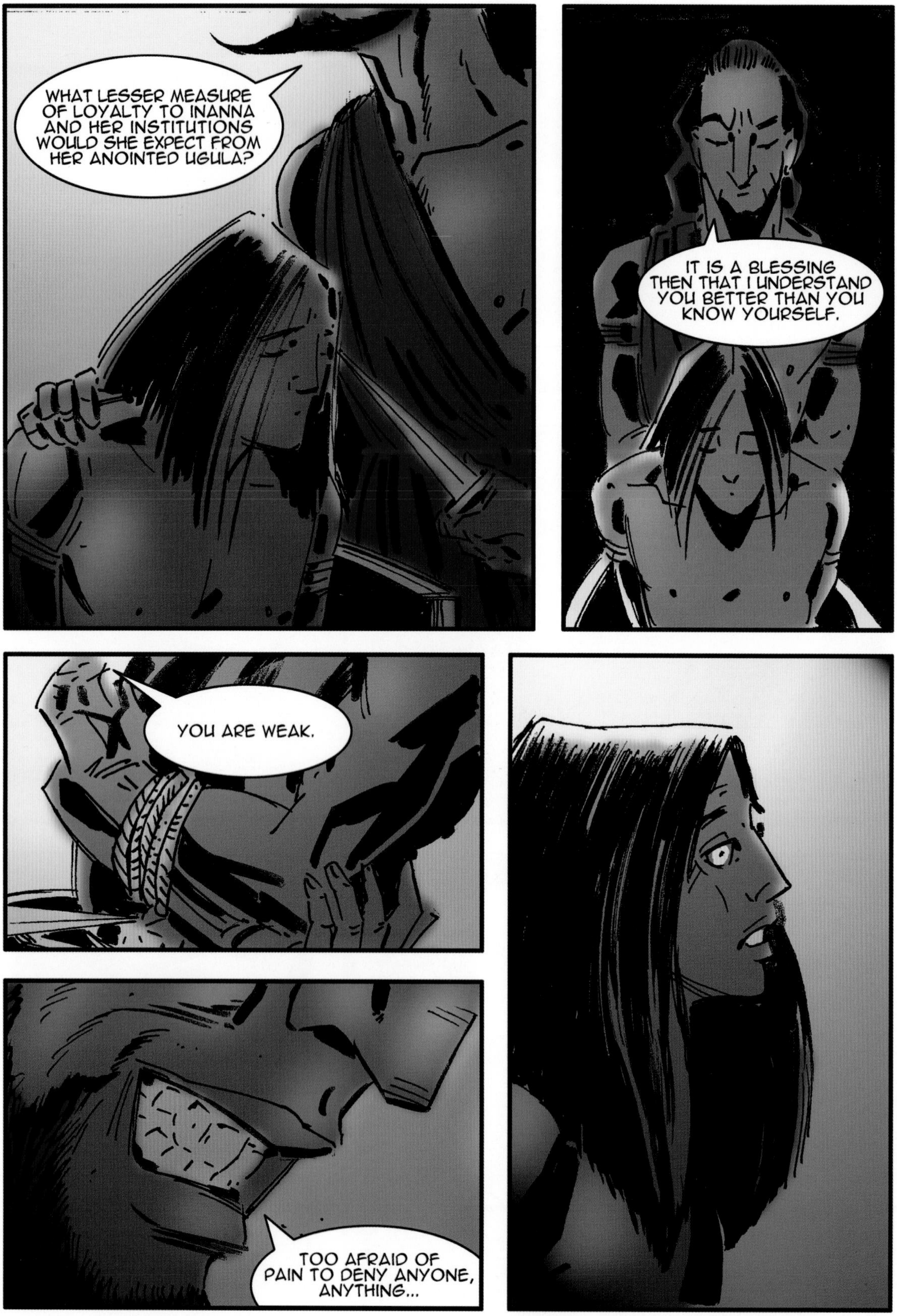
WHAT LESSER MEASURE OF LOYALTY TO INANNA AND HER INSTITUTIONS WOULD SHE EXPECT FROM HER ANOINTED UGULA?
IT IS A BLESSING THEN THAT I UNDERSTAND YOU BETTER THAN YOU KNOW YOURSELF.
YOU ARE WEAK.
TOO AFRAID OF PAIN TO DENY ANYONE, ANYTHING...

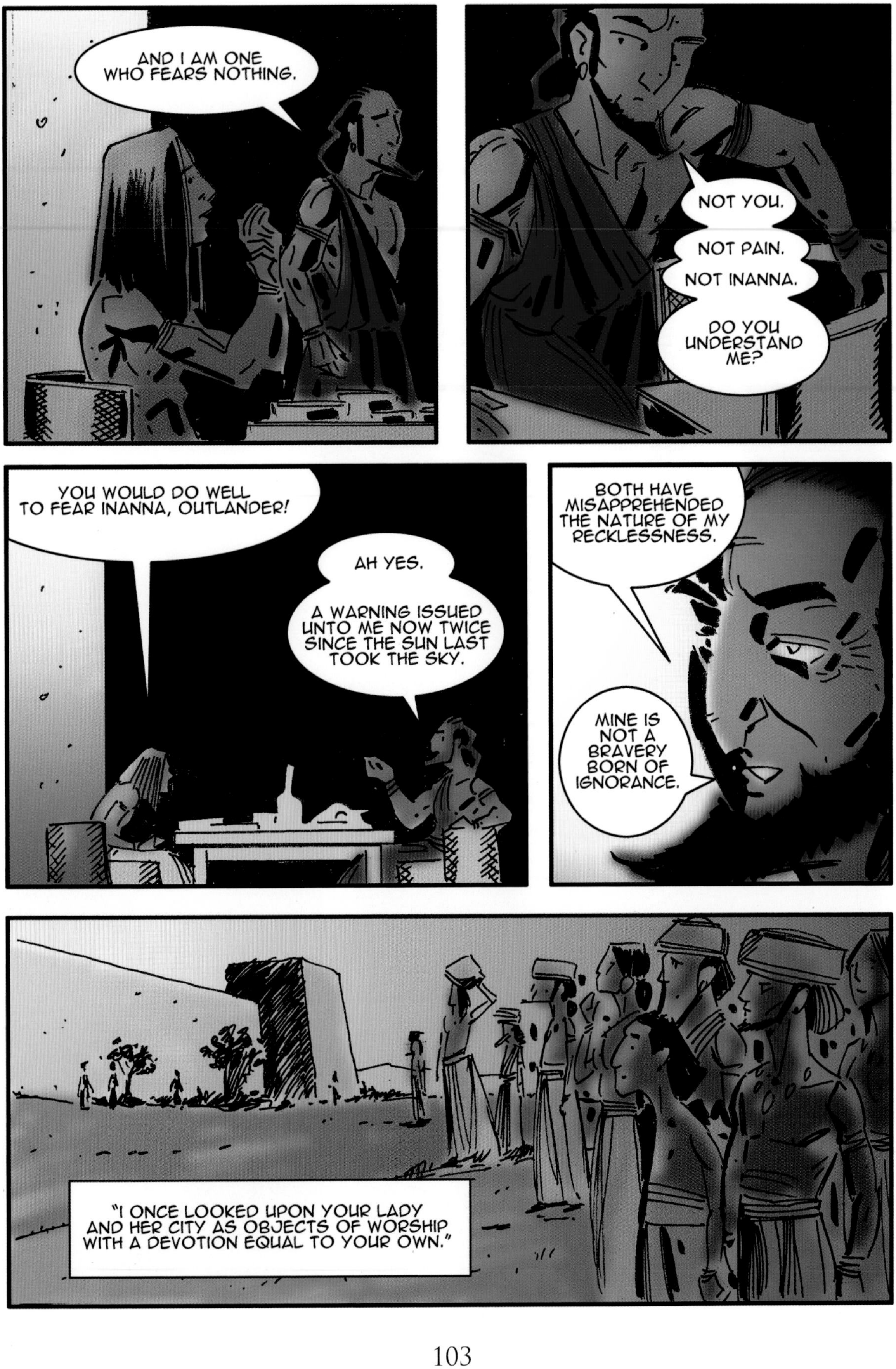
AND I AM ONE WHO FEARS NOTHING.
NOT YOU.
NOT PAIN.
NOT INANNA.
DO YOU UNDERSTAND ME?
YOU WOULD DO WELL TO FEAR INANNA, OUTLANDER!
AH YES.
A WARNING ISSUED UNTO ME NOW TWICE SINCE THE SUN LAST TOOK THE SKY.
BOTH HAVE MISAPPREHENDED THE NATURE OF MY RECKLESSNESS.
MINE IS NOT A BRAVERY BORN OF IGNORANCE.
"I ONCE LOOKED UPON YOUR LADY AND HER CITY AS OBJECTS OF WORSHIP WITH A DEVOTION EQUAL TO YOUR OWN."

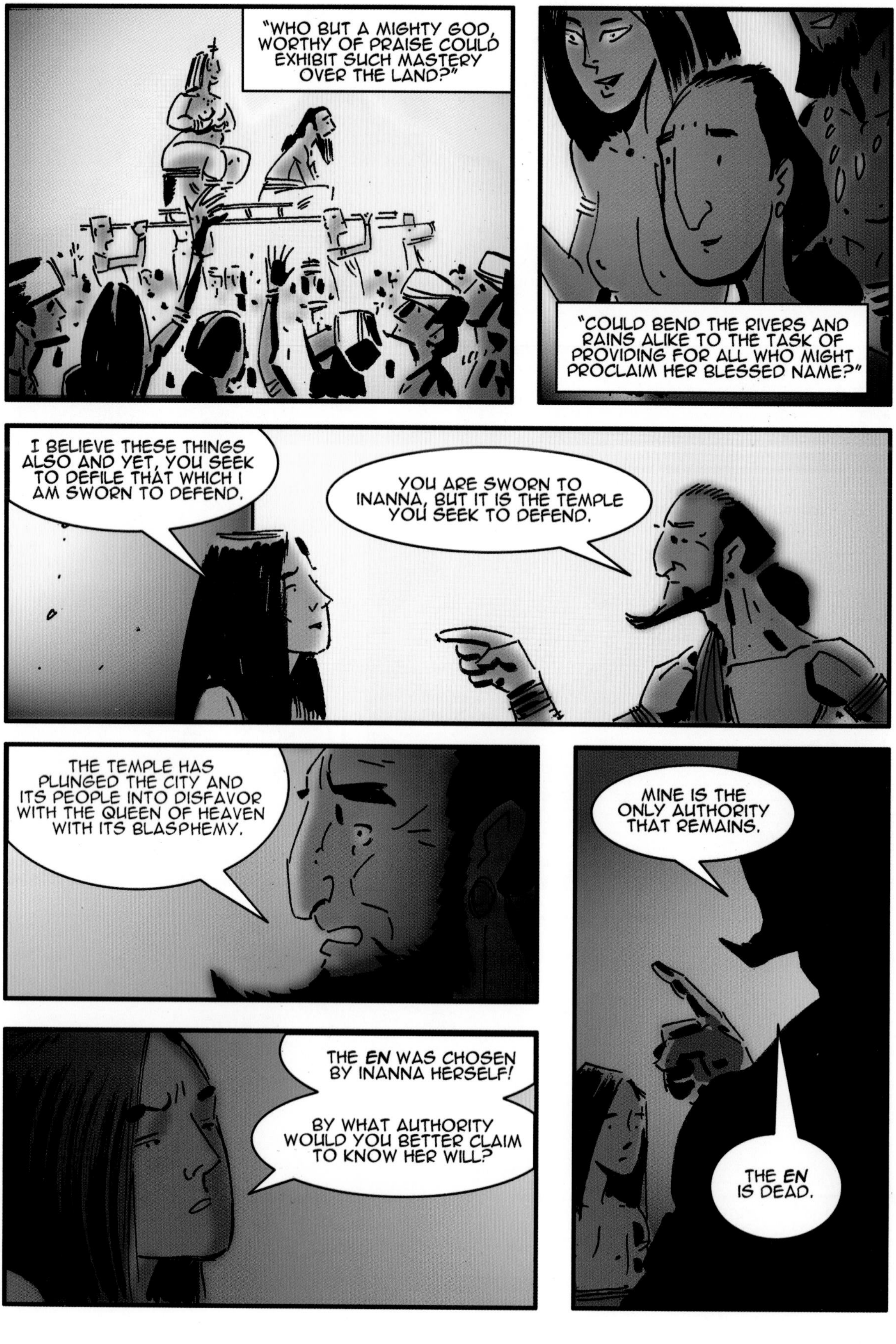
"WHO BUT A MIGHTY GOD, WORTHY OF PRAISE COULD EXHIBIT SUCH MASTERY OVER THE LAND?"
"COULD BEND THE RIVERS AND RAINS ALIKE TO THE TASK OF PROVIDING FOR ALL WHO MIGHT PROCLAIM HER BLESSED NAME?"
I BELIEVE THESE THINGS ALSO AND YET, YOU SEEK TO DEFILE THAT WHICH I AM SWORN TO DEFEND.
YOU ARE SWORN TO INANNA, BUT IT IS THE TEMPLE YOU SEEK TO DEFEND.
THE TEMPLE HAS PLUNGED THE CITY AND ITS PEOPLE INTO DISFAVOR WITH THE QUEEN OF HEAVEN WITH ITS BLASPHEMY.
THE EN WAS CHOSEN BY INANNA HERSELF!
BY WHAT AUTHORITY WOULD YOU BETTER CLAIM TO KNOW HER WILL?
MINE IS THE ONLY AUTHORITY THAT REMAINS.
THE EN IS DEAD.

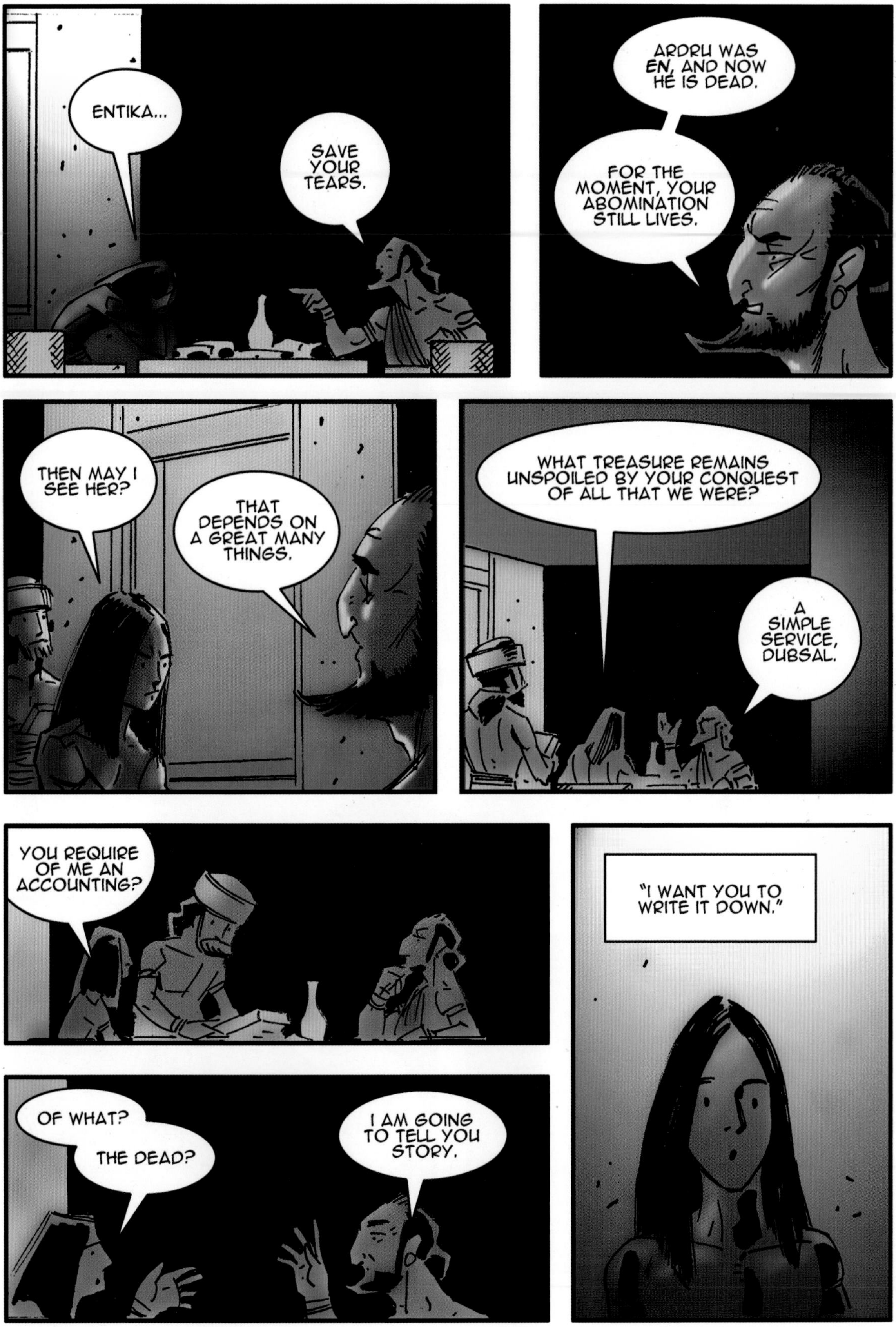
ENTIKA...
SAVE YOUR TEARS.
ARDRU WAS EN, AND NOW HE IS DEAD.
FOR THE MOMENT, YOUR ABOMINATION STILL LIVES.
THEN MAY I SEE HER?
THAT DEPENDS ON A GREAT MANY THINGS.
WHAT TREASURE REMAINS UNSPOILED BY YOUR CONQUEST OF ALL THAT WE WERE?
A SIMPLE SERVICE, DUBSAL.
YOU REQUIRE OF ME AN ACCOUNTING?
OF WHAT?
THE DEAD?
I AM GOING TO TELL YOU STORY.
"I WANT YOU TO WRITE IT DOWN."

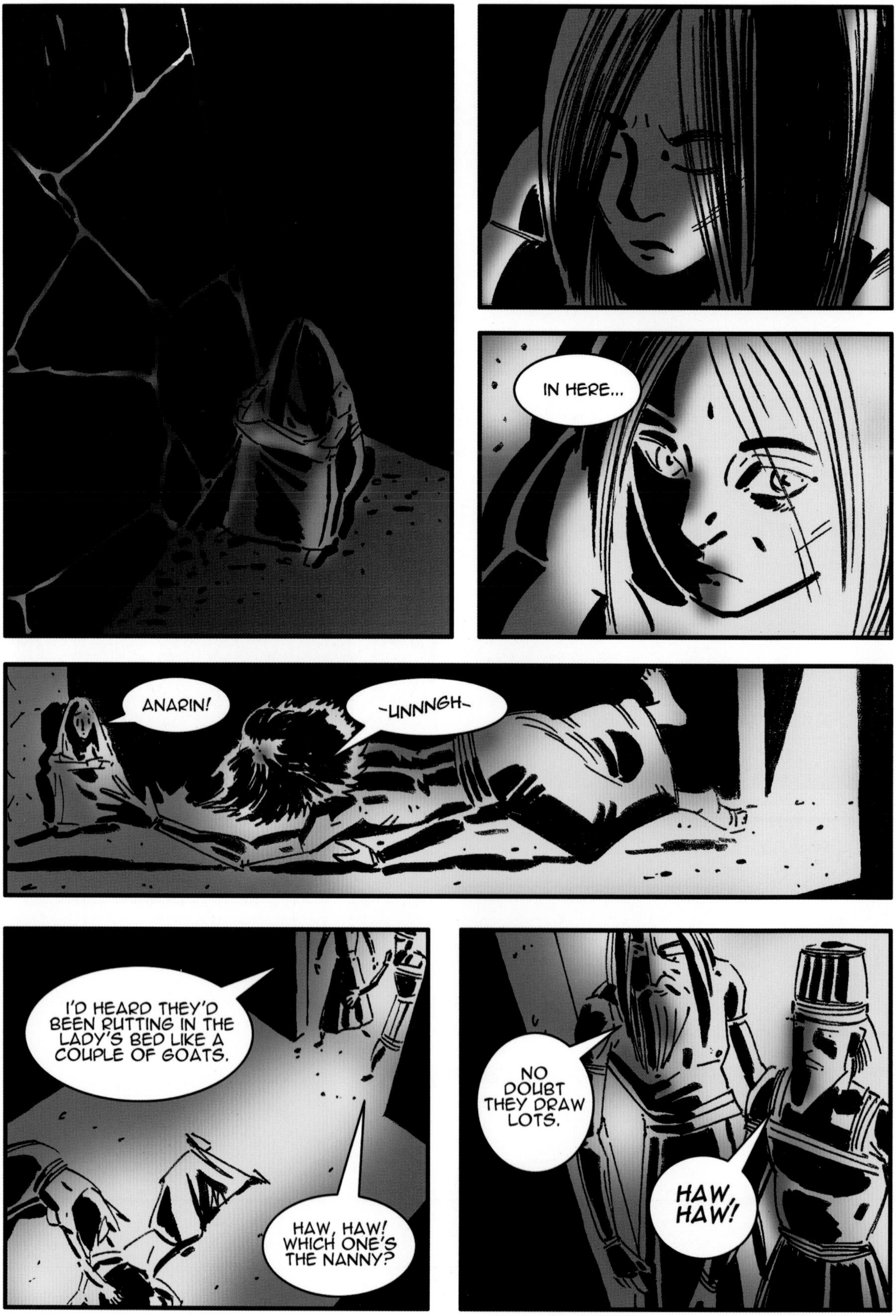
IN HERE...
ANARIN!
-UNNNGH-
I'D HEARD THEY'D BEEN RUTTING IN THE LADY'S BED LIKE A COUPLE OF GOATS.
HAW, HAW! WHICH ONE'S THE NANNY?
NO DOUBT THEY DRAW LOTS.
HAW, HAW!

DID THEY BEAT YOU?

NOT THEM.

OH, ANARIN!

NOT RECENTLY, ANYWAY.

I FEARED YOU DEAD!

THEY HOODED ME AS THE DAIS WAS PULLED DOWN.

BUT THERE WAS NO MISTAKING THE SOUNDS OF SLAUGHTER AS I WAS CARRIED AWAY.

DOES THE SANGA YET LIVE?

HE WAS NOT KEPT AMONG THE SURVIVING UGULA WHERE I WAS FIRST HELD.

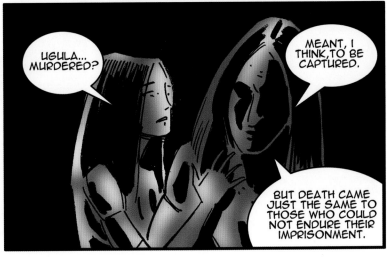

UGULA... MURDERED?

MEANT, I THINK, TO BE CAPTURED.

BUT DEATH CAME JUST THE SAME TO THOSE WHO COULD NOT ENDURE THEIR IMPRISONMENT.

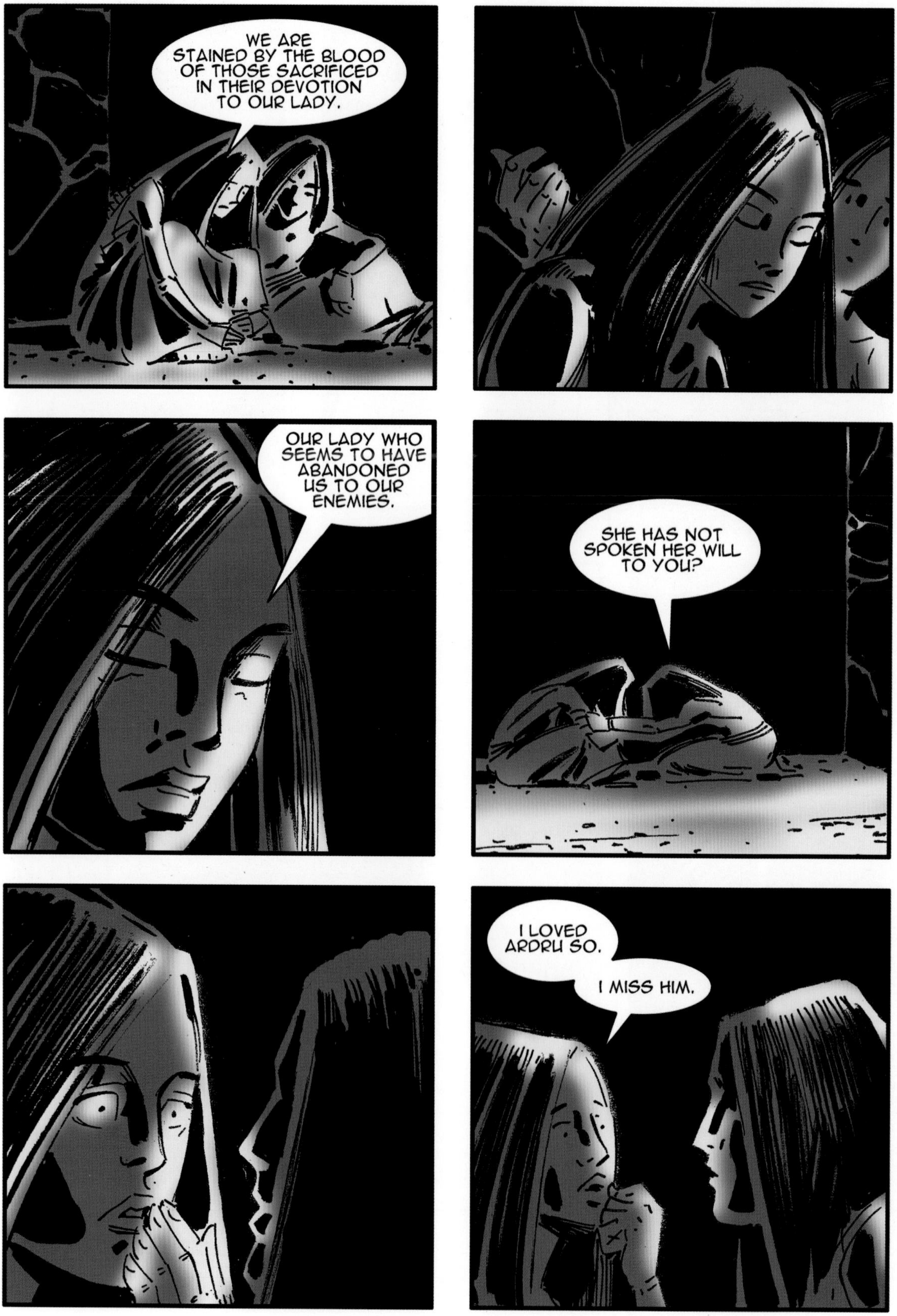
WE ARE STAINED BY THE BLOOD OF THOSE SACRIFICED IN THEIR DEVOTION TO OUR LADY.
OUR LADY WHO SEEMS TO HAVE ABANDONED US TO OUR ENEMIES.
SHE HAS NOT SPOKEN HER WILL TO YOU?
I LOVED ARDRU SO.
I MISS HIM.

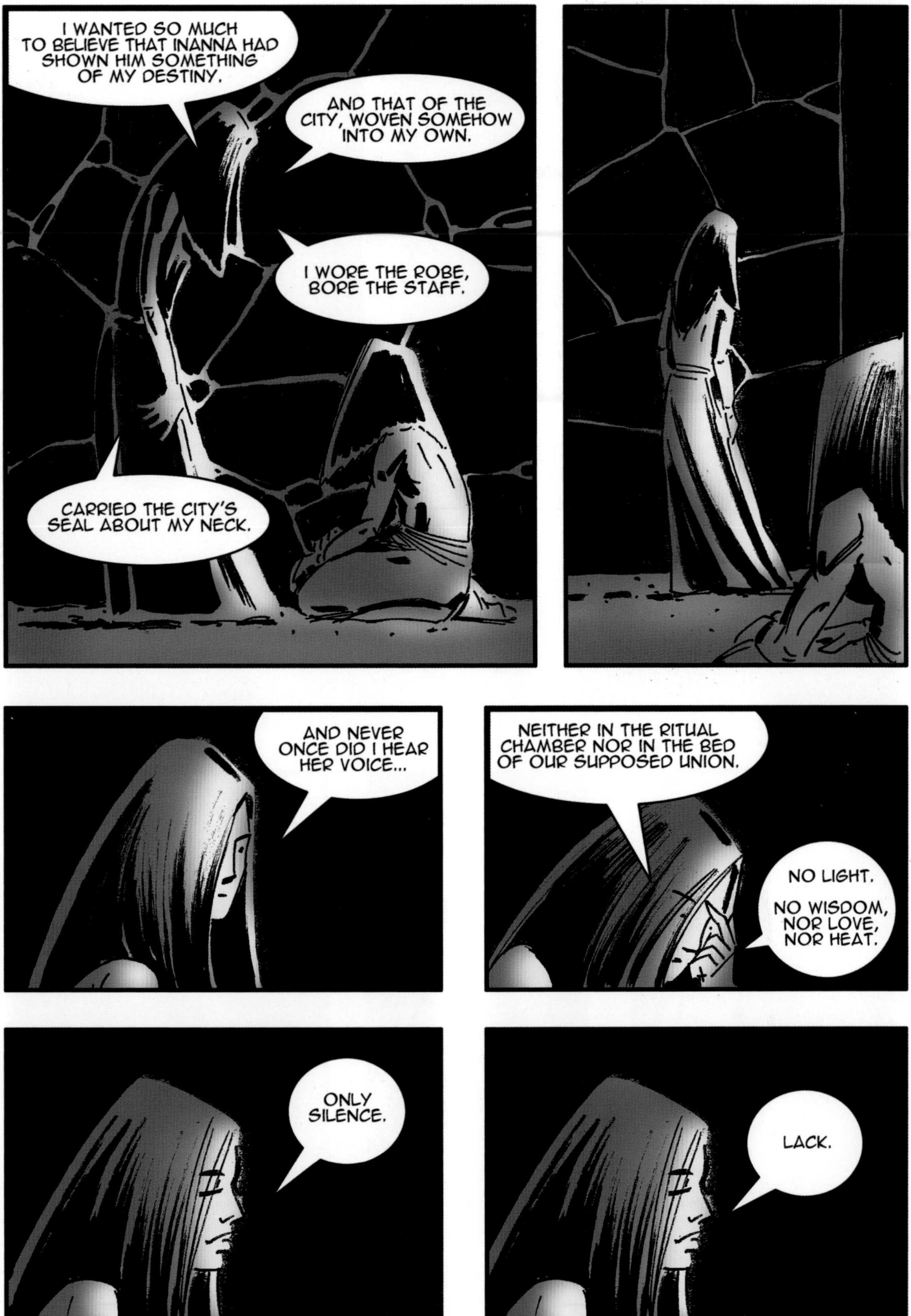
I WANTED SO MUCH TO BELIEVE THAT INANNA HAD SHOWN HIM SOMETHING OF MY DESTINY.
AND THAT OF THE CITY, WOVEN SOMEHOW INTO MY OWN.
I WORE THE ROBE, BORE THE STAFF.
CARRIED THE CITY'S SEAL ABOUT MY NECK.
AND NEVER ONCE DID I HEAR HER VOICE...
NEITHER IN THE RITUAL CHAMBER NOR IN THE BED OF OUR SUPPOSED UNION.
NO LIGHT.
NO WISDOM, NOR LOVE, NOR HEAT.
ONLY SILENCE.
LACK.

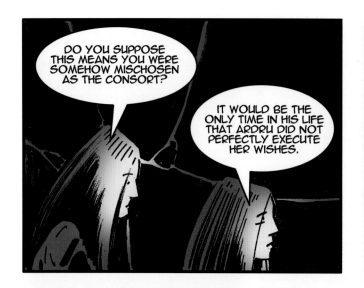

DO YOU SUPPOSE THIS MEANS YOU WERE SOMEHOW MISCHOSEN AS THE CONSORT?

IT WOULD BE THE ONLY TIME IN HIS LIFE THAT ARDRU DID NOT PERFECTLY EXECUTE HER WISHES.

YET HE WAS SO WEAK IN THOSE FINAL DAYS.

IF SOMEHOW THE DEMONS THAT DWELLT WITHIN HIM MANAGED TO DERANGE HIS SENSES.

THIS IS THE LUGALS' CLAIM.

THEY SAY THAT THEIR GOD, GERU WAS SUMMONED BY INANNA INTO THE CITY THAT HE MIGHT BECOME HER CONSORT AND RIGHT THE IMBALANCE.

THEY SET HER AFLAME BEFORE THE PEOPLE IN HIS NAME!

THE ZEAL OF YOUNG MEN WITH BLOOD STIRRED BY FIGHTING.

STILL, THE PEOPLE OF BOTH THE CITY AND THE TENTS ARE DEMANDING THE GODDESS' REINSTATEMENT IN THE TEMPLE.

HOW DID YOU COME TO KNOW SO MUCH OF WHAT HAS TRANSPIRED OUTSIDE OF THE TEMPLE?

I HAVE SPOKEN WITH BELIPOTASH, THEIR LEADER.
IN EXCHANGE FOR BEING ALLOWED TO SEE YOU, I AGREED TO TELL YOU HIS TERMS FOR SPARING YOUR LIFE.
TERMS?
HE DECREES THAT YOU ARE NO LONGER THE *EN*, DEAD OR ALIVE.
ARDRU IS TO BE THE LAST CONSORT TO RULE OVER BIRITH.
SO WE ARE TO BE RULED BY THIS BELIPOTASH?
THE TEMPLE WOULD STILL BE GUARDIAN OF THE *ME* AND RESPONSIBLE FOR TAKING THE LADY'S BOUNTY.
THE LUGALS WILL ASSUME RESPONSIBLITY FOR INTEGRATING OUR TWO PEOPLES AND DISTRIBUTING THE BOUNTY FAIRLY AMONG THEM.
AND WHAT OF GERU?
INSTALLED IN THE TEMPLE ALONGSIDE INANNA WHEN SHE IS REINSTATED AND TENDED AFTER BY HIS OWN CLERGY.
IF YOU CAN CALL THEM THAT.

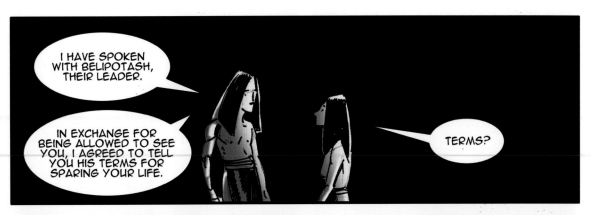

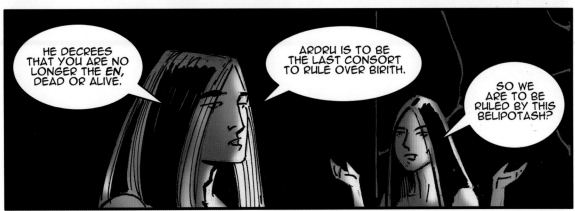

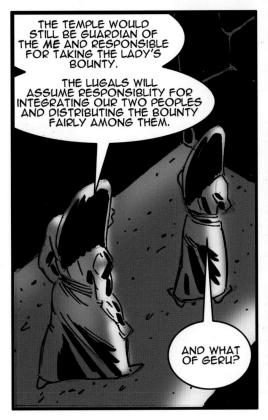

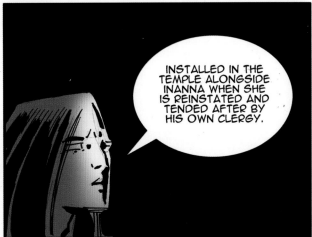

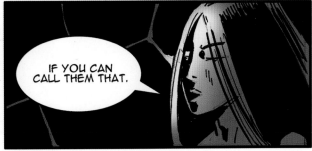

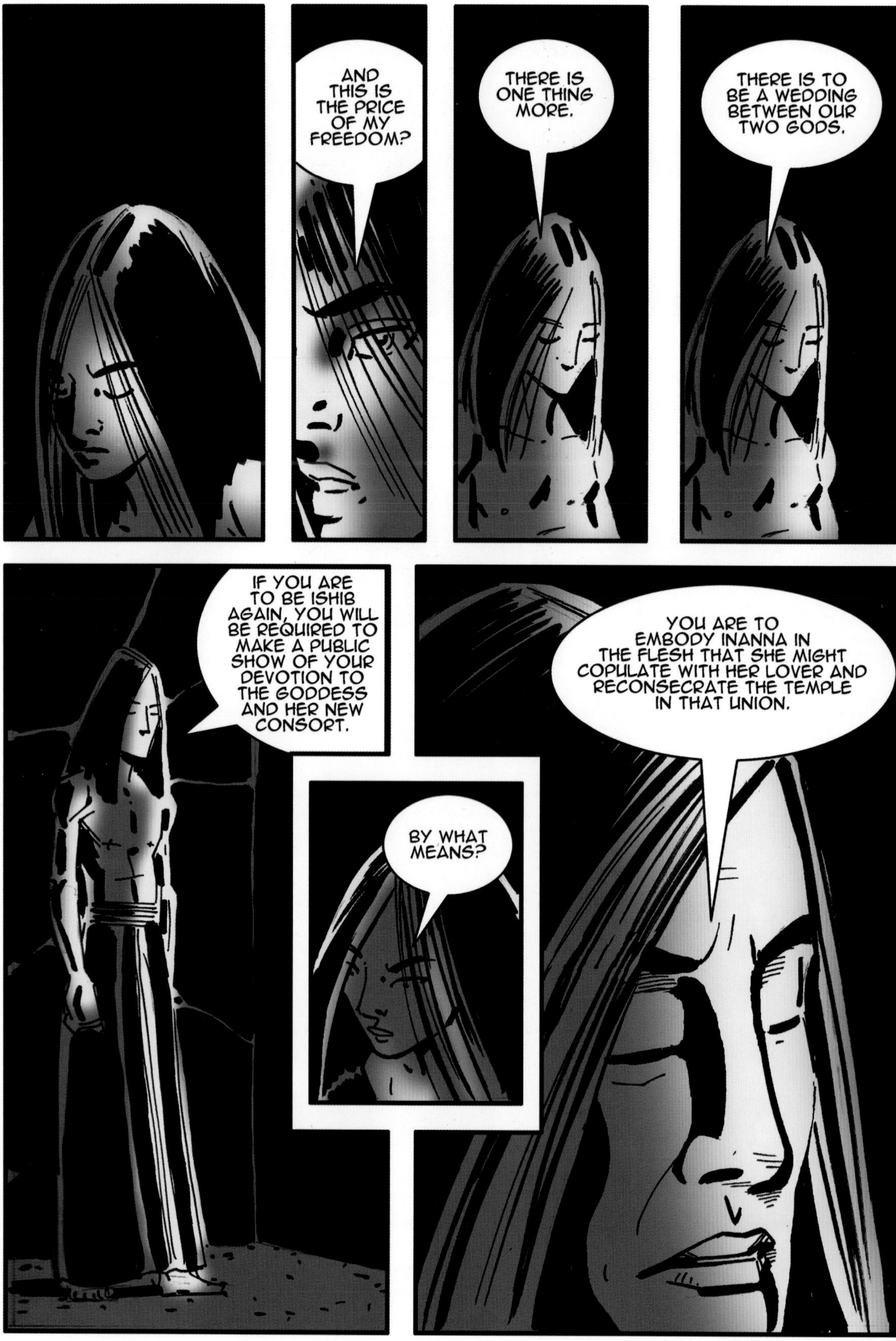
AND THIS IS THE PRICE OF MY FREEDOM?
THERE IS ONE THING MORE.
THERE IS TO BE A WEDDING BETWEEN OUR TWO GODS.
IF YOU ARE TO BE ISHIB AGAIN, YOU WILL BE REQUIRED TO MAKE A PUBLIC SHOW OF YOUR DEVOTION TO THE GODDESS AND HER NEW CONSORT.
BY WHAT MEANS?
YOU ARE TO EMBODY INANNA IN THE FLESH THAT SHE MIGHT COPULATE WITH HER LOVER AND RECONSECRATE THE TEMPLE IN THAT UNION.

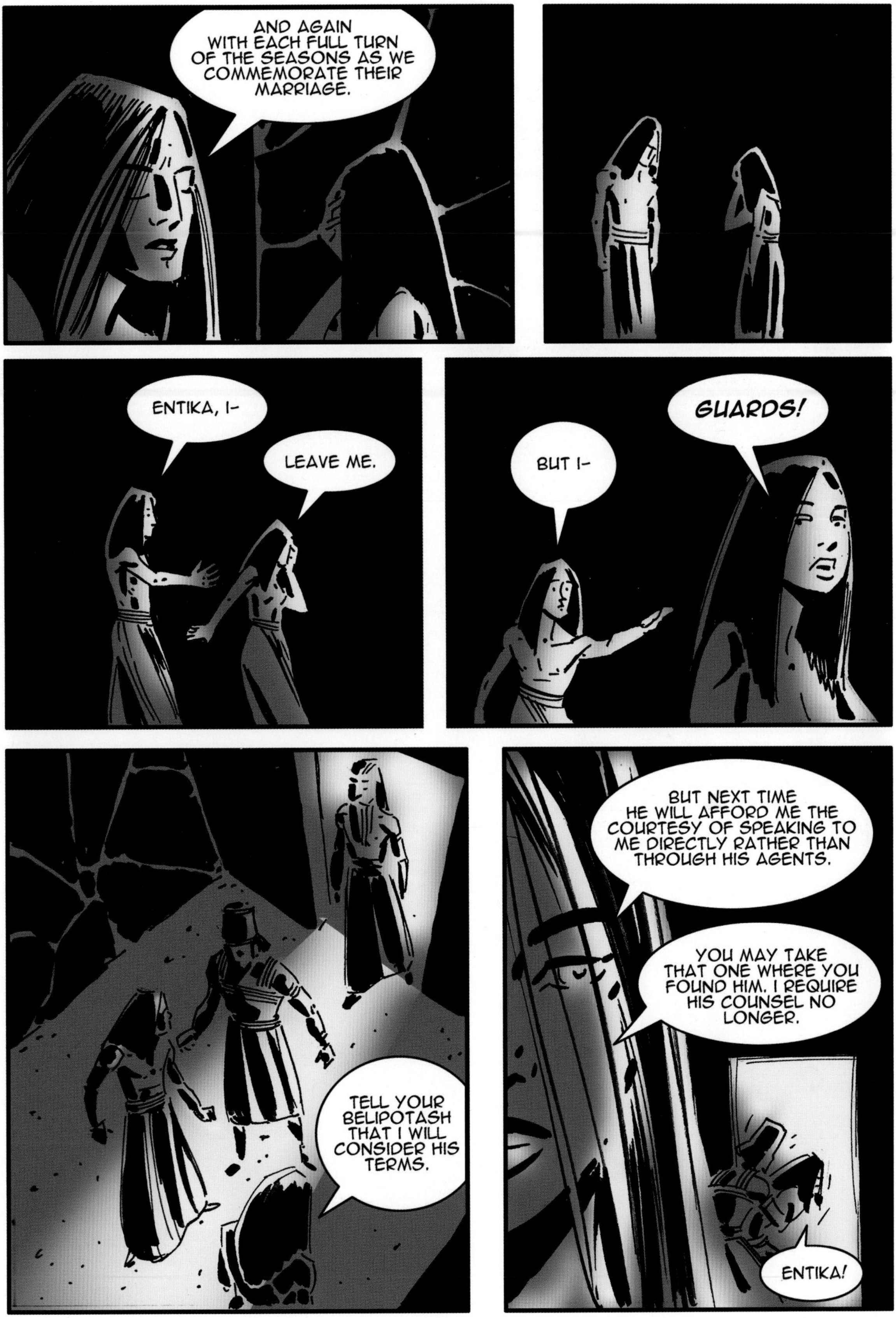
AND AGAIN WITH EACH FULL TURN OF THE SEASONS AS WE COMMEMORATE THEIR MARRIAGE.
ENTIKA, I-
LEAVE ME.
BUT I-
GUARDS!
TELL YOUR BELIPOTASH THAT I WILL CONSIDER HIS TERMS.
BUT NEXT TIME HE WILL AFFORD ME THE COURTESY OF SPEAKING TO ME DIRECTLY RATHER THAN THROUGH HIS AGENTS.
YOU MAY TAKE THAT ONE WHERE YOU FOUND HIM. I REQUIRE HIS COUNSEL NO LONGER.
ENTIKA!

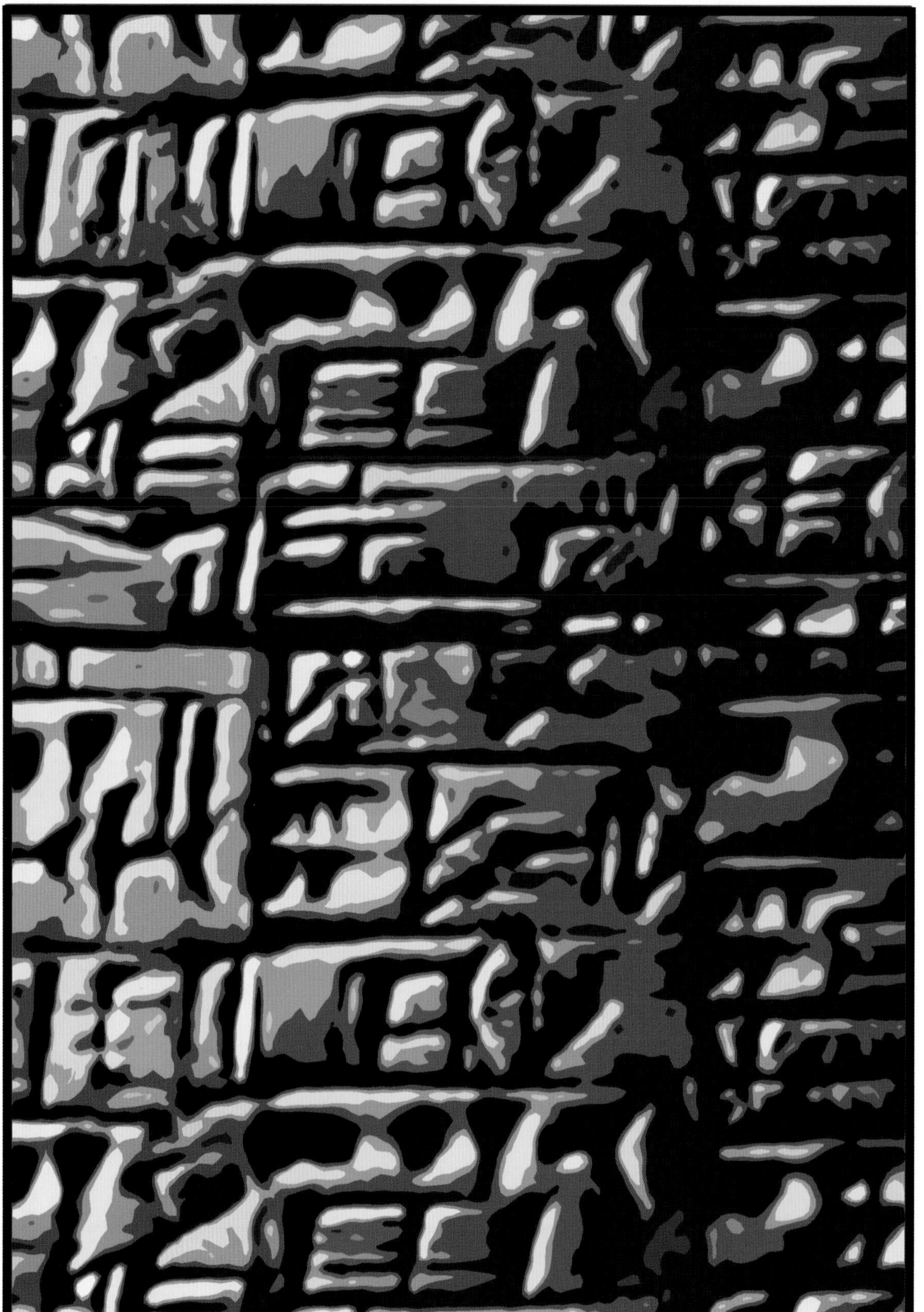

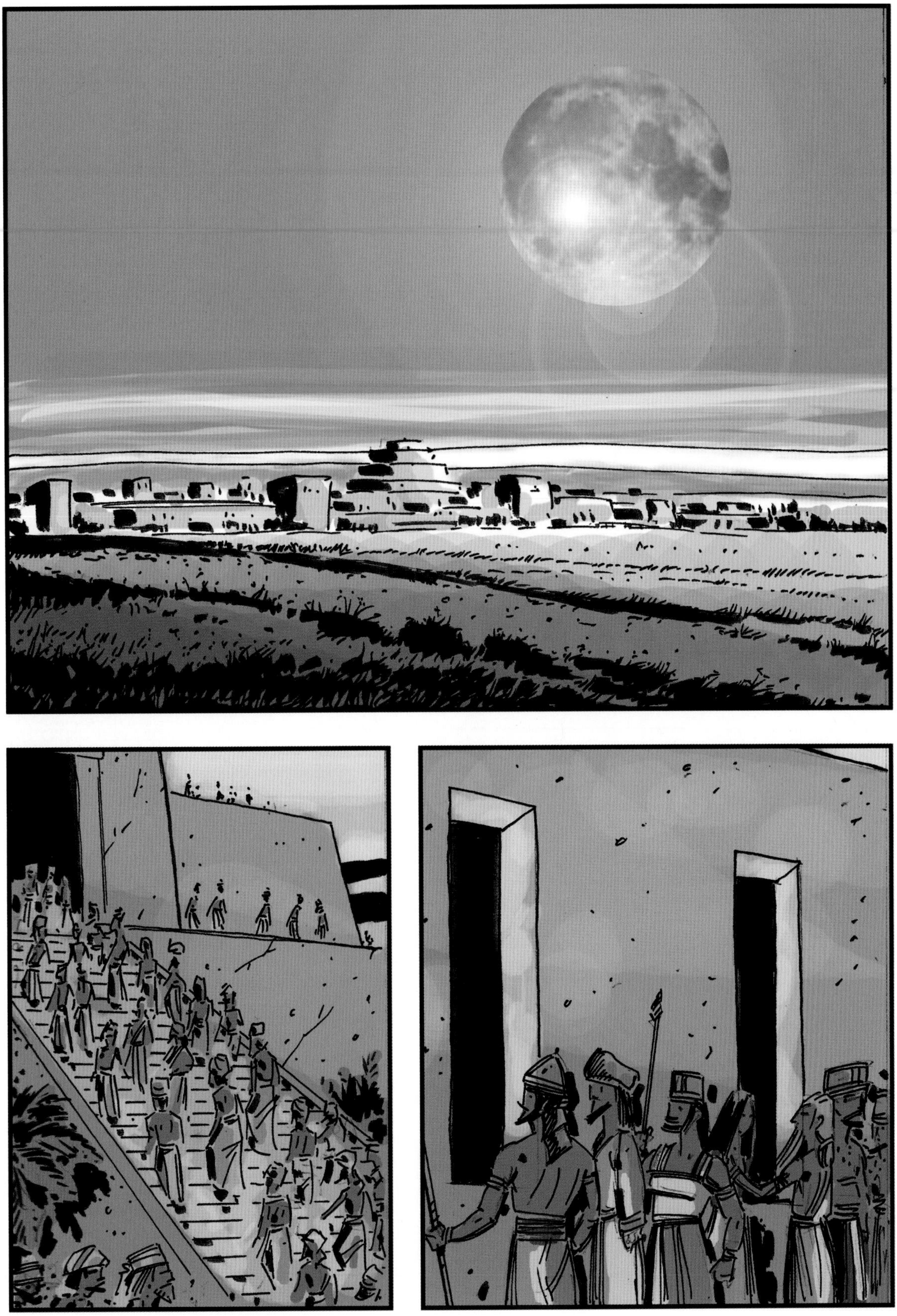

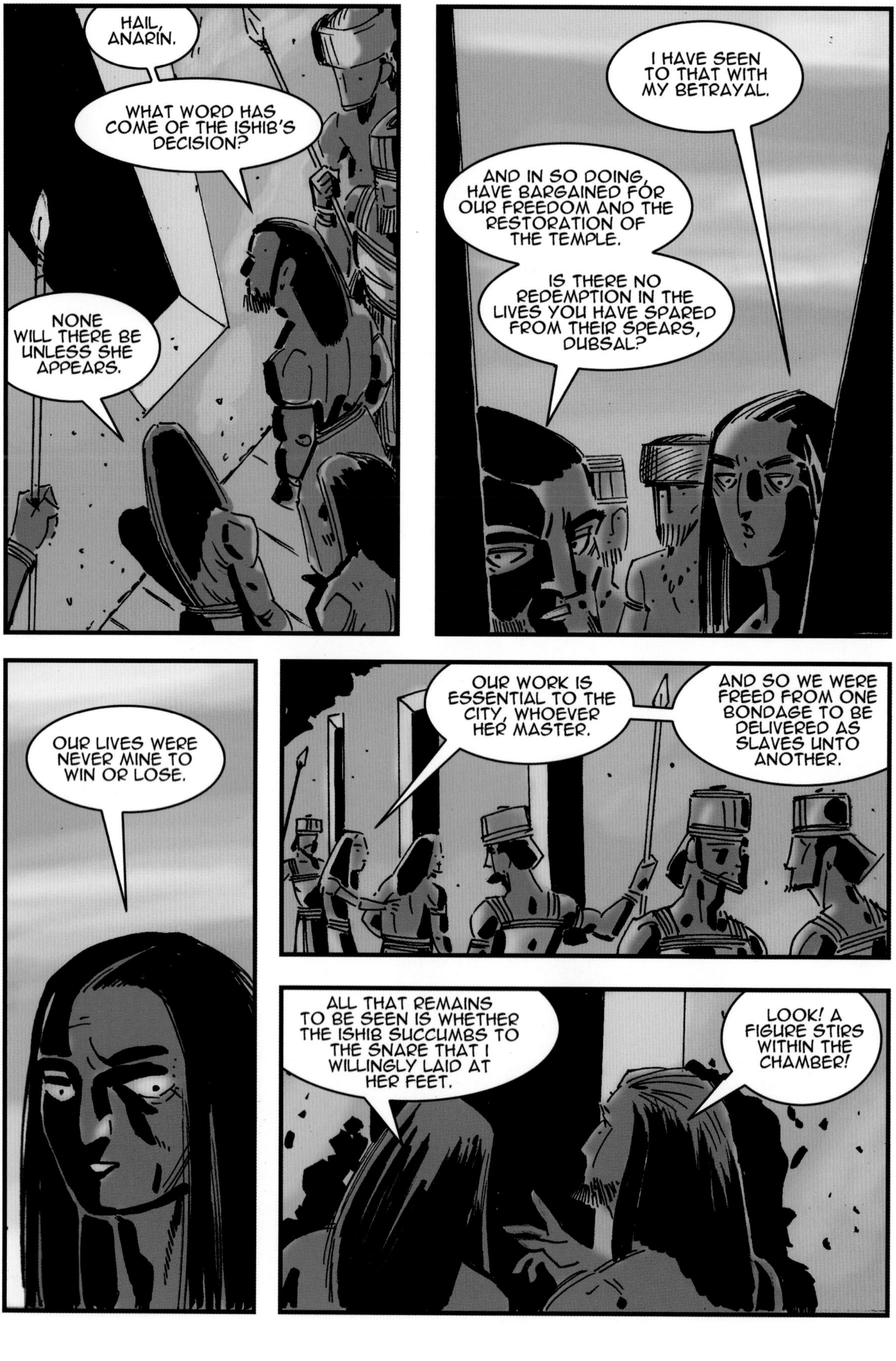
HAIL, ANARIN.
WHAT WORD HAS COME OF THE ISHIB'S DECISION?
NONE WILL THERE BE UNLESS SHE APPEARS.
I HAVE SEEN TO THAT WITH MY BETRAYAL.
AND IN SO DOING, HAVE BARGAINED FOR OUR FREEDOM AND THE RESTORATION OF THE TEMPLE.
IS THERE NO REDEMPTION IN THE LIVES YOU HAVE SPARED FROM THEIR SPEARS, DUBSAL?
OUR LIVES WERE NEVER MINE TO WIN OR LOSE.
OUR WORK IS ESSENTIAL TO THE CITY, WHOEVER HER MASTER.
AND SO WE WERE FREED FROM ONE BONDAGE TO BE DELIVERED AS SLAVES UNTO ANOTHER.
ALL THAT REMAINS TO BE SEEN IS WHETHER THE ISHIB SUCCUMBS TO THE SNARE THAT I WILLINGLY LAID AT HER FEET.
LOOK! A FIGURE STIRS WITHIN THE CHAMBER!

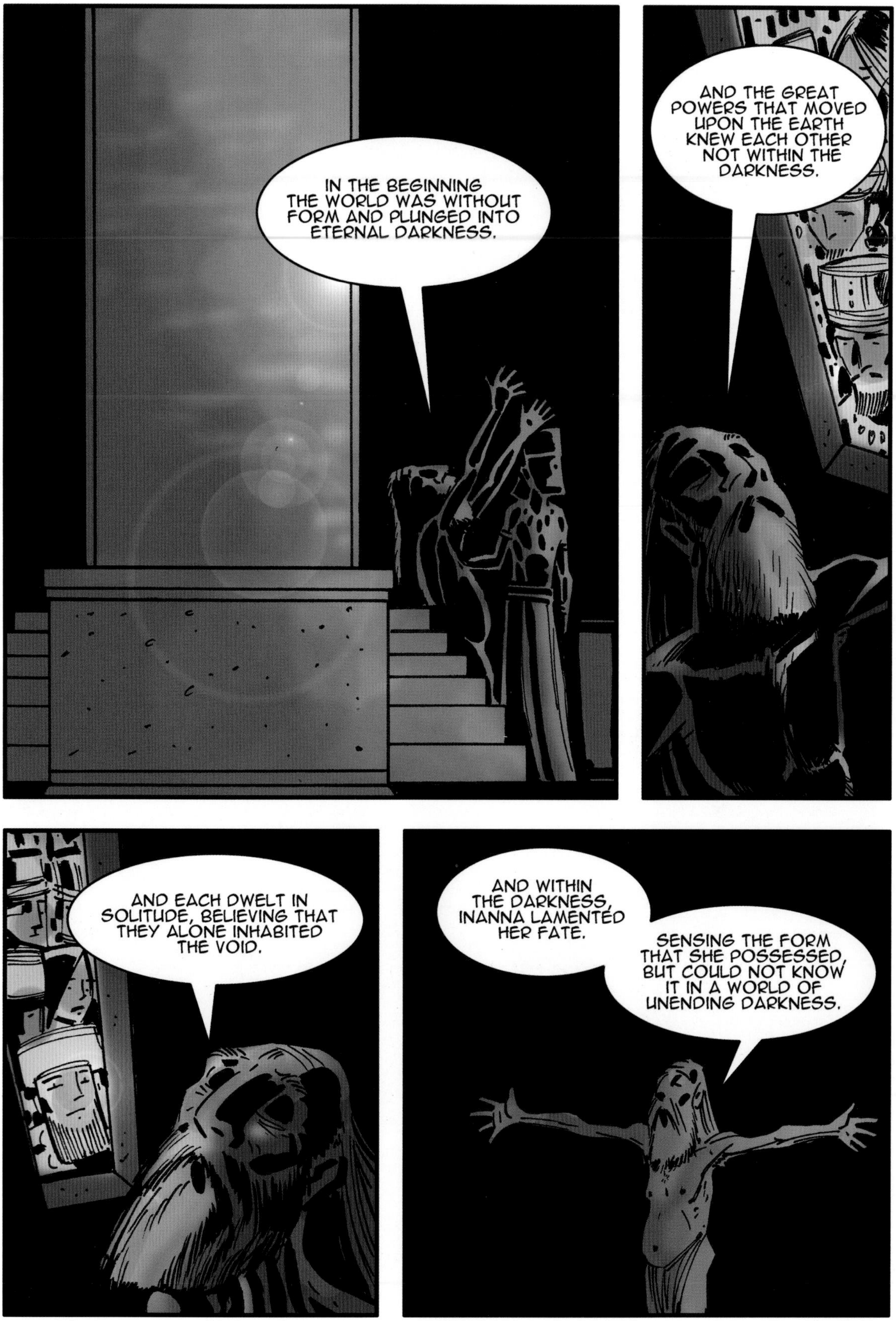
IN THE BEGINNING THE WORLD WAS WITHOUT FORM AND PLUNGED INTO ETERNAL DARKNESS.
AND THE GREAT POWERS THAT MOVED UPON THE EARTH KNEW EACH OTHER NOT WITHIN THE DARKNESS.
AND EACH DWELT IN SOLITUDE, BELIEVING THAT THEY ALONE INHABITED THE VOID.
AND WITHIN THE DARKNESS, INANNA LAMENTED HER FATE.
SENSING THE FORM THAT SHE POSSESSED, BUT COULD NOT KNOW IT IN A WORLD OF UNENDING DARKNESS.

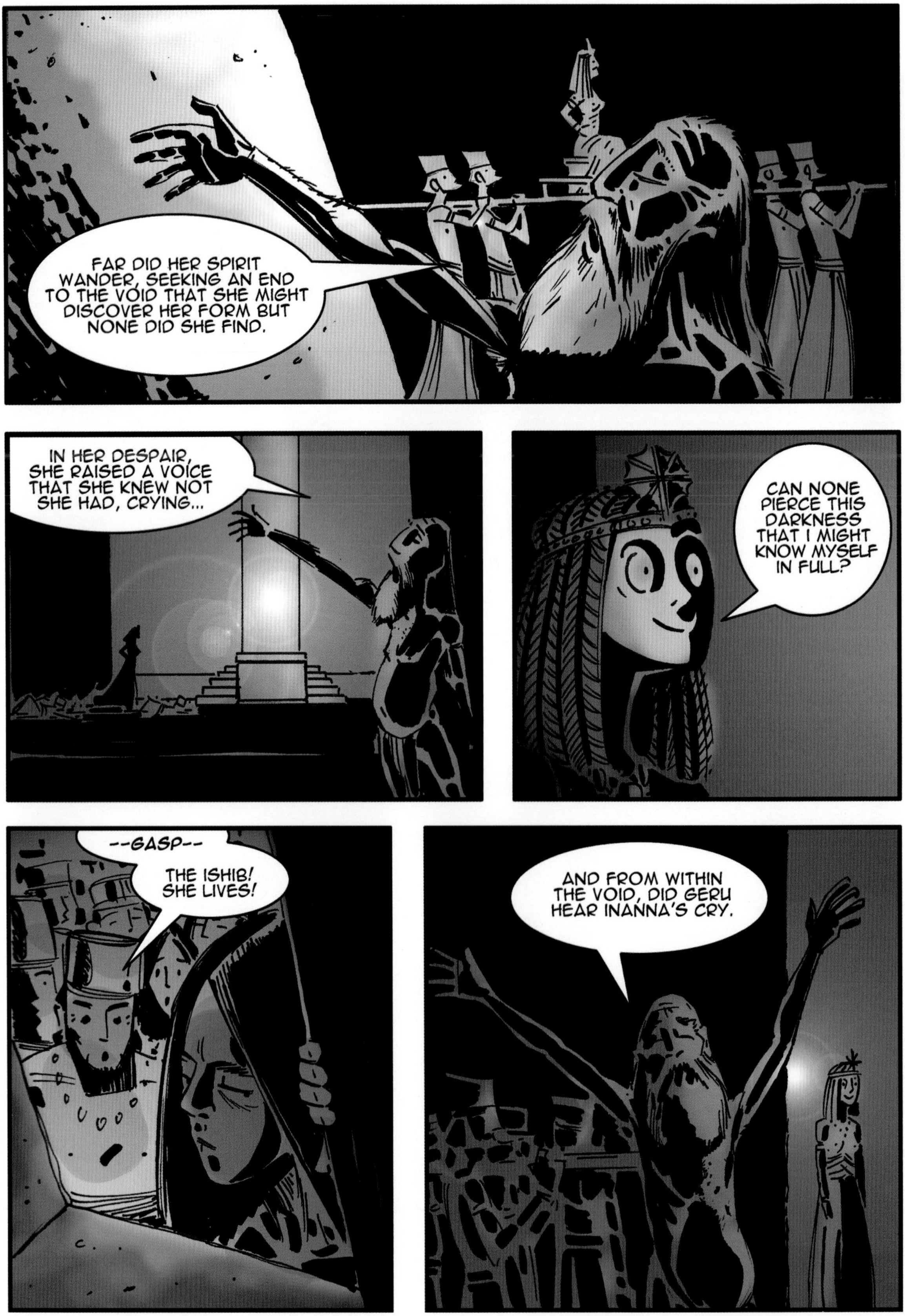
FAR DID HER SPIRIT WANDER, SEEKING AN END TO THE VOID THAT SHE MIGHT DISCOVER HER FORM BUT NONE DID SHE FIND.
IN HER DESPAIR, SHE RAISED A VOICE THAT SHE KNEW NOT SHE HAD, CRYING...
CAN NONE PIERCE THIS DARKNESS THAT I MIGHT KNOW MYSELF IN FULL?
--GASP--
THE ISHIB! SHE LIVES!
AND FROM WITHIN THE VOID, DID GERU HEAR INANNA'S CRY.

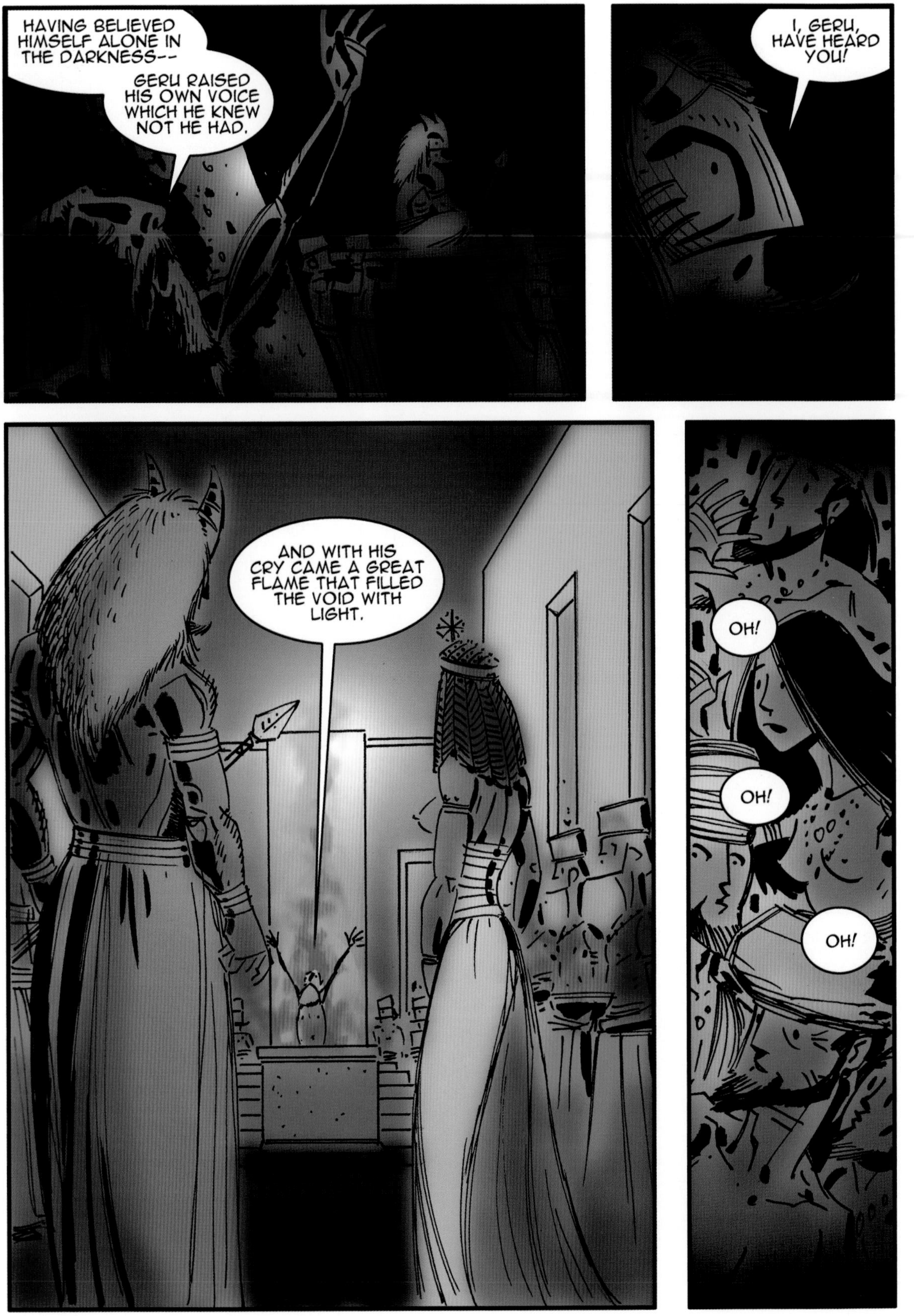
HAVING BELIEVED HIMSELF ALONE IN THE DARKNESS--
GERU RAISED HIS OWN VOICE WHICH HE KNEW NOT HE HAD.
I, GERU, HAVE HEARD YOU!
AND WITH HIS CRY CAME A GREAT FLAME THAT FILLED THE VOID WITH LIGHT.
OH!
OH!
OH!

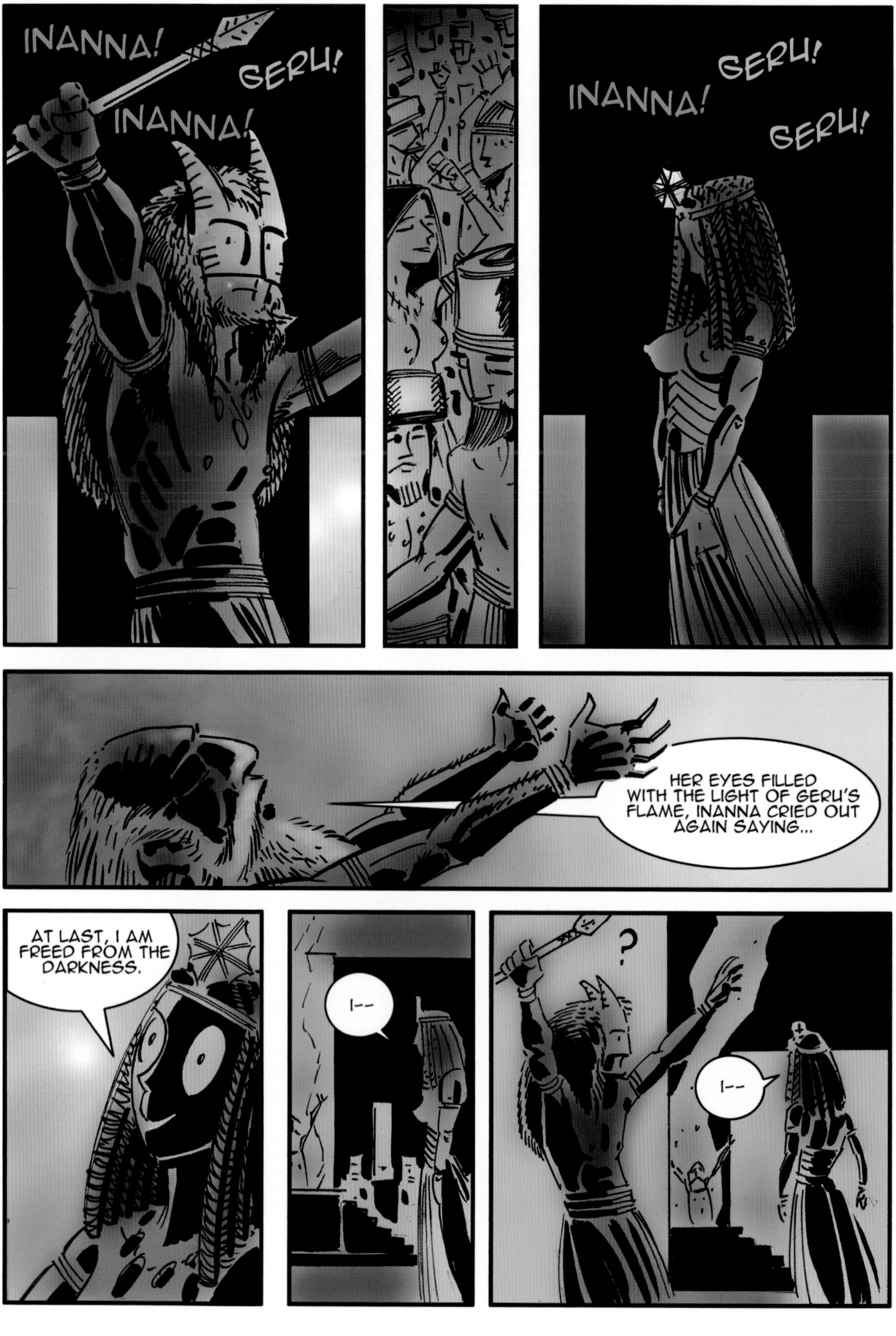
INANNA!
GERU!
INANNA!
INANNA!
GERU!
GERU!
HER EYES FILLED WITH THE LIGHT OF GERU'S FLAME, INANNA CRIED OUT AGAIN SAYING...
AT LAST, I AM FREED FROM THE DARKNESS.
I--
?
I--

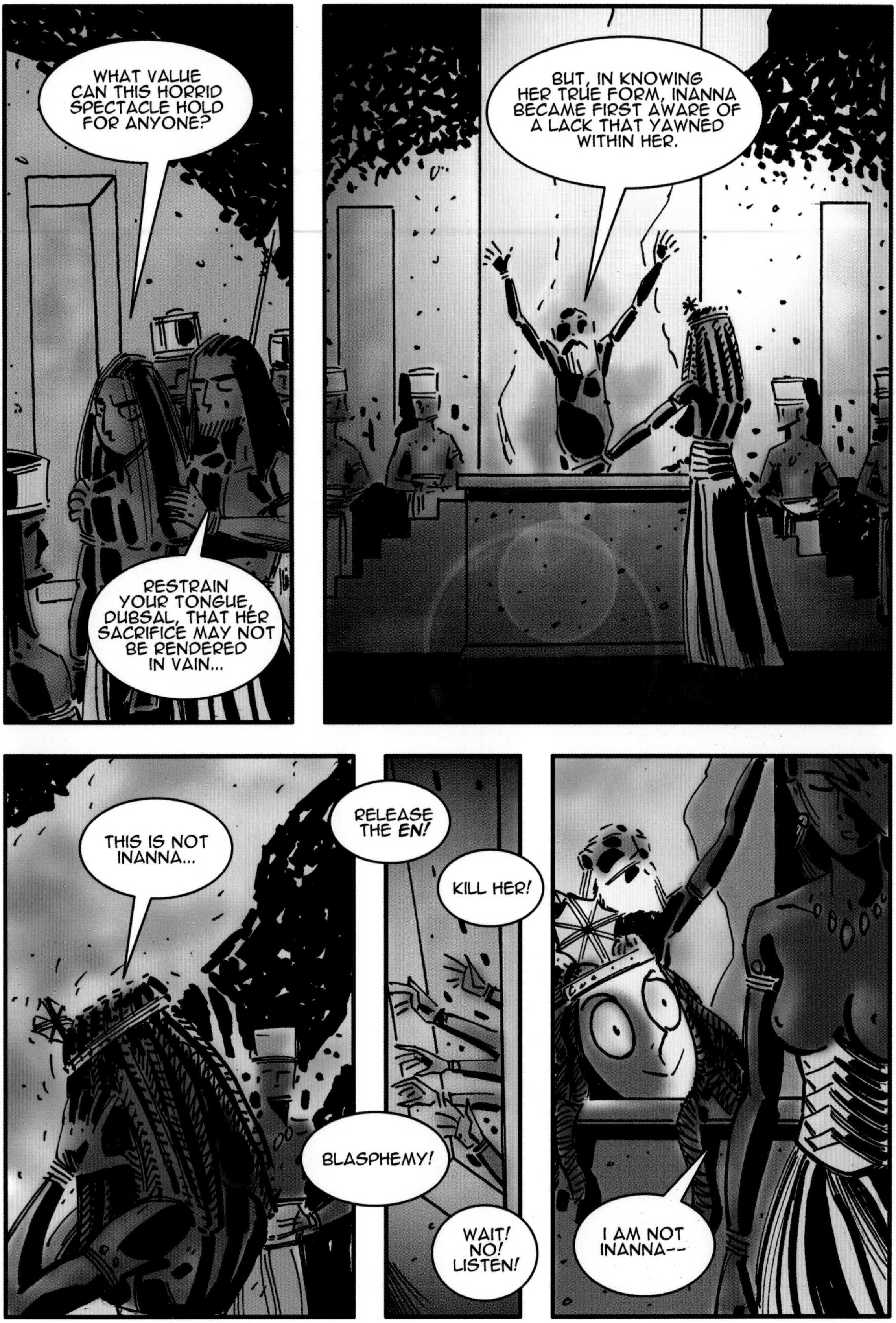
WHAT VALUE CAN THIS HORRID SPECTACLE HOLD FOR ANYONE?
RESTRAIN YOUR TONGUE, DUBSAL, THAT HER SACRIFICE MAY NOT BE RENDERED IN VAIN...
BUT, IN KNOWING HER TRUE FORM, INANNA BECAME FIRST AWARE OF A LACK THAT YAWNED WITHIN HER.
THIS IS NOT INANNA...
RELEASE THE EN!
KILL HER!
BLASPHEMY!
WAIT! NO! LISTEN!
I AM NOT INANNA--

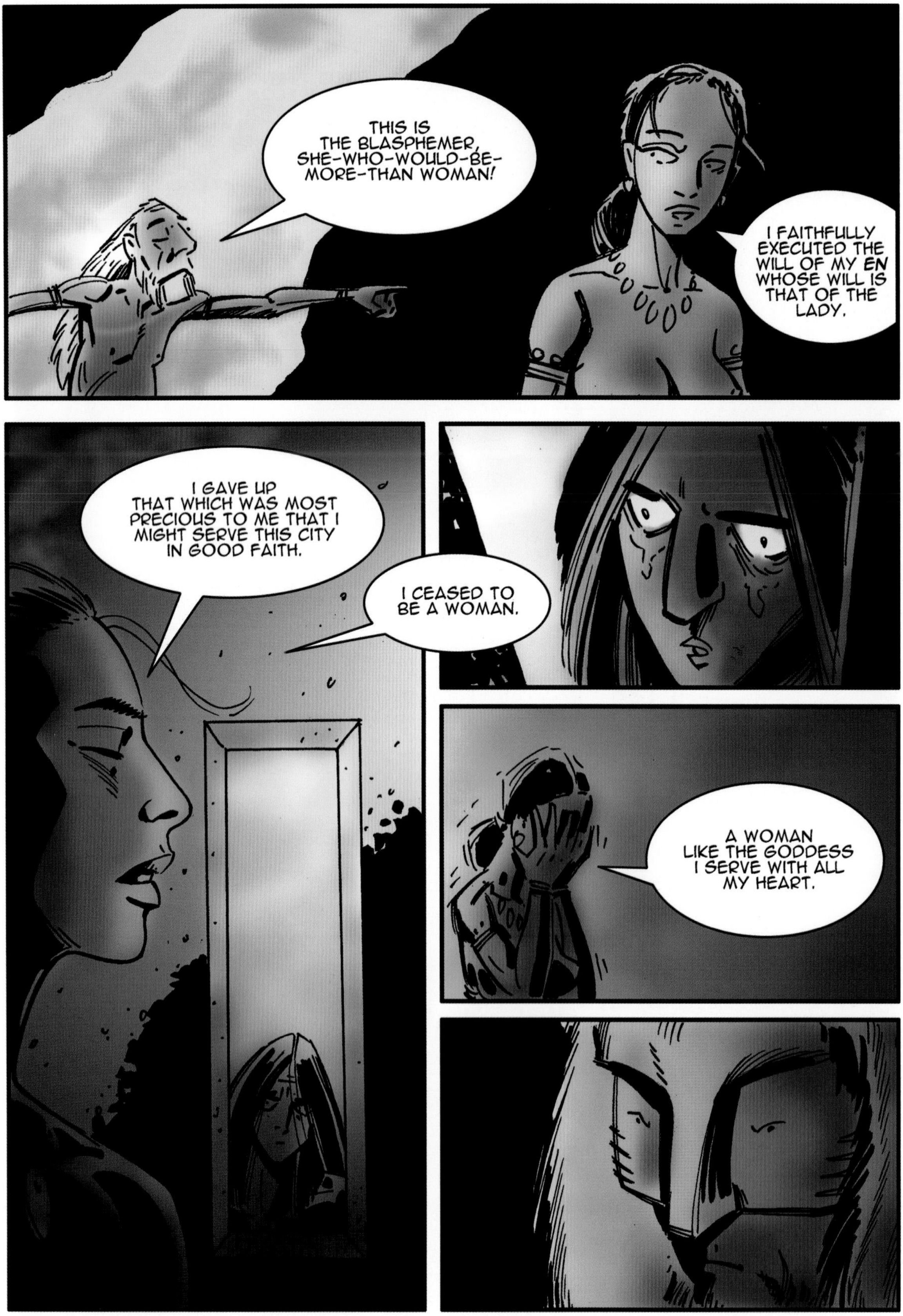
THIS IS THE BLASPHEMER, SHE-WHO-WOULD-BE-MORE-THAN WOMAN!
I FAITHFULLY EXECUTED THE WILL OF MY EN WHOSE WILL IS THAT OF THE LADY.
I GAVE UP THAT WHICH WAS MOST PRECIOUS TO ME THAT I MIGHT SERVE THIS CITY IN GOOD FAITH.
I CEASED TO BE A WOMAN.
A WOMAN LIKE THE GODDESS I SERVE WITH ALL MY HEART.

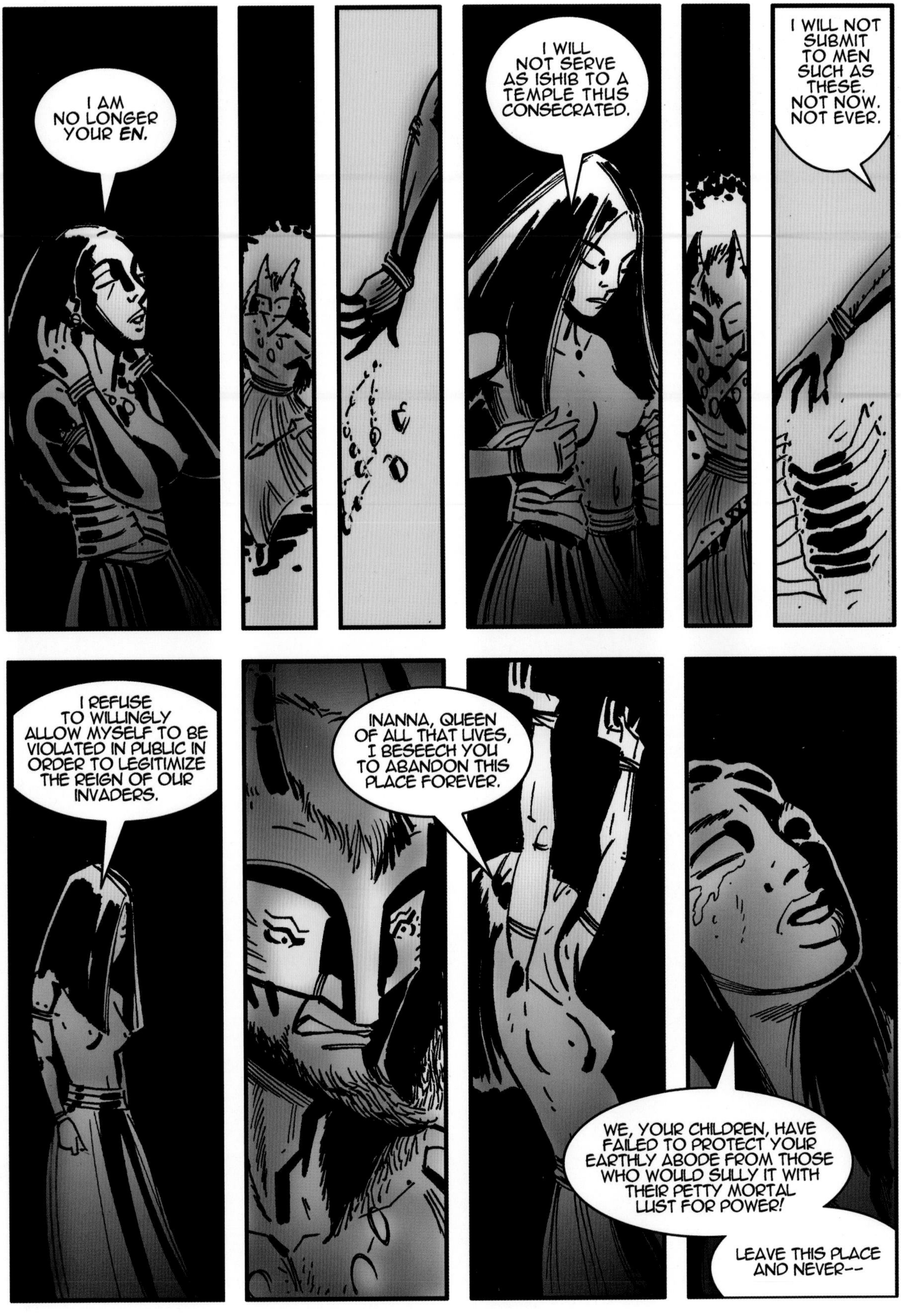
I AM NO LONGER YOUR EN.
I WILL NOT SERVE AS ISHIB TO A TEMPLE THUS CONSECRATED.
I WILL NOT SUBMIT TO MEN SUCH AS THESE. NOT NOW. NOT EVER.
I REFUSE TO WILLINGLY ALLOW MYSELF TO BE VIOLATED IN PUBLIC IN ORDER TO LEGITIMIZE THE REIGN OF OUR INVADERS.
INANNA, QUEEN OF ALL THAT LIVES, I BESEECH YOU TO ABANDON THIS PLACE FOREVER.
WE, YOUR CHILDREN, HAVE FAILED TO PROTECT YOUR EARTHLY ABODE FROM THOSE WHO WOULD SULLY IT WITH THEIR PETTY MORTAL LUST FOR POWER!
LEAVE THIS PLACE AND NEVER--

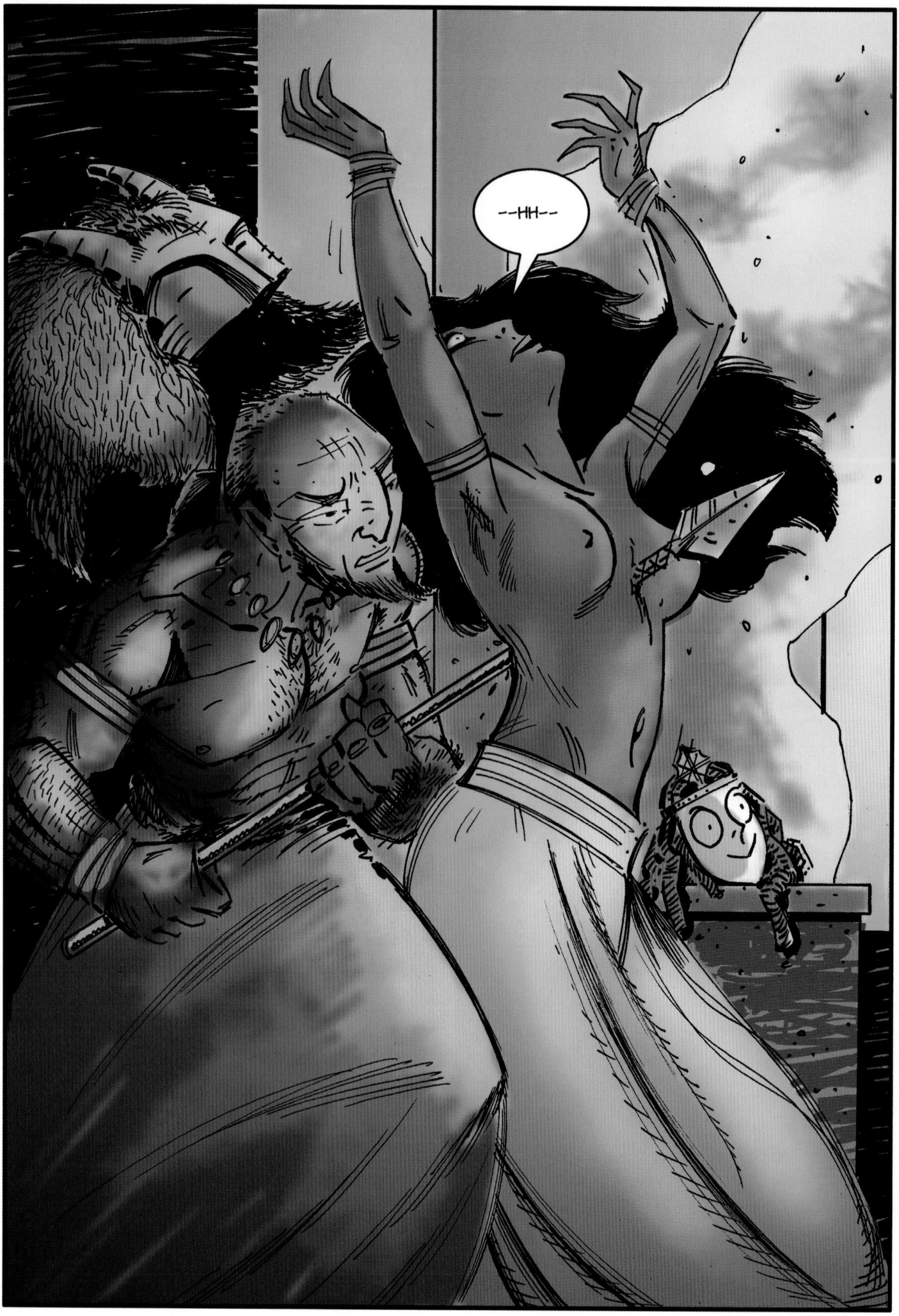
--HH--

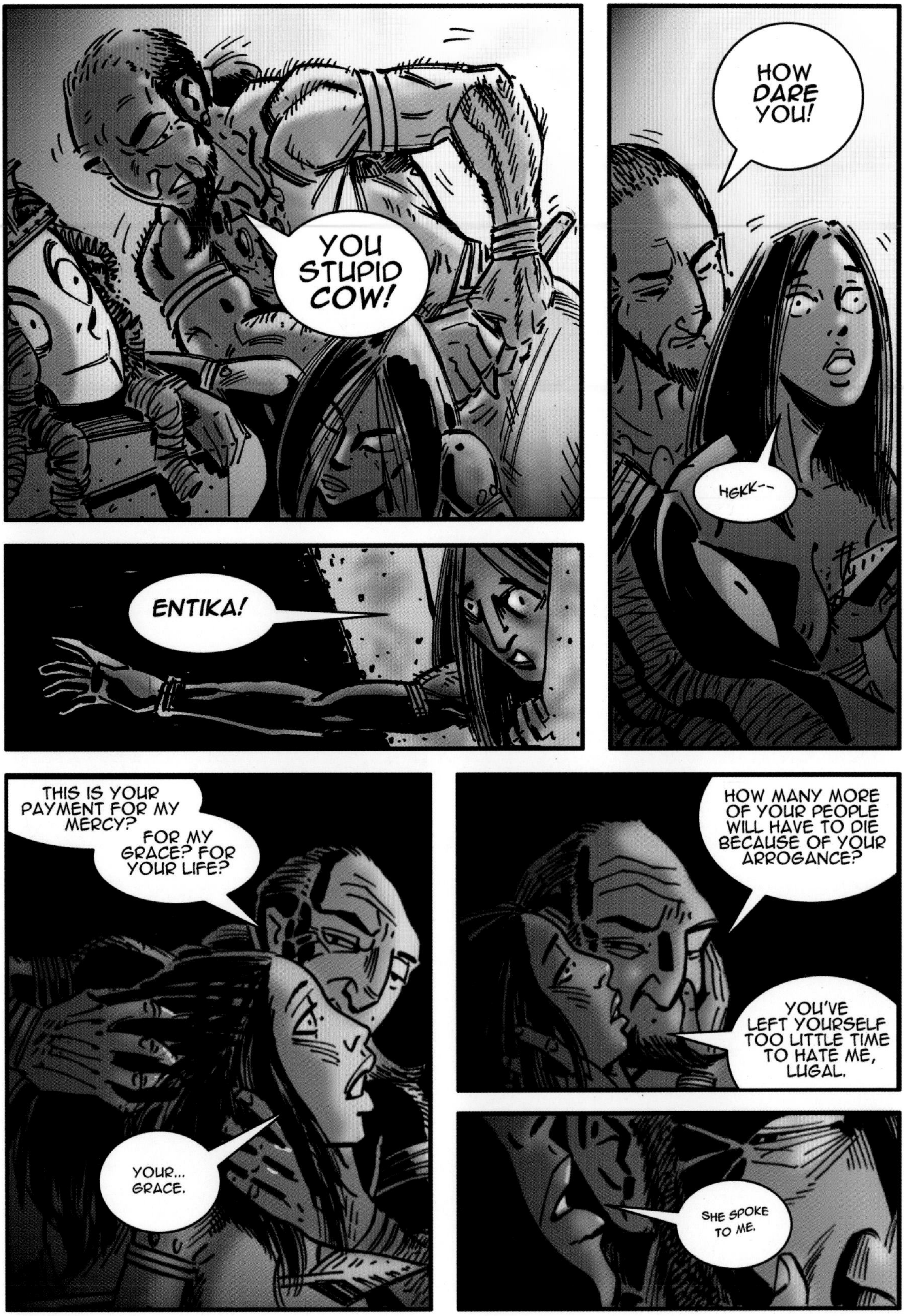
YOU STUPID COW!
HOW DARE YOU!
HGKK--
ENTIKA!
THIS IS YOUR PAYMENT FOR MY MERCY?
FOR MY GRACE? FOR YOUR LIFE?
YOUR... GRACE.
HOW MANY MORE OF YOUR PEOPLE WILL HAVE TO DIE BECAUSE OF YOUR ARROGANCE?
YOU'VE LEFT YOURSELF TOO LITTLE TIME TO HATE ME, LUGAL.
SHE SPOKE TO ME.

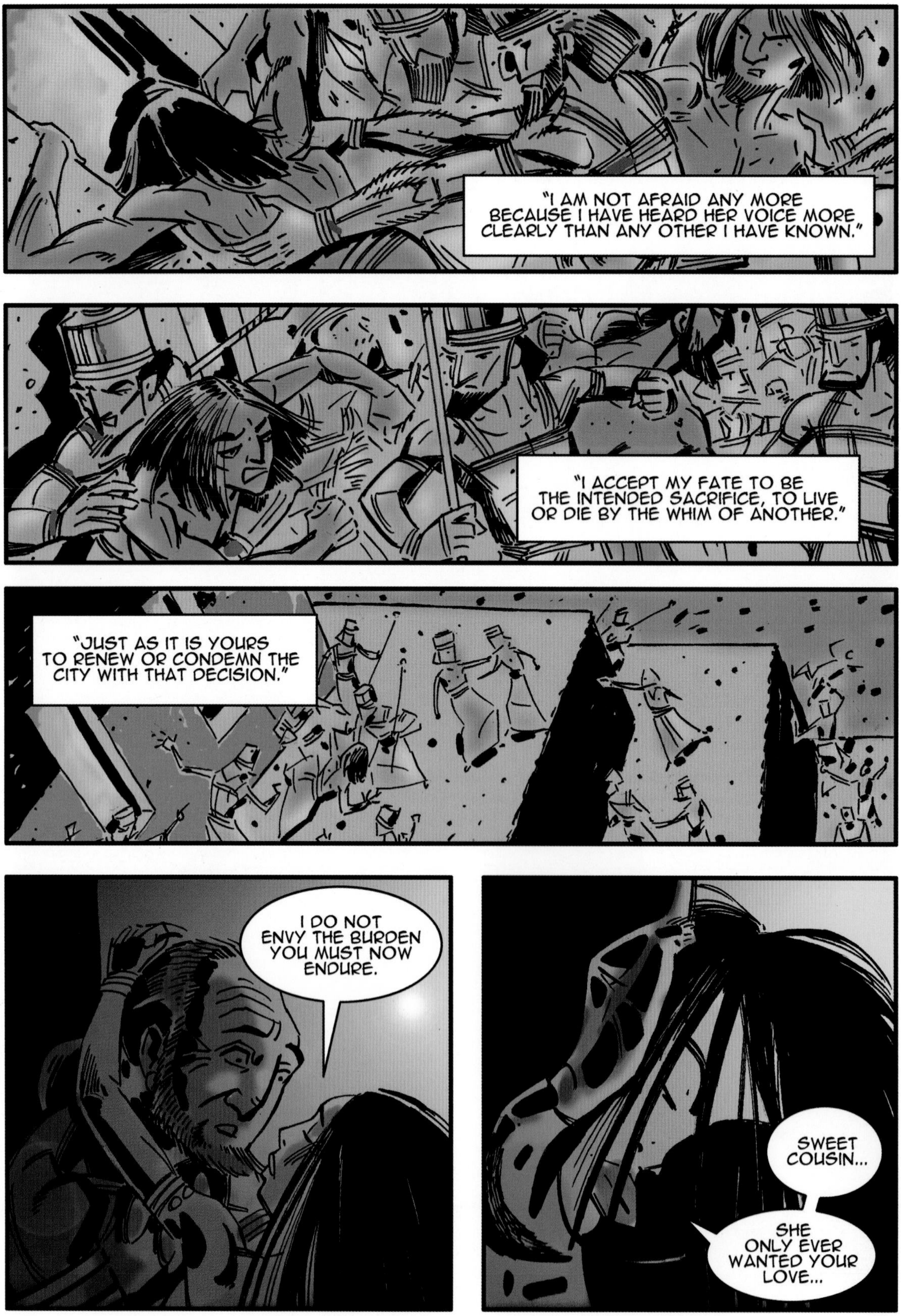
"I AM NOT AFRAID ANY MORE BECAUSE I HAVE HEARD HER VOICE MORE CLEARLY THAN ANY OTHER I HAVE KNOWN."
"I ACCEPT MY FATE TO BE THE INTENDED SACRIFICE, TO LIVE OR DIE BY THE WHIM OF ANOTHER."
"JUST AS IT IS YOURS TO RENEW OR CONDEMN THE CITY WITH THAT DECISION."
I DO NOT ENVY THE BURDEN YOU MUST NOW ENDURE.
SWEET COUSIN...
SHE ONLY EVER WANTED YOUR LOVE...

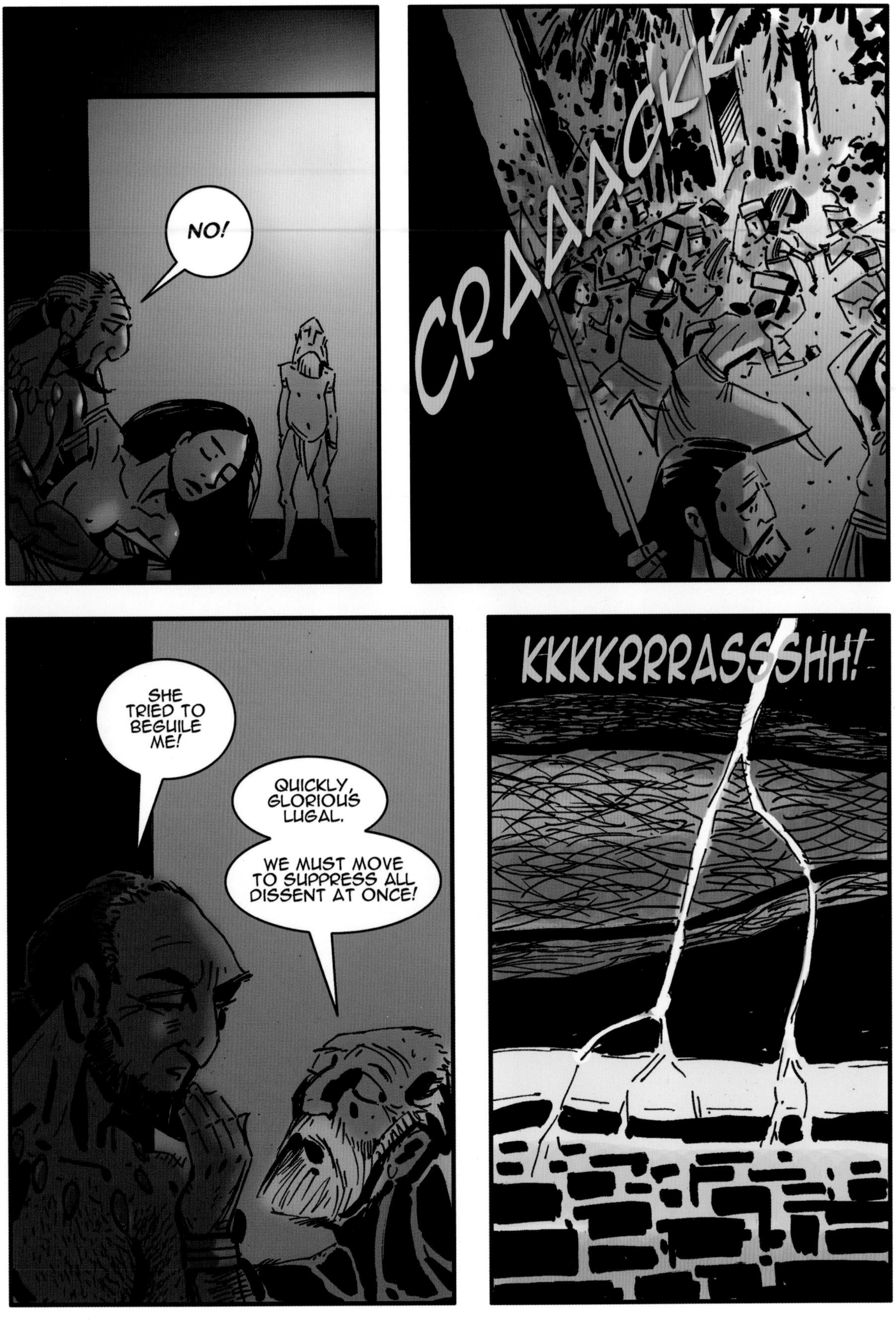
NO!
CRAAACKK
SHE TRIED TO BEGUILE ME!
QUICKLY, GLORIOUS LUGAL.
WE MUST MOVE TO SUPPRESS ALL DISSENT AT ONCE!
KKKKRRRASSSHH!

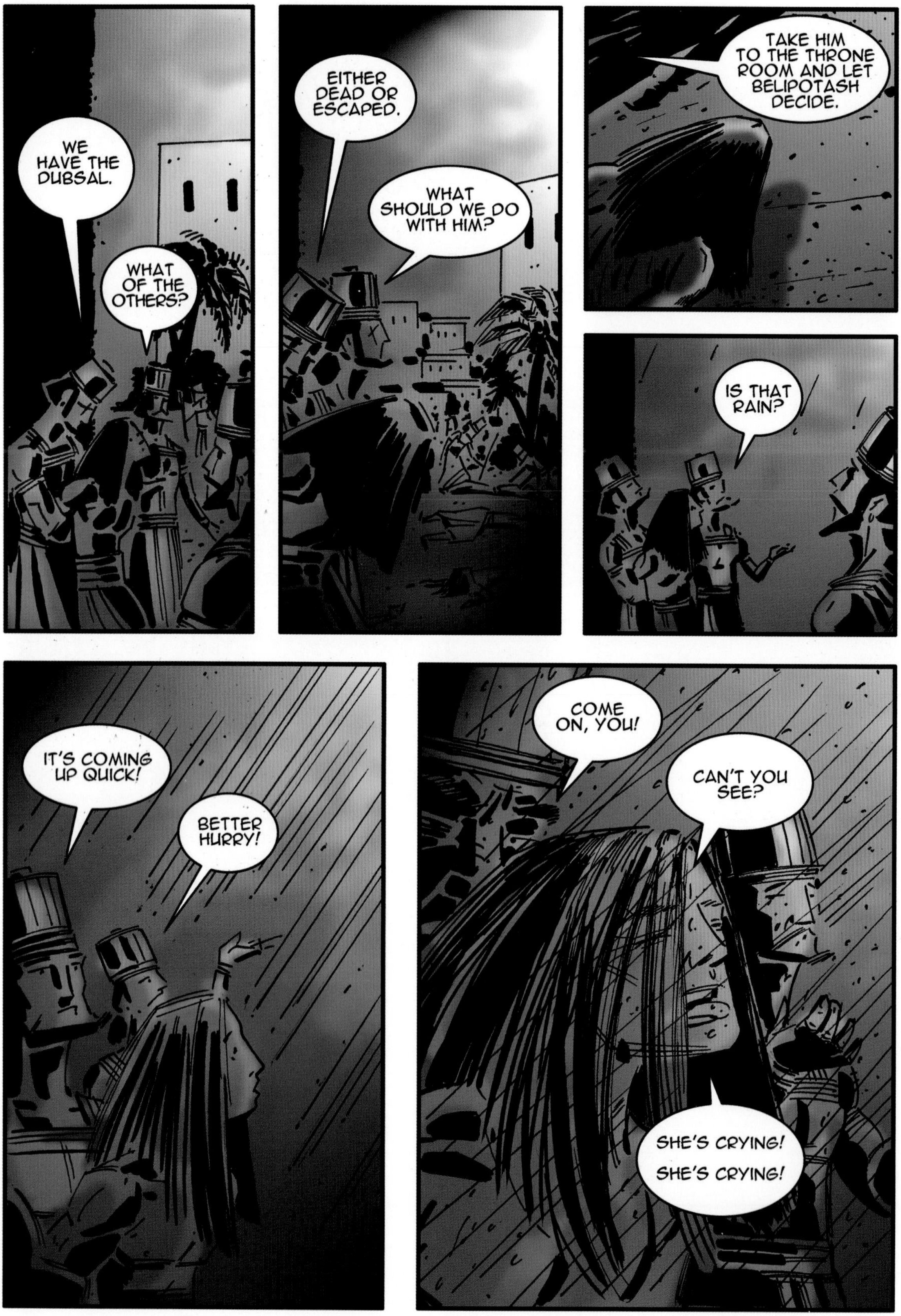
WE HAVE THE DUBSAL.
WHAT OF THE OTHERS?
EITHER DEAD OR ESCAPED.
WHAT SHOULD WE DO WITH HIM?
TAKE HIM TO THE THRONE ROOM AND LET BELIPOTASH DECIDE.
IS THAT RAIN?
IT'S COMING UP QUICK!
BETTER HURRY!
COME ON, YOU!
CAN'T YOU SEE?
SHE'S CRYING!
SHE'S CRYING!

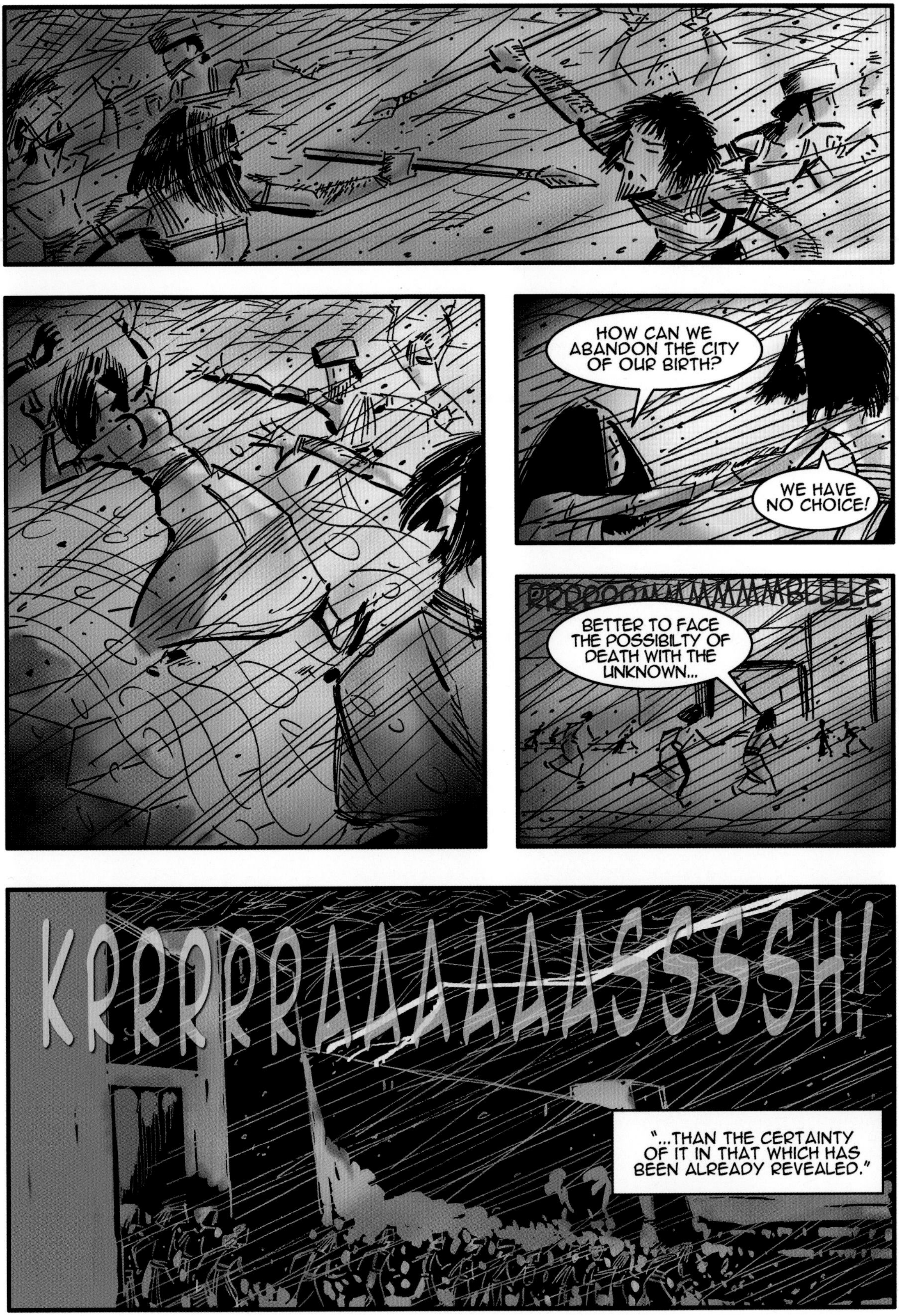
HOW CAN WE ABANDON THE CITY OF OUR BIRTH?
WE HAVE NO CHOICE!
RRRROOOMMMMMMMBLLLLE
BETTER TO FACE THE POSSIBILTY OF DEATH WITH THE UNKNOWN...
KRRRRRAAAAAAASSSSH!
"...THAN THE CERTAINTY OF IT IN THAT WHICH HAS BEEN ALREADY REVEALED."

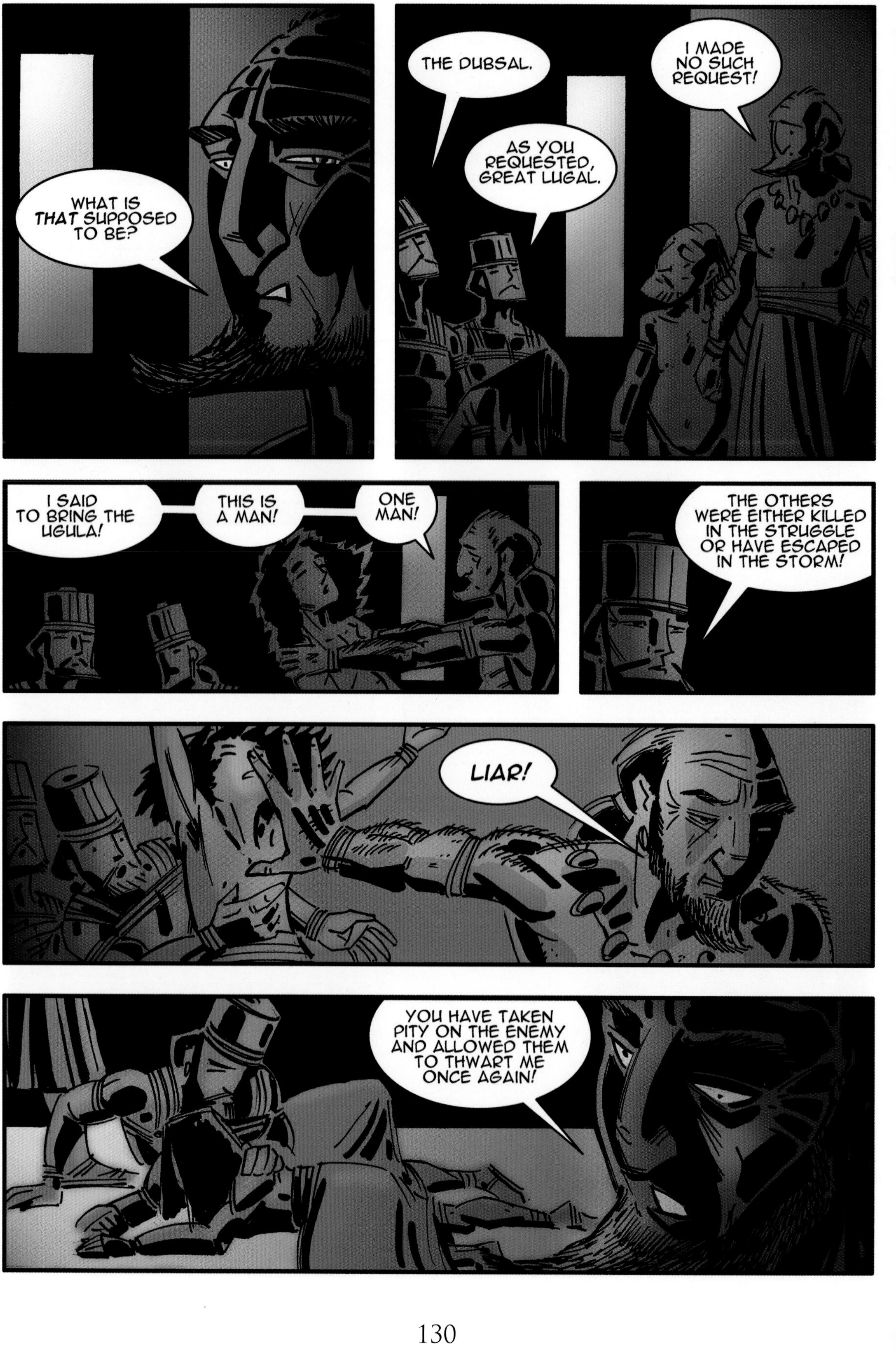
WHAT IS THAT SUPPOSED TO BE?
THE DUBSAL.
AS YOU REQUESTED, GREAT LUGAL.
I MADE NO SUCH REQUEST!
I SAID TO BRING THE UGULA!
THIS IS A MAN!
ONE MAN!
THE OTHERS WERE EITHER KILLED IN THE STRUGGLE OR HAVE ESCAPED IN THE STORM!
LIAR!
YOU HAVE TAKEN PITY ON THE ENEMY AND ALLOWED THEM TO THWART ME ONCE AGAIN!

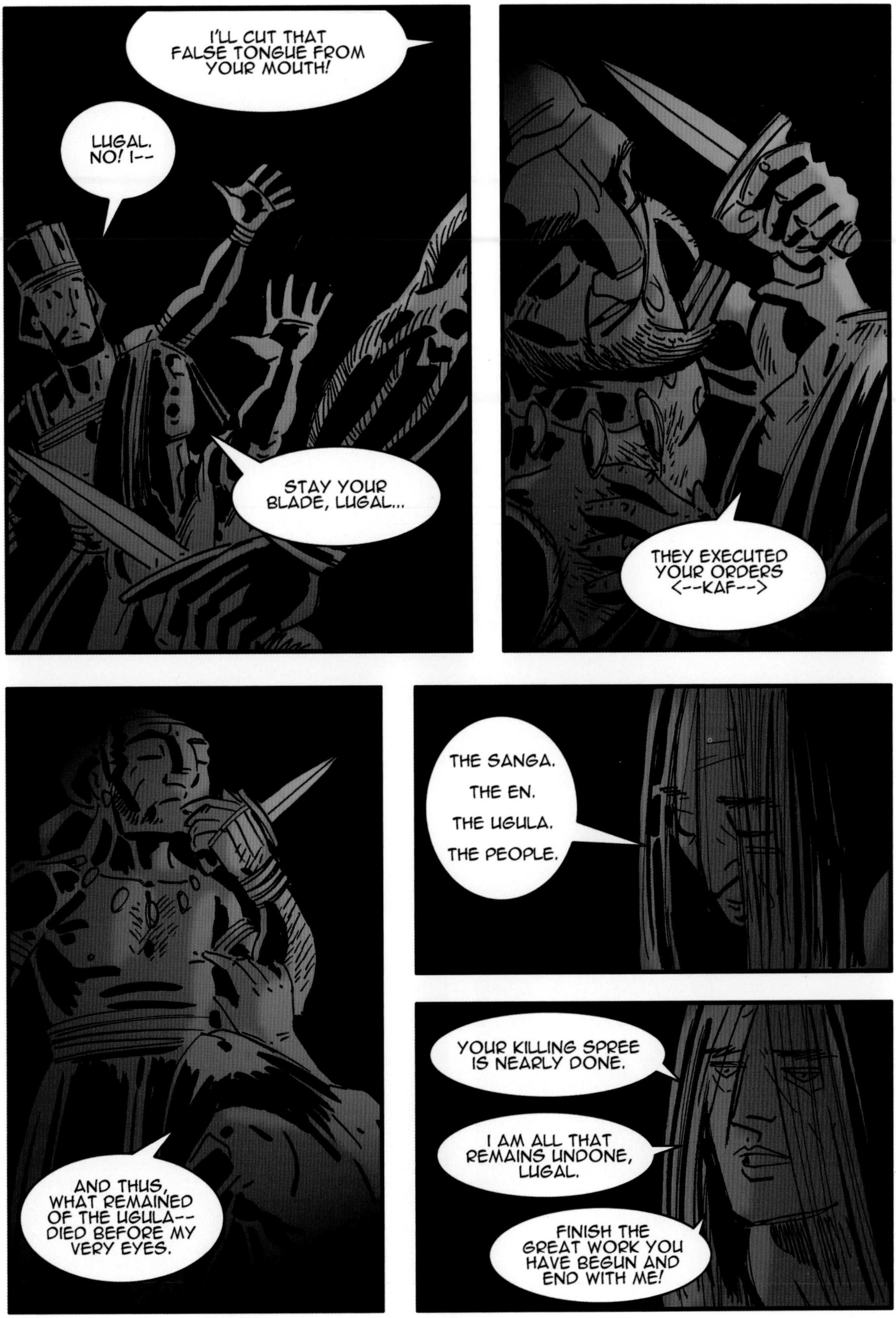
I'LL CUT THAT FALSE TONGUE FROM YOUR MOUTH!
LUGAL. NO! I--
STAY YOUR BLADE, LUGAL...
THEY EXECUTED YOUR ORDERS <--KAF-->
AND THUS, WHAT REMAINED OF THE UGULA-- DIED BEFORE MY VERY EYES.
THE SANGA.
THE EN.
THE UGULA.
THE PEOPLE.
YOUR KILLING SPREE IS NEARLY DONE.
I AM ALL THAT REMAINS UNDONE, LUGAL.
FINISH THE GREAT WORK YOU HAVE BEGUN AND END WITH ME!

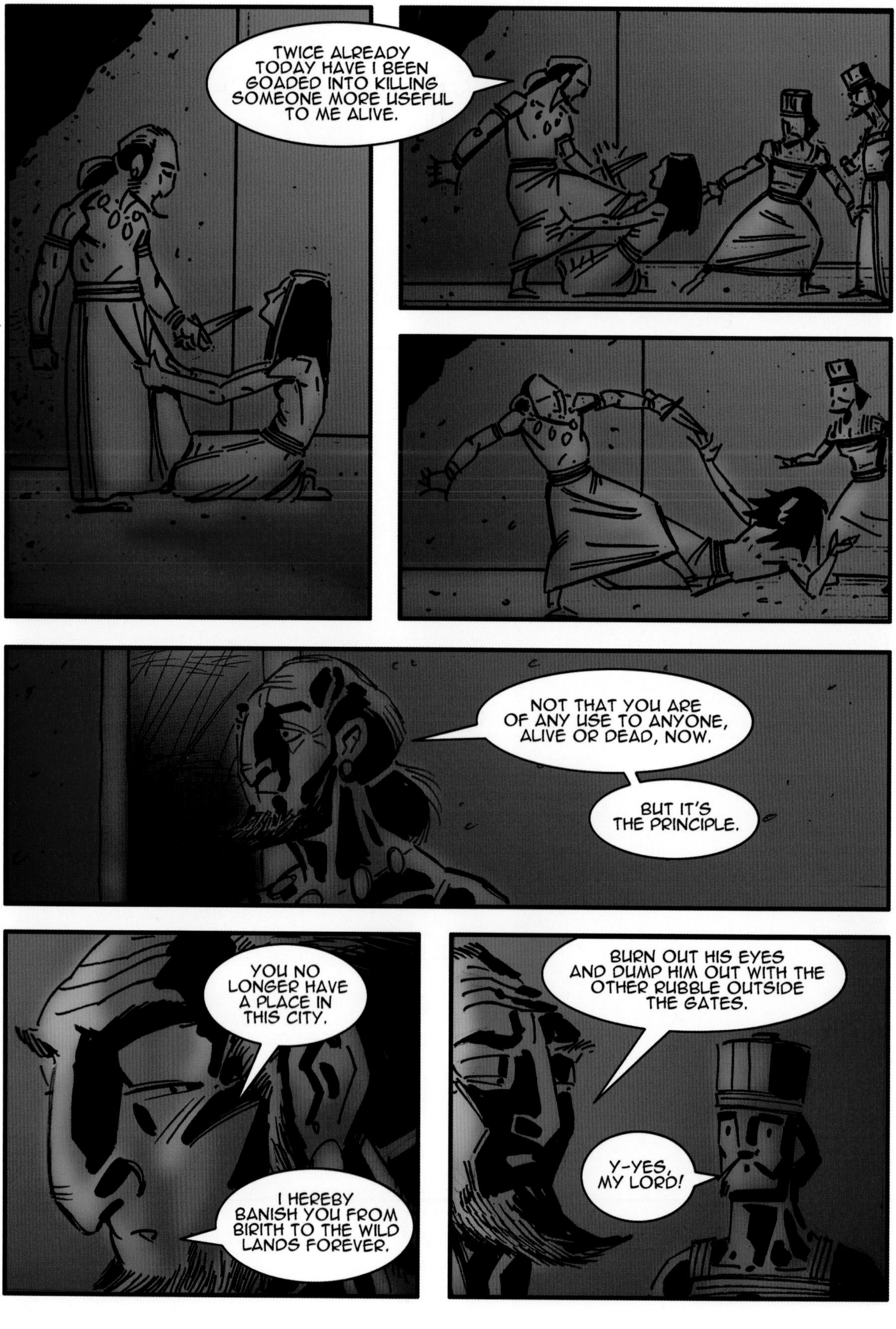
TWICE ALREADY TODAY HAVE I BEEN GOADED INTO KILLING SOMEONE MORE USEFUL TO ME ALIVE.
NOT THAT YOU ARE OF ANY USE TO ANYONE, ALIVE OR DEAD, NOW.
BUT IT'S THE PRINCIPLE.
YOU NO LONGER HAVE A PLACE IN THIS CITY.
I HEREBY BANISH YOU FROM BIRITH TO THE WILD LANDS FOREVER.
BURN OUT HIS EYES AND DUMP HIM OUT WITH THE OTHER RUBBLE OUTSIDE THE GATES.
Y-YES, MY LORD!

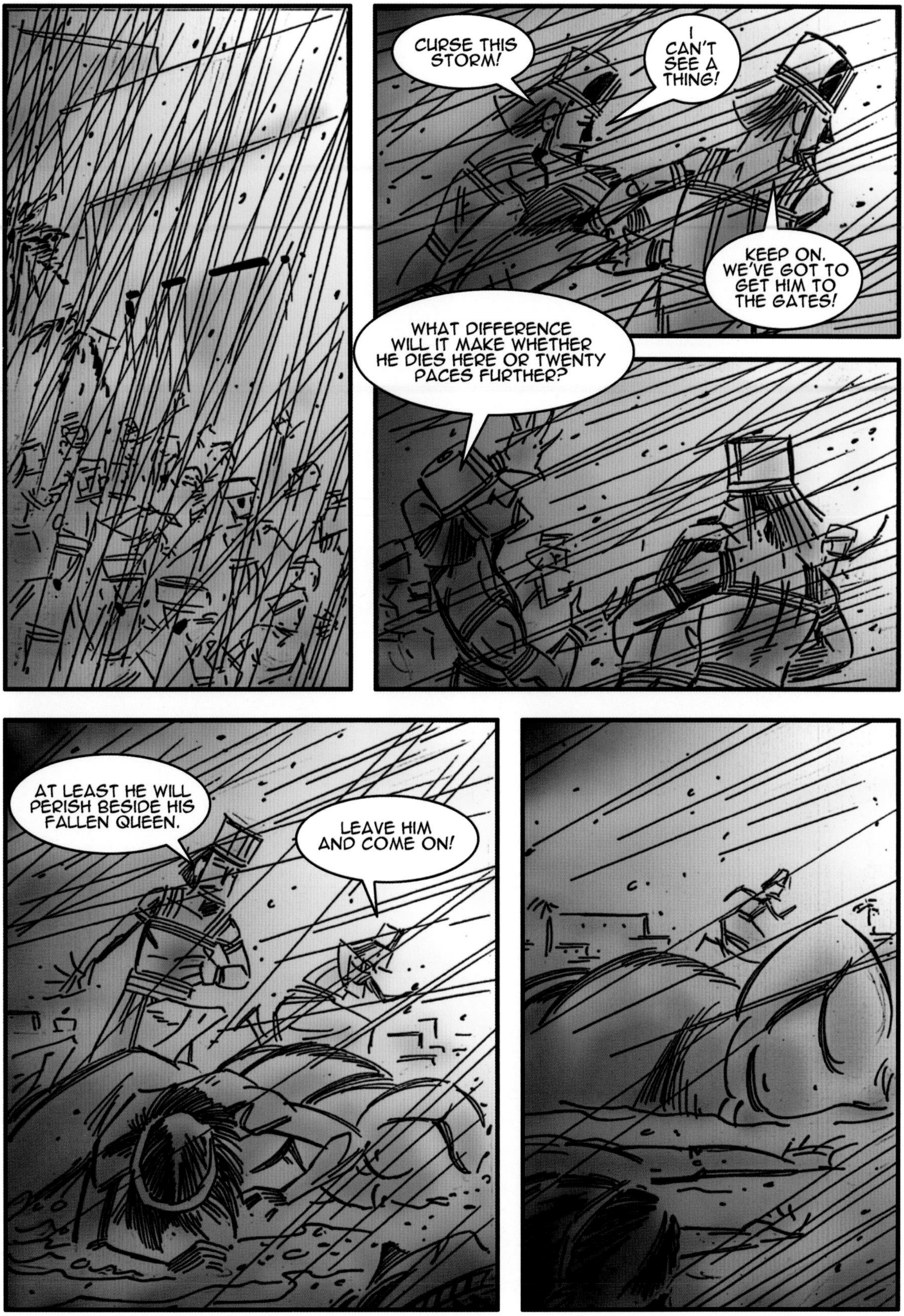
CURSE THIS STORM!
I CAN'T SEE A THING!
KEEP ON. WE'VE GOT TO GET HIM TO THE GATES!
WHAT DIFFERENCE WILL IT MAKE WHETHER HE DIES HERE OR TWENTY PACES FURTHER?
AT LEAST HE WILL PERISH BESIDE HIS FALLEN QUEEN.
LEAVE HIM AND COME ON!

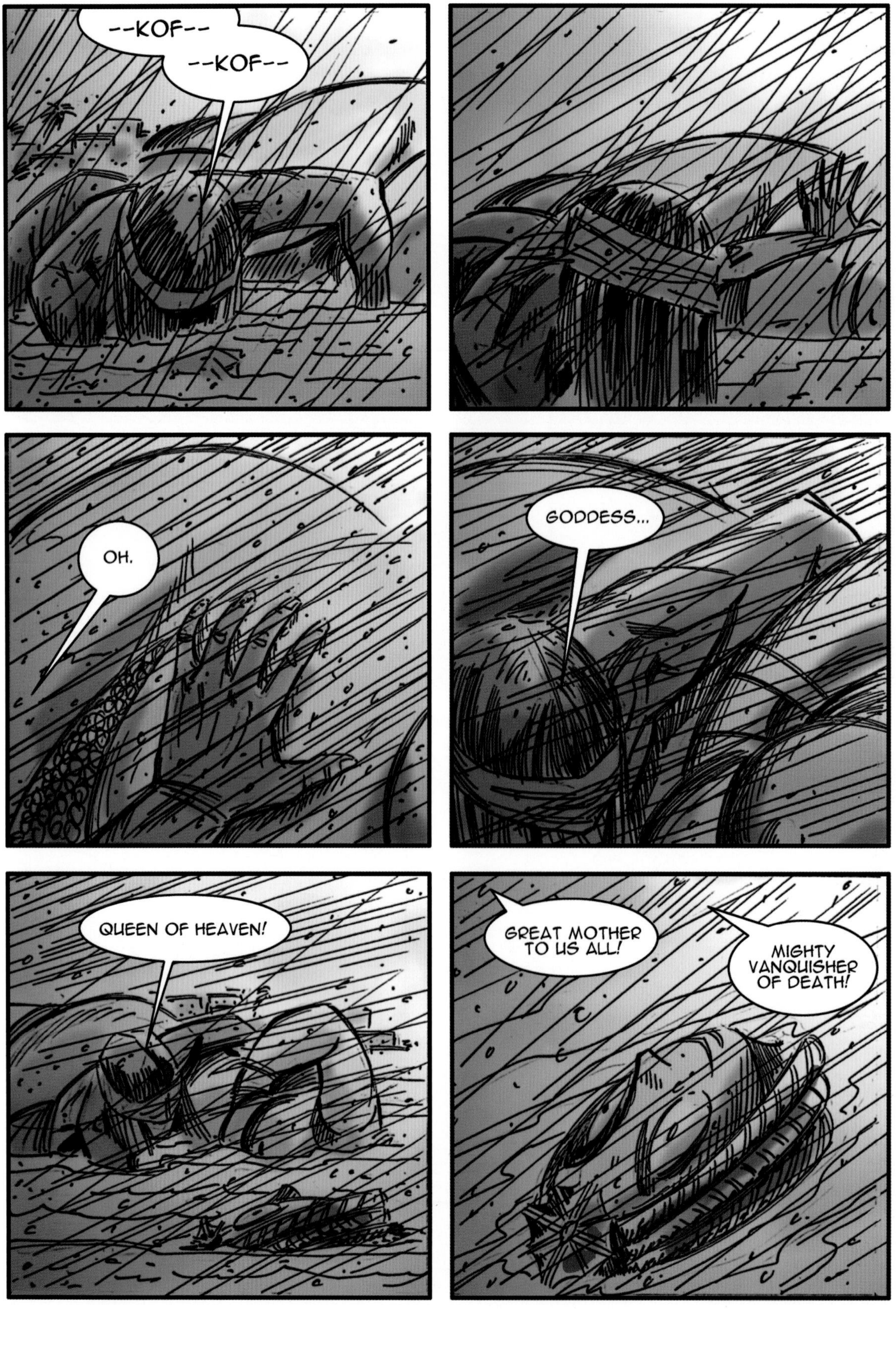
--KOF--
--KOF--
OH.
GODDESS...
QUEEN OF HEAVEN!
GREAT MOTHER TO US ALL!
MIGHTY VANQUISHER OF DEATH!

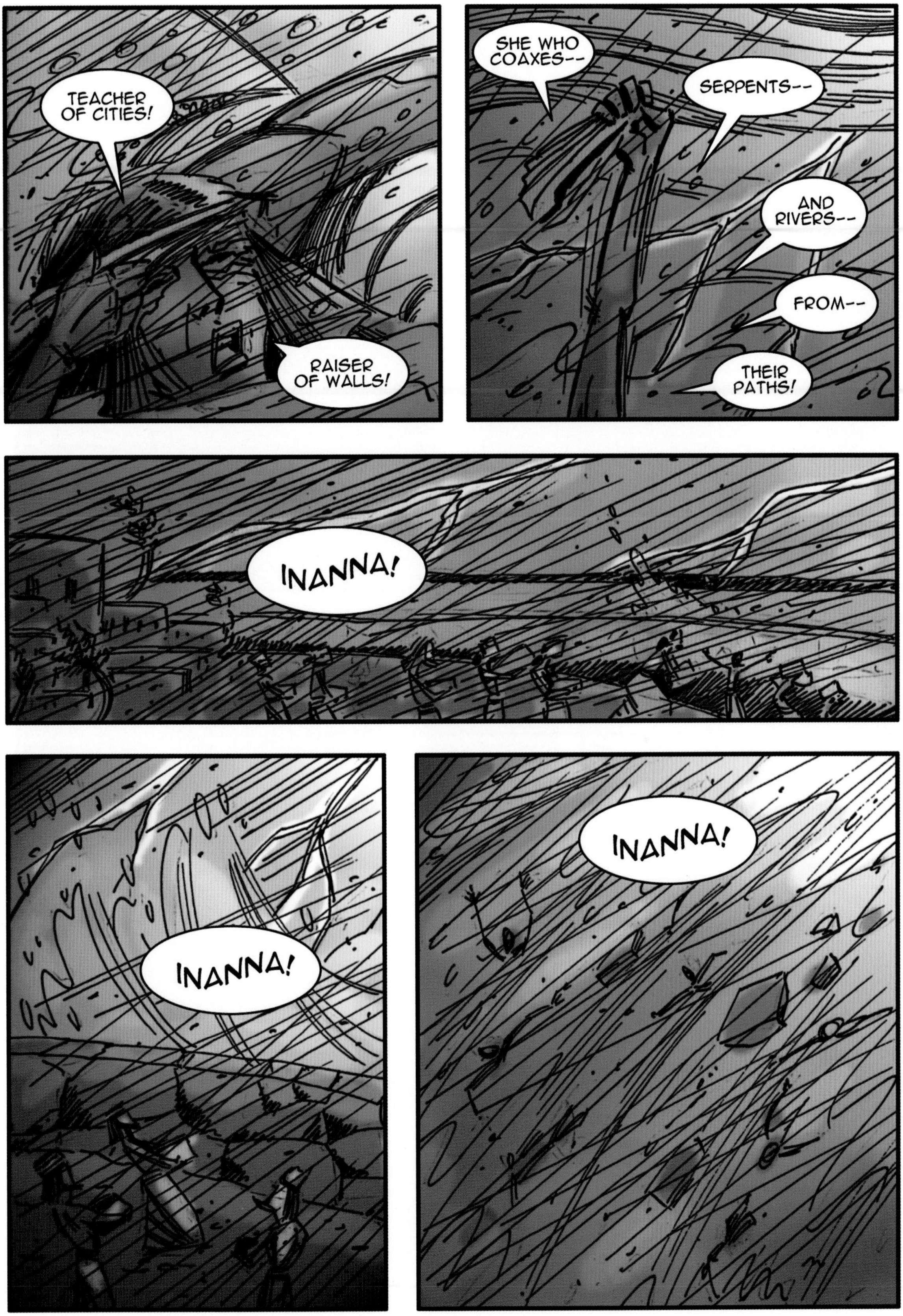
TEACHER OF CITIES!
RAISER OF WALLS!
SHE WHO COAXES--
SERPENTS--
AND RIVERS--
FROM--
THEIR PATHS!
INANNA!
INANNA!
INANNA!

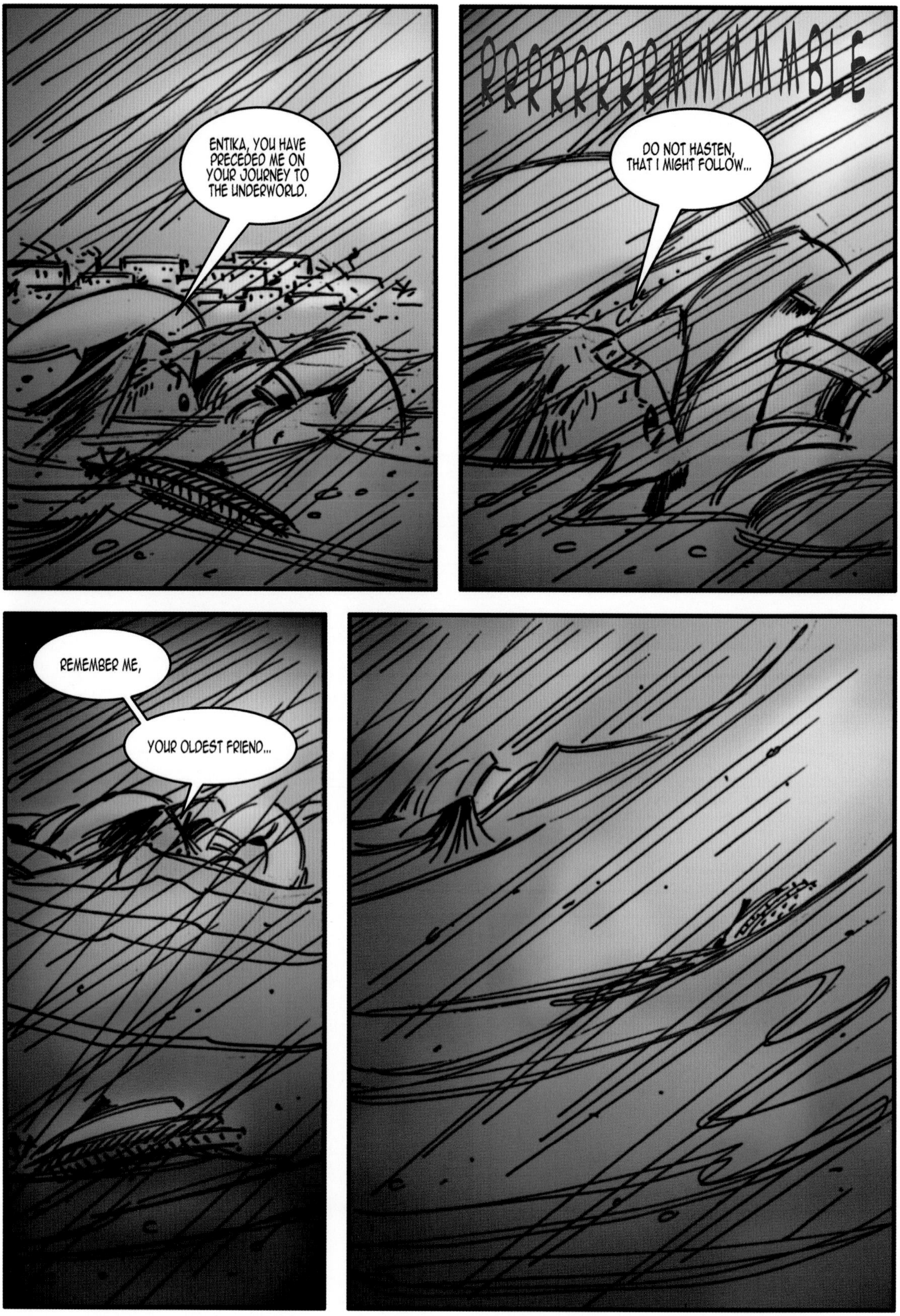
ENTIKA, YOU HAVE PRECEDED ME ON YOUR JOURNEY TO THE UNDERWORLD.
RRRRRRRRRMMMMMBLE
DO NOT HASTEN, THAT I MIGHT FOLLOW...
REMEMBER ME,
YOUR OLDEST FRIEND...

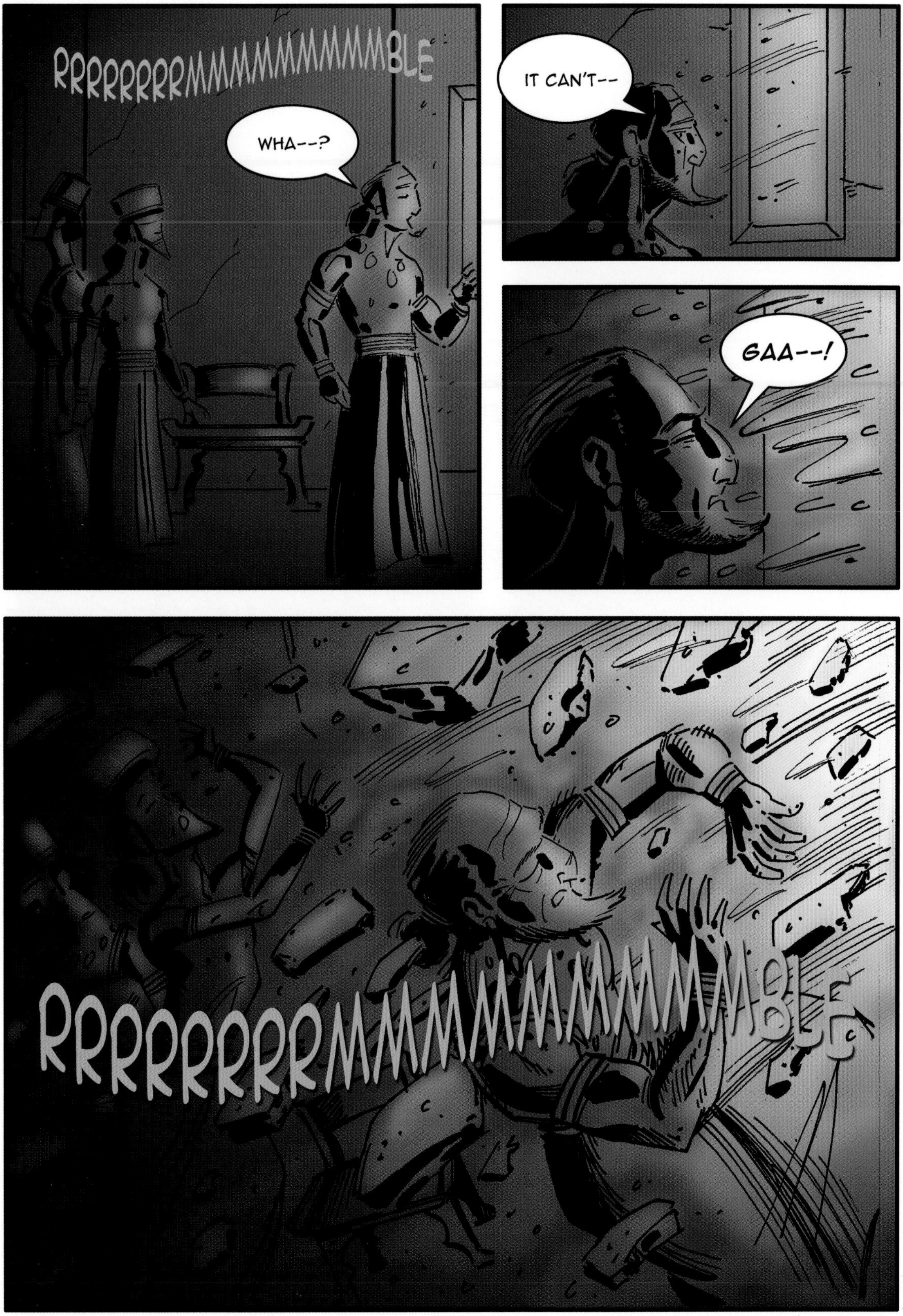
RRRRRRRRMMMMMMMMMBLE
WHA--?
IT CAN'T--
GAA--!
RRRRRRRRRMMMMMMMMMMMMMBLE

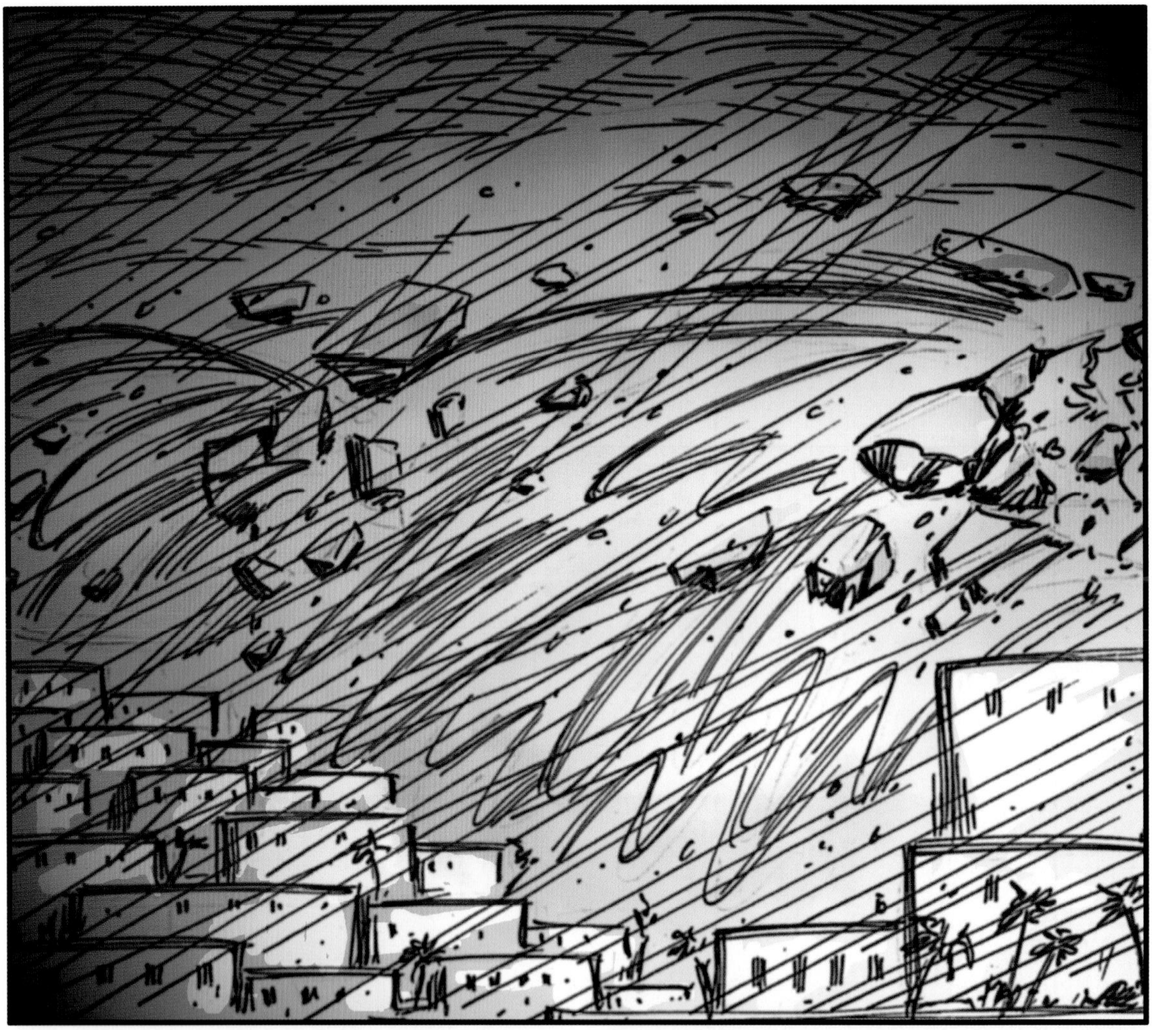

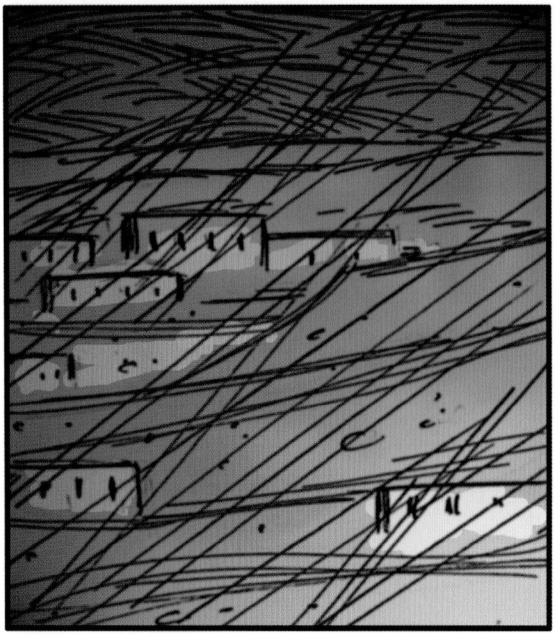

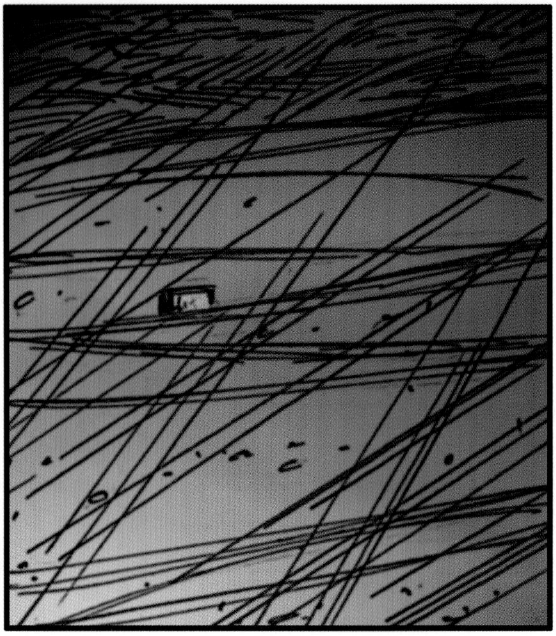

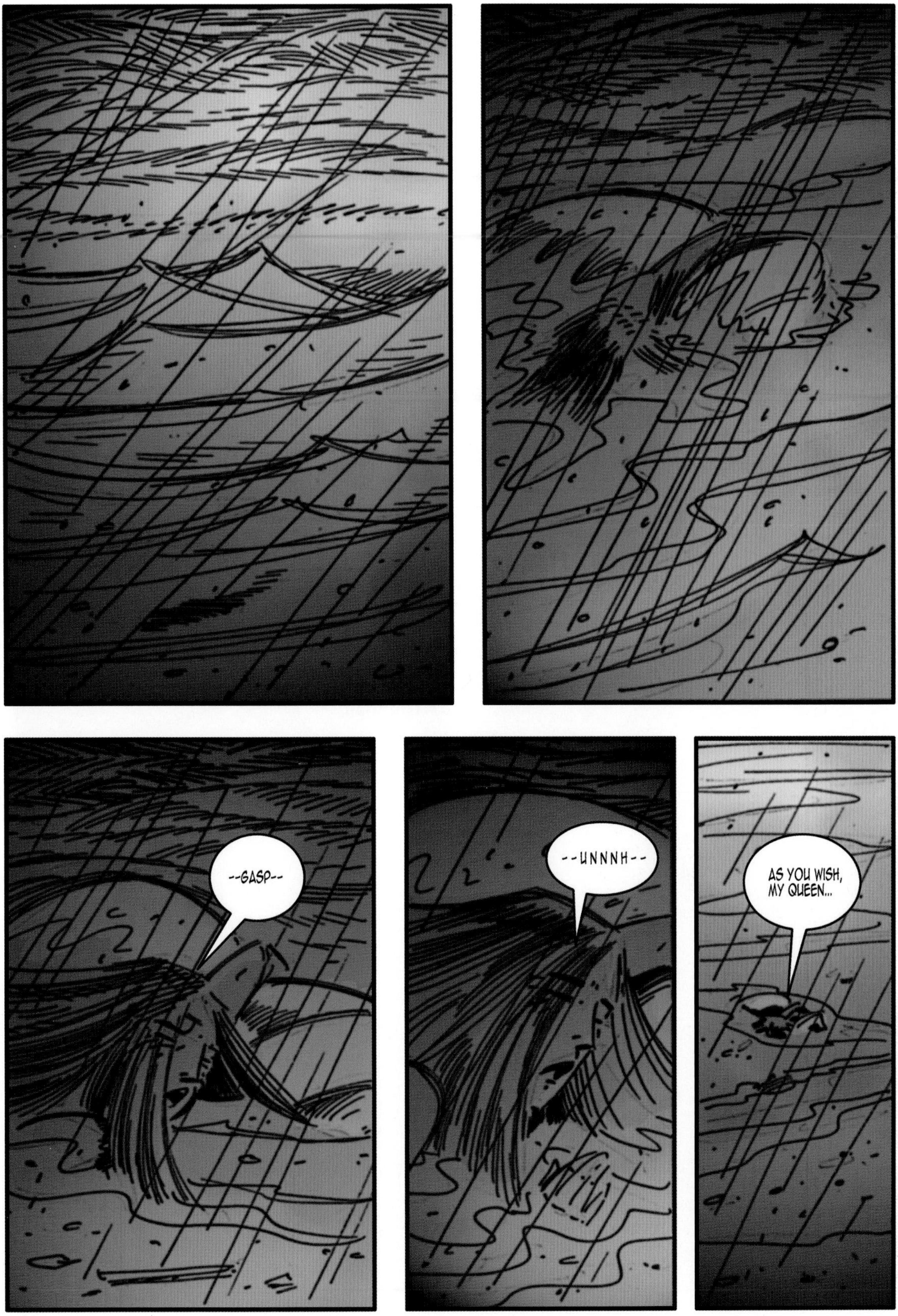
--GASP--
--UNNNH--
AS YOU WISH, MY QUEEN...

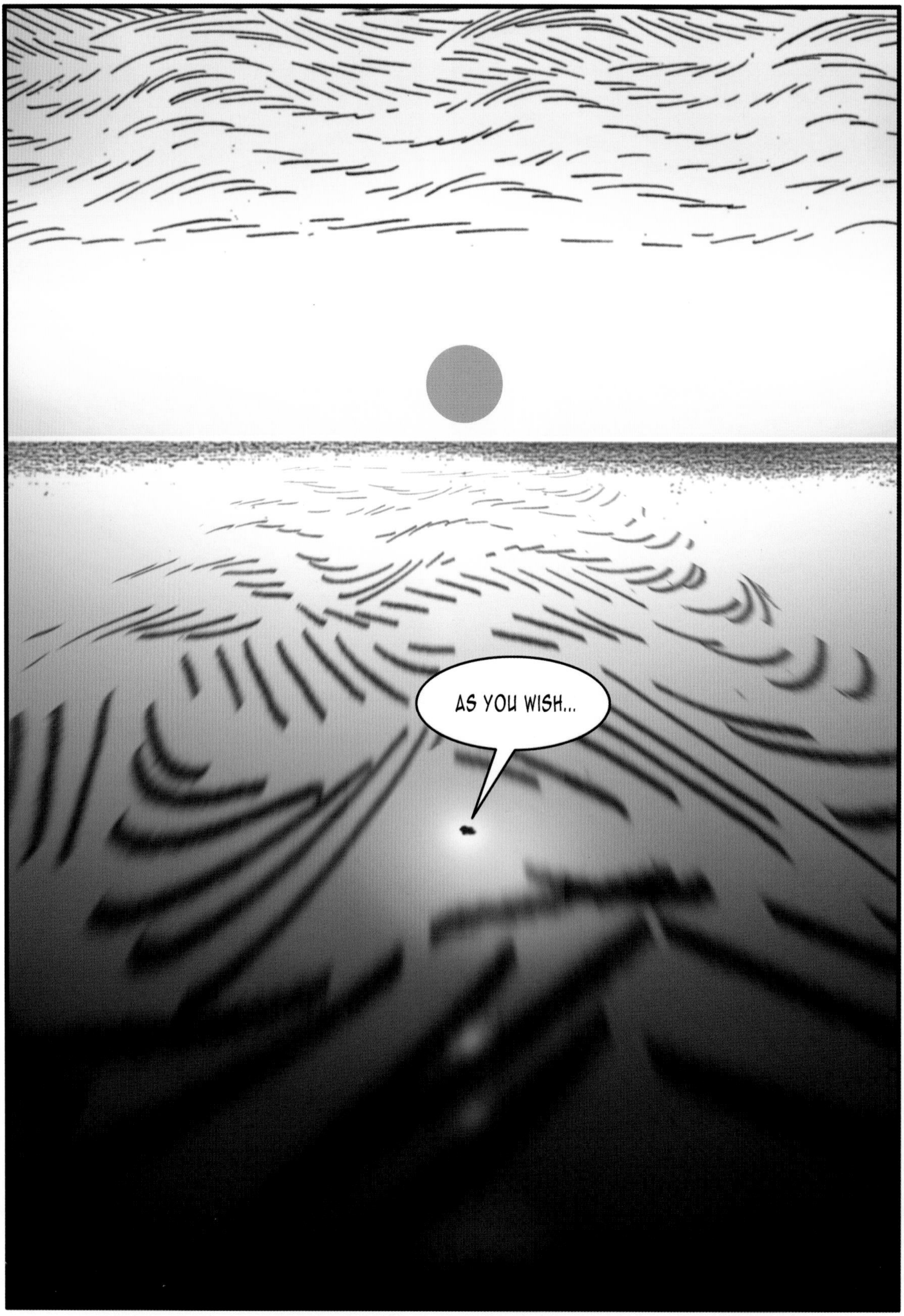
AS YOU WISH...

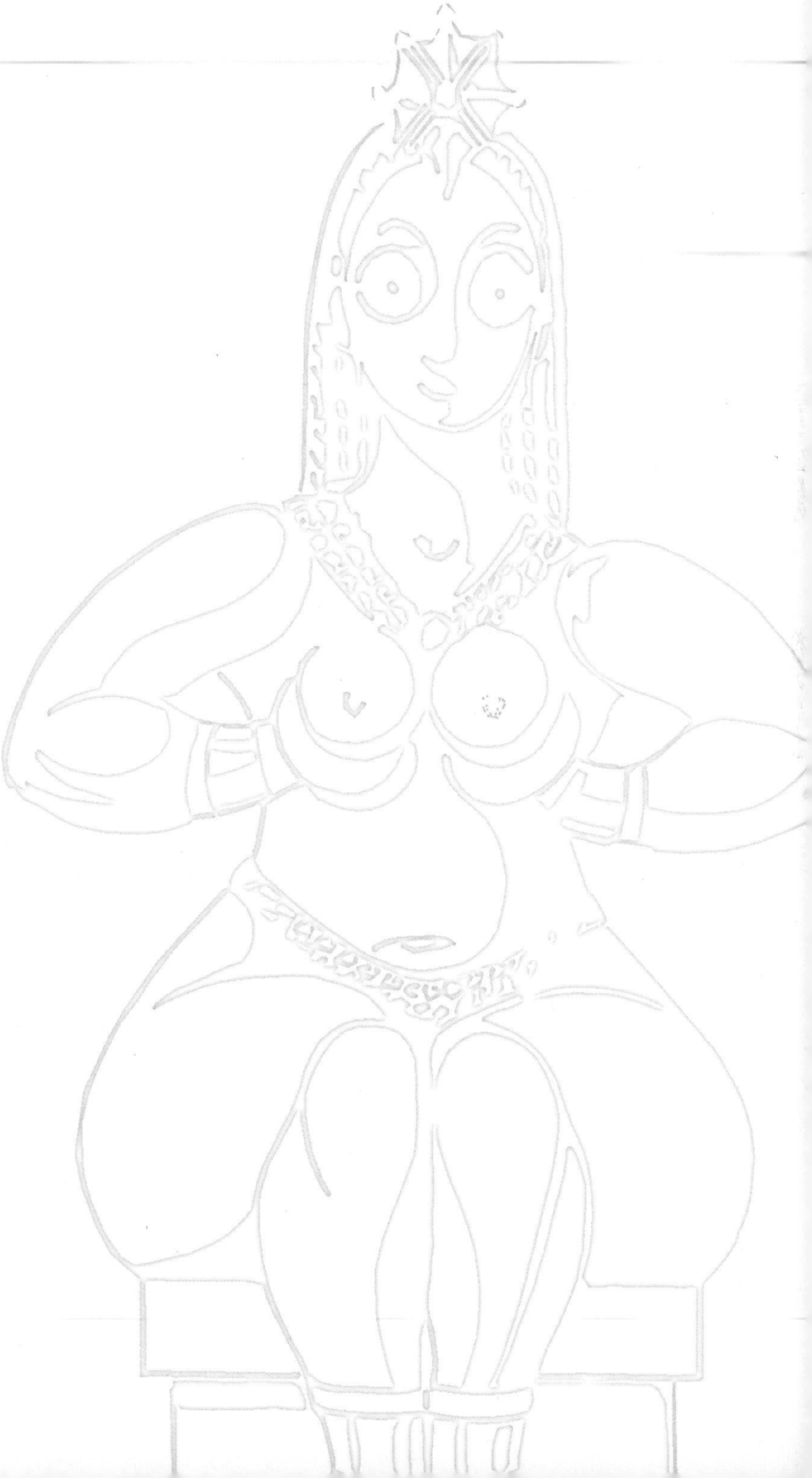

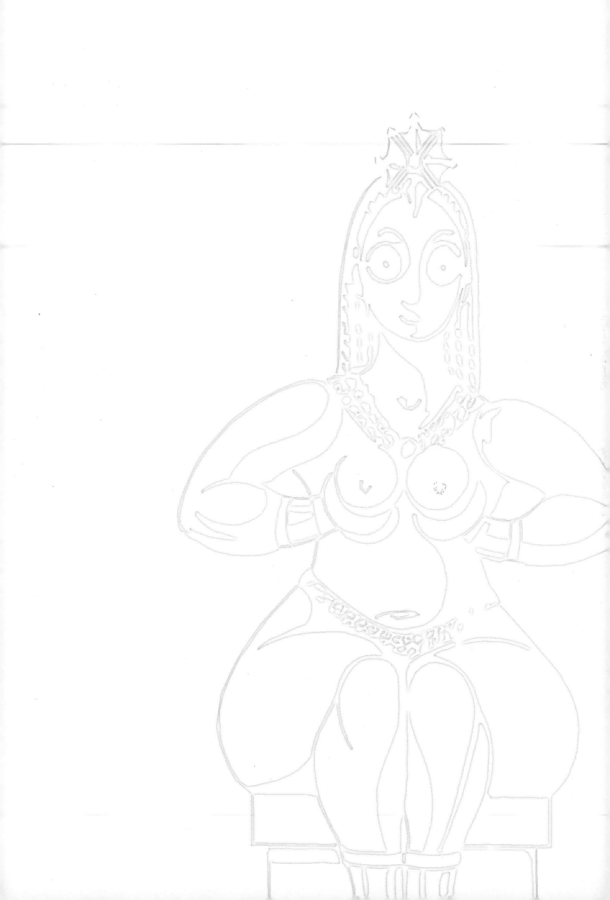

AFTERWORD

Did we get it right? The details, I mean. The research, the suppositions about how people lived, what they wore, and how they behaved towards one another, did we get it right?

Probably not. We probably got it completely wrong. As for instance, with the nudity. The art that the Sumerians left us show that both men and women often appeared in skirts, and jewelry, but without shirts. In later eras of their long history, women and eventually men of the upper classes took to wearing garments that crossed over one shoulder, like a Roman toga. In one sculpture left to us, a woman is portrayed with one breast covered, while the cloth crossed over her other breast but under the nipple. That struck me as distinctly uncomfortable, and I declined to show anyone wearing that particular fashion affectation. But we have this evidence that someone, at some point, did wear her clothes in that manner, so I was at least partly wrong.

What I chose was to show both men and women in a variety of clothing, as befits a period of change. Religions tend to conservatism, thus Entika and the servants of the temple dressed in the old style for rituals, if not always in the day-to-day business of the city. Belipotash was a powerful man of the new style, and he dressed the part.

It would be uncertain to say that nudity and sex held a different meaning for the Sumerians then it does for us. But they seem to have handled it differently. The connection between the sex act and fertility was as clear to them as it is to us and they embraced it without shame in their conceptions of the divine. The Inanna dinghir that was the focus of temple worship reflects this as she proudly lifts her breasts for our contemplation. My drawing is modeled on a Sumerian sculpture of Inanna, a goddess of youth, love and war.

But no matter how informed by research it may be, *Inanna's Tears* must still reflect the era in which it was produced. Thus Entika's forced compliance with a ritual act of sex appears to us as an intended rape, and her ultimate rejection of it an undoubted act of courage. There is a clear erotic content to the scene. Entika is never more lovely, and Belipotash looks strong and manly, at least until his impulsive murder of her.

How can we be sure that ritual sex meant to Entika what we imagine it did? Did she see it as a rape? Did she accept it as erotic, or merely as duty? It's not clear. Her rejection of the ceremony was based not on the act as a sacrilege to her body, but as an insult to her goddess. She was a husband to Inanna, not her surrogate.

I strongly suspect that Belipotash found the prospect of the ceremony to be an erotically-charged act of dominance, for Entika was once nubile and politically powerful. Although, he may have had no intention of ever bedding, or allowing another, to bed her again. Sex and power and dominance have ever been entwined.

A key part of our task as readers of historical fiction is to separate and distinguish local cultural forms from the eternal human dimension, not only in the arenas of sex and power, but in the full gamut of human activity. Was the young woman with the exposed nipple a tease, or an innocent? Did a youth of Sumer view the Inanna dinghir with demure reverence, or speculative interest? We can only conjecture.

—MPMANN

ABOUT THE AUTHORS

ROB VOLLMAR is a writer of and about comics. His first graphic novel, *The Castaways* was nominated for an Eisner Award in 2002. His second graphic novel, *Bluesman* was completed in 2006 along with a re-release of *The Castaways* in 2007. Vollmar is an associate contributing editor for World Literature Today magazine and resides in Norman, Oklahoma. *Inanna's Tears* is his first graphic novel in collaboration with artist and co-creator mpMann.

MARVIN PERRY MANN began his comics career inking *The Trouble With Girls* (Malibu Graphics). After a departure into furniture-making and 3D modeling and animation, he returned to comics in 2002, digitally producing a 240-page silent comic strip and two flipbook animations for *Pause and Effect: The Art of Interactive Narrative* (New Riders). He is the artist and co-creator of four original graphic novels published by Archaia: *The Lone and Level Sands*, *Some New Kind of Slaughter*, *The Grave Doug Freshley* and *Inanna's Tears*. He lives in California.